THE BIO-
ASSASSINS

NONFICTION BY GERALD L. POSNER

MENGELE

WARLORDS OF CRIME:
Chinese Secret Societies—The New Mafia

THE BIO-
ASSASSINS

Gerald L. Posner

McGRAW-HILL PUBLISHING COMPANY

New York St. Louis San Francisco Auckland Bogotá
Hamburg London Madrid Mexico Milan Montreal
New Delhi Paris São Paulo Singapore
Sydney Tokyo Toronto

1 2 3 4 5 6 7 8 9 DOC DOC 8 9 2 1 0 9

ISBN 0-07-050611-6

Library of Congress Cataloging-in-Publication Data

Posner, Gerald L.
    The bio-assassins / by Gerald L. Posner.
        p. cm.
    ISBN 0-07-050611-6
    I. Title.
    PS3566.0672B5   1989
    813'.54—dc19   89-30306
                                                        CIP

Book design by Kathryn Parise

To my muse, Trisha

THE BIO- ASSASSINS

CHAPTER 1 ≥———————

She pulled the curtains back slowly, as if by delaying she could improve what lay behind. But it was the same. Three months and no change. The putrid odor of death filled the cubicle. She reluctantly looked at the body strapped onto the bed in front of her. His wrists and ankles were bound tightly by knotted nylon cords. She was told they were for his own protection, to stop him from inflicting more damage to his body. She looked at the greenish-purple skin puffed over each side of the restraints. One ankle strap was speckled deep red, dry blood, the result of a shackle slicing the soft part of his Achilles tendon. Now, as she had many times before, she thought of untying him. She tried to imagine what would happen if he was free, the involuntary spasms that racked his body allowed to run their course. Yet she knew it was never going to happen. She would not reach over and undo the cords. It had to end without her interference.

She sat on the orange plastic chair next to his bed. Behind her was the rhythmic electronic beep of the nearby pulse monitor. She glanced at the bank of machinery lined against the wall and marveled at the array of devices they used to stop him from dying. There was the oscillating bright green light that indicated his heart was strong, and the assortment of plastic bags filled with clear liquids that trailed down thin tubes ending in needles stuck into his arm. But the room was dominated by one machine—a gleaming steel cylinder topped with a pulsating rubber sack that mimicked an accordion. It expanded and contracted once every two seconds. It sounded like someone in the middle of an asthma attack. From its side a thick ribbed tube extended over the bed's metal rail and into his mouth. She could see where it passed down his throat, bulging his windpipe just under the skin's surface. The tube was secured with wide strips of adhesive tape, pulled tightly across his chin and cheeks. Although the tape was regularly changed, a festering infection had erupted around it. Near the infection were patches of raw, irritated skin from the cheap electric razor they used daily on him. Saliva rolled out of the corner of his mouth and down the tube onto his hospital gown. He was drenched in sweat. She looked at his hair, matted across the damp skull. She remembered more grey, but in this fluorescent-lit cubicle it seemed dark brown. Strange, she thought. Death hovered near this room. Yet she was almost more concerned about his hair color than if he stopped breathing. Whether he lived or died was beyond her control. She was not going to allow herself to go mad worrying. Suddenly her thoughts were interrupted by the bed rattling. His body was heaving.

For ninety days she had made the same visit. Past the two baby-faced military guards at the entrance, past the battery of doctors and nurses that filled the corridors, and inside this cordoned-off section. It was as depressing as a hospital could be. They had put him into a small room painted the universal color of government hospitals, a sickly pale green. But these walls had not been painted in a long time. They were covered in grime accumulated from hundreds of illnesses and deaths. A lone fluorescent tube cast the light. It made people look as green as the walls. She hated the room. She hated the equipment that kept him alive, modern medicine's version of the inquisition. But most of all she hated it when his body started shaking.

He was in the middle of an attack. His 200-pound frame had been whittled by 50 pounds, but his body could still put on a show of strength. His head flopped back and forth to the side, each violent turn yanking the tube in his mouth. His chest continued lifting off the bed and slamming back to the wet mattress, partially pulling out the intravenous tubes from his arms. His legs twitched, the restraints tightening with each spasm and cutting into his already infected skin. The iron lung worked overtime, its mechanical hiss picking up speed to maintain the momentum of the attack. The metronome-like heart monitor emitted a faster and shriller beep as the green lines shot across the computer screen like a supercharged video game. She touched his face. She wanted to stop him. But her palm slipped off his clammy cheek as his head jolted to the other side. And all the while his eyes were glued wide open. His dilated pupils gazed through layers of pain-killing drugs. But the doctors assured her he was comatose. His eyes were open but nothing registered. He was living dead. But they would not let him die. Not yet. They wanted him alive.

Drops of blood formed at the corners of his mouth, the tube's gyrations splitting his lips. Suddenly the beep of the heart monitor and the whoosh of the mechanical lung were overwhelmed by a persistent loud buzzer. The machines were trying to talk to the doctors. Their patient was dying.

The first doctor almost knocked her over when he hurtled through the curtains. Two other men in white gowns were just a step behind. "Hold him firmly," screamed the first man. "Nurse, 10 milligrams of Valium IV, and load him with Dilantin, now!"

Two of them tried to hold him flat on his back. They pushed against the heaving chest. The wide eyes, the eyes that were not supposed to see anything, were staring at her. A nurse ran into the room holding aloft two syringes.

She had seen enough. They would stabilize him. She had no doubt about it. They had done this almost every day since he had arrived. And when the drugs wore off, the demons that thrashed his body would have another chance to split him open at the seams. She could hear the creaking of the bed and the muffled orders as she walked down the hallway. She glanced at a man in a suit and tie talking to the military guards. Every day it was someone new. There was not a familiar face among them. She did not even bother to say hello. Her mind was busy. She was going to church. She had a lot of praying to do. She was going to ask God that the wretched man in the bed should die.

Three months earlier
London
December 13
10:00 a.m.

It was London's first major winter storm. Fifty-mile-per-hour winds, nonstop sheets of rain and hail, and a deep grey sky made the mid-morning seem like dusk. The torrential downpour had cleared the roadways of most holiday traffic, allowing the bright red British postal van to speed along Regent Street and toward Piccadilly. Special deliveries were not unusual in Green Park, one of London's most fashionable neighborhoods. The cream-colored Georgian mansions that lined the narrow roads were the homes of an assortment of government leaders, business magnates, and the aristocracy of the British capital. Messengers, administrative aides, and government postmen delivered packages of importance around the clock.

The postal van slowed near the Ritz Hotel and turned left onto Arlington Street, a private lane. Inside the truck, the rain sounded like a thousand small beating drums. The water streamed so heavily over the windshield that the two postmen could barely see outside. The driver rubbed his long, angular face where a scar extended from the corner of his left eye to the middle of his cheek. He never understood why, but inclement weather made it itch. He had almost forgotten it today, the storm's severity forcing him to concentrate intently on the road. He leaned his head over the steering wheel and close to the windshield, hoping to compensate for the poor visibility. Finally he spotted his destination, one of the grandest homes bordering the park. A turn-of-the-century five-story townhouse, prominent for its grand stone columns, it was separated from the street by a large wrought-iron gate. He parked the van at the granite pathway leading to the front door. Both men adjusted their black rubber parkas and slid their plastic uniform caps snugly on their heads. They exited together and ran through the downpour to the back of the van. They pulled a large cardboard box from the rear and struggled under the weight of the delivery. The rain had turned to a light hail and struck their faces as if dozens of pellets were hurled at them. The strong wind cut through their clothing like a blast from a large freezer. They braced themselves and sloshed to the gate. One of them leaned his shoulder into the intercom.

A hoarse, American-accented voice pierced the static on the box, "Identify yourself."

"Special delivery from Lisbon. We're from the Golden Square post office."

Nothing happened.

"Please hurry. It's very heavy, mate, and the bloody weather's killing us."

A low, steady buzzer sounded. The shorter postman, with a chubby, pale face, pushed against the massive gate and it slowly opened. Both lowered their heads as if to shield themselves from the slashing hail. They knew that when the gate opened a magnetic hinge fired an electronic circuit that triggered hidden cameras to snap pictures of anyone approaching the mansion. These men did not want their faces captured on film.

At the top of the steps they noticed the raised bronze plaque set into one of the stone columns. It proclaimed the building to be the "International Society for Research of Childhood Cancers." In a city filled with hundreds of organizational headquarters, this one did not rate a second glance. Drenched, they wiped their faces and rested under a glass awning. A peephole on the front door popped open and a pair of tiny eyes, sandwiched between a thick forehead and fat cheeks, stared at them.

"We just need a signature, mate, and we'll be on our way. Bloody storm's already got us nearly an hour behind."

The door opened revealing a lavish interior. In front of them was a man resembling a retired boxer. His compact body and broad shoulders advertised his strength. Dressed in a navy blue Notre Dame sweatshirt, a pair of khaki pants, white socks, and battered penny loafers, he looked like he had just arrived with an American package tour. His nose was spread across his solid face. It had clearly been broken several times. There was nothing nice about him. The scarred postman did not like men who had necks thicker than the top of their heads.

"Go on," he muttered to them. "Put it down by the desk and I'll sign whatever you've got." His eyes were alert and scanned the front of the house and then watched every movement of the delivery men. He closed the door to block out the storm. The two again walked with heads lowered, knowing that a video camera recorded their every move. They stopped next to an ornate Louis XIV desk.

"Come on you guys, you're dropping water and mud all over the frigging place, step back over here to me," the retired boxer shouted. As the scarred man stepped toward the staircase, the other postman walked back toward the front door.

"Hey, what the hell do you think you're doing?"

It happened in an instant. The scarred one walking toward the staircase leaned over as if he dropped something. He reached under his parka and whipped out a .45 caliber MAC-10 machine pistol, fitted with a silencer. He knew he had only one shot to get it right. He yanked the pistol under the staircase and placed a bullet into a four-inch square black box. It was the main circuitry for the video surveillance system. The hollow-point, steel jacketed bullet found its target, slicing the main cable. In a fortified basement, a bank of video monitors flickered for a moment, and then went dark.

At the same time, the shorter postman grabbed an eight-inch combat knife from under his slick parka. Before the boxer could react, the postman slammed a knee into his victim's groin and hammered his face with the knife's broad handle. There was a grunt of excruciating pain as the American spun backward. The attacker raced after him and crashed the steel toe of his workboot into the knee, shattering the bone as the boxer dropped to the floor. The intruder jumped on top of the dazed American and shoved the blade of the knife against the fat man's neck.

"Listen, you're going to help us or you're going to die!"

At that moment, a crackled voice came over an intercom by the desk.

"Harry, is everything okay up there? We've lost the picture. I think it must be the goddamn storm."

"That's right, Harry, you're going to tell the man everything is okay," the postman commanded. "You're going to get us downstairs or I'm going to carve you up. Take your choice. Now!" Harry's face was bleeding and contorted in pain. His smashed knee was killing him and the ache spreading from his groin was making him sick.

"Fuck you!" Harry spit into the attacker's face, and he flinched. The knife's edge moved away from his neck for a split second. It was all the time he needed. Harry lunged forward with all the strength he could muster. He butted with his head and caught the knife-wielder full in the face. He could hear the crack of the nose as it broke against his forehead. His assailant reeled back and cried out in pain and shock. Blood splattered from his nose and mouth. Harry reached behind his sweatshirt for his Colt .45 automatic pistol. But before he could get it, the scarred gunman at the staircase whirled around and lifted the machine pistol. Five muffled pops cut the air as the slugs tore into Harry's fleshy backside.

Again the intercom crackled. "Harry, what the hell's going on up there? I don't like it when I don't hear anything from you."

Harry was propelled backward, his body sliding across the marble floor and slamming against the front door. He rolled over to look at his killers and once again summoned the strength to reach for his pistol. But his attacker had recovered. He yanked a silencer-equipped 9-millimeter Uzi machine gun from under his parka. He lifted the nozzle and squeezed the trigger, splitting Harry's forehead in two. As the fat body collapsed across the floor, a voice came from the landing.

"What's going on down there? Some of us are trying to get some rest." A young man with curly blond hair appeared at the top of the stairs. He looked drowsy, as if disturbed from a deep sleep. He shuffled halfway down the circular staircase before putting on a pair of wire-rimmed glasses. He saw the two postmen with automatic weapons at the same moment he saw Harry's crumpled body in a widening pool of glistening red. He turned to run, but two .45 caliber bullets cut into his left leg, exploding the kneecap. His body slumped onto the stairs and slid to the bottom of the landing.

"Harry, if you don't answer me in a minute, I'm going to sound an alert to headquarters' security desk." Again the intercom carried the voice belonging to the security guard sitting in front of a half dozen blank video monitors. "If you're just screwing around they're going to put our asses in the wringer."

The two gunmen sprinted to the young man. The scarred one grabbed a handful of hair and yanked his head into the air. The wounded man's eyes were dilated and he was breathing heavily. He was going into shock.

"Listen real good if you want to live. You do what I say right now or I'll finish what I began!"

He violently shook the young man's head and the dazed eyes rattled. He grabbed him by the belt on his pants and dragged him to the desk across the room. The punctured leg left a trail of red on the floor. The scarred killer grabbed the young man's hand and slammed it flat against the desk. Then he pressed the knife's blade across the knuckles.

"Now, when I push this button you're going to tell the guard downstairs that a couple of postmen came to deliver a package and one of them has keeled over. You think it's a heart attack. Your fat dead friend over there is helping the poor sick postman and that's why he's not answering the intercom. If you don't do it just as I told you, then I am going to cut your fingers off and stuff them down your throat until you choke to death. Now let's see if you're not quite as stupid as that dead piece of shit in the corner."

The other gunman reached over and pressed the intercom. The young man was terrified. Nothing came out of his mouth. The blade was pressed harder.

"Uh . . . uh, Pete, eh, it's me, Malcolm. We've got a problem up here."

"What the fuck is going on? I can't see anything and where is Harry? You sound terrible."

"Yeah, yeah, terrible." The knife was pushed deeper, the skin was about to burst. "A couple of mailmen, uh, they came with a delivery and one of the guys, eh, it kinda looks like he might have died. I think it's a heart attack. Harry's working on the guy but it doesn't look good."

"Harry doesn't know anything about saving anybody," said the voice over the intercom. "I'll come up with one of the doctors. Just sit tight."

"Nice work, kid," the scarred man smiled. Then without warning he plunged the knife into the young man's throat. The blade pierced the windpipe and stopped only when it hit the base of the skull. The dead man's eyes bulged wide as a gush of blood shot from his mouth. The killer yanked out the knife and the body dropped into a ball by the desk.

The two men tore off their parkas, revealing commando vests. On each they carried extra magazine clips for their automatic weapons, four concussion hand grenades, Beretta 9-millimeter automatic pistols, and two combat knives. They dashed to the box they had carried inside the townhouse and ripped it open. They knew the security guard and doctor would arrive in less than thirty seconds. The attackers pulled out gas masks and put them on. These were not ordinary masks purchased in an army surplus store. They were state-of-the-art. Each contained wireless microphones for easy communication. They had Darth Vader-like wraparound mirrored visors set over the eyes. A microchip embedded in the glass automatically adjusted the temperature between the wearer's perspiration and the gas in the room, always maintaining perfect vision. Minichip sensors pinpointed body heat, electronically locating people even before the human eye could see them. And the mirror finish made it impossible to identify the person inside. The attackers knew once they were downstairs, hidden cameras randomly took pictures, and the masks rendered the photos useless.

The gunmen ignored the four square incendiary devices and the six high-density plastic explosives, each capable of obliterating a floor of the mansion. Instead they grabbed four polished aluminum cylinders, resembling bloated aerosol cans. In under ten seconds the security guard and doctor would arrive. They placed the canisters in the center of the room and ran to the rear mahogany-paneled wall. Each crouched in a combat position.

"Remember, take out the guard but leave the doctor alive," an electronic muzzled voice sounded inside the gas masks.

Suddenly the mahogany wall started lifting from the marble floor. The whir of electric motors became louder as the wall slowly rose, revealing two pairs of legs. Behind the moving panel one person wore a doctor's white gown. The killers steadied their machine guns. One of the figures behind the sliding wall moved forward quickly. He bent over to enter the main floor. A middle-aged face with a walrus mustache looked into the room, "Harry, where—"

They were his only words. A 9-millimeter shell slammed into his temple. The bullet propelled the body backward. The second gunman let loose with the MAC-10. Four shots sliced into the doctor's legs, spinning him onto the floor. Red splotches spread across his pressed gown. He groaned as he tried to reach a panel of buttons. The mahogany wall had stopped moving. The two killers faced a stainless steel elevator. Hidden behind the wall, it only serviced a secret underground complex.

The second security guard was as dead as Harry. He was sprawled against the back of the elevator, his shattered head twisted as though staring back at his killers. The doctor was panicked. His breathing was erratic and his body trembled. He frantically turned between the two masked figures cradling automatic weapons and the elevator control panel just inches beyond his outstretched fingers.

One of the attackers pulled a third gas mask from the box and slipped it over the terrified doctor. He bound the doctor's hands with adhesive tape.

"Don't try to free yourself, Doc. That stuff's strong enough to hold a 300-pound man. Just want to make sure you don't do anything stupid like taking your mask off. We don't want to see you dead. Yet." He looked at his partner. "Let's do it."

They planted two bloated canisters on the staircase. Then they used keys to unlock levers on the side of the polished cylinders. They slowly pulled the levers clockwise. A small hole popped open on top of each canister.

The two men sprinted back to the elevator, carrying their automatic weapons and the other canisters. One pressed the console's Down button and the mahogany wall began closing. When it blocked out the last crack of light, the elevator lurched and started descending.

"Those little cans are filled with something you're familiar with, Doc. VX-cyber gas." The doctor looked up at the attackers. He could not see their faces, but he had no doubt they were telling the truth. He was astonished to hear the words. VX-cyber was a classified Soviet nerve weapon. According to the protocols of the 1975 germ warfare treaty the gas was destroyed. It had never been used on the public. But the doctor knew all about it. He had even seen exact replicas created. Released in small concentrations it spread quickly over a wide area. The first inhalation caused the lungs' bronchial linings to expand uncontrollably. The gas caused an instantaneous shock to the central nervous system, knocking the body into an epileptic fit. As the victim shook violently, the lungs swelled until they exploded. Certain death in less than a minute. Yet the gas had a half-life of only six minutes. In the atmosphere it was useless in ten minutes. Exposed to moisture, it lost its potency immediately. That was why the Soviets were willing to eliminate it. Its use was too limited. But it was ideal in a setting like this. The doctor knew the gas had already killed the people in the top of the mansion. If any gas escaped outside, the London storm would instantly destroy it. And in ten minutes anyone could safely enter the house and there would be virtually no trace of the killer vapor.

Suddenly the elevator jolted to a halt. The ride took less than twenty seconds. The elevator's rear panels opened wide, revealing a small, metal-lined cubicle. Less than five feet in front of them was a massive steel door, as imposing as the entrance to a bank vault. The only object in the small crypt was a thin black column topped with a sheet of opaque glass. The killers knew what they wanted was on the other side of the steel door.

"C'mon, Doc, time to go to work." One of the gunmen grabbed the doctor by his collar and dragged him to the black pillar. The doctor was about to faint, the pain in his wounded legs was excruciating.

"Hold on, Doc, there's not much you have to do. Don't conk out on us now."

He cut the tape binding the doctor's bloody hands and wiped one of the palms. "See, we know all about your little fingerprint ID machine. We can't get inside because our prints aren't in the computer's brain. So all you eggheads think once that door closes behind you, then your asses are safe because this damn device will only let a friend through. And we also know this little bugger has a special circuit to pick up a pulse, so you can't put down a picture of the print and fool it like in the old days. You can't even cut off someone's hand and place it on the glass because the fucking machine will know you're dead and won't let us in. Now wouldn't that be terrible after we've come all this way?"

The mirrored visor tilted toward the doctor. The doctor's fear kept him from speaking. Only muffled grunts of pain came over the miniature speakers inside the gas masks. The white gown was drenched in blood from the waist down. His eyes were pleading for mercy but the gunmen could not see them.

The killer grabbed the doctor's clean hand and pressed it firmly over the opaque glass. A light flashed and a toneless computerized voice came through a small ceiling speaker, "Good morning Dr. Schwartz." There was a loud click and the steel door rolled open, revealing a spotless white corridor, some twenty feet long. The scarred gunman looked at the doctor.

"Thanks," he said, and he pumped a burst of bullets into his chest.

He turned to his partner. "C'mon, let's finish this. We'll collect his mask on the way out."

They walked slowly into the underground complex. On the right was the security office; a wall of blank video screens faced an empty chair and a still steaming cup of coffee. To their left, a pair of aluminum swinging doors signaled the complex's main work station and computer room. The two killers swung into action. One ran to the end of the corridor. To an untrained eye it looked as though he had reached a solid metal wall. But the gunmen knew it was the hermetically sealed entrance to a sophisticated testing laboratory. Ground zero for their mission. No gas could penetrate the door's seals. But if their intelligence information was right, the entrance would open in less than a minute for a scheduled change of duty. They opened the locks on the cylinders and turned the levers in a half circle. Another fraction would release the gas.

On schedule there was a loud click at the steel shield.

"Here it is!" came an excited voice inside the gas masks.

The panel raised quickly, revealing a man and woman in white medical gowns, walking briskly toward the closest gunman. The two doctors saw the automatic weapon at the same moment. As panic crossed their faces the first silenced bursts hammered them. The nearest doctor took the bullets in an ascending pattern starting at the stomach and slicing toward the neck. The second doctor was struck at her jaw and ear, the hollow point bullets exiting in gaping holes at the back of her skull. Splashes of vibrant red cascaded down the sides and off the low ceiling of the glistening white corridor. The gunman grabbed the canister, sprinted down the corridor, and burst into the laboratory. On three walls were banks of scientific equipment, crammed above counters of the smoothest polished stainless steel. Three doctors shot up from their work to face the intruder. They were professionals. They rushed to destroy their specimens and records. They never had a chance.

The gunman hurled the canister. It crashed against a row of microscopes and bounced into a large display of empty testing vials, sending splinters of glass flying around the lab. The three doctors had barely moved when they doubled over in pain. Within seconds they crashed to the floor, each body thrashing uncontrollably. Screams of agony bounced off the hard walls.

At the other end of the hallway the pale gunman had set off the final gas canister. Inside the gleaming, high-tech research center, twisted among video monitors and computerized testing machines, two more scientists were in their death throes. The gunman sprinted past the convulsing victims into the computer center, where an operator was sprawled on the floor, blood streaming from his mouth.

"We've got ten minutes to wrap this," came the voice in the gas mask. They systematically set about completing their mission. They collected the bodies from the underground complex, another from the mansion's upper floors, and dumped them into the entrance hall together with Harry and those killed at the massacre's start. A small sack was opened and what appeared to be dust and dark brown chips was sprinkled under the bodies. Miniature incendiary devices were stuck around the pile of corpses. The four large incendiary packets were attached to the mainframe computers and memory banks. The six high-density plastic explosives were scattered, two on the upper floors and four in the underground complex. All the destructive devices were joined by a coordinated trip-timer ensuring the explosions and fires were orchestrated to the millisecond.

"Everything's set. One last thing and we're out of here," came the message inside the gas masks.

Inside the testing lab, the pale-faced killer settled in front of a computer terminal. He programmed a series of access codes. Their intelligence was right. The code was correct. The computer responded by releasing microchip locks on a floor hatch in a corner of the lab. The scarred gunman ran and yanked open the hatch, revealing a narrow vertical tunnel. While his partner stood guard, he climbed down a series of metal rungs until he reached a small landing. He faced a temperature-controlled metal safe embedded in concrete. He knew it was lined with electromagnetic explosive strips that would destroy the entire tunnel if there was any forced entry. He squatted in front of the safe and studied a computerized digital lock, with an adjoining keypad. Again, intelligence had given him an access code that changed daily. He pressed twenty-six digits into the keypad and when the last number was entered, the locker's door pushed open.

"We've got it!" he proclaimed.

Inside were ten plastic strips, each containing five small metal cylinders, resembling silver lipsticks. Each was hermetically sealed with bulbous aluminum caps. The cylinders contained a yellow-reddish liquid. That is what the killers sought. Stored underneath were two small beakers, each containing a clear solution and also topped with the aluminum stoppers. The gunman gingerly placed the cylinders and beakers into a leather bag designed for the operation. Each container fit into its own padded compartment and separate pouch. Although the gunman was told that everything was shatterproof, he was not taking any chances.

"I'm coming up. Reach down and take the bag."

He climbed up the tunnel and pushed the duffel through the hatch. They were on their way out. They rode the elevator for the last time, pausing for a moment by the front door.

"Are you sure you checked every room on the upper floor? No unexpected visitors?"

"No one. I was careful. Besides, we got a full count on the number in the house. You worry too much. Between the gas and blowing this place, no one's coming out but us."

The scarred killer looked at a digital display on a small square box resembling a calculator. He programmed the keypad, set the figures at "2.00," and pressed a green button at the top. The numbers began flashing down by hundredths of seconds.

They opened the front door and exited with their backs to the street, removing their gas masks under the awning. It was done so quickly that no one noticed them. The storm was still battering London. Torrential rain splashed all around. They threw the masks into a satchel and skipped down the stairs. The cameras only caught pictures of their backs. Even if the film, maintained in fireproof locks, survived the coming explosions, their identities would remain a mystery. They were inside the postal van in thirty seconds.

Traffic was light for midmorning central London. They sped by the festive Christmas decorations at Selfridge's and passed the bright holiday trappings at Piccadilly Circus. The noise of the truck and beating of the rain covered the thunder of the first explosions that ripped apart the house. Reverse-cycle detonators pulled the force of the blasts inward. Virtually no debris flew outside. The resulting fires, fueled by plastic inflammatories set among the explosives, raged until midafternoon. By then the entire complex was gutted, the dead bodies just a heap of ashes.

From the edge of Green Park, a group of men watched the fire burn out of control. They did not mingle with the television news crews that scurried to cover the story nor did they get near the police and fire brigades that manned the area. These men had been dispatched within minutes of the blasts to assess the damage. By noon they had seen enough. They left the scene in two cars speeding down Regent Street. Washington was waiting for their report.

CHAPTER 2 ━━━━━

Langley, Virginia
December 13
7:00 a.m.

Below CIA headquarters is a secluded compound. Past the armed guards, the battery of dogs, the photo and fingerprint identifiers, and a body search for weapons, iron doors open to reveal one of the Agency's best kept secrets. Inside a single room are banks of computers, rows of telephones, and stacks of terminals and video monitors. A Star Trek-like console crammed with flashing lights, buttons, digital keypads, and rows of brightly colored handles is manned by a single person. The CIA officially calls the room the "Central Emergency Response Command." Agents call it the "panic desk."

There are two basic secrets every CIA agent must know and remember: his or her code name and the telephone number to that desk. In any crisis, from blown operations to bungled assassinations to casualties in the field, the first call is to the underground bunker. On the receiving end, an experienced agent must make quick decisions to commence the Agency's emergency responses.

On the day of the London massacre, the panic desk officer was Peter Kessler, an eighteen-year Agency veteran. In a special operation in Laos in 1972, a Khmer Rouge booby trap blew off his legs. Kessler rejected early retirement and fought to stay in the Agency. Two years of agonizing physical therapy, together with an intensive weight-training program, left his upper body as strong as ever. The CIA made him the chief security officer at the panic desk. At forty-two, the muscular, black-bearded Kessler was not a man who scared easily.

"285-6702." CIA telephones are answered only with a number. The first call came before dawn. Kessler pushed his wheelchair to the center of the command board and pressed a button that placed the incoming call on a speaker.

"This is the Falcon. There's been a probable hit at Section 6, Department 2." The voice was very clear, the hiss of the transatlantic connection barely audible.

As the caller spoke, one of the world's largest computers whirred into action. It first retrieved the file of the agent code-named "Falcon" and flashed it on a computer terminal in front of Kessler. Falcon was acting of his own free will. If he was in enemy hands and forced to call, he would have tipped Kessler by giving an alternate code name. The computer also verified the sound pattern of the telephone voice against a stored microchip of the real agent's voice. An impostor would be unmasked before he could utter another word. A green light flashed in the corner of the command module confirming the caller was the real Falcon.

His photo appeared on a video monitor, together with brief background information. Falcon was a CIA case officer stationed in the London embassy, working under a State Department cover. A seven-year veteran, he had four commendations for covert assignments. Kessler reached over to a keypad and pressed in the department and section numbers that Falcon gave at the beginning of the call. Another computer terminal flickered on, revealing only that Section 6, Department 2, was a London station and that its function was "scientific research." Not much to go on, thought Kessler.

While he digested the summaries, a separate electronic switching center traced the incoming telephone number. At the same time, the world's most sophisticated battery of digital surveillance equipment swept the lines. It pinpointed any listening devices and neutralized them with magnetic countertools.

"Are you on a secure line?"

Since agents only called the panic number during emergencies, they seldom had the luxury of using CIA telephone lines, considered untraceable and free of electronic bugs. If an agent was on a public line, the panic desk officer had to disguise the call with double-talk.

"Yes. I'm calling from Section 3, the tank. This is a morning call."

Again, Falcon told Kessler a lot. "Section 3" was the code name for the American embassy in London. A yellow light flashed on the control panel as the tracer confirmed the incoming call was from the embassy. The "tank" referred to a sound-secure room found in major CIA stations. Resembling a streamlined railroad car on stilts, constructed of space-age, sound absorbing material, it provided the ultimate safeguards for any conversation. "This is a morning call" was a warning phrase, cautioning Kessler that the subject matter must be tightly guarded, even at headquarters.

"What's happened?"

"We lost all communications from the section at 1000 hours London time. Repeated attempts to open a line failed. We're having a bad storm here and it delayed a physical check until twenty minutes ago. I've just got back from the station. It looks like a total wipe. We've got fire everywhere."

"Hostile action?"

"Can't get near enough to find out. British police and fire got there before we did. But I smelled mercury. Also, most of the place came down as if it's been blasted. I'm pretty sure we've had a hostile takeout."

Kessler knew mercury was a telltale sign of high-density plastic explosives. Depending on the amount used in a blast, mercury can be detected up to an hour after the operation.

"What's the body count?"

"Can't confirm any yet, but this is the first day in two months that everyone on staff was due to be there. They had an operations meeting scheduled for later today. Whoever hit the station might have got lucky. We can't contact any agent at any location. It looks like a total hit."

"Have you alerted our cousins?"

The CIA calls agents from British intelligence, MI6, "cousins."

"Yep. Called 'em right away. Two are there now telling the local police and fire people that this is government business. More of them will be arriving together with our team to help sweep the inside, but the way it's burning it doesn't look like anyone is going to get in for a while."

"Any sign of hostiles in the area?"

"Nope. Nothing. But whoever did it had to be good. I knew the guys inside the station, and they were very solid. They wouldn't have gone down easy."

"Anything else?"

"Not now."

"Okay, go back to the scene and monitor it in person. Check back in at 1300 hours and update me then."

Kessler cut off the phone connection before Falcon even signed off. Kessler was in a rush. He was about to move one of the most complex government machineries into its emergency mode. He spun his wheelchair back and reached over to a standing computer terminal. He pressed a code across a touch-sensitive glass panel. It bounced a microwave signal to a satellite that then transmitted a hard copy of the Falcon call to the computer terminal of the chief of covert operations. All of the deputy directors were notified within two minutes. The CIA director was interrupted from a European meeting with NATO representatives and received a telephone briefing. Within six minutes of the Falcon's call, Kessler had warned all branches of American intelligence that a hostile action might be under way.

"This is Central Emergency Command. Bring me the primary files on Section 6, Department 2. On the double!" Kessler yelled into a microphone wired directly into the records branch. The files contained the section's complete history. They had copies of all transfers, written memos, orders, and directives. Records called back within a minute, a timid male voice coming over the speaker.

"Sir, there are no primary files on that section."

"Well, then bring me the secondary set and do it now!"

"Sorry, sir, but there is no secondary set either. There is nothing under the listing you are asking about."

"What the hell are you talking about? Are they signed out or what?"

"We just don't have them, sir. They aren't missing. From our system it doesn't look like we ever had them."

"What the hell's going on here?" The conversation was broken when a tall, very thin, middle-aged man ran into the panic room. He was wearing a dark grey suit that was at least a size too large. His white oxford shirt needed a wash, the oversized button-down collar was badly crumpled. The navy-blue-and-maroon-striped club tie was knotted crookedly. The black Florsheim wingtips badly needed a shine. The face was filled with anxiety. His pale skin looked worse in the underground lighting. His eyes were dark and deep-set, heavy bags under each. The hair, the same dark grey shade as the suit, was thin and plastered straight back. Perspiration made his scalp glisten between the shiny dark patches. Kessler never knew his visitor to look anything but disheveled. The man was Tony Finch, a CIA deputy director, and the chief of all covert operations. His disorganized appearance and slight physical build masked a decorated spymaster. One of the Agency's best field agents, he skyrocketed through the bureaucracy to grab control of the covert division less than a year earlier. He was an action oriented director. His operations were risky and ambitious, and he delighted in giving the KGB fits.

"I just got the flash. Do you know anything else?"

"Nothing. I can't even get my hands on the files for the section that was hit. Records doesn't have a thing."

Finch looked down at Kessler. He leaned over as if he was about to impart a great secret.

"It's okay. I'll take over from here. If it's hostile I want a team on this right away. You can do me a favor. Get me two computer tracers and also get Warrell from forensics. Then track down Richard McGinnis and get him to headquarters ASAP."

Although they were the only persons in the compound, Finch dropped his voice to a husky whisper. "Don't worry about the files. That station was a Delphi program."

Finch patted Kessler on the back and in an instant was on his way out of the panic station. That's why there was so little information in the computer, thought Kessler. Delphi programs were shrouded under the highest level of Agency secrecy. They were supersensitive and known only to the director and a few of the deputy directors. Kessler spun his wheelchair back to the command module and started locating the people that Finch wanted.

Richard McGinnis had celebrated his forty-fourth birthday just a month earlier. The problem was there had been no cake or candles, no balloons, no cards from his wife or son. Not that he expected one from his son. Twenty years had pushed them farther apart rather than closer, and he didn't expect any sign of caring. Although he was separated from his wife for four years, she still had his birthday checked on her kitchen calendar with a large red X. She didn't need the X. She knew the date just like she knew the date of their anniversary. But she kept it prominently displayed so visitors to her Virginia home would still see she had a tie to her wandering husband.

He was sure she would have sent a card. But how could you send a card into the jungle in the Congo? She didn't even know where he had been and there was nothing new about that. It was one of the reasons they split, the months of not knowing finally taking their toll. He could have been dead in some third world hole five thousand miles away or in perfect health just a couple of doors down the road. That was the problem. The uncertainty. She was a strong woman, no doubt about that. But after seventeen years of marriage the worrying had worn her down. It broke her spirit. He remembered how much she trembled and wept when she told him she was taking their son and going to her mother's house. She left with an ulcer and without any friends. He couldn't blame her. He was surprised she lasted as long as she did. But she still would have sent a card; that was certain.

It had been some birthday. He had been responsible for a group of black African soldiers dubbed the "Congo Freedom Fighters Brigade." Shit, they couldn't even shoot an automatic carbine when he took over. The average age was eighteen, younger than his son. And he was running all over 110-degree rain forests to kill some Cubans and Angolans and strike a blow for freedom. He almost got his ass shot off on his birthday because a stupid sentry forgot to set the trip-timers and a group of Cubans ambushed their base camp. Some birthday.

He stood up from the leather recliner. The television screen was filled with highlights from yesterday's Minnesota Viking–San Francisco 49er football game. But the volume was turned off. He liked it that way— the announcers' second guessing made him furious. Next to his chair was a beige Formica side table topped with an enormous bowl of Planter's peanuts and extra-crispy barbecued potato chips. It was half empty. He grabbed the skin above his belt. Shit, he could pinch a thick roll of fat. There was a time when he was solid, "like granite," his wife used to tell him. The weights, the running, the work, it kept him in peak physical condition. Now it wasn't so easy. Everything had become automated. He didn't have to chase many people, just had to aim a laser dot and press the trigger of a high-powered rifle. Didn't take a strong heart or a lot of muscles to do that.

He squeezed the roll of skin again. He knew he had to cut out some of the crap he ate. His freezer was stuffed with frozen pizzas, tamales, refried beans, and half-eaten plates of spaghetti. A girl he dated for a couple of months had tried to get him to eat "healthy." She was from California, and she had some strange ideas of what was good for you. He shuddered at the thought. She used to give him a shot of wheat grass in the morning, and he could only eat bran cereal before noon, without any milk. He was eating so many vegetables he thought he would turn into a goddamn rabbit. He had so much gas he was embarrassed to be with his friends. He never felt worse than when he was eating "healthy."

Anyway, he knew his body was still in better shape than most men his age. He was strong. He looked at his reflection in the gold antiqued mirror behind the TV. His six-foot, two-inch frame was still solid. His dark brown hair was short, but thick. No sign of baldness although a little grey was showing at the temples. His face was still good. Strong nose, full lips, and his best feature; crystal-blue eyes. It was the same all-American face that had made him a college heartthrob. Only the sun had etched in some wrinkles. He looked his age. He flexed his biceps and his T-shirt bulged. Not bad for twenty years in this back-breaking business. He leaned over, grabbed a tumbler of Jack Daniel's, and took a long swig. Now bourbon was good for your body, and no flake from California was going to change his mind about that.

The phone was ringing in the kitchen. Always thought it was a dumb place for a phone, but his wife had put it there. She chided him that it was where she spent most of her time. He meant to get another phone installed at some point, but never seemed to be home long enough to do it.

"Yeah, McGinnis."

"Well you were easy to reach. This is Kessler at CERC. Finch wants you at headquarters today. Check right into his office; he's waiting for you."

"Bullshit! Look, I've been on the road for nine months. I have two months of rest coming my way."

"It's not my call, McGinnis. He asked for you personally. We've got a problem here."

"There's always a goddamn problem! I've been back two days. I haven't even got over jet lag. Give me a break! I got to see my kid; he's pitching in a game for Georgetown today and pro scouts are going to be there. He's expecting me and I'm not going to let him down. I'll come in after that."

"Listen, McGinnis, this is Finch. We've got a stage one alert here. No bullshit. I need you, Richard. I wouldn't ask otherwise. You're the best damn guy I can get my hands on. Don't let me down. I'm waiting only for you. Everyone else is here. Now get over here and when this is finished I personally promise you double the time off, and I'll keep everyone off your back. Now get going."

The line went dead while McGinnis still had the receiver to his ear.

Those dirty bastards. Kessler calls to do the dirty work while Finch listens on a second line. When Kessler can't bring him in, then Finch butts in to feed him all that crap about how necessary it is that he comes in right away. Well, why can't Finch and Kessler do their special routine on his son. Maybe they could convince him that it wasn't so important if his father missed the biggest game of his brief pitching career.

He had no choice. He had to go in. He had worked with Finch in the field. Then, he could have told him where to go. But as chief of covert operations, Finch could order him to jump into a pile of shit and he would have to do it. But he had to do one last thing before he went. He dreaded this more than fighting the damn Cubans in Africa. He dialed the number and hoped no one was home. It was always easier to avoid confrontations.

"Hello."

"Hi, Andy, it's Dad." He looked into the living room at a framed picture of his son. It was a couple of years old, but it was a good shot. A bushy, full head of dirty blond hair and a wholesome smiling face. The teeth may be slightly crooked, and he didn't get the blue eyes, but he was a great looking kid.

"Hey, Dad, what's up? I'm just getting ready to leave. I want to warm up a little longer before this game. By the way, I heard at school that a scout from the Yankees is going to be there. What do you have to say about that?"

"Hey, that's great. But something's come up for me. I had to call you." He paused for a moment and then quickly spit out the rest of the words. "I'm not going to be able to make it . . . but I wanted to call you . . ."

"Yeah, yeah, sure, just cut it short. Something always comes up. Something is always more important than me or Mom. Jesus, I knew it! I just knew it! I told her there was no way you'd come. Man, I was a jerk to think anything was different. Thanks for nothing."

"Listen—"

The phone slammed down on the other end. McGinnis instinctively jerked the receiver away from his ear. Shit. He had to drag his body into some meeting about God knows what, and his son wasn't going to want to talk to him for weeks, maybe months. He hurled the glass of bourbon against the yellow Formica kitchen cabinets. He wished somebody had shattered it against him.

CIA headquarters was in a priority alert. Extra security guards patrolled the ground floor. McGinnis had to show his identification and still pass a photo analyzer. A lot of hocus-pocus, he thought. As if any KGB agent was going to come through the CIA's front door disguised as a pizza deliveryman. Checking the IDs and then double-checking the photos against the internal files accomplished nothing. He knew that any KGB agents inside the CIA were already well placed. They crossed that security check daily without incident. They worked for the CIA. It's just that no one knew they also worked for the KGB.

Finch's office was a large corner room on the fourth floor. Corner offices were important at Langley. They announced you had arrived at the inner power sanctum. The office looked like Finch. Newspapers were scattered on a slightly battered sofa and over a bland oak desk. The carpet was worn near the center and the vertical blinds looked like they had not been dusted in weeks. The view was nothing special. Just a bunch of trees that surrounded headquarters, and by this time of year the leaves had fallen. The room was crowded. Warrell was seated on the sofa, next to the discarded newspapers. He was one of the Agency's best forensic investigators. Two computer analysts were in a settee against the far wall. McGinnis had seen them before but knew little about them. Sitting in front of Finch's desk was a new fellow. Young, not more than mid-twenties, his chiseled face was tan. His dark hair was cut into a crew cut. Although the man was wearing a blue blazer, McGinnis could see he was broad. It wasn't fat, but muscles, that stretched his clothes. He looked like a college football player.

"Sorry I'm late but the freeway was backed up with a stalled truck."

"It's okay, take a seat," Finch said as he glanced up from behind the desk. "You can go." He waved at Warrell and the two analysts. The kid stayed. McGinnis sat in a chair next to him.

"Listen, Richard, we've got a bad one. I'm going to tell you what we know up to now. Oh, by the way, this is Jimmy Harris. He's just out of Peary."

Camp Peary is the CIA clandestine training camp in Virginia. It is where new agents are taught the tricks of the spy trade. It is also where they are trained to kill in a boggling assortment of sophisticated ways. Well, what's the kid doing sitting in a priority alert meeting with the chief of operations? McGinnis was in the same spot twenty years ago, but that was rare. Normally, it's graduation from Peary and then a couple of years in a foreign assignment. He actually didn't care what the young agent was doing there. As long as it didn't affect him.

"We've lost an entire station in London. A Delphi program. The place has been burnt to the ground. It happened early this morning, London time. We've had a topflight cleaning crew go inside. They've found a pile of human ashes and some bones."

"Ours?" the kid asked.

"It takes about a week for the doctors to do their magic with remains like that. The bones have to be compared to cross structures in the agents' files; a lot of painstaking work. We won't get positive IDs for a while. But it looks like everyone at the station was there when the place went down."

"How many?" McGinnis looked over at Finch.

"Fourteen, if we lost them all. And from the first cleaning they found some interesting items. Mercury activated plastics. They've also cleaned a microscopic residue from the remains. Some of it looks like the chemical structure for a deactivated gas called VX-cyber."

"That's a Soviet germ weapon. I've heard all about it," Harris chimed in.

Oh, shit. I can't take much more of this, thought McGinnis. It's like being back in school. Who cares if the kid knows VX-cyber gas from his elbow? The only saving grace is if the meeting is a short one. He could never stand them when they just came out of Camp Peary. They thought they knew everything. That's how he felt when he got out.

Finch looked at them. "It certainly is a Soviet germ agent. And it's not supposed to exist. Which means the Russians have been pulling us around by the noses on this one. They've had the damn stuff, and since we thought it was gone, we weren't prepared for it. And mercury in the plastics is the way Ivan always likes to do business. So they've hit us and hit us hard."

"What was this Delphi program anyway?" asked McGinnis.

"Some germ warfare research. Mostly defensive. Mostly trying to figure out ways to fight their stuff. I'm going to have you cleared for some background info. But this is more than just a hit on a station. As part of their work, our guys had developed some pretty strong chemical weapons. It was never supposed to be used. It was just part of their research. We have completed preliminary environmental tests and the area around the station is completely clean. As far as we can tell, none of it was released in the hit. As bad as that would have been, it might be worse if it's in Russian hands. If the Russkies have those weapons, I'm afraid they may be coming here to shove it down our throats. Then we're not talking about fourteen agents, we're talking about millions of Americans. I've already got a team in London finding out what happened. They'll come up with leads on the hit squad. What I want you two to do is run the main U.S. team and be prepared in case the Soviets try to bring stuff here. If they come, I want you two to close them down before we've got a goddamn national emergency."

What does he mean by "you two"? Finch expects that a kid who is not even wet behind the ears is going to be his partner on this. No way. And he was called away from his son's ball game on the slim possibility that a couple of KGB boys might be taking a flight to America with some kind of mysterious germ weapon. Give me a break. This is real horseshit.

"Why don't you just have the President call the Soviets and tell them that if their agents spread this stuff in America, it will be considered an act of war?" Harris asked.

"The President doesn't know about the London station and its Delphi task. It technically violated a couple of treaties. So the Russians know they have us cold on this one. We can't bitch about the hit since the station is not supposed to have existed and we can't go diplomatic to stop the possible germ infection. We've got to handle this one totally inside the Company and we have to do it quickly and quietly."

McGinnis couldn't stop himself. "What do you mean by 'you two' are going to do this and 'you two' are going to do that? Tony, you know I work alone and answer only to you or a case officer." He looked over at Harris. "No disrespect, son, but I'm not going to set up an operation like this with a rookie hanging over my shoulder."

"Hey . . . ," Harris started, but Finch signaled him to stop.

"Leave us for a minute, Jimmy." Finch looked at the young agent. Harris stood up and left the office, firmly closing the door behind him.

"Look it, Tony . . ."

"No, you 'look it,' Richard." Finch walked in front of the desk and hovered over McGinnis. "I've saved your ass a number of times and you know it. Now shut up and listen for a goddamn minute instead of always wanting to hear your own voice. This kid's special. He's number one in his class at Peary. He's done the best there in a long time. He even broke some of your long-standing records. It's the same thing the Agency did with you. We've been thinking of where to send the kid for his first assignment, and then this broke today. If the Russians try to bring this stuff into the U.S., you're going to be involved in the hunt of your life and you're going to need all the help you can get here at headquarters. You'll need someone working side by side with you. This is who we want next to you. The kid knows the latest Soviet tricks, he's just learned them for Chrissake, he can help you, Richard."

"My ass he can help me. And you know it, Tony. I'm supposed to be at home getting my sore ass some rest after almost a year of running around and shooting at Castro's boys in a war no one knows is taking place and no one would care about if they did know. Instead I'm called here in a big emergency to prepare for something that may never happen. You don't even know if the Russians got the damn stuff, whatever the hell it is! And then I'm supposed to babysit boy wonder out there. This is a lot of crap and you know it."

"That's it! No more! Just because you're a goddamn decorated hero doesn't mean you can't follow a simple order! This is your assignment and you're going to start getting briefed together with Harris. You're going to work with him. He's your partner, and you two are going to prepare this operation as if the Russians were bringing the germs into this country as we speak. Do you understand?"

Although Finch was slightly built, he could scream with the best of them. His voice echoed off the office walls. He was mad, and McGinnis knew there was no point in arguing. The decision might as well have been cast in concrete.

McGinnis stood up, nodded, and walked outside, slamming the door behind him. Harris was leaning against an empty secretary's desk, slowly digging paper clips into the wood veneer. McGinnis walked right up on top of him and whispered so no one else could hear.

"Listen. We're going to be working together for a couple of days. I don't want to hear about everything you learned at Peary and I don't care how much weight you can bench press or how well you can shoot at the range. I don't want to socialize with you, and if we eat together it will be because we're stuck here late. I've got twenty years on your sorry butt, and if I say it's done one way then that's the way it's done, no matter what they taught you. You go behind my back once and try to override anything I tell you and I will personally smash your face. I don't want to be your friend so wipe that silly smirk off your face. You look like an asshole. I'll meet you in the briefing room in ten minutes."

McGinnis stalked away. Harris threw a handful of paper clips across the top of the desk. He looked at a secretary at a nearby work station.

"Is he always such a sweetheart?"

"No. Usually he's in a bad mood."

"Great. If he's on my side, I can't wait to run into the Russians."

CHAPTER 3 ⇌━━━━

Paris
December 13
5:00 p.m.

The leading edge of the Atlantic storm that was battering London had crossed French territory. A steady drizzle drenched Paris. It was dusk as the dark grey Mercedes 600 limousine sped down Avenue Kléber and pulled in front of the Raphaël, one of the French capital's most regal hotels. Situated just blocks from the Arc de Triomphe, its simple limestone façade hides an ornate interior. Catering to a wealthy international clientele, its guests ranged from Italian movie directors to Argentine cattle barons to Australian real estate magnates. The man who exited from behind the limousine's smoked windows seemed a typical guest, dressed fashionably and expensively. A long, navy blue cashmere overcoat made him seem taller than his five feet, ten inches. A multicolored paisley silk scarf was wrapped around his neck. His hand-stitched, black gloves were soft kid-leather. A light grey, hand-crafted Borsalino hat was pulled low over his brow. A pair of round, wire-rimmed, dark green sunglasses rested low on the bridge of his nose. Nestled under his left arm was a thin, black leather portfolio. He took large strides, stepping over the small puddles, protecting the polish on his black Italian loafers.

The red uniformed doorman jumped to attention as the new guest passed into the hotel's lobby. He walked briskly along the plush Persian carpet past the Louis XIV marbled consoles and elaborate gilded mirrors. He stared directly ahead, not even glancing at the restaurant or the intimate, dark-paneled bar to his right, both crowded with an early evening social set. At the end of the narrow lobby he reached the hotel's single elevator. He pressed the Up button with the tip of his gloved index finger. While the elevator descended to the lobby, he paced along the edge of a hand-painted Chinese carpet. He scanned the small waiting area. Across from the elevator was the reception desk. A clerk had not even looked up from her paperwork. To the right of the receptionist was a landscape painting by Turner. He admired it. He liked the muted colors and lush scenery. Turner was a real master. Not like some of the modern and pricey junk that had passed as art at a recent exhibition he attended in Vienna. His seven-year-old son could have painted that crap. This was a beautiful painting. He speculated on its value in the hyperactive art world: $10 million? Probably more. If Van Gogh's *Sunflowers* drew more than $50 million, this Turner had to be $15 million, maybe $20 million. It would disappear inside the boardroom of some anonymous Japanese insurance company, and no art lover would see it again. People with serious money were not necessarily the most deserving owners. It took more than cash to be a connoisseur of fine art. His thoughts were interrupted by a grinding noise from the arriving elevator. A turn-of-the-century model, the luxurious mahogany cabin was covered by an iron grate door resembling a folding accordion. When it clanked to a halt, he grabbed the handle on the grating, pulled it open, and stepped inside.

He had arrived in Paris only three hours earlier. He was the contact agent in the highest priority intelligence operation of his career. Waiting for him in a third-floor suite were the two men who had finished the murderous morning in London. A third agent, crucial for the mission's next phases, had also checked in. In his portfolio he carried new identification papers. In his head he carried the next stages of the operation. Without him, the entire plan could grind to a halt.

The elevator lurched to a stop at the third floor. It missed the landing by almost a foot, but he shoved the grate open and stepped up into the hallway. A small wooden sign engraved with gold scroll lettering announced the "Bastille Suite" to the left, and he proceeded to the end of the hallway. He removed his glasses and carefully placed them into the breast pocket of his overcoat. Then he knocked on the door four times in rapid succession. He did not hear a sound, but suddenly the door swung open. He looked into an antiques-filled lounge, but he did not see anyone.

He cleared his throat. "I am here to discuss the designs for the new office building in Milan."

It was the code for his entrance. Without that, he knew the person hidden behind the door would be on top of him the moment he crossed the threshold. He placed his right hand inside his overcoat and lightly gripped his Walther PPK. As he entered the room he quickly spun around to look behind the door. There, a tall man stared directly at him, a 9-millimeter automatic pistol was pointed at his face. The gunman wore a pair of dark grey pleated wool trousers, but only a white tank top covered part of his tan and muscular torso. He noticed a scar extended from the corner of the man's left eye to the middle of his cheek. This was the leader of the London mission. He recognized him from a file photo. The gunman indicated with a nod of his head that it was all right to enter the suite. He stepped inside, and the door closed behind him.

He had not noticed the noise from the television when he was standing at the door. But once he walked inside the main room, he glanced at the screen. It was tuned to a French game show. The contestants were yelling and jumping up and down in anticipation of winning a garish dining room set. Bad taste is universal he thought as he glanced around the room. It was modeled as a nineteenth-century parlor—heavy red velvet draperies tied with gold brocaded sashes, and Louis XV furniture set on well worn but expensive Oriental carpets.

On a light green velvet settee sat a short man, dressed in a black shirt and pair of pants. The shirt's dark color made his pudgy, pale face almost seem sickly. A bandage was spread across his nose, plastered to his cheeks with wide strips of adhesive tape. He also recognized the injured man from a file photo. He was the other morning murderer. Across the room in a serpent-decorated, yellow silk lounge chair was a thin young woman. She wore brown wool houndstooth pants and an oversized white cashmere pullover. Her chestnut hair was thick and shoulder length, setting off a soft and attractive face. Large, dark brown eyes and full lips gave her a seductive allure. Her skin was smooth, almost like porcelain. But there was also a pallor that indicated her work kept her indoors for too many hours. Nothing that a little sunshine couldn't cure. She did not look like a doctor nor an intelligence agent, but he knew she was both.

"First, congratulations are in order," he announced as he removed his hat, overcoat, scarf, and gloves. He meticulously placed them on top of an empty footstool. Then he settled into an oversized brown leather club chair. The scarred gunman strolled to the television and increased the volume, insuring no passersby overheard the conversation. He then walked back to the lounge entrance, where he remained standing, the Beretta tucked into the waistband of his pants.

"The count at the target was perfect. Everyone accounted for. British and American agents were running all over the place this afternoon. There's not much left for them to scrape up and investigate. We think it's very clean."

The chubby man chuckled nervously, gently pressing his bandaged nose with one hand, as if the laughter hurt the wound. "It should be. We always like to leave things as clean as when we arrive. We don't want any complaints."

Was that supposed to be a joke? He was aggravated by the interruption but ignored it. "Let me see the liquids."

While the scarred killer went to the bedroom, the contact agent turned toward the pale killer.

"How did that happen?" he asked while nodding toward the bandaged nose.

"I blew my nose too hard and broke it."

"Cut the bullshit." He was agitated. "I don't have time for any crap!"

"Just calm down. I'm the one that should be high-strung. I was in hand-to-hand combat with a gorilla earlier today. Then I only had to wipe out a high security CIA station while my nose was busted. So don't snap at me." They stared at each other for a moment. Then the pale agent pointed toward his nose. "It got broken in a scuffle with one of their agents."

"So your blood is on the scene?" The contact agent was strictly interested in business.

"If it can be found in the ashes."

"But if they find it, they'll know you're hurt. A freshly crushed nose isn't great for melting anonymously into an international air flight, now is it?"

"I don't know. Tell me, O wise one, is it?"

The contact agent ignored the sarcasm. He would have to make a difficult decision before he left. The contingency plans for the remainder of the operation had been drawn to work with only two people. Maybe the chubby killer was too risky to move, his visible wound an advertisement to any sharp-eyed CIA personnel.

"Here it is." The scarred man returned with a leather duffel. He unzipped it and held it at an angle so the visitor could see the aluminum topped cylinders and vials, each resting in separate padded compartments.

"I don't have to tell you," the woman broke in, "but you cannot be too careful with that."

"Don't worry. Within an hour it will be on its way to America. It will arrive before any of you. As a matter of fact, doctor, your directions are being followed to the letter. The liquids will enter the U.S. under diplomatic cover, as part of a scheduled pharmaceutical delivery for the Burmese legation at the United Nations. Once past the U.S. point of entry, they will never get near the UN. You'll find them waiting for you at the New York safe house."

"Who is doing the personal delivery?" she asked without even glancing at him.

"I will. Joining me on the flight to the States will be a biochemist provided by headquarters. He's just there for insurance. In case there are problems. I do not expect any. A Burmese agent will be there for the actual clearance into the U.S., but he has no idea what he is letting in."

"I cannot overemphasize the care that must be taken with this material." Now she stared directly at him. "You've never had anything as important as this on your lap in your life. I have spent too many years waiting to work with this. We are too close to let anything go wrong. I want it there so that when we arrive I can begin my work. If you fail to get the liquids in safely, not even killing you would satisfy me."

Her face had lost its soft touch. She was now as hard as any agent he had encountered. Her eyes were impassive. She did not care whether he lived or died. She just wanted him to complete his part of the operation and then be out of her way.

He ignored the baiting. It was no use to engage her. They all seemed edgy, almost pushing for an argument. He was not going to give any of them cause to vent their frustration or anger on him. He pushed the duffel under his legs while he pulled the portfolio onto his lap and unzipped it.

"I have your entry IDs here. All belong to real people who have been eliminated within the past day. Your photos have been substituted on their passports. The work is first rate. Two of you are traveling as Americans, and one as a Swiss national with permanent residence in the States. Extreme care was taken to find passports of people who fit your general descriptions, in addition to finding people whose absence would not be immediately noted. They were all individual travelers on extended vacations. By the time these people are reported missing, your mission in America will be over and you will be home. Any questions so far?"

There was silence. He looked at her. "You will be Erica Cane. You are a computer analyst employed by Spector Vision of Sunnyvale, California. You are divorced, no children, and are thirty-three years old." He looked at her to see how she fit the age. Not bad. Although when her face was hard she looked older.

"The papers are made of opaque selenium base. When you have finished digesting the information, just wet them and they will dissolve. Make sure nothing is left behind."

"How is this room being paid?" He looked at the standing gunman.

"Cash. Prepaid for three days. Registered under a French identity that is safe. I arranged it myself."

"All right. Here's your set. You are David Colby, an independently wealthy Swiss money manager based in New York. Here is your background." He flipped a plastic folder across the frosted cocktail table.

He swiveled to face the chubby killer. "You are Peter Dillon, an insurance salesman with Prudential Life Company. You live in Orlando, Florida. Get used to this cover.

"Plan is as originally set. You'll rendezvous with me at the East Sixty-third Street safe house tomorrow at 1630 hours. The minilab you've requested, Doctor, is in place. The liquids will be ready for your handling upon arrival. The full operation commences on December 15. Any questions?"

The only sound in the suite was the screaming emanating from the television. Another pair of game show contestants had just won a dishwasher and dryer.

"Within a week you will have completed one of the most important missions ever undertaken. You will be instrumental in striking against our enemies inside the heart of the U.S. We cannot be stopped. They cannot trace the liquids or stop their entry. They are not looking for any of you. They don't even know who you are. And by the time they realize the liquids are being spread, your work will be finished. In one week you will have planted the necessary infections. And then you, dear doctor"—he emphasized the "dear" hoping to aggravate her—"will be able to monitor the results. I am sure that pleases you."

"It will please me when we are in New York. Is that all?"

"For now, that is all."

The meeting was over. He carefully wrapped his scarf around his neck, slipped into his overcoat, pulled on his gloves, and placed his hat securely on his head. He gingerly grabbed the duffel bag and walked to the door. As he stood in the doorway, he spoke in a hushed whisper to the scarred man, now David Colby. In less than a minute they finished, and the contact agent walked out the door. David Colby walked across the room and looked out the leaded windows, watching while his contact got into the Mercedes 600. The rain was coming in steady sheets. The poplar trees along the avenue swayed under strong winds that announced the storm's arrival.

"What did he talk to you about?" the woman asked.

"He wanted me to watch him as he left the hotel. If I see anyone following or observing him, I am to immediately call headquarters. But, everything is fine outside. He has left without incident."

The car pulled away from the hotel and sped down the slick streets toward the Left Bank. He turned away from the draperies and faced his two comrades. "Let's study the ID summaries and then get rid of them."

He turned off the television. They sat quietly in a semicircle for nearly twenty minutes. Each memorized the trivia in the file folders, trying to adapt to the identities that would gain them unnoticed entry to the U.S. Dates of birth, relatives, personal quirks, brief medical histories, schooling, and an abbreviated personal history. There was enough information for them to handle anything from a casual conversation to an intensive questioning by the U.S. Immigration and Naturalization Service.

"I don't want these hanging around." Colby held up his file folder and looked at the other two agents. "Finished?" They nodded. "From now on we refer to each other only by our operational names. We must live as the new people. Understood?"

Again they nodded their agreement.

He walked near the window overlooking the avenue. The storm had followed them from London. It depressed him, the constant grey sky and relentless cold. If he didn't catch pneumonia from the morning's soaking he would be pleasantly surprised. He could have daydreamed at the window for a long time. There had been enough killing for one day. But his orders were clear. He forced himself to turn away from the window.

"C'mon, Peter, let's get rid of this paperwork."

His chubby comrade jumped up from the settee and gathered the ID files. They pulled the pages from the plastic folders and proceeded into the bathroom, where they tossed them into the antique porcelain bathtub. Colby pushed the rubber stopper into the drain, and turned the spigot on full-blast. Selenium-treated paper was only a year old. It was a major advance in the intelligence trade. It prevented laser and digital reconstruction of burned notes from ashes. It dissolved into a thick, milky serum that washed down the drain on its way to mix with millions of gallons of sewage under the French capital. With the exception of a young agent who got caught with a key document in a tropical rain storm in Thailand, thereby losing the information before he could deliver it, the new paper was a wonder aid. They stood silently and watched as the paper swirled, turning into its telltale, thick slime. Peter reached over and pulled out the drain stopper. In less than a minute, there was no visible trace left in the tub.

"That was easy," Peter murmured to Colby as he turned to leave the bathroom. Before he took a step, Colby reached out and put his strong hands around his friend's chubby face. He pressed his rigid fingers deep into the soft rolls of flesh, grabbing the skull in a viselike grip. He yanked his shocked comrade into the center of the bathroom, spun him around in a single movement, and slammed him hard against the tile wall. There was a dull thud mixed with the cracking of Peter's ribs. The shock of the attack, together with the smash against the wall, delayed Peter's reaction. That was all the time Colby needed. He pulled Peter's head forward several inches from the wall. Then with all his strength he crashed the back of the skull into the smooth tile. The sound of the splintering bone filled the small room, and Colby felt warm blood stream over his fingers, which gripped the victim's head.

Peter's arms, which had started to flail in self-defense, dropped to the side of his body. His eyes rolled backward in their sockets. Colby quickly placed one hand over the front of his victim's face and the other slipped behind to the center of Peter's back. With a grunt of strength, both arms squeezed together. The head snapped back as the chest heaved forward. A sickening crunch announced the spinal cord vertebrae had snapped. The victim's head lolled to one side. He was dead.

Colby stepped back and let the body crumple to the floor. He glanced up and saw the doctor standing in the doorway.

"It was the contact. He ordered it when he left. Nothing can jeopardize this operation. The broken nose, although a slight risk, was one that could not be tolerated. We cannot take the slightest risk. We are to leave him here as an unidentifiable.

"Our departure plans have also changed. We must go to the airport as soon as we are finished here. We will not be flying from here tomorrow. You'll be going to Amsterdam on Air France flight 605 tonight. You'll get to New York on Pan Am 804 tomorrow morning. The tickets are waiting for you at the airport under your new name. I am going to leave from Munich. We arrive within twenty minutes of each other in New York."

She just stared at him, oblivious to the still-warm body on the floor. A small pool of blood was forming around the head. "What is an unidentifiable?"

"Just watch. In this day and age of high technology, there are certain emergencies that require old-fashioned methods. As a doctor you might find it a little crude, but I'm sure you'll agree it's effective."

He lifted the lifeless body over the tub's edge. Head first it slid to the bottom. "While I do this, you can clean the blood on the wall and floor with some toilet paper. Then flush it away."

He rolled up his sleeves and pulled an ivory-handled straight razor from his pocket and snapped it open with the flick of his wrist. Then he bent over the body and, starting with the dead man's right hand, grabbed each finger and deftly sliced off the skin that formed the fingerprints, carefully placing each layer of fresh cut skin into a neat pile at his feet. When he finished cutting the fingertips off both hands, he started on the face, ripping off the bandage that still clung to the nose. She watched him, surprised at the speed with which he worked. It was obviously not the first time he made a body "unidentifiable." The razor then moved to the face. He skimmed over the cheeks, through the lips, around the forehead, into the eyes, and across the ears. Within five minutes, all that was left was a shimmering red mass, an indistinguishable blob where once there had been features.

"That's it," he announced as he stood. "No fingerprints. No face. The French police will mark it up as a horrible murder. Maybe terrorists. Maybe an irate lover. Maybe drugs. But all they will know is it's a man, his height, weight, race, blood type, and maybe his age. That will still fit millions of people. This file will be closed, unsolved, very soon."

"What about his hair color, or eye color, or even footprints—they are as good as fingerprints. What about his teeth? They can match his dental records. If he has an extensive medical history on x-rays they can match him up with body scans." Her medical training was evident.

He was not fazed. "The footprints are useless. There are no data bases with that information. Even with his entire foot, there is nothing they can match him up against. As for the eye and hair color, it fits millions of people. Since they don't know whom they are looking for, it's just too general to help any investigation. The teeth and body x-rays are similarly useless. Since they have no idea who this is, and there is no standardized computer base for dental or body x-rays, there is no way they can identify him. What are they going to do? Start to ask for dental charts from hospitals and private practitioners around the world in the hope that our dead friend is in someone's files? Even if half his bones have been broken in his body, which hospitals or doctors' offices, in which countries, do they start checking with in the hope they may find a match? It's impossible. No police force will be bothered with even thinking about that type of insurmountable task. If I wanted to eliminate any trace, then I would cut off the head and feet. And all I would have accomplished is a torrent of blood and the problem of more waste matter to dispose of. Do you think it would look unusual in the lobby of this fine hotel if my duffel bag dripped blood along the carpet as I left this evening? Oh, no, taking a head is much too messy in this setting. What I've done is fine—without a face and without fingerprints they are stumped."

"What about the parts?" She glanced at the small pile of cut skin as she threw the red-soaked bundle of paper into the toilet.

"I know of a public incinerator not far from here. It's for small parcels. This will be perfect. I'm going to wash and clean up this mess. Why don't you gather your papers and get out of here. Your flight at Orly is only two hours away."

She took less than ten minutes to prepare her bag. He was scrubbing his hands furiously by the time she gathered her coat and walked to the front door. She had been noticeably quiet since the killing. "Don't be bothered by the change of plans with our dear comrade we are leaving behind," he called to her without looking away from the sink. "This week is what you've waited five years for. It is going to be straightforward and simple. You know the liquids. With your help I can pass them easily. We are not going to be stopped." He looked up at her. "You're going to give a new meaning to 'Typhoid Mary.' "

He thought he noticed a small grin.

"Now get out of here and I'll see you in New York tomorrow."

The door slammed shut before he finished his send-off.

CHAPTER 4

McGinnis was restless. He should have stayed in the Congo. At least there he could play by his own rules. Back at headquarters, the dense bureaucracy suffocated him. Worse thing you could catch in the jungle was a bullet. Didn't even have to be an enemy bullet—the damn "freedom fighters" were such nitwits that they could just as easily put a bullet in your back while crapping in their pants from nerves during a good firefight. At least you knew what you were up against in the field. But at headquarters you never knew who the enemy was. He had always hated the gamesmanship required to move up in the Company. Good field agents had to kiss ass from their station chief all the way up the Langley ladder. If you didn't butter up the right people you were almost insured a lousy field assignment. If you weren't a team player, the chance of getting a supervisory job at Langley was remote.

That was always McGinnis's problem. He preferred to play the game alone and by his own rules rather than those established by some damn desk-bound analyst whose closest encounter to real field work came once a year at the firing range. For Chrissake, he was on the scene—he knew how to handle the situation better than some twenty-eight-year-old political science Ph.D. who made decisions after sifting through dozens of technical reports. That's how we got our ass kicked so many times before—agents overruled their best instincts because some dope from headquarters thought it should be done another way.

So the agent does it headquarters' way and then ends up blowing a good cover, a deep source, or worse yet, gets himself killed. McGinnis had promised himself a long time ago that if he was going to die for his country, it was going to be his mistake that caused the end, not some analyst he had never even met.

He was going to try and keep his mouth shut during this briefing. His strong opinions were one of the reasons he wasn't at a higher rank and pay. Good agents performed their assignments—quietly. McGinnis did what he was supposed to, and then bitched to everyone about the mishaps and close calls. If people didn't like what he had to say they didn't have to listen. But he was damned if he wasn't going to express his opinion. He had as much right as the four striper sitting next to him. It was America for godsakes. He might as well be inside the KGB if he couldn't raise a little hackle once in a while.

His wife had always told him to keep his big trap shut. Well, it wasn't such a bad flaw. She once told him that he spoke out on purpose. According to her, he was subconsciously trying to scuttle any chance of promotion to a comfy desk job at headquarters. She said he was a born and bred field agent and until he was killed, or too old to perform, he would be on assignment. "If you were a cop you'd still be walking the beat at fifty-five instead of being a lieutenant inside a stationhouse," she always told him. Not such a bad idea. But he wasn't convinced that his desire to be an active agent had anything to do with how outspoken he was.

He had been the same at school. He almost got kicked out of Annapolis for having written an article criticizing the Secretary of Navy's plan for additional carrier strength at the expense of a tactical submarine fleet. Things like that just weren't done. But he had done it, published the article, and nearly got his ass handed to him by the commander. Only some strong lobbying from his professors, and his solid academic record, saved him the boot. Now, he sure as hell wasn't trying to subconsciously do anything when he wrote that article, other than point out an error he thought the Navy was making. "What about that?" he used to ask his wife. She just ignored him. She had taken a night class on introductory psychology at the New School and she saw some deep double meaning in everything he did. Nope. He wasn't buying it then and he wasn't buying it now. He was not outspoken just because he did not want a desk job, although he dreaded the thought of being stuck inside headquarters all day with most of these candyasses. Maybe he wouldn't shut up after all today. Why should today be any different than before? Hell, he was already feeling better. If he had something to say, he was going to say it.

"Well, hello, Richard. I didn't know you were back."

McGinnis glanced up to see Neal Phillips, a brigadier general who served as deputy director for intelligence. His department was responsible for all the neatly typed analyses that were the bane of an agent's life. Phillips was past army retirement age, but he was not about to let go of his power at the Agency. He was proud of telling associates that they would take him out of Langley feet first. Phillips had looked the same for the past twenty years. He still wore his light brown hair in a flat top. He always had a broad, fleshy face, but the advancing years had sagged the skin in clumps along the jaw line. He reminded McGinnis of a bulldog. No, that wasn't fair, McGinnis thought. Bulldogs were a fine breed.

"No, sir, they brought me back, and I just got an invitation for this little party."

Phillips could not stand McGinnis. Early in his career, McGinnis worked for Phillips, then a colonel, in Laos. Phillips wanted to kick him out of the Agency. That was 1966. He had been forming frontline counterinsurgency platoons among the northern hill tribes. It was backbreaking work, and a number of agents were lost in skirmishes with the Reds. Phillips personally gave McGinnis his first "eliminate with extreme prejudice" order. He was supposed to take out Ngam Touby, a half French/half Vietnamese chieftain who ruled a dozen strategically placed villages like a feudal warlord. Touby was extremely independent and a little too nationalistic. The bottom line was that he would not let agents use his villages for staging operations nor would he allow his people to join the counterinsurgency movement. To headquarters, that meant Touby was a through and through Commie. Some whiz kid, who barely knew where Laos was, had figured out that if Touby didn't love the stars and stripes, he must love the hammer and sickle. The solution was to eliminate him and thereby send a message to nonsympathetic chieftains that it was healthier to support the Americans than the Communists. The order filtered to the Saigon station chief, who passed it to Vientiane, where it found its way to Phillips and finally to McGinnis.

He was twenty-two years old, and had been working for the Agency for six months. The spooks grabbed him straight out of Annapolis where he had graduated at the top of his class. At Camp Peary he broke some long-standing endurance records and came out again as number one. His reward was a twenty-two hour, kidney crunching flight to Saigon on a cargo plane filled with electronic equipment. He was isolated in the damn hills of southeast Asia, 100-degree-plus heat every day, and not a woman in sight. To make things worse he was working under Army jurisdiction and that was enough to make any midshipman sick to his stomach. And to top it off, Phillips had just given him his first kill order, and it wasn't an easy one. Touby didn't trust anyone and traveled with a wall of bodyguards. If the hit was too clearly an American job, it could create political problems with other hill tribes. So Phillips wanted everyone to think it was a U.S. job, but he was adamant that no one should be able to prove it.

McGinnis stalked Touby during a week of night surveillance near the Thai border. He selected a Russian AK-47 long barrel assault rifle as the kill weapon, hoping that would cast a cloud over the allegiances of the killer. The hit was going to be a single shot at almost four hundred yards. It was damn difficult. On the day the hit was set, the winds were nearly forty miles an hour from an impending monsoon. He could have made it. He was sure of it. But he went with his intuition and scrapped it. It had been nagging at him all week. He knew the problem with Touby was not political loyalty. Instead, Touby's opium business had been hurt by the encroaching war, and he blamed all foreign powers for his business decline. McGinnis contacted two friends working for a CIA-front company, Air America. They were ferrying illegal weapons shipments all over southeast Asia. He wondered if they could ever jam a couple of crates of raw opium in there as well. No real harm done. Once Touby got paid for it, McGinnis didn't care if the U.S. Army confiscated it at the next airstrip. He just wanted a satisfied chieftain. If Touby was happy, he would be better alive. He simply wasn't a Communist. He was merely a disgruntled capitalist.

The Air America boys came through with flying colors. They told him they were flying opium throughout South Vietnam, Laos, and Thailand. The "black gold" of Asia helped buy the loyalty of many hill tribes. Somehow Touby wasn't a priority case. With McGinnis's assistance, Touby became a priority case. With that news, McGinnis visited Touby and laid out an offer. Business would boom if he allowed a few Americans into his villages and if he encouraged some of his able-bodied young men to fight the Communist threat. Otherwise he kept control of his towns, but his business would continue to go into the toilet, and sooner or later someone would probably put a bullet between his eyes. It was an easy sell. Touby jumped at the opportunity, and later in the war he personally joined the counterinsurgency forces. By that time he was ecstatic with his American business partners, and the thought of egalitarian Communists ruling the area shocked him so that he was willing to fight for his homeland. He was last reported to be somewhere in Malaysia, where he retired with a couple of suitcases of gold.

McGinnis thought he had done a bang-up job. Didn't have to execute a high-risk kill that would have produced an uncertain successor. Instead, with a little back-room maneuvering and the help of some friends, he made a firm ally. Phillips was infuriated. He wanted McGinnis out of the Agency and into a court martial court. If it wasn't Phillips's idea it couldn't be any good. McGinnis was called curse words he had never heard before. The Army sure spoke a lot worse than the Navy. But McGinnis was a big deal for a new agent. He had been given the Laotian assignment because headquarters wanted to put the whiz kid to the test. Everyone, even the analysts, had to admit that his results were good. Within one month of his "deal," U.S. planes were ferrying military supplies to Touby's villages and Laotian draftees were entering the counterinsurgency platoons. If there was a gripe, it was with McGinnis's unorthodox change of operations without proceeding through proper channels. But weren't agents supposed to make instantaneous in-the-field decisions depending upon changing circumstances? Of course, but not when you were only six months into the job. Weren't the results exactly what the operation sought? Yes, but Colonel Phillips should have been consulted. It went on like that with the internal affairs people for days. Finally, they noted in his file that he went beyond the scope of his orders, but they placed a commendation next to it. His personnel jacket had since filled with similar conflicting citations. He was transferred out of Phillips's command and put into a group run by "Wild" John Harriman, a Texas madman who was notorious for running the meanest operations in southeast Asia. He had a great five years with Harriman. But Phillips never forgot that first encounter. As they both moved along in the Agency, Phillips looked for a chance to knock McGinnis. But McGinnis had so many supporters that Phillips always had to back off.

Despite his big mouth, he pulled the best assignments because he was the best. The Agency was smart enough to put its top talent on its most sensitive matters, even if the agent was a maverick.

"Well, it's good to see you here, Richard. I am sure we can use your talents," Phillips said as he walked around the conference table to take a seat.

Bullshit. He means that as much as he wishes the Redskins would go 0 and 16. Phillips probably voted against his inclusion on the team. But Finch had overriding authority, and it was his call. Finch valued his own reputation too much to risk an operation by using mediocre talent.

McGinnis looked around the room as it filled up. The main briefing area at CIA headquarters is a simple affair on the second floor. A large rectangular room, without windows, it is finished in oak paneling that covers two-foot concrete walls studded with antieavesdropping and scrambling devices. A large Chippendale-styled conference table, surrounded with comfortable dark green leather chairs, takes up most of the middle. There is a large projection screen at the front, and the podium is to the right. Everything is state-of-the-art. When the projector is turned on, the lights automatically dim, and the podium swivels to face the direction of any question addressed from the conference table. McGinnis shook his head as he looked at the gadgets. A lot of electronic hocus-pocus that surely cost the taxpayers a pretty penny and did nothing but make some local contractors rich. McGinnis thought of the numerous times he had to justify an expense voucher with the dumbbells in accounting. Something was not right with a system that made those money choices.

"Hiya, Dick." Oh, shit, it was Jimmy Harris. The kid had just pulled up the chair next to him. Look at him, for Chrissake, he's chewing gum a mile a minute and he actually appears to be looking forward to this meeting.

"It's Richard."

"Oh, that's much better. At least you're talking to me. Hey, I had a cousin named Richard whom I never got along with. You know, the typical family stuff. Couple of fistfights. Oh, well, you don't want to hear that. So anyway, why don't I call you McGinnis, 'cause I can't stand calling you Richard."

This is unbelievable. He is supposed to work with this kid? He was sure Phillips had something to do with this. It must be Phillips's idea of sweet revenge. In some crazy way this was his worst nightmare—getting stuck with someone as rambunctious as he was when he got out of Peary.

"Fine. Why don't you just shut up for now. The briefing is about to start."

McGinnis glanced around the room as if he was looking for someone. He was impressed at the high-ranking brass that had been summoned. Three deputy directors were at the table. Rear Admiral Andrew Hamilton, a go-between for the Agency and the Joint Chiefs, was seated next to Major General Tony Roberts, liaison to other federal agencies, like the FBI. John Fitzgerald, a retired Navy commander, was the Agency's unofficial middleman to outside contractors, persons, and companies that performed work too dirty even for the CIA. The electronics division was represented by Nigel Hodson, a Brit who had served with American special forces during the Vietnam war. Most people in the Company thought he was a borderline psychotic, but even his critics admitted he was a damn genius when it came to computers and electronic surveillance. He had almost single-handedly moved the Agency into the forefront of the twenty-first century. As for being psychotic, McGinnis thought most good intelligence operatives might be on the borderline. It was, one needed little reminding, a job where excellence was measured by the ability to deceive. Stealing other people's secrets was a professional requirement. Killing in the name of patriotism was often necessary. The best agents were unfettered by emotions, guilt, or conscience. It was unlikely the job attracted "normal" people, whatever the hell that was.

McGinnis was impressed. For Finch to summon this crowd, there was a big operation brewing. He would never put his reputation on the line unless the information about the Soviet operation was solid.

"Excuse me, gentlemen, but I want to make this very brief." Finch had settled in behind the podium. All attention focused on the front.

"Gentlemen, we have a stage-one alert based upon a likely total Russian hit of one of our stations earlier today. As you will hear, we are going to be mobilizing for an immediate response to what we believe may be the second part, and main goal, of the Soviet operation. Due to certain constraints placed on us by the work our London station was involved with, this must be a unilateral Agency response. We will be focusing on countering a suspected Soviet operation in the continental U.S. That is normally FBI or NSA ground. Not this time. We will do it on our own."

"Does that mean we aren't going to get any help from the uniformed boys?" Admiral Hamilton broke in.

"That's about right, Andy. We aren't going to be able to go to the Army, Navy, or anyone on this one. It's ours to solve. If we isolate an operational Soviet team inside our borders, then we can use help in rounding them up. But we have to do the searching on our own. Let's get going, okay? First, our operation has been code-named "Fire-cracker." That's the internal name all communications will go under."

McGinnis couldn't believe it. What a ridiculous name. In the old days the deputy director would pick an appropriate code name for the operation. Some real thought went into it. Now the deputy director just fed the request for an operation's name into one of Hodson's computers and the machine spit out a random code. It didn't matter that it made no rhyme or reason. It was supposed to keep the Russkies on their toes since the name had no logical connection to the operation. They need a million dollar computer to come up with "Firecracker"? He must be in the wrong line of work.

"I will be dealing with each of you directly on Firecracker. I will serve as coordinating officer for the entire operation and you'll be able to get me here most of the time."

McGinnis was impressed again. A deputy director almost never served as the coordinating officer. It required eighteen to twenty hours a day. Usually an associate director or even a senior case officer handled that task. It could only mean that the Soviet operation was such a threat that Finch wanted to run this one personally. He had established his reputation as a top-notch field agent. He was not away from the streets so long that he would have lost any of his instincts. Things were looking up for the first time. McGinnis looked forward to working with Finch once again.

"I will talk to each of you later as to your specific tasks. I just wanted to cover some background information with everyone at the same time. Nothing gets past this room. Everyone else that you need to involve in Firecracker will be on a 'need-to-know' basis. Only those of you in this room are authorized to receive more information."

The lights dimmed as the curved projection screen lit up with a picture of a grand townhouse.

"That was the CIA station before today. It was a single assignment station. Research and development of defensive bacteriological weapons. Now, all of you know that we cannot produce offensive weapons as a result of a 1975 treaty with the Soviets. But before that treaty was signed you also know that we had a lot of R & D going on in offensive bacteriological weapons. We were way ahead of Ivan, and that was one of the reasons they pushed so hard for the treaty."

"You aren't going to tell us that station was involved in offensive weapons, are you?" John Fitzgerald chimed in from the rear of the table.

"Not exactly." You could tell when Finch was uncomfortable. He would unconsciously tap his left index finger against the desk or table in front of him. It was striking the podium at a steady beat. "It's not quite as clear-cut as that, John. You see, some of the scientists who were working on offensive weapons before the treaty were among the brightest guys we had in the Agency. What were we supposed to do with them? Fire them because the politicians signed a piece of paper with the Russians? Put them into research for herbicides to help the Drug Enforcement Administration fight coca and opium crops? It would have been a terrible waste of some topflight talent. So a Delphi program was formed around them. I don't need to tell you that Delphi files are closed to everyone but the director and the deputy directors. But what I can tell you is that part of this group was assigned to southeast Asia. There they worked on defensive chemicals in battlefield conditions."

"You mean they tested their new germ ideas on real people?" Admiral Hamilton broke in.

"That's not what I said, Andy. There may have been some in-field experimentation which I am not at liberty to discuss. To the extent it took place, it took place on a limited scale and with no wide-ranging repercussions. While one part of the Delphi was in Asia, the other was set up in London under the guise of a center researching childhood cancer cures."

These guys are real beauties, thought McGinnis. How do they come up with some of these ideas? That was certainly a sick one.

"The London lab was directed to concentrate only on defensive development. All within the proper confines of the treaty."

"If it was all treaty sanctified, then why didn't we put it into our major bacteriological lab out in Utah?" Phillips leaned over the table.

"Because we didn't want this lab subject to the Russian inspections mandated by the treaty. We were afraid of leaks and we wanted one high-tech lab that wasn't under Ivan's scrutiny. The London station fit the bill. The British knew it was there and MI5 kept a nice fatherly watch over it. We learned nearly ten years ago from a Kremlin source that the KGB knew about the London station's existence. They knew, and our own politicians didn't. We don't like that situation, but no one here was willing to tell the President that, under a previous administration, there was a technical violation of a major international treaty because we thought we needed more security for our operations. The shit would really have hit the fan."

"So why didn't the Soviets leak the word to the White House?" Phillips asked.

"They had a better idea. They started their own separate lab, near Pietrogansk, in Soviet Asia. It violated the treaty, just as our London one did. We both had violations and were unable to complain about them. We eventually got a lab technician inside Pietrogansk and the reports were pretty discouraging. Lots of offensive research. Our man was killed in an industrial accident after three months. We were never able to get anyone else in. Security is unbelievable and the workers are watched almost around the clock. The fact that the Russians had Pietrogansk up and running, and we were in the dark, caused a panic at headquarters. It was decided to let the London lab open a small offensive effort."

First big mistake, thought McGinnis. You can't tell a bunch of eggheads wearing white smocks that they can do just a little bit of something. They don't understand reasonable restraints. Scientists get obsessed with pushing the frontiers of science and all that junk. Given an inch, he was sure they had taken the proverbial yard.

"Well, the London station went beyond its mandate. Some of the key researchers made lab breakthroughs that appeared major. The only way to verify their significance was to field test. We now know they falsified reports indicating that research was proceeding much slower than it actually was. Since almost nobody here understood what the hell the technical reports said anyway, they were, unfortunately, accepted without a lot of double checking. It was a Delphi program and that means they had a lot of leeway."

McGinnis rubbed his forehead. I knew it. More bad news is coming from this London station.

"Unknown to headquarters, the lab started some live testing in several Asian countries."

"How the hell could that happen without general support from headquarters? I mean how could a bunch of scientists in London get the logistical support to spread some bacteria halfway around the world without us knowing anything?" Hamilton's voice trembled with incredulity and anger.

"First, Admiral, you have to remember that half the London team had worked in southeast Asia on their first independent assignment. They had developed a lot of solid contacts in the governments and the military. They had their own direct lines to a wide assortment of independent contractors who assisted them under the belief that they spoke with the full authority of the CIA. Second, remember that the weapons we are talking about are germs and microbes. They are the tiniest battlefield weapons ever developed. A doctor carrying a vial of potent microbes can infect an entire community if he plants the germ in an intelligent manner. We are not talking about dozens of support people needed in order to conduct some limited live testing."

"So what the hell were they testing, and what the hell for?"

"They thought they had made a gigantic breakthrough. They had developed, in the laboratory, a microbe that revolutionized bacteriological warfare. I am going to turn the podium over for a moment to Dr. James Christian. Some of you know him from our scientific analysis team downstairs. I want him to give you a layman's understanding of what we are dealing with here."

McGinnis had almost missed Christian, hidden behind the podium. He was easy to overlook. Standing slightly under five feet, five inches, his gaunt frame weighed little more than 120 pounds. Always looking sick, his skin covered in a yellowish pallor, he was the chief researcher for the Agency's internal scientific development. His duties were wide-ranging, from the latest field gadgets to the testing of new operational drugs and chemicals. Although he was balding, he kept his fuzzy brown hair long on the sides and back. He adjusted his thick, black eyeglass frames as he strode to the podium. McGinnis sized him up. An underweight, mad professor if there ever was.

"I've reviewed the history and development status of this virus, code-named by the London researchers as K-7." McGinnis had forgotten how high-pitched Christian's voice was. He closed his eyes for a moment and concentrated on what the doctor was saying. "Dr. Steven Schwartz headed the breakthrough team, and the virus in question is the fifth tested strain they had developed."

Big deal, McGinnis thought. How the damn thing got its name is really going to help us do something about it. Let's get to the point, Doc.

"Deputy Director Finch has asked me to give you a brief overview. This is a very complicated virus, so my short explanation is not going to do it justice. The virus is based on advanced recombinant DNA splicing techniques which generate mutant organisms that wildly proliferate in the body."

McGinnis grimaced. What is he talking about? This is a layman's explanation? Finch must be kidding.

"The virus was designed to enter the body as free oxygen radicals, highly reactive chemicals that naturally form in the body. Those in the virus are charged with an excessive number of negative electrons. Under close laboratory study, it is almost impossible to distinguish the virus's radicals from those naturally produced by the body. In the lab it merely looks like a mutation of the body's own chemical structure. This makes it an almost perfect biological weapon since the infected population can't even prove that the resulting disease was the consequence of an intentional infection. It just might be the body's system mutating to a new but deadly state."

"Excuse me, Dr. Christian. Could you tell them how it was designed to work on the body?" Finch gently prodded from his seat at the side of the podium.

"Of course, I'm sorry. As I was saying, since the virus's free radicals are similar to those produced by the body, they are unstable and highly reactive. They also have an instinct to survive. In order to do so they must counter their excessive negative electrons with a matching set of positive charges. To do this, they latch on to other molecules in the body and pair off the positive electrons from those molecules. When the virus's free radical steals a positive electron from another molecule, it renders that molecule unstable, prompting it to restore order by stealing a positive electron from a neighboring molecule."

McGinnis wondered if the virus killed its victim by boring them to death with Chem 101 facts and figures. He was sure half the high brass gathered in that room did not understand what the hell Christian was talking about. If this was the layman's version, he would dread to hear how these doctors spoke when they were alone. No wonder you had to go to medical school for eight years. It took that long just to understand what the other person was saying.

"Thus, a deadly chain reaction is started in the body. As the molecules have their positive electrons stolen in rapid succession, cells are ultimately destroyed. Natural enzymes, which normally guard against this type of deadly free radical assault, are overwhelmed by the large infusion of negatively charged radicals in the weapon's virus. Also, K-7 was treated with a series of minute DNA alterations, which have inalterably modified the surface structure of the free radicals, rendering the body's other natural antibodies ineffective."

"So if I can interrupt to see if I'm following you," Admiral Hamilton broke in, "you mean this K-7 looks like a natural substance produced in the body, so you couldn't even tell that you've been artificially infected. Is that right?"

"It's very difficult, Admiral. I'm still not sure if it's possible to pick the virus out of a group of infected people."

"Let Dr. Christian finish, Andy," Finch interrupted. "I think he's about done, and then we can let him go. It should be clear in a minute."

Fat chance. Give Christian another minute and McGinnis was sure there would be twenty more questions.

"Thank you. As I was saying, once the virus enters the body it causes this rapid cell destruction and molecular damage, which in turn leads to destruction of the body's proteins, collagen in the joints, and neurotransmitters in the brain. Within six months, muscles atrophy, joints stiffen and hurt as though from advanced states of rheumatoid arthritis, and the victims suffer from mental disabilities similar to the late stages of Alzheimer's."

McGinnis knew everyone in the room understood this part. Death and destruction was the universal language at headquarters.

"Also, metabolism is hindered, allowing the victim to bloat with liquids, and blood flow is reduced to muscle tissues causing constant pain and aching in the lean body mass. Crucially, the virus's free radicals oxidize the fat in cell membranes—when the integrity of the cell is violated, the cell is rendered as vulnerable to penetration as a house would be if the doors and windows were left wide open. This greatly increases the body's susceptibility to autoimmune diseases.

"Death results from a complete body meltdown. Death from K-7 is extremely painful, and the body is totally disabled in the final stages. The victims linger in a vegetable state for up to a year before the body turns itself off by dying."

McGinnis spoke out for the first time. "Doc, you make it sound as though this virus is like an electronic Pac-man going around your body and eating molecules and blasting cells."

"That's a very good analogy." McGinnis was proud of himself. "It's like a slow Pac-man death."

"Thanks, Richard, for the mental aid." Finch stood up and approached the podium. "Dr. Christian, why don't you just mention the infection figures and the antibody status in a couple of sentences."

"Surely. As best we understand it, the virus is passed through sprays in the air or through plantings in food or water. It has a very short half-life, and its effectiveness is good only for two to three hours. Then it loses its potency. Once it infects someone, we believe they may be contagious for two to three weeks. We are not completely clear on infection from person to person, but it appears that the virus may pass similarly to hepatitis—sex, close contact, sweat. It's contagious, but not as rampant as a flu bug.

"As for the antibody front, we have had no success. We don't think the London lab had any breakthrough either. We think the route to pursue is to counter the extreme negative charge of K-7's free radicals. We're just not having any luck on this aspect. For us—"

"Thank you, Dr. Christian." Finch had moved to the podium to retake control of the meeting. "Are there any questions for the doctor before he leaves?"

Neal Phillips straightened in his chair. "Just one thing. Have you ever seen anything like this K-7 before? Do you think the Soviets have anything like it?"

"No on both counts. This is a totally unique bacteriological weapon. It's ingenious in its structure, effect, and potential power. We don't have any evidence that the Soviets were nearing this type of break-through. This is a dream for a chemical weapons program. It certainly makes a lot of sense, to me at least, that the Soviets would risk a lot to find out more about it. And—"

"Thank you again, Dr. Christian, but I want to finish this briefing in short order." Finch was anxious to get Christian out of the room. He was a master of controlling the amount of information he wanted everyone to have. Dr. Christian had obviously given enough background. "Please close the door firmly behind you."

Once Christian was buzzed through the steel-reinforced door, Finch continued.

"So you can see we are dealing with something that is unique. We now believe that death is a certainty to those infected. But the London lab wasn't sure of that in the beginning. Well, you all know that projects can look one way in the lab and then perform completely different in the field. So their first goal was to test it on small population samples, to monitor its spread and measure the means and rate of infection. All of you also know that a weapon is only good if the enemy has trouble developing defenses against it. With bacteriological weapons the enemy is the general medical community and the defenses are antibodies and vaccines that counter the germ. Our London boys were convinced the only way to test the unsuspecting medical establishment was to release the new germ, start some infections, and then see how easy or difficult it was to curb. Well, that caused a real problem. The new germ surpassed their expectations. The rate of infection was fast and steady. And from a strategic viewpoint, the local medical community was unable to come up with any effective treatment after nearly four years of reported cases."

"Four years?" Hamilton was incredulous. "You mean to tell us that those pinheads conducted four years of live experimentation without anyone here knowing anything?"

"That's exactly what I'm telling you, Admiral. When we found out it was only because the London lab was so excited about the performance of their little discovery that they came to headquarters, to me to be precise, and suddenly spilled the details. They then incredibly asked for a major infusion of funds to develop the virus to attack-stage readiness. Of course, we were outraged when we heard what was going on. We shut that specific germ program down. We stopped the Asian experimentation. We transferred some key people responsible for the offensive program."

"What about shutting the whole place down?" The Admiral was getting testy.

"It wasn't that simple. We didn't want to tip our hand to the Soviets that we had a major problem. The London lab didn't just spend all its time on the new germ. It also had significant, legitimate defensive research underway, and it would have been thrown out of whack by closing the lab. We had nearly $40 million invested in the best possible equipment, most of it custom designed to fit inside the townhouse. We thought we had shut off the problem, and there was no useful purpose served by closing the whole damn place. Aside from this one digression, the place was within its mandate."

Pretty fucking big digression, thought McGinnis.

"What was the damage report from the Asian experiments?" Hodson was speaking for the first time, his clipped British accent sounding clearly across the room.

"That is classified under the Delphi codes. It has nothing to do with your necessary background. Suffice it to say that the virus is every bit as good as the London lab expected it to be."

McGinnis didn't like to think of that. Classified. *Every bit as good as the London lab expected it to be.* That sounded ominous if you were living in Asia. He had been around these guys long enough to know why they hid certain things and what they meant with their double-talk. Finch was telling them that a whole shitload of people had been infected with this new virus. He should definitely have stayed in the Congo.

"Our immediate problem relates to what happened earlier today." The picture on the screen switched to a series of black and white shots of a devastated inner structure. McGinnis analyzed each picture as it shot across the screen. Very professional work. Explosives placed at key structural points to maximize destruction. Plastic inflammatories wired for a complete gutting. Obviously planned well in advance.

"A gas spectrum analysis has picked up mercury vapors left at the site," Finch continued. "Scrapings of a retired Soviet nerve gas, VX-cyber, was detected by the cleaning squad. So don't tell me anything, Admiral, about what our people were doing in London. The Soviets were obviously still holding onto VX-cyber, a gas that was banned years ago. No one else ever had that gas. Mercury is also an old Soviet trade-mark with that type of explosive power. No one else had the intelligence to monitor our station so closely that they would know the single day in two months that every agent was scheduled to be there. The camera and sound recordings were lost in the fires. So all we have is the physical evidence, and it all points to a Kremlin job.

"Because of the crisis caused by this large scale hostile takeout, we have run the risk of contacting the Robin."

The Robin was a CIA legend. For a decade, he was the highest ranking CIA mole inside the Kremlin. Agents only knew his code name. No one aside from the director knew his actual identity. The Robin almost always chose the method and time of transmission. When the Agency contacted him, it increased the risk of exposing his clandestine role. Such a move highlighted the seriousness of the crisis caused by the London wipeout.

"We have just received an answer through our ambassador's office in Moscow. The Robin knows nothing about this operation. Not a single rumor. Nothing. That means it can only be performed out of the VKR, and that, gentlemen, is extra trouble."

McGinnis did not like the thought that he would have to clash with VKR agents. Regular KGB was bad enough. But Voennaya Kontr Raz-vedka was the most brutal division in Russian intelligence. It special-ized in worldwide Soviet terrorist operations. Its agents were the equivalent of fundamentalist Islamic suicide bombers. They were willing to die for the cause, but only if they took a couple of "imperialist dogs" with them. The VKR boasted some of the best Russian agents. They were top-notch operatives who had access to the most sophisticated and modern killing equipment in the KGB's arsenal.

"The Robin has never had a good line inside the VKR." Finch sounded apologetic. "It doesn't surprise me that they could pull this off and he wouldn't know a thing."

"But what is the purpose of eliminating our entire London station?" Phillips interjected. "What is it going to gain them but a like-kind retaliation?"

Finch took a deep breath. "There is one final wrinkle. We have reason to believe that some of the virus used in the Asian experiments was not destroyed in 1985 when we ordered it."

Hamilton let out a low whistle. He was not trying to be disruptive. He was just nervous.

"The information is classified under the Delphi program, but we are virtually positive that enough of the virus was stored at the London station to infect a large population sample."

"How large?" Hamilton was holding his head in his hands.

"Since we are not absolutely positive about the rates of infection and the ease of transmission, we have to be conservative in our estimates. But we believe it could be a batch large enough to infect two to four million people. From there the virus would have to independently support itself for growth."

A general hush fell over the room.

Hamilton surged ahead in his inquisition of Finch. "Do you mean to tell me that when the VKR hit our lab, they released bacteria that could kill off most of London?"

Finch's left index finger was rapidly tapping the podium. "Andy, I almost wish I could tell you that was the case. If it's possible to be worse, it is. When we discovered the existence of this runaway program in 1985, we confiscated what we thought were all of the virus's supplies. We destroyed all of it except for 20 milliliters, just enough to chemically isolate, test, and reconstruct its makeup from the ground up. We know what the bugger looks like from a chemical viewpoint. This morning we sent two medical squads to London and they swept the area with a fine-tooth comb. The virus doesn't just disappear once it's released into the atmosphere. Although it's not infectious after a couple of hours, traces of its unique molecular bonding survive forty-eight hours. Nothing is there. That means if VKR hit the lab, they also got our little

wonder virus. VKR will take some of it home to analyze in the moth-
erland. But those bastards operate on the premise that havoc and destruction is good. Chaos is even better. If they have it, I can bet my
professional reputation that some of them will be coming here to plant
the virus into our general population."

"How do you know the virus was there?" Phillips was hoping for an
out. "Maybe the medical boys are coming away with clean scrapings
because there is nothing to find?"

"No chance. Our team found a separate subterranean tunnel and
locker built for a small supply of secure liquids. That was not on the
original construction plans. Our London scientists went the full ten
yards to protect their pet project. That room was penetrated. I'll guarantee you that is where the germs were kept."

Was this really important enough to miss his son's baseball game?
McGinnis still wasn't sure.

"Now, let me tell you what we have to do," Finch continued, after
a sip of water. "If I am right, and VKR is on its way here with some of
that virus, then we are in a whole shitload of trouble and we've got to
get our asses moving. What makes this one tricky is that we have to
mobilize a lot of people without telling them too much about what is
going on. We don't want the press and the politicos getting wind of
this, and I think you can all understand why. No one will understand
the existence of the London lab. And if they hear about the Asian
experiments, all shit will hit the fan. Since the White House is clean
on this one, they would hang our balls out to dry. And a lot of them
over there would relish doing it. We're not going to give them the
chance. I am personally going to be briefing the White House later today.
Andy, you'll be there because the Joint Chiefs will be. Just be prepared
to hear a different report. They will be told that we lost an intelligence-
gathering station in London. We will still point a finger to the VKR and
will tell them that General Phillips's intelligence boys have picked up
a possible VKR movement toward U.S. borders. All we are doing is
mobilizing in the contingency that the VKR tries anything in the States.
Now that's not too far from the truth. If these bastards just take the stuff
back to Russia, then we have no immediate crisis and no one is the
wiser. Even if the VKR sends some agents here with the virus, and we
intercept them or the germ before it is spread, then again we are in the
clear. But if the VKR gets inside and then starts spreading, we will
claim total ignorance. You should know that we are already preparing
predated intelligence files that will show the chemical structure in

question was actually a Soviet invention and violation of the treaty. That should give us plausible deniability."

McGinnis hated that phrase. "Plausible deniability." You could do anything so long as you were clever enough to devise a good, watertight alibi. It was just fancy intelligence talk for "cover your ass."

Finch kept talking. "Any spread of that germ against U.S. citizens will be considered tantamount to an act of war. We may still be the heros if we find the sons of bitches before they kill too many people."

"And there isn't a hope of an antibody?" Hamilton sounded like he was almost pleading.

"No, as Dr. Christian told you, we never got that far. We do not believe the London lab did either, but now with everyone dead, we will not get a chance to check on their progress. They were supposed to start on that work in 1985, but we have no evidence they did. Although we had a physical sample of the virus in our hands by '85, we never put resources into discovering an antibody or vaccine. To the extent this stuff is spread, it's going to kill."

The room fell silent for a minute while Finch turned off the projector screen. The lights automatically brightened.

"We all have a lot of work to do. Remember, I will be the coordinator on Firecracker. The other deputy directors will be assisting me and providing me their full resources. The director will be checking with us around the clock. General Phillips is going to get us summary sheets on recent VKR operations so that we can look for methods and means. Admiral Hamilton will be working with me in keeping the military and Joint Chiefs off our backs. John Fitzgerald is arranging for some independent medical talent that might be helpful if we get to the infectious stage. Commander Hodson is going to have his computers tap into those of Immigration and Naturalization. Starting an hour ago they are getting access to every person crossing a U.S. point of entry. Then it's analyzing those names against all existing U.S. and Interpol files. Maybe we can pick up some early warning signs. He is also developing a large-scale spectrum analysis for use on his pride and joy, the Cray 2. That program, by the way, Nigel, is it ready?"

"By midnight it will be up and running," Hodson announced with conviction.

"That program will analyze hundreds of millions of atmospheric particles gathered by dozens of wide-range monitors scattered around the country. Then the Cray will crunch those particles into their constituent parts and compare it to the virus's chemical structure. This virus causes mutant alterations in the atmosphere. The computer will hopefully pick up on those changes. If it works as Nigel plans, then we will know about the germ's release within a couple of hours. We could isolate infectious areas and stay only a step behind the killers.

"The actual field work will be coordinated by Richard McGinnis. You all know him. New to the field team is Jimmy Harris. He's one of the bright new boys on the block and the director personally wanted him cleared and in on this discussion, just in case any of you had questions about why he is here."

McGinnis couldn't believe it. This kid had the luck of the Irish. Was he related to the old man in the center office? He must be kissing some pretty high-ranking ass to get this white glove treatment. McGinnis congratulated himself on keeping his mouth shut for most of the briefing. He had only asked a single question. It was almost a record. But he felt the urge coming again. He had to say something else.

"So is that it, gentlemen? We all have a lot to do." Finch looked around the room.

"Yes, I just want to make sure I got it all right." McGinnis cleared his throat. Finch frowned. "What you're telling us, Tony, is that an entire station not only surpassed its mandate, but it went out of control. And instead of terminating that station, we gave it a new set of rules and hoped they would follow those. They didn't. Meanwhile, they played little games like infecting a 'classified' number of people in Asia. And while we weren't smart enough to know our own station had this killer germ, the Soviets knew. And today they took our station out, grabbed the germs, and are either on their way back to Russia or some of them may be coming here to stuff it down our throats. And since you are not sure, you aren't taking any chances. Right?"

"He does have a way with words." Phillips grinned and leaned back in his chair at the end of the table.

"Richard, that's exactly why I chose you." Finch stared at him. "It takes you one minute to say what it takes me thirty minutes to say. Aside from your characterizations, some of which I do not agree with, you've got the general idea. And I am sure everyone else does as well. So why don't you and Harris go to the war room, and I will see you there in a bit. Admiral, why don't you stay. I need to talk to you for a moment. Everyone else can go and get their sections going. I'll be making the rounds tonight."

McGinnis stood and stretched. What an asshole. The VKR may not even be on the way here. Why the hell would they risk direct infections in the U.S.? They just pulled off a coup by getting the damn stuff. They may be slightly mad. You had to be touched in the head to be in the VKR. But they weren't complete madmen. At least the Commies pulling the strings in the Kremlin weren't totally crazy. He was sure the batch of germs was on its way to the chemical lab that Finch mentioned was somewhere in Siberia. They would analyze it and break it apart so they could re-create it. And meantime, the Agency would work on an antibody from the small sample of the virus they kept. After the Russians spent millions of dollars on re-creating our virus, and we spent millions of dollars countering our own discovery, then we would have a Mexican standoff. What a perfect waste of life, time, and money.

McGinnis coughed as he was slapped hard on the back.

"Nice going, McGinnis." It was Harris, with a big smile spread across his face. "That was a real nice summary. You have a knack for getting to the heart of the matter."

Harris dropped his voice as though he was about to impart a secret. "You know, I wanted to tell you something. I saw you drinking a lot of coffee before the briefing. I counted three large mugs. You know how bad all that caffeine is for you at this time of day?"

"Who the hell do you think you are? Jane Fonda or something? Give me a break. I'm still alive and I've been drinking it for thirty years. Don't break my back over the little things."

"Hey, I was just trying to be helpful. I mean I never ceased to listen—"

"C'mon, Harris. Follow me and keep your mouth shut."

"Where are we going?"

"We're going to see how much you really learned at Peary, whiz kid."

CHAPTER 5 ━━━━

New York City
December 14
4:30 p.m.

He had always hated Kennedy Airport. It was crowded, noisy, and dirty. A microcosm of the city only twenty miles away. It was not as efficient as European airports, to which he was accustomed. New York did not make anything easy for the arriving traveler. The customs officials were surly, the baggage handlers rude, and the airport staff indifferent. After waiting twenty minutes in freezing winter air for a battered yellow taxi, one then had to endure a harrowing ride over potholes, past errant drivers, and through streams of traffic before settling safely into the hectic city of eight million.

"Passport."

It had taken Colby forty minutes to reach the front of passport control. He wasn't sure why headquarters had given him Swiss citizenship with a permanent U.S. residence card, but he assumed it was the closest physical match they could find. As a foreign national he had to clear U.S. customs twice. It was an added risk. He slipped the blue passport of Switzerland, together with his I-90 entry declaration form, across the Formica-topped counter. Colby studied the passport control officer. He seemed a typical American. His face was slightly pudgy, almost nondescript. There was an Irish strain running through the American, or so Colby thought. This man wore dark brown spectacles, sported a fuzzy mustache, and appeared terribly bored with his work. Probably had five children and a nagging wife waiting for him at home. Colby imagined the little suburban house, the family gathered around the all-important television, watching some intellectual dribble like *Miami Vice*. He was glad he never married. He never had any desire to share his life with another person. No need to feel wanted. He had loved only once. Nearly fifteen years ago, he had just turned twenty, and she was an ideologue as firmly committed to the cause as he was. They were soulmates through their violence. But the violence that brought them together also finished them. She died at twenty-two from a bomb that exploded prematurely, intended for a passing convoy of NATO representatives. He had not cared for anyone since. He viewed emotions as a weakness. Relationships created dependencies. More weaknesses. Weaknesses killed you in his business.

"How long were you abroad, Mr. Colby?"

"Nearly three weeks."

"What was the purpose of your trip?"

"Business in England and Germany."

"And what do you do?"

"I'm an investment adviser."

"Where's your home here?"

"In New York, on Fifty-fourth Street."

The official barely glanced at him. He turned to the large loose-leaf file folders in the corner of his desk. These books contained the names and passport numbers of travelers with security clearance problems. There were thousands of names on the prohibited watch list and it was updated daily. For the world's most technologically advanced society, customs still protected the borders as it did at the turn of the century. Colby thought it was ludicrous.

The customs officer adjusted his glasses and started flipping through the pages, checking first by passport number and then by name. The telephone rang at the desk before he finished the search.

"Riley here."

Colby was proud of himself. He knew there was Irish blood in those ruddy cheeks. He could only hear one end of the conversation. A lot of "hmmm" and "yes." There was no good-bye; he just hung up. The customs man closed the file folders. No "sorry" or "excuse me." Just as he remembered Kennedy Airport and Americans. Rude.

"Mr. Colby, could I ask you to step behind the desk with me?"

The words ignited Colby's defense mechanisms. What was wrong. There had never been a problem with a cover identity. Suddenly Colby heard a noise to his right, inside the clearing lounge. He turned to see two uniformed police, together with two burly men in suits, running at full speed. They were fifty feet away and moving fast toward his area. He tensed. He snapped back to the customs officer who was staring at him.

"Mr. Colby, just for a moment, it will be better for you back here." The customs officer reached out to take Colby's arm, but Colby moved a step back and stayed free of his reach. He spun back to face the charging men. All four were coming straight at him. He did not have a weapon. Something must have been blown. His mind raced. He had to react immediately or they would be on top of him. Two had weapons drawn. His reaction was instinctive. He would wait for the first to hit him and then try to use that body as a shield against the others.

"Mr. Colby!" The customs officer's shout sounded distant. He concentrated on the four men. He had to get out of the airport and to the safe house.

They were just in front of him, shouting, "Out of the way! Down! Out of the way!"

The first plainclothes agent hit Colby with a stiff right arm and pushed him back against the customs counter. Colby started to kick out with his left leg. He was about to catch the agent in the kneecap when he realized they were running past him. It rushed over him like a wave, the cold sweat of relief breaking out across his face. They were not after him! He yanked his leg back as the first uniformed cop crashed through his customs control booth, the tip of his foot missing the racing legs by inches. The other three burst past him. He spun to his left. The four men chased a young Hispanic woman past the baggage carousel and tackled her near the exit. Her suitcase went sprawling, slamming against the far wall, exploding in a small cloud of white dust. Drugs. Damn it! It almost cost him his life. His heart was pounding. The adrenaline was pumping hard.

Now it made sense. That's why the officer had received the call. Notification they would be coming through his control booth. That's why he wanted him behind the desk, to avoid the chasing police. They did not know who he was.

He had almost engaged four U.S. drug agents. He had almost blown the entire operation! What a hole Kennedy was! He never had a good feeling about it. This just confirmed it.

"I am very sorry about that, Mr. Colby." The customs agent looked very concerned. "I didn't have much time to warn you. And they didn't tell me they would be charging through like that. Is everything all right? We have no control over these things, you know. Are you okay?"

Colby looked flustered, but as a professional, he was in complete control. "Yes, fine, thank you. It's just that I've never seen anything so violent before." He looked back to the baggage room. "It's quite unsettling; I'm sure you can understand."

The police had handcuffed the young Hispanic woman and were pulling her roughly from the room. Dozens of arriving passengers milled around; many of them seemed shocked. What a wonderful welcome to America, where the wild west still lives. Colby found that thought quite amusing. These people would have stories to tell for days.

"Yes, I'm sure it is quite upsetting. Are you sure you're okay? Is there anything I can do for you?"

"No, no. Everything is all right."

"Well, here's your passport. Welcome back home."

The ride into the city was uneventful. It gave Colby time to relax. He needed it. Eight and a half hours in the crammed economy section of a Pan Am 747. As an investment advisor, he should have been flying business class. It was stupid to put him in economy. It tried him unnecessarily before the start of a difficult operation. For people who were supposed to be very smart, sometimes his superiors did some dumb things. His flight proved it.

He rested in the rear of the taxi. Or at least he tried to rest. Every couple of minutes a pothole caused his head to bounce off the back seat. The driver had a radio talk show on too loud. Callers were irate over some kind of player trade the local baseball team, the Yankees, had evidently announced. People wasted so much effort on unimportant issues. It was something that Colby did not believe in. Wasting your energy on trivial matters. These callers might be dead in a couple of weeks, the result of the work he was about to start. Yet they weren't trying to enjoy their miserable little lives. They were working themselves into a frenzy over some sports figure. Idiots. Deserved to die.

He had almost always had the belief that the people he killed on his assignments were somehow less than worthy of living. He despised most people. He simply did not see the good attributes that supposedly existed in most of the human race. Instead he saw stupidity, closemindedness, callousness, hatred—these were the character traits of human nature. As far as he was concerned he was not much better. No one was. He just was smarter than most. It had been his curse even as a child. He was the brightest student in his little town school, skipping three grade levels on his way to excellence at the university. His mind was as strong a weapon as his body and hands. It was also his handicap. He saw things that others could not, realized things they were too slow to appreciate. While his classmates still fretted about the local hockey scores, he recognized the need for violent revolution. He despised the intellectual inferiority that marked the other students. Even his parents, wealthy bureaucrats who were snobs in their own right, chided him for being a terrible snot. His disdain for other people led him to treat most with contempt.

The only exception had been his first and only love. She was an intellect. They spent hours talking about the inevitability of worldwide Marxist revolution. They dissected the failures of Stalin's great programs and analyzed the pitfalls of Mao's cultural revolution. He could talk to her like no one else he had ever met. And when they made love it was what sex was supposed to be for him. It was hard and mean— nothing gentle about either of them. Together they came to the attention of one of the world's largest intelligence organizations. They were prime recruits. Bright, physically daring, and disenchanted with their lives. They relished their new careers. They were still getting to know each other when she was killed. She was blown up beyond recognition in a little town outside the Hague. He didn't even find out about it for two weeks. The Dutch refused to release the unidentified body, dissecting it and freezing the remains in a police morgue. With her death, his budding emotional growth had ceased. He turned completely to his work. Obsessed and driven, he excelled at his new assignments. He became a master of death. It complemented his disdainful attitude for most of the world. Now he played the role of God. He could take life. And he did. Often. But this assignment was the most important of all. The most daring. It was his chance to inflict death as if by a plague from the heavens. It would be as if he had a miniature atomic bomb in his briefcase. He could selectively let it kill millions of people. That imparted a power to him far beyond his 9-millimeter pistol. He put his head against the back seat of the taxi. He felt totally relaxed. A warmth came over him. He felt good. He was about to cause havoc and death in America.

It took less than thirty minutes to get to the East Side of Manhattan. A lush, forty-block radius of multimillion-dollar apartments, high fashion clothing boutiques, and overpriced, trendy restaurants, often better for their architecture than their food. The East Side was also the home to the mission's safe house. A simple four-story limestone townhouse on Sixty-third Street. It was in the middle of a row of similar town-houses, and its light beige exterior melded unobtrusively into the ad-joining buildings. He had the taxi drop him off at Sixty-fifth and Park. Although darkness had settled since he left Kennedy, he preferred to walk to the safe house. Better not to take any chances. Besides, the fresh air would be good for him before he sat down with "Ms. Erica Cane" and the contact agent. He needed a clear head for this evening's planning session.

It took him less than ten minutes to walk to the safe house. He had forgotten how cold New York could be in the winter. His ten-ounce check worsted suit and a lined raincoat were not warm enough. The electronic sign on top of a Park Avenue skyscraper flashed "18" degrees. But it felt much colder. The wind whipped down the broad avenues and small side streets and seemed to claw at his face. Again he worried about his health. Combined with yesterday's soaking in London, if he didn't succumb to pneumonia it was a testament to his strong consti-tution. Despite his discomfort, he paused for a moment in front of the townhouse. He knew that the two iron eagles set on each side of the staircase hid sophisticated security equipment. The one on his left contained a miniaturized infrared camera that snapped pictures of any-one approaching the house. Images were then displayed in control booths inside the safe house and at a downtown security station. The pictures at the downtown center were automatically fed into a main computer storage bank and compared to tens of thousands of photos of known agents, terrorists, political activists, and the like. If there was a match, the townhouse would know who the visitor was before he announced himself at the door. Colby thought back to the operation at the London lab the morning before. It seemed much longer than thirty-six hours ago. Those cameras were not hard to bypass. He was sure that a skilled team could eliminate these with little difficulty.

The second eagle contained a digital microchip recorder. It pin-pointed sound waves from conversations near the front door and com-pared them to a digital sound chip system in another computer terminal. This allowed the security department to isolate voices when it did not have matching photos. Sometimes the picture of an agent or terrorist was ten years old. The photo computer could not make a match. A good facial disguise could thwart the computer's photo identification.

But a voice pattern was like a fingerprint. The passage of time could not alter it. Trying to disguise it could not hide the voice print stored in the computer memory.

He reached the landing and noticed an arrow pointing to a buzzer. It was a single button that was hard to push in. It would not budge by merely leaning into it or pressing it lightly with your knuckle. You had to take the tip of your finger and push it hard. That allowed a light sensitive recording strip to make a copy of the fingerprint and simultaneously transfer it to the stored files in the downtown security center. Even with a partial print, the high speed computers could reconstruct the entire print with a digital marker, and then find a matching print within a minute.

Good security, all of it, but not enough to keep out a top agent. Colby thought of how he would gain access. A good facial disguise, total silence, and gloves worn for the winter air would frustrate millions of dollars of modern identification equipment.

He wasn't in the mood for games. He took the glove off his right hand and firmly pressed his index finger against the buzzer. The door swung open in less than a minute.

"Welcome, Mr. Colby." It was the contact agent, the man who had given Colby the murderous order in Paris. He was wearing a pair of forest green corduroy trousers and a long-sleeve red polo shirt. Colby had remembered him as being taller. He also noticed a roll of fat above his belt. The contact agent had seemed trimmer the day before in his neatly tailored European suit. Colby despised intelligence agents like that, and he had seen many of them during his career. They ran around carrying directions for the faceless supervisors at headquarters. But they could never carry out a mission of their own. He was sure the agent he had to kill in Paris was a better man than the one who stood in front of him. He would relish an order to take the last breath from his body.

"Come on inside. You've got an hour to nap and then we start the final briefing. There's a lot of work to do."

Colby walked inside without saying a word. The door slammed behind him on an unsuspecting New York.

CHAPTER 6

Paris
December 14
10:00 a.m.

It was a stroke of bad luck for Colby and his team. The Hotel Raphaël
had been used by the contact agent many times in the past. Its lacka-
daisical staff and management had always provided an ideal backdrop
for any rendezvous. It had been a logical meeting station after the London hit. There was no way to know that within hours of their departure
the hotel would be crawling with agents from the Service de Docu-
mentation Exterieure et de Contre-Espionage, known as SDECE for
short, the French equivalent of the CIA. Any chance that the mutilated
body in the Bastille Suite would pass simply as a horrible but unsolved
crime vanished with the arrival of the SDECE agents.

   Colby was the unwitting victim of middle east politics. The French
government had been involved for nearly nine months in sensitive and
secret negotiations with the Iranian government regarding the fate of
four French hostages held in Lebanon by pro-Iranian fundamentalists.
The Iranian demands were two simple ones: the release of ten billion
francs frozen in a joint French-Iranian power plant project along the
Riviera, and the resumption of French arms sales, especially Exocet
missiles. An eleventh-hour demand was thrown into the negotiations
by the Islamic Jihad, which held the hostages—a direct ransom payment
of $15 million. Initially the French government refused to negotiate the
release of its hostages. But as the presidential elections drew near,
opinion polls revealed overriding public support for the hostages' free-

dom, and politicians interpreted that as a mandate to strike a deal with the terrorists. Indirect talks began in April, and by the summer Iranian parliamentary representatives and French ministers were covertly ferrying between Paris and Teheran. The months of hostage diplomacy taught the French that extremists do not negotiate—they simply demand. The Iranians and the Jihad never budged from their original conditions. Instead, the French government gradually began accepting the Iranian terms as the only feasible alternative to the hostage crisis.

During the last week of November the French notified the Iranians they would meet the demands so long as the hostages were released by Christmas. Foreign Minister Valmain, orchestrating the French efforts, had a good sense of dramatic timing and knew that Christmas freedom for the prisoners would boost his party's chances in the upcoming election. Mohammed Rijav, the top aide to the Iranian Speaker of the Assembly, Adnan Jajantani, scheduled a mid-December trip to Paris in order to finalize the details of the payments and arms sales. Both countries wanted to avoid a public spectacle. Rijav planned only two quiet nights in Paris. Instead of staying at the Iranian embassy, the object of eavesdropping devices from at least half a dozen nations, the French decided it was best to treat Rijav as a simple tourist. They booked him and his seven-person entourage into the Hotel Raphaël. Situated close to the SDECE's security department, the French decided that the Raphaël offered the best protection and privacy for the Iranian negotiating team. During earlier visits, the Iranians had stayed at a variety of Right Bank hotels, without a single incident.

Unfortunately for Colby and his team, Rijav was scheduled to arrive at the Raphaël on December 15. That meant the 14th would be used by security forces to sweep the hotel in preparation for the visit. The SDECE agents did not expect to find anything. The Iranian negotiations were a well-guarded secret, and so far had been leakproof. But the French could not take any chances. A strike against Rijav or his staff would scuttle the hostages' release and exacerbate tensions between the countries. There were enough pro-Shah exiles in Paris to ensure that the security forces could not relax.

Half a dozen SDECE agents arrived at the Raphaël at 6:00 a.m. Three of them began a floor-by-floor electronic sweep of the hotel. A pair of agents, with dogs trained to sniff explosives, started on the roof and began working toward the basement. The final agent, Serge Ropac, was the youngest on the team. At twenty-five, the baby-faced operative had only been with the SDECE for two years, after having spent three years in the army's special forces. As the agent with the least seniority, he was assigned to the task considered the most boring and least important—a review of the hotel's guest cards and room records. But Ropac did not mind the work. His passionate patriotic zeal was often mocked by his fellow agents, but no SDECE assignment was below the dignity of the young intelligence officer. The fastidiousness with which he approached his work paid off on the morning of December 14.

At 9:15, Ropac noticed the first discrepancy. It was a cash prepayment receipt for one of the hotel's most expensive suites. A cash payment stood out by itself; most of the guests at a deluxe hotel paid by credit card or travelers check. But heightened suspicion was cast on the Bastille Suite rental because three days were paid in advance. Virtually no one paid $1100 a day before they absolutely had to. Ropac knew he had discovered a warning light. Instead of following up on the lead on his own, his training required that he call for a senior agent. That was the next bad break for Colby. The agent who was sent from headquarters was Jean-Claude Bouchet, an investigative legend in French intelligence.

Tall and thin, Bouchet was the central casting image of a suave French lover. In his mid-fifties, he still bore the handsome features that were his trademark. A chiseled, strong face, offset by grey eyes that almost sparkled, he wore his light silver hair brushed straight back. He was born into a wealthy, aristocratic family, owners for six generations of one of France's most respected vineyards. His two brothers had done what was expected of them. They had followed the family footsteps into the winery. But Bouchet had rebelled. He was not satisfied by the provincial confines of the Loire Valley, and on his eighteenth birthday he volunteered for the French army. His family was disgraced, and his father pulled every possible string to obtain his son's discharge, claiming he was not mature enough to reach such an important decision. But nothing could be done—Bouchet was of legal age, had volunteered for the service, and he did not want to leave. Within a month he was on his way to Indochina and his father had disowned him.

He became a man during the next three years in southeast Asia. The pampered son of a lucrative family dynasty, he lived and worked with men who were from a wide and harsh mix of the French lower classes. He joined the paratroopers and excelled in combat. When he had first arrived, the soldiers in his unit had called him "petit bonhomme" (pretty boy), but once they saw how he could fight, they dropped the mocking title and he became one of them. On his twenty-first birthday, the French garrison at Dien Bien Phu surrendered. It was as though he had thrown away three of the most important years of his life.

He returned to France but did not adjust to civilian life. Shunned by his family, he felt alien in the strictures of Parisian life. Within a year he was in Algeria, battling for the last vestiges of the colonial empire. His fighting skills were further honed during three years in the brutal North African combat. By the time he was promoted to major, he had come to the attention of French intelligence. The SDECE underwent a massive expansion during 1957 and it presented many decorated combat agents with a chance to enter the intelligence community. Bouchet jumped at the opportunity to continue fighting wars, even if they were covert.

By 1959, de Gaulle had publicly announced the abandonment of the French occupation of Algeria. For the soldiers who had fought there, de Gaulle became an overnight traitor. The general in whom they had placed so much faith betrayed them by giving up the fight for the colony. The bitterness of many excellent French soldiers was funneled into an organization dubbed the OAS, a French acronym that translated as the Secret Army Organization. The OAS waged a vicious underground war against de Gaulle well into the 1960s. Financed by a series of spectacular bank robberies, as well as donations from sympathetic French, the OAS posed the most serious post-World War II threat to the stability of the Republic. The counterfight against the disgruntled soldiers was left to Section 5, the SDECE's Action Section. Bouchet was one of the first assigned to the anti-OAS squad. Since he had fought in Algeria for nearly three years, he knew many of the men involved in the anti–de Gaulle campaign. Although his sentiments lay with his former comrades, his patriotic loyalty was with the government. He reluctantly approached his new work with the same zeal he demonstrated on the battlefields of two continents.

In the Action Section, Bouchet showed the flair for a new talent. Not only was he a born field soldier, but he was a natural detective. Methodically, he tracked down his former friends. He was responsible for the investigation that uncovered Marc Rouvelle, the sadistic trigger man for the OAS, at a fleabag hotel just outside of Cannes. Almost single-handedly he exposed the stunningly complex OAS banking system. An underground grouping of gold dealers, currency exchangers, and import-export companies, the system was the brainchild of some of France's brightest accountants. It shielded and moved millions of francs, allowing the OAS to fund its war against the Gaullists. Bouchet developed a network of informants and, combined with a detailed analysis of a mountain of paperwork, finally unmasked the rebels' financial backbone. Once its money lifeline was destroyed, the OAS's chance of pressing an effective fight was finished. Bouchet's growing reputation was enhanced further when he was personally decorated by de Gaulle for his success in tracking down the six OAS operatives who had been involved in the June 1961 assassination attempt against the French president. By the mid-1960s, his colleagues had dubbed Bouchet the "bloodhound."

Almost thirty years of SDECE work had still not diminished his enthusiasm. Even though he was summoned at a late hour and the Atlantic storm made driving treacherous, he was not upset by the call from his superior officer. It took him nearly thirty minutes to drive across Paris in his early model Peugeot. He pulled into the hotel's driveway and flashed his government identification as he left the car. The doorman stiffened to attention. The hand-engraved card was issued only to officers in the French security apparatus. It guaranteed that his battered car would not be moved to make room for an arriving limousine.

He walked briskly down the corridor toward the manager's office. He liked the Hotel Raphaël. Always had. Although he had never married (most of his girlfriends said he was married to his work), he had courted many women at the intimate, wood-paneled bar off the main lobby. It was much too nice a hotel for an Iranian "dignitary," but then he would be happier if the Ayatollah's representative never set foot on French soil. He just didn't believe that negotiating with terrorists was right. It was common knowledge inside Section 5 that Valmain was anxious to obtain the hostages' release at any cost. He shook his head in dismay. The government was pandering to the Iranians. SDECE agents had been assigned to perform a security check that should have been the province of the police. It was probably nearing the culmination of the government's efforts. It was the only explanation for why they had called him personally to attend to a minor, last minute hitch. Unless he gave the okay, the Iranian would never set foot in the Raphaël. But he doubted he would find anything that would halt the visit. Someone had paid cash for a suite for several days. Probably some old fool with too much money for his own good, entertaining a young girl for a private tryst. He could imagine the pleading once he personally checked on the suite's occupants; "Oh, please, Mr. Inspector, please understand that I hope this will not be mentioned to my family; it is really not a matter for the police." Well, at least he was satisfied that he would not be at the hotel for a long time. It was midmorning and he hoped to keep a luncheon appointment with an old army buddy from the Indochina days.

He paused for a moment outside the manager's office and admired the Turner painting. It was such a peaceful scene. He imagined its beauty took away some of the pain for guests who had to pay extravagant bills at the adjoining cashier's desk.

"Ah, Ropac, I have been summoned here on your word and I hope it is worthwhile," Bouchet announced as he walked in behind the young agent.

Ropac jumped to his feet. Bouchet seemed to tower over the five-foot, six-inch junior agent. "*Oui*, Colonel Bouchet, I have only one room that seems unusual to me, and it is a suite. All the other sections have signaled a go-ahead. The hotel is secure from every aspect except the guest list."

"Have you checked the guests' names versus their credit cards or travelers check vouchers and verified with the companies that the information listed on the passports is correct?" Bouchet removed his trench coat and folded it neatly over a wooden chair in the far corner of the office.

"Yes, Colonel, and with the eighty-four occupied rooms, seventy-nine are foreigners. Of those, there are forty-six from EEC countries, twenty-nine from the United States, and one each from South America, Canada, eastern Europe, and Japan. Except for the EEC countries, all the others registered with passports and, as part of the hotel policy, all of them had to give an imprint of a credit card, no matter how they intended to settle their final bill. The passports double-check with information from credit card companies, and further examination, within the time I've had, confirms the employment data. I am not suspicious about any of these people. I am only having trouble confirming some sources with the South American, but I intend to personally visit him. As for the EEC visitors, I have run Interpol files as well as checking police identification folders in respective countries, and the result, I am pleased to report, is nothing unusual. The EEC visitors have been easier to check as to their employment, and all match their hotel identity cards. We don't have any problem with them.

"As for the remaining six rooms, including the suite in question, they are held by French citizens. I've cleared five of the six, and it is not surprising that the one question mark relates to our mysterious friend in the Bastille Suite. He registered two days ago under the name Maurice

Lebens. His credit card voucher was imprinted with an American Express card in his name. His biographical information filled in for the hotel is confirmed and matches the credit company. His place of employment, Citroën in Marseilles, has not seen him at work in two days and did not send him here for business."

"Is he sick?"

"This is unusual. They have received a telephone call for the past two days, reporting Lebens as sick for work. But the call was not made by Lebens. It was from a man who claimed he was a friend and that Lebens was too ill to speak on the telephone, much less come to work. There is no answer at his house. No wife or children, so if he's not there, it should be empty. Maybe he's playing hooky for several days in Paris?"

"What position does Monsieur Lebens hold at Citroën?"

"He is an accountant, middle level from what I am told."

Bouchet slowly shook his head at Ropac. "Think of what he earns a year as an accountant at Citroën. No more than 150,000 francs. And you believe that our elusive Monsieur Lebens is going to spend 7000 francs a night for a hotel room when the company is not paying for it? There is no woman in Paris worth ten percent of a man's salary for a three-day love feast. Young Ropac, whoever is upstairs, I can assure you it is not Monsieur Lebens. You should notify the local gendarmes in Marseilles to visit his home. I think our accountant may have run into foul trouble. Now let's go upstairs and find out why."

CHAPTER 7 ≽══──────

New York City
December 15
6:00 a.m.

Erica slept only two hours. The briefing had lasted until midnight and then she spent half the night in the makeshift basement laboratory encapsulating the virus into miniature, self-dissolving capsules. Each capsule was no larger than a kernel of corn. Constructed of a resilient acrylic-polymer base, the K-7 pills resembled tiny dosages of vitamin E. But these pills were potent killers. Each contained enough virus to infect more than a thousand people.

The contact agent had offered her the assistance of a biochemist during the virus transfer stage. But she had refused. She wanted to do the final preparation alone. Transferring the virus from the steel cylinders stolen in London to the new capsule containers was a straightforward mechanical job, similar to beginners' assignments in pharmaceutical courses at medical school. The only difference was that Erica's equipment was some of the most sophisticated manufactured, all quadruple sealed with tungsten liners to prevent even microscopic leakage. As long as she took her time, it was virtually impossible to make a mistake. The virus was manipulated by robotic arms sealed inside a glass case. She manuevered the arms until the yellowish, thick K-7 fluid dripped into a metal saucer attached to an electronic needle. The needle automatically aspirated the correct dosage, which she had preset into the microchip's memory, and then shot the virus into a waiting acrylic pod. The small pill was then moved by air pressure to a lithium plate where it was bombarded by a combination of ultrasound waves and high density laser beams, causing a uniform and almost impervious structural bond. The one weakness built into the acrylic's chemical webbing was a timed destructive pattern kicked off by temperatures of more than 105 degrees Fahrenheit, or contact with moisture for more than five minutes. This meant that if someone stepped on the pill or hit it with a hammer it would not budge. It had a chemical cross-structure as strong as reinforced bronze. But subjected to temperatures above 105, or placed into a tub of water, the chemical structure began rapidly disintegrating, and within twenty minutes the K-7 would be released into the environment.

When she had made seven of the mini-biochemical bombs she again reverted to the robotic arms. She slowly moved the long metal rods and retrieved the pills, which she then deposited into a separate glass chamber. With the flip of a switch the case turned a bright purple as radioactive-charged light flooded the space. If there was any error in the ultrasound and laser bonding of the acrylic cover, the radioactive tint would isolate the mistake. Imperfections in the acrylic's chemical base showed up as small but bright pink spots under the purple glow. Once the pills cleared this final hurdle, Erica pulled a lever on the table in front of her and the pills slid down an aluminum tube and were deposited into a leather-padded pouch to her left. She then placed each batch of seven pills into a thin plastic tube, no larger than a pencil. That tube had a round button at the top, and when the button was depressed the tube automatically released a single pellet. These were the tools that would allow her and Colby to complete their mission. It was tedious work and although she was tired from her flight to America, she performed her task with an alert mind.

By 2:00 A.M. she had compiled nearly thirty K-7 pellet strips. A small portion of unused K-7 was stored in an original cylinder and retopped with an hermetically sealed aluminum lid. She did not want to convert all the virus into the pellets. In case there were any unexpected developments during the mission, an unaltered supply of the virus could be an advantage. Her superiors had allowed her to utilize only a small sample of the K-7 seized in London. The rest of the virus was forwarded to headquarters even before she left Paris.

By the time she finished, exhaustion should have overtaken her. But her biological clock was at her normal wake-up time in Europe. The adrenaline pumping through her system, the result of anticipating the morning's operation, gave her a second wind. She had been inside laboratories so long that she had almost forgotten the exhilaration that accompanied field work. When she had been a young rising star in the research department of the country's largest university, she could never have imagined that she had the constitution or talent for intelligence work. Back then she would have guessed that her future achievements lay in academic journals and citations from the professional community. Even when first approached by the nation's intelligence apparatus, she was reluctant to join. Idealistic, she believed that her talents could best be used by public institutions, not the military. By the age of twenty-eight she had combined dual degrees in biochemistry and medicine into pioneering research on recombinant-DNA theories. Most academics and hospitals thought her work was a waste of time on esoteric research that was best saved as cocktail party chatter. But she knew better. She knew that she was at the frontier of a new science—the molecular reconstruction of the human body. By unlocking the key to the human DNA structure, the entire race could be genetically improved. Her work was her obsession.

It was why the intelligence agency finally won her over. The doctors involved in the country's bacteriological research were the only ones who understood and appreciated her work's importance. They knew that unlocking the DNA theories could lead to the development of ethnic weapons, drugs that only attacked weaknesses in cells peculiar to certain races or ethnic groups. The government offered her what no private enterprise could. Almost unlimited amounts of money, the newest and best equipment to work with, and dozens of other doctors who not only admired her work but encouraged her ambition in challenging the forefront of a major new field. They also did not care that she was a woman. In the private sector she had to fight extra hard to prove her worth in a male-dominated research world. But with the intelligence agency, it was the quality of her ideas, not her sex, that mattered. She liked that. That type of ego massage eventually weakened her resolve. Finally, they won her over by telling her that she could come into the intelligence underworld for a couple of years, advance the state of her research, and then return to public life. It was an offer that was too good to refuse.

In retrospect she knew it had been a lie. They would never have allowed her to enter the nation's most secret programs and then simply return to a regular lifestyle. They would have stopped her, probably at any cost. But there was no need to find out what extremes they would have resorted to. She never wanted to leave. They had put her through six months of rigorous training, as much as any new recruit. Although she was expected to serve her country inside a lab, they also wanted her to have operational capability. It had surprised her when she found the physical training the most gratifying. Nearly ten years ago, at the beginning of her career, she had led two difficult field tests of an early strain of dengue fever. They had involved specialized infections against Moroccan air force bases. She had excelled during the operations and had relished her time in the field. It was her last outside mission. Once they put her inside a laboratory, they realized her value. Now she was finally in the field again, and they had trusted her with the most important chemical operation of the twentieth century. Mass infections with a marvel of a weapon. From the first time she heard about K-7 she had welcomed the opportunity to work with it. Now the time had arrived, and her mind was charged with anticipation. The excitement caused her fitful sleep. Finally, at 4:30 in the morning, half an hour before the alarm was due to ring, she surrendered to her active mind, abandoned the idea of sleep, and got up.

She did not know that Colby was already awake on a separate floor of the townhouse. He had also slept sporadically, which was unusual for him. But he did not mind having the extra time to prepare for the start of the morning mission. He took out a battered brown crocodile bag, opened it next to the sink, and slowly took out the contents. He knew them by memory. If need be he could have worked from the case in the dark. Once everything was arranged in a neat row along the top of the sink, his work began. First he meticulously shaved with a straight razor, using the large mirror over the sink to guide his eye. Then he grabbed a small plastic tube and stepped into the black marble shower stall. With his right hand he turned on the cold water. It splattered against his scalp, ran through his hair, and streamed over his body. Ice-cold water. He always used it. It was a shock to his system and tensed his muscles but he was convinced it made the blood flow faster. After twenty years an eccentric habit became a necessity. The numbing, wet, cold water awakened his senses. He squeezed the tube into the palm of his hand and worked the brown liquid into a lather in his hair. In less than a minute he let the water wash the solvent from his scalp, a dark brown foam dropping into the basin and running down the drain.

He had enough. He turned off the water, stepped from the shower, and threw his head back, a spray of water arching across the floor. At least the mirror in front of him was a good size. The dye was a good one also. His medium blond hair had turned a uniform dark brown.

There was no artificial red sheen, no stains along the skin line. The scientific department at headquarters had invented this coloring agent. A mixture of vegetable extracts and synthetic dying agents, it was the most natural hair color devised. It could be washed out with a mild cleaning solvent at any time. And if the assignment called for the impersonation of a particular person, headquarters could match the dye to the victim's identical shade.

He dipped his fingers in petroleum jelly and then rubbed it into his scalp. He plastered his hair straight back, a deep part set along the left side. A look in the mirror confirmed the accuracy of his eye. This was the easiest part for him. Almost chameleonlike, he had always been able to adopt faces and personalities with little effort. He considered himself an artist, his canvas human flesh. The scar on his face, the result of a policeman's billy club in a West German peace demonstration, had proven a limitation. But the scientists had again come to his rescue. They developed a liquid makeup that covered the scar to anything but the most intense scrutiny. It evened the skin on each side of the cut, blending the face into a smooth mask of human color. Now the disfigurement almost worked to his advantage. Anyone who knew he had a scar would first look for that. With the makeup, his face was unmarked. That would ensure that he was almost always eliminated as a suspect.

He grabbed the small jar to his left. He had used it so many times in the past that he felt it had almost become part of him. In less than a minute he had smoothed the makeup across his face and into the scar. This batch had been blended with a beta-silicone color tint to slightly darken the skin tone. The skin's pigmentation changed evenly over his face and neck.

The last changes were simple. With an eyebrow pencil he deftly filled in the edges of his own eyebrows, making them appear bushier but natural. The final phase was the eye color. His were a deep green, a color most people wanted to be born with. For an agent it was a disadvantage. The best agents were anonymous men. Their ordinary features made them forgettable. They merely blended in and out of crowds and no one could remember what they looked like. Nondescript brown eyes were ideal. Sea green was too memorable. With a well-practiced hand he popped the colored contact lenses into each eye. A few blinks, a drop of eye solution, and the contacts settled into their proper fitting.

He looked in the mirror. He was no longer a fair-skinned Nordic, distinguished by his scar and the striking color of his eyes. His thin, light-colored hair looked thick and dark, held straight back by a layer of grease. His lightly tan skin looked more deeply bronzed. His new brown eyes looked quite ordinary under his bushy eyebrows. His new appearance would work well. And finished in less than thirty minutes. He was proud of his work.

He started on his final preparations. He neatly packed some clothes into a black leather duffel bag. A pair of grey, wide-wale corduroy trousers, a pair of black wool pants, two cotton tab-collared shirts, a solid burgundy silk tie, a dark green pullover Shetland sweater, and a brown tweed wool jacket, complete with suede elbow patches. He neatly folded several pairs of underwear and socks, and placed a pair of black loafers and a pair of black Reebok sneakers into the side of the case. Finally he slid in his toiletries kit, jammed with everything from toothpaste to Band-Aids. He zipped up the duffel and placed it on the floor near the door of his room.

From the mahogany armoire at the end of the bedroom he pulled a navy blue jumpsuit. It was emblazoned with a large orange patch that proclaimed "Consolidated Edison Co." He slipped on underwear and stepped into the jumpsuit. He then grabbed a heavy pair of workboots from under the bed, sat on the edge of the mattress, and pulled them on. He surveyed the room a final time to ensure he did not miss anything. Satisfied, he clutched his cases, closed the door, and started down the circular staircase. His "tool kit" and a very special can of Coca-Cola were waiting for him.

Erica had packed her clothes into a light blue vinyl overnighter. One black jersey dress, two pairs of pants, a white cotton blouse, two short jackets, bras, and several pairs of panties were stored for the upcoming trip. She had dressed in a pair of dark brown trousers, a beige turtleneck, and a brown houndstooth jacket. Khaki, patent-leather, flat shoes completed her outfit. Next to her luggage she placed the leather padded box that resembled a shaving kit. It was the mission's entire supply of K-7. That was everything. She knew the contact agent had a small canister for her. It was time to pick it up.

"Are you ready?" It was Colby. Or at least a second version of him.

"My, a good night's sleep did wonders for you. You're like a new person." He did not even crack a smile. She guessed it was too much to hope for a sense of humor before the sun was up. She stared at him for a moment. He was memorable, but any identification based on his current disguise would lead investigators far afield from his real face.

"I've been ready for twenty minutes," she told him as she reached into the closet and grabbed a camel overcoat.

"Good." Colby grabbed her case. She lifted the padded kit of microencapsulated pellets. "Let's do it." He repeated the same phrase that had kicked off the murderous row at the London townhouse just two days earlier.

The contact agent was waiting for them in the paneled, main floor library. "Your canister"—he turned to Erica—"and your diverter"—he looked back to Colby—"are waiting for you in the car.

"The CIA is looking for an entire army of agents coming across their borders. They are never going to expect just the two of you. Without interference you should have no problems. I'll see you by the end of the week.

"An agent is waiting for you in the car. He is briefed only insofar as his limited role. That is to drive you to the hotel, wait until you are both back in the car, and then on to the airport. Your flights do not leave until 2:00 and 2:20. You should have no problem making them with plenty of time to spare. I will give you the coded signal over the car's telephone once we have a go. You are to contact me only if there is a change of plans due to events at the scene. Remember, the car phone is fitted with a scrambler, but cellular lines can't be totally secure so beware of open talking."

Erica broke into a small smile. "You sound like a den mother. Now are you sure you have your lunch packed with you, and are you dressed warm enough, and . . . Honestly, we went through this three times last night. It is going to be simple."

The contact agent nodded his agreement. "You're right. Get going." Colby grabbed a yellow plastic rain poncho and pulled it over his jumpsuit. "Good luck" were the last words they heard as they left the safe house.

It was 8:10 when the forest green Oldsmobile 98 pulled away from Sixty-third Street. The windows were tinted a dark grey, shielding the driver and occupants from the outside world. But in a city filled with limousines, the vehicle did not rate a second glance. Colby and Erica sat in the rear. They were silent, and the driver, a young Hispanic man who looked like he had been on the losing side of too many boxing matches, did not say a word. Manhattan's reputation for the world's worst traffic was well deserved. It took them nearly twenty minutes to travel fifteen blocks.

"There it is," the driver nodded to his right.

Even in the midst of a series of skyscrapers, the Waldorf-Astoria Hotel is a grand building. They had approached the rear of the hotel on Lexington Avenue. The only sign of any unusual activity was a couple of uniformed police standing in front of the gold-tone revolving door.

"Keep driving," Colby muttered as his trained eye scanned the sidewalk, windows, and adjoining buildings for other signs of extra security. He saw none. "Go around the corner two blocks from here and then pull to the curb."

The middle of December in New York is the height of the Christmas holiday season. Parties, galas, and benefits are conducted at an annual record pace. The Waldorf is usually booked, a year in advance, for the entire month. December 15 was no exception. The governor was hosting a fund-raising gala in the Grand Ballroom. The guests included 1500 of the wealthiest and most powerful people in New York City, a who's who of power politics in the Democratic party. The $1000 a plate seats had been gobbled up months ago by real estate developers, stock market barons, advertising tycoons, and a cross section of the city's power elite. Those people were not only the inner circle of New York's political and economic life, but they were also the core of New York's glittering social scene. They were the "A" guests for the finest holiday parties and events of the season. Once infected, they would unwittingly be contagious for several weeks, enough time to carry them through the upcoming Christmas, Hanukkah, and New Year's parties. Enough time to come in contact with thousands of new victims, most of them the upper echelon of America's seat of capitalism. Headquarters had a copy of the guest list for the Waldorf luncheon. By tracking the individuals about to be infected with K-7, Erica could monitor the virus's effectiveness. A live experiment on a controlled group—New York's aristocracy.

The driver made a right on Forty-seventh Street and pulled to the curb. "If you are not back in thirty minutes, I'll be in for you," Colby told Erica.

She paused for a moment once she stepped out of the car. "Don't worry. I'll be back."

She glanced at her watch as she hurriedly walked the two blocks up Lexington Avenue toward the Waldorf. 8:40. As long as she finished her work by 9:00, Colby should be on the scene by 10:00. They were on schedule. She bundled her hands deep inside her camel overcoat and pulled her head into the collar in a futile attempt to ward off the twenty-degree temperature. Paris had been cold, but nothing like this.

A stiff twelve-mile-per-hour wind made it feel below zero. By the time she passed the two young policemen at the hotel's side entrance, her face felt frozen. They didn't even look at her. They were doing their best to stay warm, walking in small semicircles and clapping their gloved hands together. Since the luncheon was at noon, guests would not be arriving for several hours. Security was not yet at full force.

She stood for a moment inside the small rear lobby while she caught her breath. She reached inside her right overcoat pocket and felt the cold steel cylinder, no larger than a cigar, which had been given to her in the car. The sooner she finished the better it would be for Colby. Without hesitating, she took off her overcoat, folded it over her right arm, and proceeded up the escalator. She briskly walked past the arcade of glitzy jewelry and antique salons, and into the grand main lobby. As she strolled through she could not help but admire the imposing art deco architecture that soared from the floors to the top of the painted ceilings, forty feet above. A couple of uniformed police stood surveying the crowd near the entrance to the Turkish inspired Peacock Bar. She appeared no more than a mere tourist on her way to the passenger elevators.

She walked past the main lobby, beyond the elevators, straight toward the Park Avenue lobby and the entrance to the Grand Ballroom. Before reaching the ballroom she turned left by the cloakroom and passed a door that was marked with etched glass as "Ladies Lounge."

Inside the pink marbled bathroom, a small, heavyset black attendant stood in the middle of a row of doors. Behind each door was a private toilet and sink. It was luxury of a bygone era, each woman provided with her own private bathroom. Only three of the six rooms were occupied, and the uniformed attendant moved forward and opened a door for Erica. But the last stall, at the far left end of the bathroom, was the one Erica needed, and it was occupied.

"Not yet, thank you." Erica smiled at the attendant. "I must wash my hands first. I spilled coffee on them."

"You can wash them in there, Madam." The attendant gestured toward the empty stall.

"I'm sorry, but I'd rather wait for a corner stall. I don't like people on both sides of me."

The elderly black woman did not seem surprised. After twenty-seven years in the Waldorf's main floor bathroom, she had passed the point of being shocked by almost anything. She had heard the snorts of coke addicts and the grunts of masturbators, had had her toilets stuck with the syringes of heroin users, had found discarded pantyhose, and, on one occasion, even a pearl-handled derringer. Nothing surprised her. At least not an eccentric request for a corner toilet. One regular had her own stall "reserved" every weekday morning at 9:30 where she would sit, smoke a cigarette, and read the *Daily News*. It took all types. As long as she got a tip she didn't care what they did. Unless they were up to something illegal or causing a toilet to back up—those things caused problems. Otherwise they could do what they wanted.

Erica waited for a minute, self-consciously standing by two mirrored vanities near the front of the lounge. The wait seemed interminable. She glanced at her watch. 8:46. A flushing toilet caused her to turn toward the stalls. The closest door opened and a fashionably dressed matron emerged. The attendant did not even ask Erica if she wanted to use it. Two other women passed her to enter the toilets. What if the other corner stall became available first? How would she explain that to the attendant? She could only use the one on the left. What would happen if the toilet was out of order? A little change like that could foul up the entire start of the operation. Again she looked at her wrist. 8:48.

"Madam." The attendant's call made her spin around. The elderly black woman gestured toward the rear left door. It had swung open and a young girl was walking toward her. She had not even heard the toilet flush.

"Thank you, thank you," Erica muttered as she walked briskly toward the stall.

She closed the door and latched it. Directly in front of her, three feet above the toilet, was a twelve-inch-square aluminum screen. It was the reason Erica needed that stall. It was the only vent in the ladies bathroom that was connected to the main cooling system that ventilated the lobby, the ballrooms, and all the public lounges. The vent recirculated air on an hourly basis, pushing air into the bathroom for an hour, and then sucking air back into the system for an hour. From 8:00 to 9:00 in the morning the vent pulled air out of the ladies lounge and recirculated it in the main cooling tanks before sending it through the rest of the hotel. The other three vents in the ladies lounge were part of a secondary cooling system, which worked in tandem with the garage and the storerooms. Erica moved toward the rear wall and pulled the small steel cylinder out of her overcoat pocket. She rested her coat over the top of the toilet tank and pulled a needlelike plastic tip from the breast pocket of her blazer. She slid open a metal lid on top of the cylinder and slowly inserted the plastic needle. Then she bent the thin catheter and squeezed it through one of the vent's small openings. With her free hand she pressed a rubber button on the bottom of the cylinder. When she put her ear next to the can she could barely hear a tiny hiss. When she straightened up she could not hear a thing. There was no risk that the attendant or even the person in a neighboring stall could hear any unusual noise.

She glanced at her watch. 8:52. The canister would take another four minutes to empty. It contained destostat-12, a partially hydrogenated vapor that re-created specific odors over a wide area for a short period of time. Chemically adapted to clone the structure of other scents, destostat-12 could make a convention hall smell like a fruit market, or a church smell like a sweaty locker room. When released into the air it took nearly ten minutes to gain strength as carbon dioxide in the atmosphere activated its odor. From the point of full activation, destostat-12 lost its potency over thirty minutes. At the end of half an hour, the chemically planted odor had disappeared. The canister that Erica plugged into the vent had been altered to smell like natural gas. By 9:06 the Waldorf would think that a gas leak had struck. Within two minutes the day manager would institute a written set of emergency procedures. Erica had committed them to memory. First he would start an evacuation of the public parts of the hotel, including all restaurants, lounges, shops, hallways, and lobbies. While some of the staff helped move those people from the warmth of the hotel to the frozen air of New York's streets, the remainder of the staff would start the laborious task of evacuating guests from their rooms, floor by floor. By the time the staff had started the room evacuations, the manager would have telephoned the emergency section of Con Edison, New York's power supplier. Because of liability insurance limitations, the Waldorf was unable to use its internal maintenance staff on only two types of problems—natural gas leaks and electrical fires. With a gas leak, the fire department would not be notified until the Con Ed team arrived at the hotel and assessed the seriousness of the situation. That could be determined only in one location. The single gas dependent section of the otherwise totally electrified Waldorf was the 4400-square-foot main kitchen in the lower level. The gas leak could not have happened at a worse time for the hotel. The kitchen was in the middle of preparing the luncheon for the governor's 1500 guests.

8:56. Erica pulled the canister away from the screen, took off the plastic needle, and slid the metal cap securely over the top. She put the parts into her overcoat pocket, picked up her coat, and left after flushing the toilet. She paused for a moment by the bathroom attendant and fumbled in her pockets for small change. Finally she plunked two quarters on top of the dollar bills gathered on a small white china plate. You could tell by the attendant's face that she was unhappy with coins. Only green paper pleased her in these inflationary times.

Erica retraced her steps to the exit on Lexington Avenue. Before stepping outside she slipped on her overcoat and checked her watch. 9:01. Five minutes until the panic struck.

At 9:06, by the time Erica arrived at the car on Forty-seventh Street, the destostat kicked on like clockwork. You could see guests and staff alike sniffing the air as if doubting their own sense of smell. Short conversations back and forth. More sniffs of the air. Someone called the day manager out of his office. The final sniffs. A look of panic settled over the manager's face. A gas leak in a hotel holding thousands of guests and expecting the governor, mayor, and half of the city's bigwigs for lunch was a real emergency. The procedures were followed to the letter of the written rules. After commencing the complete evacuation procedures, he picked up the telephone and dialed 683-8830, the emergency line at Con Edison.

An intelligence agent sitting inside the basement at the Sixty-third Street townhouse was waiting for that call. The townhouse had tapped into the Waldorf's switchboard nearly a week earlier. There had been no hitch in monitoring the thousands of calls placed daily in the hotel. With modern intelligence's tools, tapping the switchboard was a simple procedure. Because of the multitude of lines, a hotel's system is an open invitation to a computer tap from any remote switching center, like the one New York Telephone maintained at Fifty-sixth Street in midtown Manhattan. Through a paid informant at that location, the townhouse had obtained the Waldorf's computer access code. By duplicating the code in its own computers, the townhouse made the Waldorf's system believe they were one and the same. Everything that transpired over the Waldorf lines played simultaneously over the townhouse's computer lines.

"This is Con Ed Emergency Service. . . ."

"Hello, Con Ed. This is Marvin—"

"All lines are busy now. Your call is being held in the sequence in which it was received. Please hold on the line until a service representative can assist you. This is a recorded announcement and will not be repeated."

"Oh, for godsakes! I don't believe it. Jesus . . ."

"Hello, Con Ed Emergency Service. This is Peter Dalton; what is your customer account number?"

"This is Marvin Scheitzer at the Waldorf-Astoria. We have a gas leak!"

"Is it confirmed as a leak?"

"Everyone in the hotel can smell it for godsakes! I have already started to move people outside. You better get someone here immediately!"

"I am going to put the call in right now. We can get a team to you within fifteen to twenty minutes."

"That's too damn slow. Get someone here earlier!" Scheitzer slammed down the receiver.

The moment the line was disconnected, the agent in the Sixty-third Street townhouse telephoned the cellular box in the car holding Colby and Erica. Colby picked up the receiver. "It's a go," came the toneless voice over the line. Colby did not say a word. He put down the phone, picked up a large metal case at his feet, and left the car. He walked quickly up Lexington toward the hotel. Erica did not say a word to him. She knew he did not like talking before he went into action and that he thought send-offs like "good luck" were stupid.

Within one minute of the original call from Scheitzer to Con Ed, while Colby proceeded to the hotel, the agent at the townhouse telephoned the emergency section at the power company.

"Hello, Con Ed Emergency Service, Robert Seigel here; what is your account number please?"

"Yes, this is Marvin Scheitzer at the Waldorf. Let me speak to Peter Dalton please. I was just speaking with him."

"One moment, sir."

It took less than ten seconds. "Dalton here. I've got the call out. A team should be there in ten to twelve minutes—"

"Hold on, hold on. I am happy to say you can cancel the emergency squad. It is not a gas leak. It looks like some damn cook had left a couple of the main burners on after the pilot had gone off. For some reason it smelled much worse than it was. I am a little embarrassed but I guess we overreacted a little here."

"Are you sure you do not want our squad to come over and verify that everything is all right, Mr. Scheitzer?"

"I am sure, Dalton. We just got a little nervous over here. We've got a lot going on and this was the last thing we needed today. I'm sure you can understand. Thanks, but we really don't need anyone. We've got the governor coming over today and between the private security and the police, your fellows would just get tangled up in a real mess."

"I can understand 100 percent. I am glad you didn't hesitate to call us when you thought there was a problem. Better to be safe than sorry when it comes to gas. It is certainly a big relief to hear that you do not have a problem. If we can be of any assistance, feel free to call us anytime."

"Thanks, Dalton. Merry Christmas."

"Thanks, Mr. Scheitzer, happy holidays to you too."

As soon as the line went dead, the agent tapped in another seven digits. The phone was answered on the second ring.

"Waldorf-Astoria, how may I help you?"

"Mr. Scheitzer, please, this is Mr. Dalton at Con Ed. This is an emergency call!"

In less than thirty seconds a nervous voice came over the phone line. "We're getting him, just hold on one moment."

"Scheitzer here. The smell is real bad, what's the news on your team?"

"Not good unfortunately. We've got a gas leak in the financial district and another uptown on Park, and a team isn't going to get to you for at least thirty minutes. But I've got one of our best technicians, Dave Bolton, less than a block away from you. He's just checked and cleared a leak report at the Roger Smith Hotel around the corner. I've buzzed him on the beeper and he should be to you in less than two minutes."

"I don't care if you send me one guy or twenty as long as they find the leak and stop it! He better get here soon!"

At that moment Colby arrived at the Lexington Avenue entrance to the hotel. A steady stream of evacuees was pouring onto the icy sidewalk as he approached one of the two young policemen.

"Con Ed, emergency gas crew," he lifted his parka to flash the orange decal on his jumpsuit. The policeman looked at him. In one hand he held a large tool kit. In the other a can of Coca-Cola. Damn cold to be drinking soda pop the cop thought. It takes all types. He waved him through.

"Come on, folks, give the man a break here. Step back just for a second, don't push, everyone will have a chance to get outside. Just let the man through. There you go, pal. Good luck."

Colby nodded and smiled. He paused for a second near the escalator and gingerly deposited the Coca-Cola can into the trash receptacle to his right. Unknown to the policeman that ushered him in, Colby's Coca-

Cola can was an integral part of the morning's operation. It was packed with a colorless and odorless fire gel. At the appointed second, an electrical detonator inside the can would spark the gel, causing a momentary flash, and then a small but steady fire. The garbage can would be enveloped in flames, causing a secondary panic during the evacuation through the Waldorf's rear lobby. Every distraction worked to Colby's advantage.

As he rode the escalator to the main floor, past a solid stream of descending, nervous guests, he took a strong sniff. Ah, the destostat-12 was working well. If he didn't know better he would have thought that all of them were about to get blown sky high. He unwittingly retraced Erica's steps, past the high-priced boutiques and into the main lobby. Dozens of people were hurrying past him, all on their way to the exits. He scanned the large room until he noticed the brass sign announcing the manager's office. He was halfway to the office when someone grabbed his arm from behind. He instinctively tensed.

"Hey, I was calling you. Are you the Con Ed guy or not?"

He turned to look at a dapper man in his early fifties, his silver hair matted with sweat. He was impeccably dressed in a navy blue suit, his starched white shirt and maroon tie evidencing none of the stress that was written on his face.

"Yes. I'm Dave Bolton."

"I'm the manager, Mr. Scheitzer. Do you smell it? Do you?"

"Yep, I sure do. You better take me to the gas source now."

"Yes, yes, of course. This way, just follow me."

As he cut a criss-crossing path through the nervous evacuees, Scheitzer kept mumbling half to himself and half to Colby. He couldn't understand how a gas leak could happen at the Waldorf. The hotel had spent almost a hundred thousand dollars as part of a multimillion-dollar renovation and installed a backup and safety system that was supposed to catch gas leaks before they happened. What the hell had happened to that system? Could it be found before some idiot lit a cigarette or a spark flew from a piece of scraping metal? His muttering almost blended in with the constant murmur of noise from the departing guests. Colby remained quiet and merely followed several steps behind.

Through the main lobby and to the rear of the hotel is the service elevator servicing the main kitchen. The doors were open and waiting for Scheitzer.

"It'll take just a moment and we'll be there," a nervous Scheitzer told

Colby. "Wait 'til you get there. It's strange but the odor almost seems worse upstairs than it is down there. Is that possible?"

Not only possible but probable. While destostat affected the atmosphere uniformly, gas rises and so does the implanted odor. "Remember, gas rises. So even if it starts down there, it's normal that you'd smell it worse upstairs."

The kitchen was exactly as described to Colby. Almost as large as a city block, the spotless space was filled with large, industrial ranges, cutting and dicing tables, sinks and multidoor refrigerators, and hundreds of gleaming cooking utensils. Scheitzer cut through the long room toward the left rear wall. He stopped short of a large pipe and valve protruding from the wall. Scheitzer shot his hand out toward the pipe almost as in disgust.

"Here it is! Here's your gas source and main connection to the hotel." He looked over at a dark green computer module in the far corner. "And that little martian is the special device that is supposed to monitor gas pressure and density and warn us beforehand if there is going to be a leak. So much for that. And—"

"Mr. Scheitzer, this is really good enough for a start. Give me five minutes here and I'll tell you if the leak is coming from here." Colby glanced at his watch. 9:14. Twenty minutes until the destostat lost its potency.

"Well, where the hell else could it be coming from?"

"We've had instances in which the gas leak is from an adjoining building, or an underground main, and the odor is so strong that you're sure it's from your place. You might be lucky and this could be someone else's problem."

"Since I'm evacuating this hotel, it's become my problem one way or the other, my friend. I'm going upstairs for a second to see how everything's going. Bo Svelna, our maintenance chief, will stay with you here. He's got a walkie-talkie to me so if you've got anything just let me know. Are you all set?"

"All set," Colby answered as he pulled the yellow rain parka over his head and set it on a wooden kitchen block several feet from the gas pipes. "Oh, by the way, when the rest of the Con Ed team arrives, just send them down here."

"Don't worry. I'll bring them down personally."

A middle-aged man in the blue uniform of the Waldorf maintenance department walked toward them.

"Here's Bo now. Bo, here's the Con Ed fellow. Let him work, and give him a hand if he needs it. I'm going upstairs."

Colby looked at the broad face, the thick neck, the protruding temple. Slavic. Romanian. Maybe Hungarian. You could tell that he was not happy to be near the source of a potentially disastrous explosion. People who did not work with gas had a natural, and realistic, fear of its destructiveness. As foreman, Bo had the responsibility to oversee the Con Ed crew. It was not a job for which he would have volunteered.

Colby bent over his tool box, snapped it open, and pulled out a metal rod with a large bulbous gauge attached to one end. It looked like a high-tech turkey baster. He reached into the second shelf of the box and pulled out a set of multicolored wires, finished with suction cups. Bo had seen an earlier, more rudimentary version of these tools during a gas panic nearly ten years earlier. He vaguely remembered the emergency team attaching the wires to seals along the gas line and then the gauge somehow pinpointed the trouble spot. He wasn't sure how it worked, but last time they had zeroed in on the source of the leak in less than five minutes. No problems. No explosions. He hoped it would be as easy this time.

Colby took one of the wires and plugged it into the tip of the metal rod. He attached the other end, together with a metal clip, to the main connecting line between the city's underground gas reserves and the kitchen's supply. Then he quickly placed the other wires around the first seal on the gas pipe. The device was the latest tool used by utility companies around the country to quickly isolate the source of leaks. The sensitizers isolated the electric charge from the escaping gas, measured its velocity on the gauge, and directed the worker toward the malfunctioning component. Colby turned his wrist to look at the watch. 9:19. Fifteen minutes left.

He flipped the switch on the gauge, and the needle shot into the red danger zone. How was Bo supposed to know that this gas spotter had been modified to shoot into the danger zone no matter how many times it was activated? Only if Colby reversed the wire hookup would the monitor read in the green safety range and report no gas leak.

"Holy shit!" Colby loudly exclaimed. He stared wide-eyed at the gauge. Bo leaned ever so slightly toward Colby trying to peek at the gauge, but trying not to show his nervousness.

"Something has happened?" Bo asked as nonchalantly as possible, his neck straining to look at the instrument in Colby's hand.

"Something's gonna happen if we don't do something right now! You've got enough gas in here to blow the place apart. You've got a main line leak coming straight from the underground into the receptor valve."

Bo wasn't sure he understood what was wrong but he was sure he understood that it was very dangerous.

"So what can you do about it? Should we wait until the rest of your team arrives to fix this? Maybe it's better we go upstairs now."

"No, we can do it here. I need to turn off the receiving unit and then cauterize the valve at the exit point. You've got a big problem, but fortunately it's a straightforward one. I think I can fix this one quickly."

Suddenly the crackle of the walkie-talkie broke the tension in the room. "Bo, Bo, do you read me?"

"Wait a minute." Bo sounded apologetic as he nodded at Colby. He turned partially to the side and held the receiver to his mouth.

"Bo here."

"Bo, it's Marvin. We've got a fire of some type in the Lex lobby. People are screaming and everything and running back up the elevator toward the lobby. We are having trouble getting down there with extinguishers. What can we do?"

Colby gave Bo his best expression of shock. His voice rose in excitement. He concentrated on keeping his American accent perfect. "You've got to get up there now! If it's in the lobby you are real lucky because that's where I came into the hotel, and with the open doors there's a lot of fresh air. It's probably diluted the gas's concentration enough that you won't get an explosion. But you better get up there and make sure that once they get the fire under control they pull everything onto the street. If they try to bring it back inside the hotel, this whole place could go! Also, they've got to open the doors and every window on that side of the lobby!"

Bo looked like he was about to hyperventilate. His breath came in quick gasps. "I'll make sure there is no explosion." He turned back to the walkie-talkie. "Mr. Scheitzer, it's Bo. Just get the maintenance crew there and have them put the damn thing out. I'll be right up to take over. Don't do anything, but put the fire out for now."

"I couldn't make out the last part of what you said. We've already called the fire department."

"Forget about it, I'm on my way up," Bo screamed into the receiver. He then turned to Colby. "I'll be back in a minute. Here's a spare walkie-talkie." He yanked a second unit dangling from the back of his work belt. "Just press this yellow button if you want to talk to me."

Colby watched Bo walk between the kitchen counters and into the elevator to the main floor. He looked at his watch. 9:27. Seven minutes left. The intensity of the gas odor had already substantially subsided. Colby had to act quickly. He reached into his tool kit, removed a long hammer, and started screwing the hammer head off the wooden handle. When he pulled the head off, he turned the handle upside down and out slid one of Erica's special cylinders filled with K-7 pellets. He knew exactly where to go. He had memorized the lunch for the governor's holiday party. Shrimp in dill sauce as an appetizer. Grilled chicken breast, accompanied with a julienne of vegetables and new potatoes, all covered in a light tomato cream sauce, as a main dish. Of course there was a tossed green salad with fresh strips of carrots and radishes. And dessert was pineapple upside-down cake served with petit fours. Cups of coffee to wash it all down. The governor's favorite blend. Mocha Java beans had been used especially for the luncheon.

He left the gas tanks and moved past a long counter topped with defrosting T-bone steaks. Near the rear of the cavernous room he turned left into the kitchen's second hall, the main cooking room. He sprinted to an enormous Sub Zero refrigerator and opened the doors. In front of him were large plastic vats of a thick red paste. Tomato sauce, accented with a little garlic and parsley, salt and pepper to taste. From a single briefing he knew the details of the kitchen's operations. Colby knew that this sauce had been finished from freshly pureed tomatoes less than an hour earlier. An hour before it was to be served at the luncheon, light cream would be added and the entire concoction would be brought to a boil before being served. More than enough heat to release the encapsulated K-7. Into each vat Colby released a pellet. Five in all. Anybody who tasted the sauce would be infected.

Suddenly the walkie-talkie dangling from his belt loop crackled on. "Hello, Con Ed. We've got everything under control up here. Hello, do you read me? Hello, this is Bo."

Colby depressed the button on the side of the walkie-talkie and raised it to his mouth. "I read you, Bo. This is Bolton, Con Ed."

"It was only a garbage can fire and we've got it all outside. By the way, there is a lot of smoke smell here, but even upstairs they are saying that the gas doesn't smell so bad. The fire department is here and they think it is real mild. How are you coming?"

"Okay. I think I've just about got it. I've cut the flow and I'm about to finish the inside of the tube. Just a few more minutes."

"I'll be down in a couple of minutes. But Mr. Scheitzer just took the elevator down. Should be there any second."

Bo had just finished the sentence when Colby slammed the refrigerator's doors shut. He jumped and ran to the far side of the kitchen to a large industrial coffee machine. Pausing for a moment, he listened for the elevator but could not hear a sound. He flipped open the top of the coffee machine, and a large screen-mesh filter jammed with mounds of ground coffee greeted him. The machine was capable of making nearly 1000 cups of coffee. One of the largest and quickest units on the market, its brewing process also reached the required temperature to activate the K-7. The remaining two pellets were shot into the mounds of ground coffee. He slammed the lid back on the machine. Between the sauce and coffee, Colby was sure that 1500 infected guests would be walking out of the Waldorf later that day.

He sprinted back to the main room, and as he neared the gas pipes he heard the elevator doors open. 9:35. One minute to go and the destostat would be entirely gone.

"Well, Bolton, if it's not one thing it's another." It was Scheitzer, worse for wear. "When I heard we had a fire I thought that was it. But it was small and nothing happened with it. Tell me something good. I can't take much more of this."

Scheitzer rested for a moment, leaning against a countertop. He looked as though he hoped the worst was over. "It smells much better. Does that mean that you have good news for me or does that mean I am just getting used to the damn stuff?"

Colby gripped the electric wiring as he glanced at the hotel manager. "Your sense of smell is real good. I've caught it at the source. It was an interior seal leak from the main line. It had ruptured pretty well but I've resealed it with a super caulking. It will hold longer than the rest of your pipes. It's solid. But the service section will still send a crew out to put in an entire new piece." Too late for your luncheon guests, Colby thought. By the time Con Ed realized someone had impersonated a repairman at the Waldorf, his mission in America would be accomplished and he would be safely home.

"Are you sure that everything is all right for today? This couldn't happen again, could it? I've already got the press arriving upstairs to report on this damn gas leak and the evacuation. And I've gotten a dozen calls asking if the governor's lunch is canceled. I've told them that it is on. You better not make a liar out of me."

"You're in great shape. You can let everyone back in here if this test goes as well as I think."

Colby reattached the wires and rubber sensitizers. Again he heard the elevator. It was Bo and a fire captain, who was decked out in his thickest rubber parka. That was good. He must be dying of the heat in that coat. He wouldn't want to stay long.

"The maintenance man tells me you had a leak coming from down here," the fireman said, moving close to Colby.

Colby did not look up while finishing the wire attachment. "Yep. Inner seal. But I've redone it."

"That was fast," marveled Bo.

"You've got to be fast in this business," the fireman retorted.

Well, thank you, Colby thought. He couldn't have answered better himself.

The fire captain looked at Colby. "Are you sure you got it all?"

"That's what we'll see right now." Colby turned to the fire captain. "Do you know this device?"

"Sure. Foolproof detector. We only have one in the entire department. I'd love to have some more."

Colby turned toward Bo. "Bo, tell the captain where this gauge read when we tested before."

Bo shook his head as if still in fright. "Way up in the red. It was danger. Real danger."

Colby turned back to the fireman. "It's all yours, captain. Give it a twist."

The captain took the metal rod and gauge from Colby's hands. He flipped the switch at the end of the gauge. The needle didn't move. No gas leakage. He flipped the switch to a second setting. The needle jumped along a second scale to 1550 psi. Fifteen hundred and fifty pounds of pressure per square inch. That's exactly what the main line should receive from the city's gas supply. The new seal was doing its job.

"Nice work, kid," the fireman said as he handed the device back to Colby. He turned to the hotel manager. "Your system is good enough to run on, Mr. Scheitzer. If I were you, I'd run as little gas as possible down here until the Con Ed boys can get in to put in the new stuff. But I know you fellows can't close shop. Bring the guests back in." He looked at his watch. "Hell, it's only 9:47. You've still got plenty of time to get ready for your bigwig party today."

"Oh, sure, thanks a lot. I've also got a couple of hours to lose this migraine that has started." It was Scheitzer's first faint smile. "Let's go upstairs, Mr. Bolton. I need you to sign some papers before leaving and you might as well call the main Con Ed number to arrange for the team that will replace the parts."

Colby packed his tools, grabbed his rain parka, and joined the others in the elevator to the main lobby. While walking to the manager's office he passed several cooks, the first contingent of returning workers, moving toward the rear elevator. One of them noticed his bright Con Ed uniform and shouted "Thanks" across the lobby.

Colby managed a tight smile. "Bon appetit" was his muttered response.

CHAPTER 8

CIA Headquarters
December 15
12:30 p.m.

McGinnis hated waiting. It was the worst part of any operation. But in a stage one alert, being stuck at headquarters was about as bad as it got. Everyone on the alert team slept in the "dorm," a spartan underground complex lined with bunk beds. Together with an adjoining locker and steam room, television center, and a cafeterialike dining hall, the dorm was supposed to engender esprit de corps among the troops. It also ensured they were available twenty-four hours a day for breaking developments. Thus far, he could have been on the beach in Waikiki and they wouldn't have missed him. There had been nothing to report. Since the grand briefing forty hours earlier, they just sat around waiting for the Russian suicide terrorists to land. McGinnis wondered whether they had decided to do a little shopping and sightseeing before killing off half the country. He still had doubts they were coming. But Finch wasn't taking any chances, and told them that the alert would stay in effect until midnight. That meant that if the VKR had the common sense to stay away for at least the next twelve hours, McGinnis could actually get a good night's sleep in his own bed. It also meant that he would not have to spend another evening with Jimmy Harris. The kid's enthusiasm was commendable, but only in small doses. McGinnis just didn't have the spirit for it.

Since the war room was quiet, Harris was trying his damnedest to make small talk, something at which McGinnis had never excelled. Tell me about your days in southeast Asia. What was the toughest assignment you ever had? Would you choose the same career again? What have been the biggest changes since you started in the Agency? For Chrissakes, it was like nonstop twenty questions. The kid may have meant well, but he sounded like a goddamn reporter doing a book instead of a partner breaking in a new assignment. And what the hell did he mean by "What are the biggest changes since you started in the Agency?" It made McGinnis feel like someone's grandfather. Had twenty years of field experience made him such a relic that new graduates were seeking his historical analysis of how the Company had changed? He had told Harris that the biggest change was that Camp Peary didn't teach new recruits how to properly occupy their time preparing for their upcoming assignments. If they did teach things right, Harris would shut his mouth and keep reviewing the files on recent VKR operations and the declassified memos on the London lab. That shut Harris up—for ten minutes. Then he would ask a question about something he saw in one of the files. McGinnis would grunt an answer. Then another couple of questions. In a minute, he would be jabbering away again. Oh, please God, just twelve more hours and freedom, McGinnis thought. He would be free of Harris and his constant optimism. Free of the windowless war room packed with computers, communication equipment, and digitized-laser wall maps. Free of the specter of the VKR.

Suddenly the buzzer sounded on the console next to McGinnis. That signified that someone had just passed through the war room's outer security perimeter. A steel reinforced sliding door was the final barrier to entry. It was cleared only after the person seeking access placed their right eye against a concave mirrored lens set onto the door. All authorized personnel to the war room had the blood vessel patterns of their eyes digitally encoded into the security computer bank. Reliable as a fingerprint for identification, the retina scanner compared the blood vessel pattern on the eye against those stored in the computer's memory. Since no two retinas are alike, a perfect match is required for entry. Once the retina scanner cleared the person for entry, the name of the new arrival appeared on a video terminal inside the war room. The green lettering flickered across the display terminal seconds before the steel door began sliding toward the ceiling. Nigel Hodson was paying a visit.

McGinnis had never felt comfortable inside the war room. With all its high-tech gadgetry it was like an adult video arcade, but without the fun. The man who had single-handedly designed it was now joining them. Hodson and McGinnis were friends. But as far as intelligence work was concerned, they were opposites. McGinnis still believed espionage was best performed with the tried-and-true methods of vast networks of agents, informers, and moles. He was convinced that a well-timed bullet was as powerful as any computer program. Hodson believed that agents with guns were the relics of a bygone era, and that a good computer could penetrate as much of the enemy's secrets as could one hundred Mata Haris. The Brit's machines increasingly ate larger slices of the Agency's annual budget, and they seemed to fill almost an entire floor at headquarters. In Hodson's presence, McGinnis felt like an antique battlehorse. He had a disturbing feeling that Hodson's philosophy was the future path for the intelligence trade. McGinnis was glad he wasn't going to be around for that many more years. He wanted to retire as a field agent, not a goddamn computer operator.

"I don't have much for you," Hodson sighed as he swung a chair in front of him and plopped into it. "We've just finished the checks on entries into the U.S. since the London hit. Finch wants me to update you."

McGinnis put down the file on a recent VKR terrorist team that was believed to have assassinated Chilean Archbishop Julio Graves. A nice, bloody little job.

McGinnis studied Hodson for a moment. The dark circles under his eyes and the pallor of his skin were caused by too many days indoors. McGinnis had not seen him at the dorm. He had probably spent the night with his computers, trying to pinpoint any irregularities at our borders in the last forty hours. Harris had closed the file he was reading and pulled a chair next to Hodson. McGinnis noticed the sharp contrast. Harris, although only a decade younger than Hodson, could have passed as his son. He had a youthful vigor that Hodson had lost. The Brit's brown hair had turned mostly grey. His receding hairline had turned into an official bald spot. His teeth were stained a deep yellow, the result of nearly twenty years of four-pack-a-day smoking. McGinnis remembered the frequently discarded blue packs adorned with a sailor, Player's cigarettes. Those English really knew how to make cigarettes that killed you. None of this low-tar-and-nicotine crap. They believed that if you were going to smoke, you might as well enjoy it and die young. If Hodson's teeth looked like that, McGinnis shuddered at the thought of what his lungs were like. Hodson had given up smoking at least once a year for the past five years. The average time away from the cancer sticks averaged one week. He was always trying a different gimmick to kick the habit. Hypnosis, group therapy, positive thinking, vitamin supplements, you name it and Hodson had probably tried it. This year it was acupuncture, administered by a seventy-seven-year-old Chinese herbalist in the back room of a fruit stand in Georgetown. Hodson claimed this time he was cured of his addiction. McGinnis would bet five dollars to one the abstinence wouldn't last past the holidays. But at least he wasn't smoking now, and that meant that the health and exercise buff, Harris, would not have anything to complain about in the windowless war room. McGinnis hoped that when he was next to Harris he did not look as terrible as Hodson did. No, he was sure he didn't look that bad. He had his arms crossed in front of his chest and flexed his biceps by squeezing his left arm. It was still tight. He was all right. It must be the endless hours glued to a video terminal that turned Hodson into an aging mole. Give Harris ten years in this job and it would be interesting to see how he weathered the wear and tear. From here on it was downhill, *wunderkind*.

"Can you grab me a cup of coffee, mate?" Hodson asked as he turned to Harris. The kid nodded and went to get it while Hodson continued. Harris hadn't said a word so far. The lack of sleep must be catching up with him. Thank God for a little sleep deprivation.

"Since Finch assigned my department the little task of checking everyone crossing our borders, I've pulled a Cray 6 into the job full-time. In the last thirty-eight hours we have had 129,876 people cross our borders. Legally, that is. That's airports, ships, and cars at the Canadian and Mexican entrance points. If the VKR sent their team in by an illegal crossing over Mexico or Canada, we're dead. If we can't pick up illegal aliens, we can't be expected to pick up espionage teams crossing the Rio Grande. Also, if the Soviets were planning this for a very long time, they might have followed one of their favorite past tactics, and that is have a team already in place here in the U.S. If we're dealing with agents who have lived and worked here for several years, under deep cover, then all our computer crunching was for naught. But with those caveats, let me tell you what we have discovered."

"You don't expect to find a Soviet agent traveling under a known pseudonym, do you?" Harris chimed in as he placed the paper cup of black coffee in front of Hodson.

"Cream next time, old boy, but thanks anyway." Hodson took a sip and then continued. "No, of course not. But Richard here may well remember, we once helped the Dutch foil an East German sabotage squad when one of the agents landed at Schiphol Airport under a valid Dutch passport with a matching photo. The only problem was that the passport belonged to a banker who had been killed in a mysterious car accident a couple of days earlier near Munich. An informer had tipped us they could be coming into Holland on that day, and we ran the same type of massive software program that we have been doing in this case. The minute someone enters the country, the computer picks up the names from airline arrival lists, shipping passenger logs, and license checks at the drive-in borders. Those names are run through identification lists maintained by the government, and cross-checked with data in driver's license bureaus, IRS information files, police arrest records, passport office files, and employer and credit data banks. For arriving foreigners, Interpol files are accessed, as well as the European Economic Community's general ID base, and we pull in a combination of our INS records as well as police files from nearly sixty-eight countries.

"Now, not every state has computerized their driver's license bureaus, the passport office files are notorious for poor maintenance, and some third world countries don't even know if the person in question is a citizen or not, but by cross-checking so many disparate sources, we can pick out the trouble spots. If somebody comes into the U.S. with a passport that should have expired, or that lists inaccurate home or personal information, or that belongs to someone we show is in prison, in a rest home, or even dead, then we know we have follow-up to do. Those become our target cases. You'd be surprised how we have tripped up otherwise elaborate operations because someone didn't pay attention to a small detail. I've seen cases in which they are so damned concerned about the actual operation inside the target country that they screw up the easy part—getting across the borders. Sometimes they'll pick a cover identity for an agent months in advance because the person fits their agent's physical description. Then, when the operation starts, they fail to check on whether anything has happened to the person whose passport has been copied. In the unlikely instance that he's had an accident, or been killed, or arrested, it will kick up on our computer with a warning flag. It's the little things that can trip you up in this business."

Hodson was perking up. He loved his work, and once he started talking about his machines and how well they worked, he seemed to draw on an unseen energy source. McGinnis had gained respect for him when they worked together on half a dozen earlier assignments. Originally skeptical that computers had any benefit in intelligence work, McGinnis was convinced that in the hands of someone as talented as Hodson, they were a wonder tool in the spy trade. While McGinnis was convinced they certainly did not replace the intuition of a good agent, he knew they were indispensable in a technological society. When his son entered college, he bought him a personal computer as a gift. It was called the Osborne Executive and had set him back almost $3000. It was the best on the market according to the young salesman who had guided him through the otherwise indecipherable computer showroom. Less than two months after he purchased it the Osborne company went bankrupt and the computer was outmoded by a new generation of equipment. His son recently told him that you could now buy a computer half the size, with three times the power, at only a third of the cost. That he understood. He got a lousy deal. But he didn't know much else about them, except that the Cray 6's, which Hodson worked on, were the most expensive, at $11 million each, and the most powerful in the world. With the way the CIA used computers, it was unlikely that Cray would join Osborne in the bankruptcy courts.

"Out of the 120,000 plus arrivals we coughed up 246 irregularities. Not bad for a day of combing the files. So far we have eliminated all but twelve of the inconsistencies. One hundred and forty-seven were due to errors made by the passport agencies in transcribing information from applications to the finished product. Thirty-eight were due to input errors in existing computer files—those highlighted problems which resulted only from wrong data sitting in some agency's file. Forty-nine have problem passports from their host countries. Of those, three are wanted by Interpol for currency violations, and the rest are an assortment of bureaucracy foul-ups, plus a few cases of suspected narcotics trafficking. But there's not a Russian agent among the group. That you can rest assured of. We still have twelve that are giving us some problem, and none of them are on U.S. passports. We might have a couple of instances of totally fictitious names being used, and we are in the process of physically tracking down those arrivals. They are probably just illegal immigrants coming into the country. It's highly unlikely that the Soviets would resort to a fictitious name. It just jumps out too easily at customs. We think the problem group is probably just part of a sophisticated alien smuggling ring. Within a couple of hours local police forces who are doing some follow-up for us should have an answer."

Hodson was like a computer himself. He never referred to a note. The figures came out of his mouth as if a microchip inside his brain pumped them through his vocal cords. McGinnis remembered Hodson had always been like that. He was the one agent you could count on to remember all the details at any briefing—the type of agent that the Soviets would give anything to bring in. If they could ever get him to talk, there was a wealth of information stored between his rather prominent ears.

McGinnis leaned back in his chair. "So what it all means, Nigel, is that you gave your machines a real good workout, but they have probably come up with nothing more than a typical day—a few drug smugglers and a couple of illegals trying to make it into the land of golden opportunity."

"That's exactly right."

"So what did Finch say when you told him that you didn't have one entrance that bore a VKR trademark?"

"He shrugged and said he wasn't surprised. He thinks they have had this planned for a long time and the team is either in place or it's coming in on real clean passports."

"Oh, that's great. So why the hell did he have you do all that work then?" Harris broke in.

"Because otherwise I have nothing else to do in the beginning of one of these bloody things. So instead of just making a nuisance of myself I might as well keep checking the entry points for inconsistencies. Hell, if it ever turned out that a VKR team entered our borders, and there had been a chance to stop them because of a mistake on their paper work, there would be some major questions to answer if this program was not being run."

McGinnis turned in his seat to face Harris. "It's the 'cover your ass' philosophy. You better do everything, even if you think it might be a waste of time. That way no one can blame you for leaving any stone unturned. It's why we have such inflated payrolls around headquarters. Half the people around here just perform useless tasks that covers someone's ass up in a fifth-floor office. And I'm not talking about you, Nigel."

"I know you're not, Richard, and even if you were I wouldn't take any mind. I think—"

Again the buzzer sounded on the console next to McGinnis. They all looked at the green video monitor that would announce the identity of the authorized visitor. In less than thirty seconds "Tony Finch" flashed on the screen. He burst inside.

"Hodson, get your ass moving back downstairs. Your spectrum system just picked up atmospheric disturbances. According to your machines, it matches a chemical structure that it is identifying as K-7! Your damn program looks like it might be working!"

All three men inside the war room rose as if on cue. Hodson was the first to speak. "Where is it?"

"East coast. The warnings are sounding in the tristate region, around New Jersey and New York. The machines are trying to isolate the atmospheric alteration by pinpointing the sensors to the highest chemical alteration."

"If I've designed the bloody system correctly, we should know within one hour of the original disturbance, a location that will be within a quarter mile of the infection site. We're only in trouble if there's been widespread spraying. Are we sure it's K-7?"

"Come and look for yourself. Your computers are ringing all the right bells indicating they have spotted something that matches our missing virus. Come on, let's not waste time talking. Come back downstairs with me. Richard, contact the New York office and let them know you and Harris will probably be up there shortly. Don't tell them anything except that we may need some follow-up on the ground. This operation has been activated. Once we get a handle on what's happening, you two will be on the road. . . ."

Finch finished the sentence as he left the war room, Hodson in tow, the steel door slamming shut and cutting off his last words.

McGinnis couldn't believe it. A release of K-7 somewhere near New York. The damn VKR really was run by crazies. Well, at least the waiting was over. McGinnis liked action. He couldn't tolerate sitting around and twiddling his thumbs. While he wouldn't be getting to sleep in his own bed, at least there was work to do and he liked that. And now that the infection had been spotted in the States, he recognized the importance of the operation. No more small talk, no crossword puzzles, no more rereading of two-year-old files. This was the real McCoy, and his system responded like a well-tuned machine being turned on.

He looked at Harris, standing, waiting for some direction. "Come with me, kid. It's time I showed you how it's done different here than in the classroom."

CHAPTER 9 ⋛━━━

Paris
December 15
3:00 p.m.

Jean-Claude Bouchet paced in small circles around his spartan fifth-floor office. He paused for a moment in front of the dirty windows and stared at the cluster of bland 1950s-styled buildings that surrounded him. He was in French intelligence's headquarters, on the Boulevard Mortier, close to Porte des Lilas, a seedy little suburb north of Paris. But the bloodhound's eyes were not focused on anything in particular. His mind was racing through the events of the past thirty hours.

Based on the information provided to him by the young agent, Ropac, he had expected foul play. But he did not expect to find a corpse in the Bastille Suite. And he certainly had not expected to be greeted by the horror inside the suite's bathroom. During his career, Bouchet had both seen and done his share of killing. Although he had been good at it, he never relished it as did some of the men with whom he served. He knew there was nothing glamorous about pushing the last breath from someone's throat or watching their head explode inches in front of you. Television and movies all too often idealized death. Most young people seemed to think that in combat, men only died in slow motion, soft sunsets glowing around them, with beautiful music in the background. In reality it happened in a second, and the brutality overwhelmed your senses so much that eventually they were numbed. It finally deadened your soul. After a while you could kill as easily as you could make a pot of coffee in the morning.

That had always amazed him. How human beings adapted to the worst situations. Concentration camp survivors, famine victims, murderers, all eventually described their experiences in a way that made them sound normal. At one point in his career, killing had become normal for him. That's when he knew it was time to come in from the field. It was time to sit behind a desk at headquarters and use his analytical mind to do what he did best—piece together the pieces of the puzzle that no one else could even see.

But the fact that killing had become second nature to him once did not mean that a dead body couldn't still send chills down his spine. And yesterday's corpse was grotesque enough to send shivers through the most hardened agent. There had been no telltale odor when they entered the suite. The kill was so fresh that too little time had passed for the stink of decomposing flesh. The living room and the bedroom had been clean, almost too clean. When people checked out of hotels, they usually left the rooms in a terrible state, knowing that maids would have to thoroughly clean for the next guests. In the Bastille Suite everything looked as though it had been wiped spotless, the effort of someone who wanted to leave without a trace. He almost expected the bathroom to be empty as well, but he knew it wasn't when the young agent went in first. He heard a grunt, the sound someone makes when they are about to vomit, and he immediately knew a dead body had been discovered. Running into the bathroom, he stopped wide-eyed and focused on the shiny red mass spread out in the porcelain tub. At first glance he didn't know that the fingers had been sliced to eliminate the prints, but he could tell that the face had been peeled away from the naked body. Blood was splattered across the tub and against the rear wall. When Bouchet had looked at the young agent's ashen face, he recognized the nausea overtaking him. He grabbed Ropac by the arm and sprinted him outside the suite.

"After you've been sick, come back in. I need you to start getting people for me."

It was cruel, but Bouchet's instincts had instantaneously taken over. He could not allow his young sidekick to become sick in the suite. By throwing up into a toilet or sink he could destroy valuable traces of forensic evidence that the laboratory might be able to salvage. If he was going to get sick he might as well do it down the hallway, away from the scene of the crime.

While Bouchet waited for Ropac's return, he knelt close to the tub and studied the body. No marks on the front of the body, no visible knife or gun wounds. The head, or what was left of it, was twisted at a sharp angle as though staring toward the door. The neck was swollen on the left side and a dark purple and reddish discoloration had formed under the puffed skin. The neck had been broken, the bloodhound would bet on it. He studied the face. It had not just been mutilated. It had been skinned as a furrier would skin a mink pelt. Somebody had deftly removed the 7 millimeters of outer skin revealing most of the muscle tissue and skull. The eyes were gouged, the glistening sockets adding a touch of surreal horror. When he diverted his stare from the empty sockets he noticed the fingers for the first time. He lifted the corpse's right arm and studied the skillfully cut skin that eliminated any identifiable tips. Very professional. The bloodhound knew that only a handful of people specializing in death possessed the gruesome skill to finish a kill in this manner.

His young assistant had returned just as he was about to start jotting down notes. Ropac was still very pale and had obviously lost his breakfast. Bouchet ignored the illness. He lost no time in ordering him to retrieve the necessary components for the investigation. As the senior SDECE officer on the scene, Bouchet automatically became the temporary operational chief. First he notified headquarters that the Iranian entourage must be diverted from the Hotel Raphaël. The corpse could well be the hallmark of terrorists eliminating a dissenting member from a pending operation. French intelligence could not take a chance with the Iranian visitors. He then had the night staff of the Hotel Raphaël summoned from their homes to return to the hotel. Together with the day staff he wanted to question everybody concerning the people who had come and gone from the Bastille Suite. He had discovered long ago that the best way to conduct these interrogations was in large groups. Often one employee would remember something that would trigger another's memory. Questioned alone they often failed to remember anything, sometimes sheer fright blocking their recall.

Bouchet also ordered a forensic team from headquarters to come to the hotel to sweep the suite. The SDECE forensic team was like no ordinary police squad. Armed with state-of-the-art detection devices, they obtained microscopic scrapings and chemical tracings that helped identify colognes, perfumes, or medications, all of which might help to pinpoint the killers. Most importantly, if they found even loose hairs in the room, they could reconstruct genetic DNA patterns from the follicles. This allowed them to get a biological fingerprint for the people that had been there. With radium-filled, time-lapse screens, the lab could even estimate how long ago the hair had been removed from the body, which helped determine whether the hairs belonged to recent visitors who might have been at the scene near the time of death.

Finally, Bouchet had summoned a medical team. Not only did he want to have a thorough autopsy, but the bloodhound knew that a full and detailed skeletal x-ray might help identify the body that the killer wanted left as an enigma. If the bone structure exhibited an unusual x-ray history, Bouchet might be able to identify it through existing medical records. Before the rest of the team arrived Bouchet had taken a handkerchief, covered his right hand, and pried open what was left of the mouth. The teeth were covered in blood, but they were still there. Dental x-rays would also be taken and could be crucial.

A pigeon fluttered in front of the window, only inches from Bouchet's face, and it broke his concentration. Turning away from the soiled glass, he shook his head as he ended his daydream about the scene at the Raphaël. He sat behind his large, battered, oak desk, which occupied almost a third of his small office. He glanced for the tenth time at the initial computer reports issued by the forensic laboratory and the medical team. The Bastille Suite had provided a gold mine of information. Twelve different hair samples had been identified. The protein had been synthesized, then chemically separated into its molecular state, and finally fed into complex computer programs that took less than an hour to identify the genetic code, the DNA number sequence for each strand. The twelve samples belonged to eight men and four women. Five were dated by almost four weeks, two of them nearly two months old. These were eliminated as belonging to earlier guests. Three others, belonging to two women and a man, had been eliminated as a result of hair samples taken from the employees at the hotel. Two maids and a room service attendant fit those three strands. Subsequent questioning by Bouchet had eliminated them as suspects. That left four strands, three belonging to men and one to a woman. One matched the hair found on the corpse. According to the radium time-lapse test, the final three people, two men and a woman, had been in the room at or near the time the victim was killed. They were Caucasian and between thirty and fifty years of age. The woman had natural dark brown hair. One of the men had black hair and it was also his natural color. The final unidentified man might have been the killer. His hair follicles were found not only in the suite, but extensively in the bathroom and even on the corpse. His natural hair color appeared to be a light brown, almost a dirty blond. Attached to each hair sample was a long strip of white paper resembling a calculator output, and printed across it were the thousands of characters that constituted the unique genetic code for that person. Whether the hair was dyed purple or the head was shaved, if Bouchet could obtain a follicle from any other location he could now identify whether one of his suspects was there with as much certainty as if he knew them and personally saw them there. In many ways it was better than a fingerprint, because the quarry often did not even know he was being hunted.

There had been no fingerprints at the scene. The killers had swept the surfaces clean, even eliminating any prints left by the hotel staff. If it had not been for the arrival of Bouchet and the SDECE, the police investigation would have been frustrated by the absence of fingerprints. Bouchet wondered how surprised the killers would be to know that they had left behind a fingerprint of a new age. Even if they knew about DNA identification, how could they possibly have known that the full resources of French intelligence would be called into an apparently isolated murder case. It was their misfortune to have chosen the Raphaël.

The bloodhound looked at the medical report next to him. Again a gold mine of information. The victim was somewhere between twenty-five and thirty-five years of age. Caucasian, muscular in a beefy way, the body was filled with unusual characteristics that might help identify it. There were two bullet wounds, one near the kidney and one in the left thigh. Both were old wounds that had been very professionally fixed. They should be on file in a doctor's office somewhere. Maybe even a military file if the wounds were war injuries. The body also showed the signs of four broken bones, including a nose that had been broken twice. And the real help was found in the right thigh. The hip flexor was swollen and the bone had been cut and shaven to eliminate a childhood case of osteomyelitis, a potentially degenerative bone marrow disease. According to the medical report it was a rare disease, occurring less than one time in 100,000 newborns. The field had been substantially narrowed. The bloodhound was looking for the medical records of a Caucasian man between twenty-five and thirty-five, with evidence of a broken nose, a smashed right index finger, a fractured left ankle bone, a compound break of the right shoulder bone, two distinct bullet wounds, and the evidence of an unusual disease, osteomyelitis. The mouth further narrowed the search to someone with two full caps, eight fillings, and surgically removed wisdom teeth. It was a distinct medical profile.

The question was where to look. If the files were stuffed away in some country doctor's office, the bloodhound would never find them. But if they were in a central computer file he might have an identification within a couple of days. He had placed his bet on the military services. He had already sent confidential, emergency action cables to the intelligence branches of the Americans and seven European allies asking for comprehensive checks of their military personnel data bases to see if the corpse was a former soldier. He also sent a request to Interpol for assistance with known criminals. He wasn't quite sure where to proceed next, but he would not have to decide until the first requests were returned without a match.

Bouchet leaned over and pulled open the top drawer of his desk. He reached inside and grabbed a small pouch of black tobacco, emptied a thimbleful into the head of his briar wood pipe, and stuffed it deeply into the well burnt crevice. As he lit the pipe with the thin, silver lighter that had belonged to his father, the pungent odor of cheap French tobacco filled the office. He leaned back in his chair and grabbed the final file folder on the desk. It was a separate report issued by the forensic laboratory. It also had "Confidential" emblazoned across the front page in bold, red letters. He flipped it open. He had read its contents several times but it still surprised him. The technicians had scraped the bathtub and the plumbing under the tub. Their microscopic findings uncovered a key item. It had nothing to do with the body. It had everything to do with Bouchet's world of cloak and dagger. Selenium-treated paper had been dissolved in the tub, at or near the time of death. Bouchet knew that selenium paper was an intelligence trade tool employed by fewer than a dozen agencies. The killers in the Bastille Suite were no ordinary murderers. Unless they had stolen the paper, they had a connection to one of a handful of the world's most sophisticated spy agencies. What they were doing in his city he did not know. But the discovery of the selenium paper presented him with an additional challenge. Someone connected to his trade was killing people in his territory. He was determined to discover who they were and why they had been in Paris.

He had already sent confidential requests to the intelligence agencies of the NATO powers, as well as Interpol, asking for information on any operatives distinguished by a trademark of leaving corpses peeled like a piece of fresh fruit.

The knock on the door interrupted his thoughts. "Come in."

It was Serge Delon, a senior director of Group 5, the Action Directorate for the SDECE.

"Good afternoon, Jean-Claude. I have read the reports you had generated. I do not think this had anything to do with the visit for our Iranian friends, do you?" Delon grabbed a straight-back wooden chair in front of Bouchet's desk and plopped his lanky, six-foot frame into it. As he waited for an answer he pulled Gauloise filterless cigarettes from his breast pocket and shook one from the pack.

"No, I agree." There was no uncertainty in Bouchet's voice. "I just do not feel it was connected to the Iranians, although I cannot eliminate it as a possibility yet. But I do not feel it. Yet, we could take no chance, it was better to divert them."

"Oh, no doubt! I am not questioning the wisdom of changing the plans, although it was a logistical nightmare. They ended up at the Crillon, which is much nicer than they deserved. But it had to be done the way you did; they could never have gone to the Raphaël." Delon reached over to the desk and grabbed the silver lighter. After lighting the cigarette, he drew a couple of long puffs and continued. "Do you have anything back yet on your requests to other agencies?"

"Nothing yet."

"What do you know about the hostile action that took place in London several days ago?"

"Just what I was briefed on earlier this morning. That we have a source inside MI5 that has told us that an American station inside the British capital was utterly devastated. Evidently no mere accident, but possibly a combative action, with an undetermined loss of life, all apparently American agents. That's all I know. Why? Do you believe there is any connection? I can speculate, but I do not know enough."

"Well, let me tell you a little more. To be precise, the American station was taken out on December 13, the morning of the same day that our corpse was killed inside the Raphaël. Our contact tells us that the word on the American station is that they were involved in some type of covert research, maybe special weapons, although the Americans call it a central research base. I wouldn't trust the U.S. description for a second. Tell me, Jean-Claude, does that pique your curiosity?"

Delon respected the bloodhound. He wanted to see his mind in action.

"It certainly must be followed up. Consider the facts. We have a friendly power that suffers a hostile and overt military action. That in itself is very rare. None of us have these types of cases very often. So that makes the day itself a special one. Any other unusual intelligence activity must be studied that day. The Raphaël murder would seem totally unconnected if it were not for the traces of selenium paper. That single item marks the room with an intelligence imprimatur. Less than an hour from London, same day, a brutal murder. Could have been part of the operational team that acted in the morning in London, or maybe a second team that was supposed to strike in Paris and something went askew, or even a support team that had a last minute problem. Of course, it could also have had nothing at all to do with the American problems in London."

Delon smiled. He could almost hear Bouchet's brain wheels grinding. "So, Jean-Claude, what do you intend to do?"

"I'll start by checking every flight from Heathrow and Gatwick to Paris for that day. If they were part of the London operation against the U.S. base, then they would have had to fly here in order to make it in time for the evening. The ferry crossing would have been too slow. I'll see if we recognize any names. I can have that done downstairs and it won't distract from my other work. I'll also check with the Americans to see if they have been able to scrape any fragments from their wreckage. If they have any, I'll match it against what we have found. As you know, we have unlocked the genetic codes for people we think were at the Raphaël during the murder. We can always match those codes against any the Americans might have." Bouchet paused for a moment, drawing on his pipe as he stared at the ceiling. "But I must tell you that I find it difficult to conceive why a murder squad would strike in London and then travel to Paris to kill off one of its members."

"You've been in this business long enough to know anything is possible. Let me tell you one last factor which you might find interesting. Our source in Langley has told us that the place is crazed. There is a special alert, but no one outside of a small circle seems to know what it's all about. It was coincidentally called late the same day the American station in London was destroyed, and it is still on. As far as we know, no other American station was hit anywhere. No Soviet station has been involved in hostile action. The Americans appear to be gearing up for something important but our source doesn't know what. It's possible the team you have uncovered in Paris was an American team trying to stop the hostile action that took place in London. They might have known something was about to take place but had the wrong information on its time or location. It's also possible that, as you speculated, the Raphaël episode had a connection to the London hit team.

Or maybe we are just dealing with two totally separate coincidences and we are rushing down the wrong path. One way or another I would love to know what our friends in Washington are up to. I'd also like to know more about what happened to them in London. The good news in all of this is that you will be able to help me, and help your investigation at the same time."

The bloodhound took another long puff on his pipe. It was seldom possible to advance the investigation while trying to serve the interests of the Action Directorate. They were often different interests.

"We don't know what the American inner circle is working on but we know the people on it," continued Delon. "Tony Finch appears to be the coordinator and you know I've never gotten along very well with him. That mad limey Hodson is running their machines and he's no good to anyone or anything but his computers. But they have had the good sense to include your old friend Richard McGinnis."

The mention of McGinnis's name brought a smile to Bouchet's face. He had worked with him on several intricate cases in the past. They had both nearly gotten their heads blown off in southeast Asia when they stumbled into a booby-trapped opium refinery. Although their friendship was built on respect for the other's talents, they were different in important ways. McGinnis acted on instinct, often impetuously. Bouchet prided himself as a thinker, analyzing the options and then choosing the most rational route. They arrived at their decisions in fundamentally different ways, but when they worked together they always seemed to agree on what should be done. A good agent was the same, no matter how he did his work. McGinnis was a solid man, even if he was a bit rambunctious and outspoken. But the bloodhound had found those traits particularly American, and thought they were an integral part of what made him like McGinnis so.

"There's no guarantee that McGinnis will tell me anything."

"I realize that. But he is the best chance we have for quickly discovering what is happening in Washington. If he thinks you have something for him, he will jump at the chance to work with you. If the Americans are not sure who struck at them in London, he'll be begging to see any Paris connection, no matter how tenuous. Gather your reports. You're going to pay your friend a visit. He's still in Washington as of this past hour. You are going to catch him before he gets into the field and we lose him. We will tell Washington when you've arrived that you are dropping in for an operational security visit."

"I won't be there until the middle of tomorrow morning, even if I get a flight out tonight."

"No, you'll make it. You should thank this emergency for imparting a little luxury. You'll be on Concorde, my friend. You're leaving in one hour and will be in Washington before dinner."

In an agency known for an extremely tightfisted budget, it was a major concession, and imparted the importance with which the directors viewed the assignment. Delon noticed the surprise register on Bouchet's face.

"Don't be so impressed, Jean-Claude. Remember, the Concorde is part of our national airline. It doesn't cost us a franc, no matter how you fly."

Bouchet still savored the moment. Major strings had to be pulled in order for a government employee to take a supersonic flight. Concorde to see McGinnis. The investigation had already taken a turn for the better.

CHAPTER 10 ⟫———————

San Francisco
December 15
10:00 p.m.

It was 1:00 in the morning in New York. God knew what time it was on their biological clock in Europe. But both Colby and Erica knew they were utterly exhausted. They had slept only a few hours the previous night. Up before dawn, the Waldorf operation had emotionally and physically drained them. Upon its completion they were driven to Kennedy Airport for separate flights to the West Coast. Neither slept during the six-and-a-half-hour journey. They were supposed to touch down at 8:30, but dense fog at San Francisco International Airport kept their planes circling for almost an hour. At one point, it appeared they both might be diverted to San Jose, adding an additional two-hour drive to their odyssey. But the fog finally cleared and they touched down in San Francisco.

Both carried their own travel bags, Erica's containing the leather kit safeguarding the remainder of the virus. They looked much more like a rumpled pair of travelers than terrorists on their way to rendezvous with a local contact. They almost seemed to slouch through the modern red-and-white corridors of the TWA terminal. Yet Colby's eyes were different from those of his fellow travelers. They darted from side to side searching for the man who matched the photo he had been shown at the New York townhouse.

"There he is." Erica nodded her head toward the upcoming Avis counter. Standing less than twenty feet away was a middle-aged man of average height, with curly brown hair and a neatly trimmed mustache. Erica thought the deep scarring on his face must be the result of a burn. The man stood in the rear of a small group of people waiting for the arrivals from New York. His khaki slacks and dark purple polo shirt blended in perfectly with the casual dress of the Californians surrounding him. He spotted Colby and Erica almost at the same moment she saw him. Pushing his way through the small throng, he reached for them with outstretched arms.

"Hiya, folks, how was the flight? Good to see you." Before Colby or Erica could respond he leaned forward and gave Erica a sloppy wet kiss on the cheek and then threw his arms around Colby in a bear hug.

"Cut this silliness out immediately!" Colby hissed through his teeth as he tensed and tried to pull away.

"Oh, darling, isn't it just wonderful to be out here for a couple of weeks with friends?" Erica gave her most ingratiating but plastic smile and nodded for them to move along.

The agent released Colby and stood back. "Can I help you carry anything?"

"No! No!" they responded, almost in unison.

"Okay, don't be so uptight. You can carry it. Just relax and follow me. I'll take you to the car."

They followed him through the terminal, along the "People Mover Belt" and into the multistory garage. The whole time they endured a nonstop conversation about how glorious the weather had been, how well the local football team was doing, and how scared everyone was over a recent prediction by a psychic that a major earthquake would devastate California within a week. Both Colby and Erica merely glanced at each other and rolled their eyes in dismay. They were too tired to give a damn whether the entire state fell into the ocean, even if they were in it at the time. They took an escalator to the third floor and followed their escort until he stopped at a navy blue Jaguar sedan, with dark grey windows blocking any interior view.

"This is it," he proudly announced as though he were showing the car to two prospective buyers. He fumbled with the keys only for a moment and then opened the rear door.

"Please make yourselves comfortable." As they slid in he sprinted around to the driver's side, unlocked his door, and jumped inside. He turned halfway in the seat to face them.

"Sorry about all that bullshit out there, but believe it or not you attract less attention out here if you are a little boisterous. No one gave us a second glance. But if you're too furtive you are sure to stand out like a sore thumb. This is the 'mellow' part of America, so relax.''

"Fine, fine. Save the explanations." Colby's voice sounded raspy. "We need a good night's rest. Give us the material so we can get going.''

"I am, I am, don't worry." He pulled a black nylon gym bag from under the front seat and unzipped it.

"Here's everything. First your credit cards, issued under your traveling names, all from major California banks. I have a driver's license for each of you. Yours"—he looked at Colby—"is an international one issued here by the Frisco AAA.''

"You broke regulations by leaving the material unattended in the car while you picked us up," Erica broke in.

"What?"

"You heard me. You broke regulations by leaving that bag here while you were in the airport. What if this car was stolen and the material was lost for the mission?''

"Hey, you've got to be kidding. I thought you wanted to get through this quickly? What am I, back in school or something? This car has a kill switch and one of the best alarms in the market. No one is getting in here. Your stuff is safe, so what's your bitch?''

"She's right," Colby chimed in. "But right now I don't think it's something we have to dwell on. Just give us the materials.''

The agent looked at Colby and Erica. First they can't wait to finish and then they start to cite technical regulations. What a charming pair. He had no idea what their mission was and had no desire to find out. He was only briefed on a need-to-know basis. Headquarters had decided he needed to know very little. The sooner he was finished, the better for all of them.

"Here is the photo of Father Enrique Vasquez. He arrives on Varig Airlines from San Salvador tomorrow at 8:00 a.m.''

Colby took the photo and spoke while he studied it. "You are sure no one else is picking him up?''

"Absolutely. Originally the Catholic archdiocese was sending a car and driver to bring him into the city. But we've called them and told them that Father Vasquez was going to be met at the airport by friends from the Humanitarianism in Central America movement in Berkeley. We insisted that this was the way he wanted to be met. They said that as long as the good father is at the church by 10:00 there is no reason to panic. Things don't get under way until a little after 11:00.''

"The Catholics didn't insist on sending someone to help a blind priest?"

"Not at all. That's part of his claim to fame. Not only has he stood up to the death squads, but he is notoriously independent. This is one blind guy who evidently likes to think of himself with a pair of eyes. They almost sounded relieved that some acquaintances were going to pick him up."

Colby held the photo in front of Erica. "So what do you think?"

"The glasses are so big that they hide half his face. The rest of the face is pretty plain. It should be easy for you. Right?"

"From a distance I'll look like the photo. I just don't want people who know him getting too close to me."

Colby turned to face the agent in the front seat. "How well do they know him in San Francisco?"

"You're safe. Remember, he's known for his stance against the military in El Salvador. His picture has been in the paper enough; he's big news. You know, 'Brave peasant priest challenges military despots.' But none of the people in the church up here have ever met him. They've invited him up because they want to meet him. This will be their first time."

"What's the rest of the schedule after the mass?"

"They have a press conference for him at 2:00 and a private audience with the cardinal at 3:00. So there is enough time to take him to the hotel after the mass. He's staying at the Hyatt Regency at the Embarcadero."

"What else do you have for us?" Erica asked impatiently.

"Here is $2000 in cash, in various denominations," he said as he gave Erica a white envelope. "And here are your SIG Sauer P226s."

He handed them two suede pouches.

"Each is as ordered. No serial numbers or identifying markers. Each is filled with a sixteen-round clip of hollow point 9-millimeter parabellum shells that have been acid stripped so they won't leave any unique ballistic characteristics. Even the firing pin marks won't be identifiable. The bullets are mercury tipped and when they hit a target they go off like a quarter stick of dynamite. Nasty little suckers."

Colby pulled out the dark grey pistol and studied it. Similar in style to a Colt .45, the SIG Sauer was half the weight of the American pistol and packed twice the firepower. It was one of Colby's favorite weapons, and he had personally requested it for the mission. He slipped it into the back of his waistband. Erica rested the gun on her lap.

"And here's an update from New York. It arrived three hours ago. It's on coded tape, as ordered. You're supposed to read it upon arrival."

He handed a thin white strip of paper to Colby. "That's the last item I have," the agent announced. On the strip of paper were a series of alphabet letters strung together in a seemingly random format. Only by unlocking the letter code they had memorized in New York could they understand the message.

Colby rested quietly in the back seat while he studied the paper. Erica started playing with the SIG Sauer. She looked at the agent. "No one can see inside these windows, correct?"

"That's correct."

She took out the clip, checked the chamber slide and trigger action, and popped out one of the bullets to study its smooth casing. Suddenly Colby threw the note toward her. "I am too tired for this. I can't make heads or tails of it. You do it. You're better than me anyway at remembering the code. I'm going stir crazy in here and I must stretch my legs outside the car."

Erica was so surprised that she didn't even respond before Colby unlocked the door and stepped outside. For a moment, he leaned against the rear door, the back of his navy blazer pressed against the grey glass. She was as tired as he was. He would hear it from her later. She grabbed the note and studied it. It took her less than three minutes to decode it. Why that dirty bastard! She glanced out the window and watched him pace near a water fountain, slowly drawing on his favorite cigarette, Dunhill menthols. You take care of it. Sure. I am too tired. Ha. Why, it was his idea of a little joke. This is definitely something he would find amusing. That little bastard. She would get even later. She stared at the roof of the car's interior.

"Is there anything I can help you with?"

Erica looked at the agent. "Yes, actually you can. There is something you must do right away."

She reached down to the duffel bag at her feet. She unzipped it and fumbled around for a moment. He leaned slightly over the seat. Suddenly her hand shot out of the case. She was clutching a long, blue metal knitting needle, its tip pointed straight up. There was no time for him to react. In a millisecond the sharpened end pierced his left eye and rammed deep into the crevice of his brain. His torso lurched backward, crashing his head into the steering wheel, and then fell to the side of the seat and halfway onto the floor. She looked over at him, the body still twitching from the nerve shock. Nearly six inches of the needle protruded from his eye. A steady stream of blood ran down his face and onto the car's plush carpeting. His mouth was frozen halfway open, in the process of forming a scream that was never uttered.

She reached over and flipped off the windshield wipers, which had been turned on when his body slammed into the dashboard. Then she put her pistol inside her purse, grabbed both Colby's case and her own, and quickly surveyed the garage before leaving the car. Colby had a grin from ear to ear as she stormed over to him.

"Were you able to make it out?"

"I'll report you for this, you son of a bitch!"

"Oh, my, my now. Our dear doctor has quite a temper."

"Don't fool around with me, asshole." Her voice trembled with anger. "You knew it was a kill order. No loose ends. We know that. It confirmed what we both suspected since Paris. But it was for you to do."

"Oh, don't take it so seriously. Please. No harm was intended. We're in this together. You can handle yourself, I knew it. I was nearby in case anything went wrong." She was not placated. He could see she was furious, her rage masking her nervousness. He tried talking to calm her. "I couldn't see inside with the windows. I didn't hear a shot. How did you do it?"

"How could I use a gun with the noise it would make? Huh? Tell me. I had to use one of the shears we passed as knitting needles."

"Oh, that was a nice touch."

"Asshole." She turned away from him.

"Look, while you pout, I am going to wipe any prints from that car and then lock the doors and throw away the keys. They shouldn't find him for a couple of days, by which time we'll be far from California. Let's get moving before we attract attention. Not many people seem to stand in the garage and converse."

Their ride into San Francisco was in silence. Erica thought of the kill she had made. She had not taken somebody's life with her own hands in more than a decade. And then she had only killed once. Although she developed death in the laboratory, she found it disturbing face-to-face. Colby was glad she was preoccupied with the airport murder. He could barely concentrate on driving the rental car through the freeway maze to their hotel. His eyes were heavy, his body aching for sleep. The oncoming headlights on the freeway were a constant sleep inducer. He fought to stay alert. He widened his eyes and clenched his jaw, hoping to wake himself. At one point he even pinched his arm, the pain helping to refresh him for a moment. He completed the last portion of the thirty-minute ride in a semidaze. By the time their car pulled into the circular driveway of the Fairmont Hotel, a few minutes before midnight, he was exhausted.

Colby registered the room under his name and placed the requisite imprint of a credit card on his Bank of America VISA. Two porters hustled across the gilded Victorian lobby to offer assistance with their luggage, but the weary couple politely declined. They walked past the lobby bar blaring American jazz, through the Venetian room hosting comedian Jackie Mason, and to the rear of the hotel. There they took the glass-enclosed elevator ride to their tenth-floor room. Past the third floor the elevator rode along the outside of the hotel. Already perched on top of one of San Francisco's tallest peaks, it commanded a breathtaking view.

"It looks so peaceful," Erica almost mumbled to herself.

"We'll have something to say about that." She could never tell whether it was a twisted sense of humor at work or inflated machismo that made him utter such corny phrases. She assumed it had to be a clever mind that had cultivated a cutting wit. He smiled at her. My God, he must be tired, she thought. Almost a sign of gentleness.

The view from their adjoining rooms cleared the nearby buildings on Nob Hill and presented them with unobstructed sights of the bay, the Golden Gate Bridge, and Alcatraz, just a dark dot in the distance. It took them a few minutes to unfold their clothes. Erica carefully placed the padded kit with the virus under the side of her double bed. Colby placed a small clock next to his bed and set the alarm for 5:00 a.m. He then telephoned the receptionist and requested a wake-up call for the same time. He always believed in a backup for every part of an operation, even something as simple as getting up in the morning. A malfunction in his traveling clock could cause him to miss Father Vasquez's arrival. That would be the end of the San Francisco operation. He never overlooked the smallest details. It was one reason he was still successful in a business with a very short career span.

As he washed up in the bathroom, Erica came into his room and sat on the edge of his double bed. Dressed in a pair of loose shorts and an oversized T-shirt, she seemed to stare a hole through the bathroom door. Her body ached from the traveling and the strain of the mission. She had been as tense as a board when she had planted the destostat earlier at the Waldorf. It seemed like days ago instead of a mere eighteen hours. She arched her back and pulled her arms behind her, clasping her hands together and stretching her muscles. Waiting for Colby in the car on Forty-seventh Street, she almost expected to see police or plainclothes agents running toward her to make an arrest. When she saw the bright yellow Con Ed raincoat sprinting toward her, she finally relaxed. Although she was as independent as a person could get, she felt safe with him. It didn't mean she couldn't do the operation without him—it just was comforting to have a partner who was very good at what he did. In a perverse way she was pleased that he had allowed her to make the airport kill. He was too professional to jeopardize any part of the mission unless he was absolutely sure of what he was doing. So when he decoded the message and saw it was a kill, he would have done it there, himself, if he had any questions about her resolve or ability. But instead he had just left her alone. No worries about her panicking. No doubt that she could eliminate another trained agent, a young man, physically stronger than her. His confidence in her made her relax. It was like he had told her at the airport, they were indeed a team. They served very distinct functions in the operation, but they were strong together.

She didn't know when it came to her. But suddenly she was sitting on the bed alternating between thoughts of her aching body and her satisfaction with the operation's progress, and the next moment she was thinking about seducing him. It surprised her. He wasn't particularly attractive or unattractive. She hadn't even looked at him that way. She respected his strength and talent, but she certainly didn't care for him. It was not affection that made her mind race and her heart beat faster. She had no illusions about meeting her soulmate. She was at nerve's end, racked physically and emotionally. She just wanted good, relaxing sex. No attachments. No love. And it would only work for her if she made the choice. She was long past allowing a man to seduce her. She decided when and whom she wanted to screw. And she decided it was time for Colby, whether he knew it or not.

When he came out of the bathroom, he still had on his black trousers, but he was bare-chested. His chest advertised his strength. Broad pectoral muscles, a flat stomach, and muscled arms. He would do nicely.

"We've got to be up in several hours, so you better get to sleep," he wearily announced to her as he rested on the edge of the bed.

She had already walked over to him. She reached down, grabbed his right hand, pulled it under her T-shirt, and placed it across one of her breasts. With her other hand she reached to his lap and massaged his penis through the thin fabric. His face showed no reaction but she knew he was surprised. His hand passively rested on her breast, as though undecided whether to stop her or to proceed.

"We should sleep. We don't need this." His voice sounded husky.

"We do need this," she whispered. "Both of us do."

She could feel him respond. His pants bulged under her hand, and slowly he began massaging her breast. She stepped back and pulled off her T-shirt. He had unbuckled his pants and she helped him slide them to the floor. She pushed against his shoulders and shoved him across the bed. She reached over, grabbed his wrists, and pinned him flat. Then she climbed on top of him, grinding her hips into his. She smiled, her thick hair falling around her face and over the top of her breasts. "Now let's see how good you really are."

CHAPTER 11 ⟫═══───

New York City
December 16
10:00 a.m.

"A dead end! That's where we are. And we're going nowhere fast."
McGinnis slammed down the receiver.

"What do they have for us?" Harris tentatively asked from across the
room.

"That's just the problem. They have a big zip for us. None of the
leads from the entry searches turned up a single fact to help us. So that
means that Hodson and his precious machines wasted another day
pursuing ghosts. We've isolated an outbreak of K-7 at and around the
Waldorf, where only half of the city and state's bigwigs got together
yesterday. And what do we have besides concrete evidence of an infection? Not much. We now know that the gas leak was a phony. Our
boys still haven't found the canister that caused the odor in the cooling
system but they might come up with it. We have a copy of the recording
from the emergency line at Con Ed that shows the call from the Waldorf
manager was cancelled by an unidentified voice, sounding like a male.
Now, as if we needed confirmation, we have more evidence of the
sophistication of our adversaries. Their scientific toys are very special.
The voice that cancelled the Con Ed repair team was done by someone
who spoke into a digital voice synthesizer that broke the vocal tones
into a different and random series of sounds and then spit them out on
the telephone. The damn thing happens so fast that you can't even tell
that a machine is regurgitating time-delayed speech. Since the machine

totally changes the voice pattern, there's no way we can match it against anything we have stored in our computers. For Chrissakes, we don't even know if it was a man or a woman who called Con Ed—the voice synthesizer can reverse the sex tones as well."

Harris picked up McGinnis's thoughts and continued the conversation. "Then after the mysterious caller cancels the real Con Ed team that is supposed to rescue the hotel from an odor we now know is a phony scent, we have a knight in white armor arrive and save the day. A little diversionary fire starts in the lobby, far removed from our new friend, and he spends his time, alone in the kitchen, trying to find the gas leak. Coincidentally, Hodson's spectrum computers go mad and start sounding like a Christmas party just a couple of hours after the supposed Con Ed man is wandering around the Waldorf kitchen. So it's not surprising that K-7 appears for the first time in New York when a guy is in the basement who turns out to be a phony Con Ed emergency repairman."

"Now you're thinking, kid. But what do we have from that? We have half a dozen conflicting descriptions of what the Con Ed man looked like, and even if we knew which panicked hotel employee had the most accurate description, you can rest assured that it would be a description of a well-disguised face. So the biological team is scraping around to see if they can come up with anything. And what if they do? Even if they come up with something that doesn't belong to the hotel employees, then we have to hope it matches the tracings found in London. If we don't get a match, we don't know anything more than we did three days ago. If it does match, it means we know that at least one of the sons of bitches who smashed the London station is here and spreading the damn virus. That confirms that Finch's hunch was right, but it still doesn't give us any more info on getting any closer to who the hell the guy is. So that's what I mean when I say we're at a goddamn dead end. Any more ideas, Harris?"

Harris had turned his back toward McGinnis. He was facing the large bay windows that looked uptown. He and McGinnis were sitting in a corner office on the forty-eighth floor of One Chase Manhattan Plaza, one of Wall Street's preeminent skyscrapers. The entire floor belonged to "Milbank and Oakes International Trading Corp.," one of the city's most successful high technology brokers. The Milbank firm was a privately held company that had annual revenues exceeding $100 million, most of that generated by top-of-the-line computer sales to far and middle eastern countries. John Milbank, an attorney who had served as assistant attorney general in the Nixon administration, had cultivated excellent government contacts that he used to the advantage of his new business. It also helped that the Milbank firm was a 100 percent CIA subsidiary. Formed and operated as a CIA enterprise, it was at the forefront of the CIA's new philosophy regarding front companies. No longer did the CIA hide behind minuscule storefronts and operate tacky back-hall businesses that lost money. The new CIA had created conglomerates in fields where trade in high technology with foreign governments was critical. Not only were the new companies multinational, allowing agents to move freely worldwide without having to invent half a dozen identities and cover positions, but they were often vast money-generating machines. The Milbank company was rumored to have turned a profit of nearly $10 million during the past year. Much of that money found its way into special off-the-shelf operations that Congress could never know about and which the CIA could never fund from appropriated monies.

Harris and McGinnis were in a segregated portion of the company. The section was a fully staffed CIA station, complete with computer access to everything at Langley. Harris could almost see the entire island of Manhattan from his office perch. McGinnis kept rattling in the background about the obstacles the investigation had run into. Harris appeared to listen, but the view had made his mind wander away from the work at hand. Harris was back in New York. He was home again, and the feeling wasn't a good one.

If McGinnis had bothered to look at Harris he would have seen him transfixed on a distant sight, the 1920s, art-deco styled Woolworth Building. Harris had worked there as a newsstand clerk for nearly four years. Every day after finishing his classes at P.S. 101 he had taken the IRT line to the Brooklyn Bridge exit, walked the five blocks to the Woolworth building, and started a six-hour shift that paid $3.00 an hour. On weekends he put in twelve hours a day at a wholesale vegetable stand near the fish market at Pier 17. He needed the income for his own schooling as well as helping his mother. His father had been an Air Force lieutenant, shot down near Haiphong Harbor during the last month of bombing raids on North Vietnam. Officially, he was still listed as "Missing in Action." It was the worst fate that could befall a family. You had to be realistic and resign yourself to the fact that he was most likely dead.

Harris's mother had held a glimmer of hope that he was a prisoner somewhere in the north and one day he would miraculously reappear.

Harris had lost the hope. For him, his father was dead. But since he was an MIA, he did not even have the honor of his name being etched into the granite monument in Washington. Although 55,000 names grace the Vietnam war memorial, the MIAs are forgotten. It took seven years before the Veteran's Administration even paid benefits to his mother. The official policy was that no death benefits could be paid since he was only missing. After seven years they decided the chances that he was merely missing were so slight, they justified paying her a nominal amount.

Harris was eight when his father went down in southeast Asia. At that time McGinnis was a young agent completing his first tour of duty with the Agency, stationed less than 100 miles from the site where Harris's father was downed.

With his father gone, his mother tried to support the household, but her physical limitations proved a major obstacle. She had been afflicted with severe arthritis after Harris's birth. It slowly crippled her. By the time she was forty, she walked with great difficulty and had lost the use of her left arm. With three children to support and less than $417 a month in state and military disability, their lot was a difficult one. Both of his older brothers had dropped out of school to get full-time jobs to help at home. One was a sanitation worker, earning nearly $13.50 an hour in union inflated wages; the other was one of the smoothest talking Buick salesmen in New Jersey, bringing home more than $30,000 a year. Harris had also been tempted to drop out of school. His brothers set the example, and he wanted to earn the same money and help himself and his mother. But she was the one who persuaded him not to leave. He was the brightest of the three brothers and school came easy to him. She was desperate that he complete his education and make something of himself. A professional man, a doctor, a lawyer, it was her obsession more than his. He's sure if she had lived he probably would have stayed at it, making a safe but profitable career.

But that choice did not seem as compelling once he lost her. Both his brothers had already moved out of their West Forty-seventh Street apartment. It was four small rooms in a third-floor walk-up. Now the neighborhood was called Clinton, and multi-hundred-thousand-dollar apartments were sprouting up as quickly as freshly watered grass. When he lived there the area was still dubbed Hell's Kitchen and no one wanted to walk through at night, much less live there. They had air-conditioning units in two of the four rooms, but they were so decrepit they barely kept the place tepid in the summer. In winter, the broken window seals let in stiff blasts of arctic air. It used to take his mother nearly twenty painful minutes to shuffle up or down the three flights of stairs. That apartment had become her own prison, and as a result, it was a prison for him as well.

They had made a pact, an oath as brothers, that they would get a better place for her the minute they could afford it. His brothers claimed they were saving some of their money. Harris put aside whatever he could from the $650 a month he earned after school. But he was always sure they could have done more to help before she died. He knew his brothers had the money. But they were too preoccupied with their own lifestyles, acquiring new cars, buying clothes, or getting larger color televisions, than with their mom's agony. It was one of the reasons he was still bitter toward them. They had made an oath with him and then they had ignored it. He couldn't forget that so easily.

He had been the only one who really cared. He had planned it out. Once he got to college, a state university with low tuition that he could afford, he would start a prelaw program. His grades were high enough to get a clerk's job in a law office. From reading the *Times* he knew the salaries were high, up to $1500 a month for researching cases. If he could hold down a second job, it would pay for his own living expenses and still leave enough to move his mother out of Hell's Kitchen. He could have achieved it within a couple of years.

But it all changed when he returned home that miserable Wednesday in July. It was ninety-three degrees and humid at 10:00 p.m., one of those suffocating New York days that make you long for the frozen blasts of mid-February. Between school and work, he had been gone since 8:00 a.m. He knew something was wrong the minute he opened the door to the apartment. Later he discovered that such heat starts decomposing a corpse within six hours. His mother had been rotting for twelve hours. He remembered the odor, a stench of decay, almost like sour milk or rancid garbage. It was new to him, but his instincts told him it was foreboding, terrible news. He shouted her name. She always called out to him when he opened the door. The silence scared him. He paused at the door, almost trying to pretend that he was day-dreaming. It was as if by waiting a moment he could be back outside and by reentering the apartment things might be different. Some part of him did not want to step inside. But he did. And what he discovered in his mother's bedroom was a scene forever branded into his mind. Her room was in shambles, as though a tornado had struck down in New York City and only ravaged her ten-by twelve-foot cubicle. Her naked body was spread across blood-splattered sheets, her limbs twisted as if she were a rag doll. She was bruised across her chest and on her thighs. Part of the bed sheet had been torn and tied around her neck, bulging her eyes and puffing her tongue out of her mouth. He remembered standing there as if cemented to the floor. He didn't even feel the nausea overtake him as he vomited over himself. Then his head felt light and he was falling. A neighbor had discovered the open door and gone inside to find him still unconscious almost half an hour later.

He could almost cite the coroner's report from memory. Severe contusions to the head, back, and chest. Mutilation of the breasts. Sperm found in the rectum and vagina. It was almost as if he had been attacked. The disorder in the room, the location of splattered blood, and the skin tissue under her fingernails told the police how ferocious the fight had been. He tried to imagine how difficult it was for her to move her almost crippled limbs to ward off the attacker.

For days Harris couldn't function. Almost catatonic, he went through the motions of living. There had been an eyewitness who described a young Hispanic man leaving the apartment. Twenty-six dollars was missing from a kitchen drawer. The police had fingerprints and knew whom they were looking for in less than a week, a twenty-two-year-old drug addict with a long arrest record. Harris wanted him first. He had to know why. How was it possible to have done it to her? He wanted him for himself. But the police found him first. They found him dead of an overdose in a shooting gallery less than ten blocks from the murder.

It was as if the murderer had gotten away with it. He had brutalized and killed someone and had not paid. It filled Harris with rage, but he had no place to direct it. He left the Forty-seventh Street apartment, knowing he never wanted to see it again. Any thoughts of going to college were abandoned. High school had just been finished and he knew that was as far as he would go. Even his graduation ceremony did not draw him back. His brother the car salesman suggested he move to New Jersey temporarily. But Harris blamed his brothers for letting her live there so long that some miserable punk ended her life like that. He didn't want help from them.

It came to him less than a month after her death. The only place where he could go and start fresh was the Marine Corps. He registered at the recruiting station in Times Square and within a week was in Camp Pendleton trying to forget everything about New York. His rage carried him far in the armed services. He excelled in everything he did.

It was not long before he came to the attention of his commanding officers, and within a year they had brought him to the attention of the spooks. The CIA is always interested in young hotshots who might turn into effective field operators.

Harris had everything going for him. No living parents. His father had a distinguished military service record. No personal commitments to a wife or child. And the CIA spotted the rage that drove him. That's what attracted them to him. They knew they could direct his anger. They could sharpen him into a fighting machine, an agent whose frustration at failing to find and exact revenge on his mother's murderer could be channeled for their own purposes. By the age of twenty he was at Camp Peary and was on his way to becoming the best student they had. In his file it looked so innocuous. "Father: missing in action in Vietnam, 1972. Mother: deceased 1982, New York." It told nothing about him. That's why he knew that McGinnis did not understand. McGinnis couldn't know what drove him.

The ringing of the telephone broke his concentration. He spun around to look at McGinnis.

"Jesus, kid, what are you—standing over a heater or something? You're pouring with sweat," McGinnis said as he walked to the desk to pick up the receiver.

Harris wiped the back of his hand across his forehead. A cool dampness covered him. His heart was beating at a quickened pace. Leaning back against the windowsill, he rested. He didn't feel very good. He never felt very good when his mind brought him back to that room, that stench, that last memory of his mother. He tried to break the thoughts by concentrating on McGinnis. The telephone conversation was a one-way affair. McGinnis listened, jotted down notes on the desk pad, and grunted occasionally before putting the receiver down.

"Well, we have a genetic match from the Waldorf." He said it as though he was still contemplating the consequences of the discovery.

"What type of match?" Harris tried to bring his full attention onto the case.

"The lab boys found some skin scales in the area where the supposed Con Ed repairman worked. They don't belong to any of the kitchen help, the managerial staff, the maintenance people, or the fire captain that paid a visit. They reconstituted a computer sample of the skin and they've just kicked out a DNA sequence. It's dead on for some of the charred hair samples we picked up in London. That means our target has arrived here within the last three days and we haven't picked up a clue about who he is. All they know is that it's a male, Caucasian, and probably young. That narrows the field down to a mere fifty million suspects."

"Well what if we—"

The phone interrupted Harris's thought. McGinnis held up his finger to stop him for a moment. Harris could immediately tell that McGinnis was surprised with the new call.

"Sure, I'll wait. Put him on."

"What's happening?" Harris whispered.

McGinnis placed one of his hands over the receiver. "An old friend of mine, French intelligence, has touched down in Washington. Evidently he's come to talk to me and has been cleared by Finch that it's okay. Now Finch is only going to let someone speak to me if it's connected with our little investigation, so maybe the bloodhound has something for us."

Harris looked befuddled. "The bloodhound?"

Suddenly McGinnis put his hand up to silence Harris. Whoever the bloodhound was, he had obviously started talking on the other end of the phone. McGinnis started an animated conversation. Harris could only hear one side of it.

"Well how the hell was I to know you were coming into the States. . . . You come for more than just saying 'hello, Richard.' What do you have for me? . . . What did Finch tell you? . . . Well, that's just about it, trouble with an historical analysis unit and we think the hit squad, or part of it, might be here in the U.S. . . . What makes you think he might have visited you? . . . Well, why the hell didn't you tell me that in the first place? Shit, I've just heard the latest lab update and that's the same goddamn fellow!"

McGinnis stood up. He was clearly excited. "You bet your ass" were his final words as he slammed down the receiver. He was beaming. "We've just got a solid breakthrough. The French had a brutal murder late on the same day our London lab was hit. They found some tissue samples at the site, enough to make a biological composition of the murderer. Well, as you can imagine, nothing as big as our London wipeout stays quiet very long in a community that thrives on gossip and rumors. So the French thought they should check to see if there's any connection between their little problem and ours. And guess what?"

"Do you mean there might be?"

"Might be? Shit, it's dead on. Finch took the French DNA compositions and ran them against the ones we had compiled from London. The murdered boy in Paris was in London earlier that day. And another sample was also in London. And that goddamn guy is the same fellow who was in the Waldorf earlier today!"

"So that means if we know they came out of Paris, we've got a much smaller group of people to zero in on," Harris chimed in.

"You're quick on the uptake. That's exactly what Hodson is doing right know. He's having his computers check every damn person who flew out of Paris that night and the next morning and arrived in the U.S. in time for this morning's New York operation."

Harris was getting into it; the thoughts of his mother's brutalized body had faded away. "That means that at least with one of the Soviet team, he wasn't already in place here in the States. That means he had to go from London to Paris and then here. That's too quick for a boat. So we know it's a Caucasian male, young, and on an airplane passenger list."

"Now you're starting to sound like they may have taught you something at school."

"Just a little." Harris noticed McGinnis was grinning. He didn't look nearly so stern when he allowed himself a smile. "By the way, who or what is the bloodhound?"

"C'mon, let's get going, Finch wants us back in Langley ASAP. They think we're wasting our time up here. You're going to have an interesting plane ride. I'll tell you all about the bloodhound."

Chapter 12 ═══════

San Francisco
December 17
8:00 a.m.

They drove to the airport in silence. Erica deliberately sat on the far end of the car seat, trying to place herself as far away from Colby as possible. She did not want any contact with him. The lust that had overwhelmed her common sense during the night had abandoned her in the morning. Except for a musty odor in the room, there was no evidence of the passion that caused them to alternately brutalize and caress each other for hours.

Colby noticed her distance. But he didn't care. He did not really want her before and he was not going to fret about whether he could have her again. There were more important items to be preoccupied with. They were about to embark on a complex and arduous stage of the mission. Neither could afford the luxury of broken concentration. Four days of intense stress and little rest had caught up to them.

Erica did not want to use it, but she had little choice. She administered 25 milligrams of Benzedrine solution to each of them at dawn. It was enough pure amphetamine to keep them going through the entire day at peak efficiency. Colby had worked on it before but was reluctant to take the injection. He was familiar with the side effects—irritability, interference with judgment, heart palpitations. Maybe the most dangerous side effect was a delusion of invincibility. In an intelligence operation timed to split-second accuracy and dependent on the impeccable field instincts of the agents, an extra dose of machismo could lead to disastrous consequences. But they had little choice as they tried to clear the cobwebs from their heads early that morning in San Francisco. They were not going to meet the challenge of the day's operation unless they were artificially stimulated.

They reached the Varig terminal twenty minutes before flight 602 from Rio, with stopovers in Panama City and San Salvador, was scheduled to arrive. Colby parked their rental car on the same floor where they had left the body in the Jaguar the night before. On their way to the People Mover Belt they strolled past the darkened windows of the navy blue British luxury sedan, each of them satisfied that the body was undiscovered. Inside the postmodern Terminal A they checked the large computer information screen, and then proceeded to the gate.

One of the items discussed in the New York briefing was certainly true—the American Christmas season brought extra people to the airports to greet arriving friends and relatives. The additional traffic was a good cover for them. They did not even need to disguise themselves—they did not expect to be seen by anyone who would live to identify them. Colby was dressed casually in a pair of grey corduroy trousers, black sneakers, a plain white shirt open at the neck, and a navy blue sports jacket. Erica wore a pair of dark brown pants, her favorite khaki flat shoes, a white cotton blouse, and a short, houndstooth jacket. They had carefully chosen their clothes to look innocuous. They merely wanted to melt unobtrusively into thousands of arriving holiday travelers at San Francisco International Airport. When they arrived at the gate, they quietly blended into the group of more than fifty people waiting for arrivals from the same plane.

The flight from Brazil was a rarity for Latin American carriers—it arrived on time. The plane was packed with passengers. Suntanned faces carrying great wicker baskets full of colorful South American stuffed toys, elderly passengers beaming as they spotted grandchildren seen once a year, young vacationers dressed in wild print T-shirts proclaiming Cococabana—every type of person but a priest. As the departing crowd thinned, Colby grew slightly apprehensive. If there had been a change of plans for Father Vasquez's arrival, the Catholic archdiocese would have been informed, but headquarters might have missed the news. If Vasquez arrived on a different flight, it could ruin the day's plans. Colby stepped up on his toes to look over the heads of the other passengers. Nothing.

"You're a nervous wreck. Stop fidgeting, you're driving me crazy," Erica spoke softly to him.

"What?"

"You don't seem yourself. Don't be so nervous."

"It's the goddamn Benzedrine. I told you so. I hate it. It makes me jumpy. I shouldn't have taken it."

"Just relax. Think of it as if you drank too many cups of coffee."

"Like a hundred too many?"

Erica nodded her head toward the departing passengers. "There's our pigeon, so do both of us a favor, relax. This is California and no one is in a rush to get anywhere. Remember?"

Colby looked in the direction Erica nodded. A priest dressed in the black uniform of the Catholic church was slowly shuffling toward them. He looked very much like the recent photo Colby had seen. A small but neatly trimmed beard, the skin a medium brown, the dark thick spectacles covering his eyes, and the black hair cut short and greased straight back. He was smaller than expected. He had to be at least three inches shorter than Colby. That was the easiest way for an impostor to be unmasked. Shit. No one had told him about the height difference. Maybe he should have killed that idiot in the Jaguar himself. Should have eliminated him for mere incompetence even if he didn't receive the kill order.

Colby started to wave toward the priest, but he wasn't noticed. Father Vasquez was intently conversing with two young girls who were walking next to him.

"Father Vasquez. Here. Father." Colby waved his arm over the crowd.

The priest appeared to look into the crowd as if trying vainly to pinpoint the source of his name.

"I don't believe you this morning." Erica rolled her eyes. She whispered as she leaned into Colby. "What do you think that white stick is that he's waving? A candy cane? Remember, he's blind."

"I know that." Colby said it too quickly, defensively. It did not have the ring of authenticity. He had forgotten Vasquez's blindness. "What do you think, I've lost my mind?"

Erica wondered whether 25 milligrams of Benzedrine was too much for him.

Colby parted his way through the crowd and finally reached the still groping priest.

"Father Vasquez, hello, my name is Gunther Bergman, and I've been sent by the archdiocese to see that you get to your hotel and then to the mass on time."

Vasquez put down his black leather valise and extended his hand toward Colby.

"Señor Bergman, mucho gusto. I am very pleased to be here." The priest's English was heavily accented.

"Father"—Colby motioned for Erica to join them—"I also have with me Ms. Donna Wintour. She is the director of the women's auxiliary club for the San Francisco archdiocese, and she is arranging part of your calendar for later in the day."

"I am all yours," the priest beamed. He turned to the two girls at his side and bid them farewell. "So nice, they sat next to me during the flight here. Two college students on vacation in Rio, they were quite knowledgeable about the dirty war in my country. It was reassuring to hear such strong words from two young Americans. It's good to know that young people are concerned about their government's suicidal policies in the region."

"Yes, it must have been very nice for you, Father," Erica broke in. "Do you have any luggage?"

"Just one bag. I have my chalice with me here." He groped for the case at his feet. "It's the cup that Bishop Tanturo used the day the terrorists massacred him in the cathedral. Now I carry it everywhere with me. They have taken his life, but his work lives in all of us. His chalice is his symbol of peace, and I have brought it here with me to America."

"That's exactly how we feel, Father," Colby stated with as much conviction as he could muster. "I can't tell you how happy I was to see you step off that plane." The second sentence didn't require any effort for conviction.

They waited nearly half an hour for a battered and chipped blue Samsonite case, bound together with hemp rope. During the wait, Father Vasquez regaled Colby and Erica with tales of the peasant movement in El Salvador and the dirty war waged against civilians by the right wing military. He was a man of passion who had made many enemies in his native country. The political factions in the liberal Bay Area that opposed American involvement in Central America had invited him to San Francisco to say a special mass in honor of those who died in the struggle for independence and freedom in El Salvador. The mass would be attended by leading politicians, church elders, and citizens of conscience, all opposed to the widening secret war in the Americas. Father Vasquez was supposed to highlight the issue for the local media and help raise money for the independence movements.

Headquarters had chosen the mass for the West Coast introduction of K-7.

During the twenty-minute drive back to San Francisco, Father Vasquez wanted to know about the church in San Francisco. Erica had been briefed with a fairly comprehensive background, but she kept deflecting the discussion back to his own travails. He happily told one story after another. By the time they arrived at the Hyatt Regency Hotel at the Embarcadero in the center of San Francisco and pulled the car directly into the underground garage, Colby and Erica felt they had heard more about the activist Roman Catholic church in the third world than they ever wanted to know.

Together with the priest's luggage, Colby grabbed his crocodile case from the trunk, and proceeded to the lobby's reception desk. It took less than ten minutes to register with the young receptionist, who greeted them behind a massive grey granite desk. Father Vasquez had already received several telephone calls. With his messages and luggage in tow, they proceeded to the prelate's nineteenth-floor room. Colby gave the bellboy two dollars and dismissed him once the door was open.

"Well, Father, it's time to relax."

Vasquez had barely inched into the main room when Colby stepped in front. *"Uno momento, per favor, Padre, quidal."*

Father Vasquez smiled. "Thank you. Your Spanish is excellent. Are you a native?"

Erica stepped behind the priest and with her right hand swatted at the exposed skin on the back of his neck. In her hand was a pin, no larger than a thumbtack, covered in imoserbol-24, the fastest acting sleep agent ever developed by medical science. It sends the body into a natural sleep for several hours almost upon contact. It leaves no medical trace. Father Vasquez began collapsing before Colby could answer him. Colby's strong arms caught the priest before he struck the floor, his dark glasses flying into a corner. He slowly laid Vasquez across the top of the queen-sized bed. The milky pupils of the blind man stared at them.

"Put his glasses back on his face, will you? I don't like those dead eyes staring at us."

She was surprised. "Something actually bothers you?"

"Just do it."

"Okay."

As Erica picked up the priest's glasses, Colby checked the time: 9:10.

He had fifty minutes to arrive at the church before they would start worrying.

Erica closed the draperies while Colby propped the unconscious priest into a sitting position with several pillows stuffed behind him. Colby grabbed the crocodile valise he had carried into the room and snapped open the hand-crafted bronze locks. He slowly assembled the contents on the dresser bureau. A clear plastic container holding an assortment of different colored contact lenses; a dark brown false mustache and two strips of hair that would form a beard; a glass vial of skin-coloring lotion; his scar cover-up; two tubes of adhesive glue; a small aluminum tin of petroleum jelly, and a pair of sunglasses that appeared to be duplicates of those worn by Vasquez.

Erica was fascinated as she watched him work. She had marveled before at the finished results but had never seen him perform. He was as quick as he was good. First he stripped to his underwear. She eyed the broad shoulders and the narrow hips, both of which she had clung to during their lovemaking. She had an urge to reach over and caress him, but she didn't dare interrupt him. He would tolerate no interference once his work was under way. He squeezed a small amount of the liquid cover-up onto his fingertips. He massaged it across his scar and she marveled as the protruding gash appeared to melt into his face. Next, he grabbed the glass vial containing a milky brown fluid, unscrewed the top, and slowly spread it across his hands and then rubbed it over his face and neck.

"Get me a towel," he said. His voice was all business. "Wet one tip of it with some cold water."

It surprised her that by the time she returned, the coloring agent had taken hold, its chemical properties working quickly with his pigmentation to produce a natural brown tone. He took the towel without a thank-you and wiped some excess lotion from his neck and hands. He looked at the sitting priest, his eyes intently comparing skin tone for accuracy. He didn't even ask her if she thought it was a good match. His eyes were too professional to need any assistance. Methodically he approached the remainder of his kit. The adhesive was applied lightly around the face, and the mustache and beard were set securely in place. He reached into his case and produced a small pair of scissors. With one eye in the mirror and one on the priest, he cut the bushy portion of his newfound beard to match the trim sported by Vasquez.

"When I leave here, make sure the hair is cleaned off of this bureau. I don't want them finding any of this."

She nodded while he continued. Small amounts of petroleum jelly in his hair highlighted a sheen that matched the color of his facial hair. He combed it straight back, using Vasquez as the model. After wiping his hands on the small towel Erica had brought him, he carefully folded it into his valise. Finally he opened the contact lens case and with dexterity popped a lens into each eye. When he turned to look at Erica, she jumped with fright. His pupils were off-white, the milky disks of a blind man.

"Those are startling," she told him as though he didn't realize it.

"Just in case my glasses should fall off. Wouldn't want anyone to discover a pair of seeing eyes now, would we?"

He pulled the glasses over his face. Vasquez's lenses were pitch black and blocked any vision. Colby's were identical in every way except that his lenses were two shades lighter, allowing him to see, in a slightly distorted manner, through the thick glass.

"Well, what do you think?" He looked at Erica for approval.

"You look like his twin. Just better looking."

Colby reached into his crocodile case and pulled out a clear plastic bag containing clothes. He gently unfolded the black trousers, the black shirt, and the thin polyester blazer. He shook them to smooth the wrinkles.

"Don't worry about it," Erica told him as she wiped the top of the dresser with a handful of toilet paper. "Look at the state he's in. He's been on a damn plane for nine hours. You're supposed to look tired and rumpled."

He nodded and slowly slipped into the clothes. The collar bothered him, too stiff from an extra dose of starch. He removed it and tried to break the boardlike quality. Finally, he tossed it back into his case and strode over to Vasquez, where he yanked the collar from his neck. He snapped it around his own neck without difficulty.

"Much better," he mumbled to himself as he tied the laces on his thick black shoes. He looked at his wrist. 9:38.

"I must leave. Stay here, and I will return before 1:00. You have everything you need?"

"Yes. But you don't have everything you need. Think."

"I don't have time for games. What, goddamn it?"

"Your watch. What the hell does a blind man have a regular watch for? You're not yourself. Get his braille watch and take it with you."

Colby stopped and looked at Erica. She was good. He never made mistakes like that. The goddamn Benzedrine.

He walked to the sleeping priest, unclasped the dark green strap that held a bulbous watch with raised numbers. He placed it on his wrist and felt the face. What a way to tell time.

"Thanks." He looked at her as he walked to the door.

She nodded. "By the way, is your Spanish really as good as the priest said?"

"Like a native." Colby was not one to advertise his strengths. But if Erica had asked she would have discovered that he was fluent in half a dozen languages. So well trained that he could converse, think, and even answer questions during brutal interrogations, in the language of choice. His ear could place variations in accents and even adapt regional differences into his own speech patterns. After listening to someone for several minutes in their native tongue, he could talk to them and always elicit the response "My God, you are from my village!" It was one of the attributes that made him such a valuable intelligence asset.

He reached over with one hand and grabbed Vasquez's carry-on luggage containing the chalice, took the white cane in his other hand, and proceeded out of the hotel. It was not the first time he had played the role of a blind person. But it was the first time he had stepped into the shoes of a blind priest. He had forgotten how gracious strangers were to blind people, always going out of their way to assist in strolls across a hotel lobby, a street corner, or into a taxi. Coupled with the fact that he wore a clerical collar, the good samaritans were out in droves. Colby played the role for maximum benefit, the white cane swinging in wide arcs in front of his hesitant steps.

When he stepped outside to be placed into a taxi he stiffened at the strong wind that chilled him to the bone. Goose bumps ran down his spine and along his arms. He realized at that moment that he had not been in fresh air since leaving New York the night before. He and Erica had been in an airplane for almost seven hours, then inside the airport terminal, then the garage where they murdered their local contact, then along enclosed escalators to the rental car agency, straight in the car to the Fairmont Hotel, inside the hotel garage, and then up by elevator to the room, down this morning to the car, straight to the airport and Vasquez's arrival, back to the garage, the car, and back to Vasquez's hotel. Between a lack of fresh air for almost a day, only a couple of hours of sleep, and a large dose of pure amphetamine, it was little wonder that his body was racked with aches and pains. He needed rest. He had to get it tonight. For a moment, he paused in front of the taxi and drew a long, deep breath, hoping the crisp bay air would revitalize his sagging system like gasoline in a high-performance car. Even with the Benzedrine, he was running near empty.

The taxi driver stopped in front of St. Mary's Cathedral at 9:57. It was a relief to be on time. He gave the driver the only money in his pocket, two ten-dollar bills. Through his thick lenses he watched the driver count out the exact change for the $4.75 ride, and press the change and the extra ten back into Colby's breast pocket. What a benefit to be blind, he thought to himself. No one takes advantage of you. There is too much sympathy for the disability.

"I'll help you inside, Father," the driver offered.

"Thank you, that would be very nice."

Together they walked arm-in-arm toward the main entrance of the cathedral. Colby thought it was the oddest church he had ever seen. He was used to traditional European churches inspired by Gothic designs, complete with soaring arches studded with stained glass and decorated with elaborate statuary. This cathedral was perched on top of one of San Francisco's hills, directly across from a high-rise apartment tower. It was an ultramodern, white structure that looked like a surrealist triangle.

"Is this your first time to San Francisco, Father?"

"Si."

"Well, I don't know if you know what a flying saucer looks like, but our cathedral looks a lot like the ship that came down in a movie called *Close Encounters of the Third Kind*."

That's exactly what the damn thing looked like. Colby had seen pictures of the movie in a Czechoslovakian magazine. It looked like a damn spaceship. "I don't know what that looks like, but I have a good imagination." Even Colby's accented Spanish was perfect.

"Father, there are some people coming to greet you. I think this is as far as I have to take you."

"Thank you, my son, for your help. God bless you."

Colby could see the taxi driver make the sign of the cross as he left. Idiot. Hooked on the great religious opiate. His faith in some supposed God wouldn't stop him from dying if Colby injected him with any of the K-7 he had in the metal dispenser in his pocket.

"Father Vasquez, we are so honored to have you here with us."

Colby watched the group converge around him: several priests, one with the purple sash of a monsignor, and three news reporters, their pads held high. There were all the traditional questions about his flight, if he wanted coffee, what did he want to do before the mass started, and the like. A few more black uniformed dignitaries were only several steps behind. Colby despised them. They reminded him of the black uniforms of the Gestapo forty years earlier. Only these fascists marched to the tune of a different despot—Jesus. It was one thing Marx had right. Organized religion was an enemy of the people.

He spoke very little. He requested as politely as possible if he could avoid the press until after the mass, as he wanted to concentrate on the matter at hand that concerned a higher authority than the media. The monsignor agreed and led Colby through the cavernous, cold church to the rear sanctuary. After Colby was inside, the monsignor turned and informed the press they would have to wait until after the mass for interviews and photo opportunities. No one complained. A 2:00 p.m. news conference ensured they would have time to get statements for the evening editions.

The entourage of clerics didn't even question him when he said he was very tired from the plane trip. But they looked disappointed when he said he just wanted to refresh himself by meditating alone in the sanctuary in preparation for the mass. He wanted to talk about many things, but would they please understand and wait until after the mass. At first they tried to persuade him to rest inside the more luxurious rectory. But he politely refused, paying reference to his simple peasant upbringing. Soon they all dutifully nodded and within several minutes he was left alone with a steaming cup of black coffee in the solitude of the large, Holiday Inn–styled sanctuary.

Colby worked quickly. He walked to the vestibule near the rear of the room and pulled the purple velvet cloth to the side, exposing a small bronze door engraved with the block lettering "Pax," Latin for peace. From his trousers pocket he pulled a small key. It had been measured almost six months earlier, in the preliminary planning for the mission, then copied in New York, and presented to him after his arrival in the States. He looked over his shoulder at the remainder of the room. Empty. He pulled his glasses over the top of his forehead and rested them in his hair. It was much easier to see without them. The key slid into the curved lock, the tumblers clicked as he turned it clockwise, and then suddenly it snapped open. The door opened wide revealing a half dozen brass saucers filled with hundreds of thin, white wafers. Communion hosts. Catholics believed it was consecrated during the mass to become the body of Christ. Colby almost snarled. Rubbish. From his other pocket, he took a thin metal cylinder modified by Erica for this infection. The K-7 had been set into a hydrogenated droplet mist. Directing the air pressure canister over the hosts would deposit the virus across the wafers' surfaces. The mist was maintained in the pocket canister in a minuscule air vacuum. Once released into the atmosphere, a chemical bonding with oxygen caused a time release of the virus. As developed by Erica, the virus would be activated in an hour, a point shortly before the communion was to be dispensed. Those who touched the hosts would become infected. Those who swallowed them would be marked for death. This was certainly a day that would favor worshipers with unforgiven mortal sins on their soul. Those people were blocked by church rules from partaking in communion. Colby liked that thought. Only the most grievous sinners would survive this religious experience. Might leave a better constituency in the church that Peter built.

Father Vasquez's disability played perfectly into the infection because he seldom distributed communion at masses. Headquarters had done its research. The San Francisco archdiocese had already been informed that he would not partake in the giving of the sacrament at the celebration mass. Colby reached into the safe and pulled out an oversized host, the one that Catholic ritual required he would have to eat during the mass. He placed it behind him on a chair. It would stay hidden inside Vasquez's special chalice until it was time to use it.

One last time he looked over his shoulder to ensure that his ears were as trustworthy as his sight. They were. The room was empty. He lifted the aluminum beaker into the safe and pressed the green plastic top. The microscopic mist which deposited on the wafers was not visible to the human eye. But in less than three seconds the plastic top popped up signifying the canister's contents were empty. Erica had assured him there was no danger when emptying the contents. He had asked her so many times that she said she was willing to spray a similar canister just to calm his nerves. He believed her. No man or weapon frightened him. Although he had come face-to-face with well-trained killers, and fought his way clear of foes armed with guns, knives, and clubs, the killers he was working with now did scare him. They were the tiniest battlefield weapons and the most lethal. He did not like something that could not be seen. A bug, smaller than a cell in his body, could kill him with a long and painful death. There was no room for a margin of error on Erica's part. It was more comforting at the Waldorf when the gelatin capsules did not dissolve until a certain temperature level. Erica assured him this was virtually the same process. Just think of the oxygen interaction in the air as the heat source at the Waldorf. He did. It still didn't comfort him. Even their sex had not comforted him. He just wasn't sure that he meant any more to her as a lover than as an operational partner.

He replaced the canister into his pocket, locked the bronze tabernacle, and then proceeded to Vasquez's case. The single uncontaminated host was carefully placed inside the gold chalice, the case was closed, and then he returned to his chair in the front of the room. At 10:45, two altar boys and a priest were the first people to break the sanctuary's solitude. Within the next five minutes more than half a dozen other priests and parish dignitaries arrived. All were extremely pleasant to the retiring, quiet Salvadoran cleric who had created such a stir in his own country for his brave stance against military abuses.

The purple-sashed monsignor approached Colby as the altar boys helped him on with the silk robes that constituted the uniform for the mass.

"Father Vasquez, the altar boys are going to guide you outside to the altar. You'll be facing the congregation, and we have a packed house. A lot of concerned people in San Francisco are out there. Some government leaders, press, prominent business people. You'll meet them all at the luncheon later. They are here to wake up to the problems in your country. Bishop O'Hara will deliver a small sermon, but as you know the mass will be relatively short. Everyone wants to hear your statement this afternoon at the press conference. So unless you've changed your mind, you won't be part of the homily. Is that still the way you want it?"

"Yes, Father, it is." Although Colby could see through his glasses that the man addressing him was the rank of monsignor, he had not been told that by anyone. To have addressed him by his correct title would have signified that Father Vasquez could see more than his white cane indicated. Then suddenly he saw it. Out of the corner of his eye he noticed one of the altar boys step backward into a massive candelabra. He watched it tip over the edge of the table. He started to instinctively react, to reach forward and break its fall as it came down at the monsignor. But with split-second reasoning and body control, he forced himself to stop. If he reacted to the falling object before anyone else saw it, again he would be unmasked. He braced himself as it crashed into the monsignor, striking him across the back of the shoulders and knocking him forward into Colby. Colby let his cane fly into the air and flopped heavily on the ground. Everyone rushed to help. His glasses had been knocked off. He could see the recoil in their faces as they stared into the blank whites of his eyes. The monsignor was not hurt, and when the scolding started on the altar boy, it was Colby who interrupted and said it was all right.

"Father," the monsignor announced with a quickened pace, "I'm so sorry for that clumsiness. Are you sure you are all right?"

Colby nodded. Someone helped him put his glasses on and another brushed his clerical robes.

"You're sure?"

"Yes, Father."

"Okay. Then let's start before anything else happens. You have a packed house waiting on the edge of their seats to see a hero from the war zone."

"I am no hero, my dear brother in Christ. I am merely a soldier of the church doing what I can to save souls."

The assembled priests and dignitaries looked at each other with admiring and knowing glances. What easy fools to pull on a string, Colby thought to himself.

"Just my chalice. The chalice of peace." They guided him to his leather case. He pulled it open for the second time that morning, and gently removed the jewel-encrusted gold cup, covered with a piece of silk. Inside that chalice was the only uncontaminated host in the cathedral.

Colby had practiced it more than one hundred times. The Roman Catholic mass in Spanish. In preparation for this assignment he had attended daily mass in Madrid for nearly two months. He knew it by heart and felt as though he could do it in his sleep.

And for a while that morning the man who had killed so many people became the representative of God for a standing-room-only congregation. For Colby it was merely another cover identity in years of assuming different names and personalities. He concentrated on doing everything right. There was no room for mistakes, for the slightest error could raise suspicion.

As promised by the monsignor, the bishop's sermon was short. And before noon, the mass reached the communion ceremony. Colby raised his chalice into the air proclaiming the transformation into the body and blood of Christ. He drank the wine offered by the altar boys, and when the time came for him to consecrate the host, he took the one from inside his chalice, leaving another on the altar. An altar boy guided Colby to a pew at the side of the altar where he sat quietly, facing the congregation. Half a dozen priests had arrived, all holding chalices filled with wafers taken from inside the tabernacle. He watched as the first one crossed in front of the altar and approached the line of waiting worshipers. The priest reached into the chalice and took out a host. Colby listened intently.

"The body of Christ."

The worshiper whispered, "Amen." Then he opened his mouth and the priest placed the host on his tongue. "Amen" indeed. Colby relaxed. The virus was out. Now he only had to get back to the hotel and finish his business with the real Vasquez before anyone was the wiser.

CHAPTER 13 ═══════━

Washington, D.C.
December 17
8:00 a.m.

From McGinnis's description, Harris had formed a mental picture of the bloodhound. He was completely wrong. He expected someone short and slightly plump from years of desk work. Images of university professors in tweed jackets crossed his mind, largely influenced by McGinnis's information that the bloodhound was an avid pipe smoker. The pipe was about the only item Harris correctly visualized. When he walked into the second-floor conference room at CIA headquarters, Bouchet was waiting behind a large oak conference table. The first feature that struck Harris was that Bouchet was very slim. When Bouchet rose to greet them, Harris was surprised again, this time by his height. He was taller than McGinnis, at least six feet, two inches, and his body was narrow. And no university professor that Harris had ever seen dressed like the bloodhound. He wore a dark grey suit made of wool so smooth that it almost looked like silk. Double breasted, with peak lapels, wide at the shoulders and narrow at the hips, the suit draped beautifully over Bouchet's almost mannequinlike body. From his highly polished dress shoes to the blue-and-white-striped, tab-collared shirt offset with a deep burgundy tie, the bloodhound was impeccably dressed. In the American intelligence world, wing tips, button-down Oxford shirts, and three-button Brooks Brothers suits were still de rigueur. At CIA headquarters an Italian loafer or a brightly colored shirt was enough to make the hierarchy grimace. Compared to intelligence agents Harris was accustomed to, the bloodhound looked as though he had stepped out of the pages of a European fashion magazine. Style. That was the word Harris thought best summarized this French wonder-detective. There was even an intangible aura of class in the face. A strong jaw, sharp cheekbones, a prominent nose, and a deep set pair of dark brown eyes. He wore his thick grey hair combed straight back from his forehead.

"Richard!" There was genuine affection in Bouchet's heavily accented voice as he jumped from his chair and strode quickly in front of the table to embrace McGinnis with a solid hug. He stepped back and planted a small kiss on each of McGinnis's cheeks. McGinnis reached out, grabbed Bouchet's hand, and shook it heartily.

"Jean-Claude, it's good to see you." He stepped back and studied the bloodhound from head to toe. "You old scoundrel, you look fabulous. How do you keep it so flat?" McGinnis patted his own stomach. The bloodhound laughed.

"None of your famous Budweiser, my friend. I've always told you that white wine goes through the system faster. You just never believed me."

"I believed you. It's just that around here they have us on a beer budget. No white wine salaries." McGinnis snapped his fingers as if in disappointment. "Damn it. Talking of food reminds me that I left my coffee and danish in the war room."

Harris interrupted. "You don't need it. You've already had four cups this morning."

McGinnis sighed and shook his head. "Jean-Claude, I want you to meet the new kid on the block. He's my partner, but he thinks he's my personal nutritionist. Jimmy Harris, meet Jean-Claude Bouchet. Jean-Claude can teach you more about sleuthing in a day than the boys at Peary can in a year."

Bouchet gave Harris a firm and heartfelt handshake. "It's always good to meet new talent." It felt as though he meant it. Harris instantly liked him.

"Richard"—Bouchet turned to look at McGinnis—"let's sit down. I have a lot to tell you. I've briefed Finch on everything we know, but he has only told me a little bit. It's this damn need-to-know business." Bouchet returned to his seat on the far side of the table. McGinnis and Harris sat next to each other, directly opposite the bloodhound. "All I know is that you are looking for someone here in the States. Probably a Soviet agent. But I don't know who or what they are, or what they are doing here. Inside SDECE, we also know that you lost a London station four days ago. Finch says it was only a research center. But as I told him, it's unusual in our business to lose an entire station due to any type of hostile action. We don't fight our wars with real weapons and battlefield skirmishes."

McGinnis didn't say a word but he knew Bouchet was right. They were involved in a business where victories were posted by the obtaining of information. The biggest congratulations came for operations no one ever knew existed, not for special forces missions against an enemy site. That was something left to the military. The Frenchman didn't miss a beat but continued with his thoughts.

"Finch didn't say a word, but I know he agreed with me. To lose a whole station is extremely rare. But when that station is merely a research and collating center, then the enemy action makes no sense whatsoever. Who would want to kill a dozen or so bookworms? Am I right?"

McGinnis shrugged his shoulders as though he had not thought about it. "Let me hear you out, Jean-Claude. You know I like to hear you think out loud."

The bloodhound chuckled. "You mean you like to know what cards I have in my hand. Well, not much. It's just the way I feel about the situation. It's very unusual. So, assuming for a moment that your London station is merely a research center, an above-board overt establishment, then you must rule out a Soviet operation."

"Why?" Harris broke in.

The bloodhound did not miss a beat. "Because they have nothing to gain and everything to lose from such an action. What are they going to eliminate? Copies of nonfiction books about the espionage trade or collated, irrelevant newspaper articles from around the world? I know how these research centers work. We have them in the SDECE. A group of historians and academicians sit around reviewing everything published about the spy business. They read fiction and nonfiction. Yes?"

Neither McGinnis nor Harris responded.

"Well, the answer is yes. They read them to see if they get any new ideas. And then sometimes they will find something that parallels an existing covert operation, technique, or device. And then they must follow up on their research to discover whether the writer knows something he shouldn't or whether he was merely lucky to develop something in print around the same time we developed it in reality. Now, why the hell do the Soviets have to eliminate a place like that? I ask you, why?"

Harris answered. "Maybe the center had come across some information that was about to compromise a Soviet operation."

"Nice try. I like that. Spunk. But you see, my good friend Richard here cannot even waste his energy. He knows there is no use in answering me because I am right. There is no reason why the Soviets would destroy such a center. Research centers are notoriously unproductive. They consume large parts of the budget but return little in hard results. I am not even sure why they continue to be so popular. But they are also easily penetrated. The security is not the greatest. So why destroy a place if you could compromise it by becoming part of it?"

Neither of the American agents answered.

"There is no reason to destroy it if you are the Soviets. Or at least I have not heard a reason sufficient to convince me yet. So that leaves two options. The first is that the center was not a mere research location, but somehow hid something more dear. I could imagine a Soviet operation, if what the station had was important. But since our American friends tell us that it had nothing more than half a dozen intellectuals reading books and magazines, who am I to doubt them? I must accept it as the truth. Right?"

The bloodhound leaned over to the aluminum ashtray on his right. Resting on the edge was his briar wood pipe. He slowly started to play with the tobacco with his little finger. Neither McGinnis nor Harris looked away from the French agent. They did not want to show he had struck a raw nerve.

"And what did Finch say when you explained your thinking?" McGinnis said as he leaned back in his chair.

"A lot of 'hmmms' and 'uh huh.' "

McGinnis smiled. "Hmmmm."

"That's the right inflection, Richard." Bouchet returned the grin. "If you keep practicing maybe one day you'll move up as high as Tony." Bouchet removed the silver lighter from his pocket and struck the flame to the pipe's bowl. He started sucking on the tip, and in a matter of seconds the pungent odor of black French tobacco filled the room. Harris coughed, trying to indicate his displeasure with the foul air.

"God, Jean-Claude, I would have thought that over the years you would have at least chosen a better mixture. Phew!" McGinnis turned to Harris. "They had to remove him from the field even though he was one of their best agents because he wouldn't give up on this damn pipe. The enemy could smell him coming." He looked back to Bouchet. "I can tell you haven't met a good woman yet or she definitely would have made you abandon that habit."

"No, you are right, Richard, I have not yet met a good woman. But for me a good woman would be one who would not mind my smoking."

Harris dropped the paper clip he had been playing with throughout the meeting. As he leaned over the chair and scanned the floor, he mumbled to himself. "You should know that smoking is not only dangerous for you but also for the people—"

McGinnis held his hand near Harris's face. "Forget about the clip, kid. I'll buy you another one later. And none of that health stuff here. Jean-Claude's smoke may smell like a dead dog that's been left in the sun for a couple of days, but that's my only objection to it. I wouldn't want him to stop just because he's giving himself and the rest of the world cancer."

"If you are finished insulting my one indulgence, may I continue?" He looked at both of them. "Thank you. If it's really that important, I am sure you can discuss it later when you jog. You do that, don't you? Now don't disappoint me, it's such an American thing, this fitness craze. I would join you but I have, alas, forgotten my jogging shoes."

He smiled at the two of them. McGinnis chuckled. Harris wasn't sure if the bloodhound was serious or joking.

"Now where was I?"

Harris jumped in. "You were just telling us that you believe Finch when he tells you that London was a research center."

"Oh, yes, yes. So I must tell you that originally I had my doubts about the purpose of your center. But it is clear that if you don't want me to know any more, then I shouldn't compromise allies by pushing for more information. So if it is indeed what you claim, the second option is that the destruction was caused either by a disgruntled group of agents within the center, or from an outside party uncontrolled by any of the government players."

"Like who?" Harris leaned back in his chair.

"Like a terrorist group. A group that somehow obtained information of the center's existence, and then struck at it in order to cause problems between the member governments. If it was a terrorist operation, then it makes sense that it might be a mere research center staffed only by academicians. It is much less of a risk to the terrorists. I've checked with Finch, and he assures me that the body count in London included everyone on staff. No recent transfers or reassignments. He totally dismisses the possibility of disgruntled internal staffers as well as the idea of terrorists. As far as Finch is concerned it's a Soviet action, but I don't have access to all the facts, so I am at a disadvantage."

The bloodhound reached under the table and pulled out an antique leather portfolio. It looked like a large puffed tortilla that had been scuffed and knocked about. He carefully laid it on the table and flipped open the small brass locks on each end. He pulled out a handful of papers with a great flourish. The bloodhound was good, no doubt about that, McGinnis thought. But he had always had a flamboyant nature, which rubbed many people the wrong way. McGinnis had liked that trait. It made the bloodhound more interesting than the one-dimensional agents that often populated the espionage ranks.

"I have shown this to Finch. He has a copy of it. It was sent yesterday by confidential fax transmission while you were finishing up in New York."

McGinnis pulled the papers in front of him. "It's in French, for Chrissakes. I am sure you can summarize it faster than I can read it."

"Richard, it relates to a body we found in a Right Bank hotel the other night. To be precise, the night of the same day your massacre took place in London. I spoke to you briefly about it the other day on the telephone. Let me tell you in more detail what we found there."

McGinnis interrupted. "Are the Paris police on strike? Since when have your ample skills been used to track down murderers?"

"The SDECE had reason to use that hotel that night. I came across the body during a security check."

"Your use of the hotel had nothing to do with the body turning up?"

"No, Richard, you must trust me."

"The same way you must trust us about the use of the London station?"

"Exactly." They stared at each other for a moment. Two professionals who knew that sometimes the rules required that even friends remain in some darkness. Bouchet continued. "Now let me tell you what we found. Traces of selenium paper in the bathtub." The bloodhound could tell he had hit a nerve with both American agents. Their faces registered surprise. "I don't have to tell you how rare that is. We found a badly disfigured body that someone obviously left in such a state so that it should never be identified. And we found enough skin particles and hair follicles to make genetic fingerprints for those who were in the room besides our dead friend. Now I find out that your laboratory team was able to salvage extremely small samples of genetic material from the London debacle, and they have also obtained full DNA sequences. As you know, we have exact matches. Our dead body was in London earlier that day. One of the other people in the hotel was also in London earlier that day. Two others that we picked up don't match anything you found."

McGinnis interrupted again. "What has Finch done with this information?"

"The appropriate question is not what Finch has done with it so much as what has Hodson done with it. He's glued himself in front of those computer terminals I am not allowed to see, and he's checking everyone who flew from London to Paris that day, and then seeing who flew from Paris to New York after the murders. Or for that matter, I think he's also checking anyone who flew from any point in Europe or North Africa to New York or another nearby East Coast city. Hodson thinks the team might have covered their tracks by flying first from Paris to another city like Amsterdam or Madrid and then flew to Philadelphia or Boston and either flew down to New York or drove there. He's got his computers telling him every possible airplane or train connection that could have gotten the Paris murderers to New York. This much I know because Hodson told me. What I don't know, Richard, is why Hodson and Finch and everyone else is so damned convinced that the murderers are in New York. What do you know that I don't know?"

Silence greeted the bloodhound's question. "Just let me tell you this much for old times' sake, Jean-Claude. The DNA sequence you picked up in Paris, which we picked up in London, was picked up yesterday morning in New York. For your purposes, it's not important how or where we found it. It's just important that we confirmed it was there. I still wonder whether I should have stayed in the Big Apple. I am not as convinced as Finch that our boy left Gotham."

"Well, you know . . ."

The door to the conference room clicked open, and when it swung aside, Tony Finch stood in the doorway. He was still wearing the same suit he had when Harris and McGinnis left for New York. McGinnis would have thought it was impossible, but the suit was even more rumpled. Finch looked as disheveled as ever. He lifted his head into the air. "What is that sm—"

McGinnis interrupted. "Tony, Colonel Bouchet's pipe."

Finch looked at the desk. "Yes, yes, of course. Strong, Colonel. Good strong tobacco."

McGinnis smiled. In Finch's vocabulary, "strong" was synonymous with shit.

"Colonel Bouchet, I am going to have to ask you if I can take these two men with me for a moment. I have something to show them."

Bouchet rested his pipe in the ashtray and nodded his head as though he completely understood and agreed. He was used to comments about his tobacco and he politely ignored them.

Harris and McGinnis followed Finch quickly down the corridor, and into the rear security elevator.

"Where are we going?"

"The war room. The spectrum system has just picked up a new infection. Northern California, the Bay Area. We're working right now on isolating the infection site."

Harris spoke up. "You mean the team in New York that hit the Waldorf has moved across the country?"

The elevator stopped. "Wait until we get inside the room," Finch commanded.

The war room was bustling with activity. Hodson, his coffee-stained white shirt rolled up at the sleeves, was bent over two computer operators. McGinnis's nemesis, General Neal Phillips, was standing next to Hodson.

Finch turned to Harris. "We've got no fucking idea whether it's the same team as hit in New York. They could have sent several teams in."

"Or they might have sent one team in and had the other one, or more than one, in place in this country for some time." Phillips turned away from the computer screen. "Who knows how we're getting fucked. You fellows certainly don't have a goddamn idea. From what I hear, you two are chasing your dicks in your hands. It looks like these Russkies aren't giving you field guys a fair run for your money."

McGinnis gave Phillips his broadest smile. "Well, General, I guess if someone in your intelligence department had known about the bio-chemical work in the London lab, Harris and I wouldn't have the opportunity to screw up a chase for our own goddamn virus. Shucks, it's just one of those things."

Phillips was steaming. "Why you insubordinate little twerp." He turned to Finch. "I told you that it was a bad idea . . ."

"I am really having a quite difficult time trying to digest a lot of information here," Hodson's British accent interrupted. "I would appreciate it if you would take this little disagreement to another location."

Finch moved close to Phillips. "Neal, it's not the time or place. These fellows haven't had a lead with enough advance notice to make a good stab in the field. So stay off their backs until they have really screwed up. Then I'll help you hang them out to dry."

Phillips was about to answer, then thought better of it, and with a controlled effort kept his mouth shut as he stormed out the door.

Finch turned toward McGinnis. "Boy, he really hates your guts, Richard. He wants you to screw up so badly that he almost forgets at times that we are on the same side."

"What about me, sir. General Phillips doesn't even know me."

"Harris, you're working with McGinnis. That's enough for Phillips. If it means McGinnis has to screw up in order to please Phillips, then you might as well go down as well."

McGinnis patted Harris on the back. "He actually couldn't give a shit about you, kid. At least I don't like you."

Finch smiled. "Same old asshole, Richard. Listen, while Hodson breaks his back to find out what the hell is happening in California, I'd like you to turn some of that rude charm of yours on your old friend the frog. I don't want him hanging around our operation. You can bet he was sent by Delon to find out what the hell we are up to after London. I wouldn't trust Delon as far as I could throw him."

"Well, they do have a match with our Con Ed man and the London-Paris murders," McGinnis offered.

"So maybe they got lucky and stumbled across one of the Soviet hit team while they stopped over in Paris. But I'll tell you what I think is more likely. Somehow there was a leak from our laboratory about the genetic fingerprint we found in London. I think the French picked up on that and then just told us they found the same sequence in the Paris hotel room. All they did was take our DNA sequence and run it by us again. And we are supposed to say, 'Oh, my God, thank you so much, and since you told us that, we will tell you all about London and our operation.' Fat chance. I'm just not so convinced that the Soviets were running around Paris killing some of their own agents the night of the London hit. Why would they do it?"

McGinnis didn't hesitate. "I'm not sure why they would kill one of their own, Tony. But you and I know it happens in this crazy business. Sometimes somebody screws up or you think they've become a security risk or whatever, and they end up dead. And from the way the French found the body it sounds like it may have been a last-minute decision. And how do you explain selenium-based paper there?"

"They're telling us they found selenium paper. Think, Richard. They want us to believe there is a French connection to the killers we are looking for. I think its a smokescreen and their information is a dead end. That's my professional hunch. I just think that we've learned all we can from Bouchet, even if his info is correct. But the longer he stays here, the greater the chance he might learn something he shouldn't. Now, I had to extend him the courtesy of coming over here to see you, even though I tried to convince him that a secure phone call would have served the same purpose. For godsakes, they are so goddamn anxious to find out what we are up to, they even sent the bastard over here on Concorde. You can be sure they didn't do that so that we could have the information any quicker. They did it because they have hot pants to find out what we're up to. Well, they aren't going to find out at our expense. Just get everything you need from Bouchet and then make sure he goes back to Paris. I want it very clear to him that he has no place near this operation. You do it, Richard. He likes you."

"I'll see what I can do, Tony."

"Be sure you do it well, Richard."

Finch walked to the computer console and stood behind Hodson. The Brit turned his head and stared at him for a moment. Then he sniffed the air. Finch didn't even wait for the question.

"French tobacco. Colonel Bouchet's personal mixture. Ignore it and it will go away."

McGinnis smiled and walked into a far corner of the war room. Harris stopped by a desk, grabbed a handful of paper clips, and then joined his partner. McGinnis looked back at Finch, who was hurrying around the room shouting orders. He was one of the best field agents the Agency had. He had also shown top skills in his new role as director of covert operations. Finch was one of the few men at headquarters that McGinnis respected; McGinnis would have trusted his life to him. But McGinnis's instincts didn't agree with Finch regarding the information from French intelligence. He also knew the bloodhound. They had spent time together in the field, and their lives had depended on each other. He trusted Bouchet. The Frenchman would not feed him false information just to uncover the details of a new operation. That assumed that Bouchet knew the information was false. It was possible that he was being used by the SDECE hierarchy to pass along reports that he thought were true, but were in fact doctored. Goddamn it! The lousy intelligence trade. It could drive you crazy with the possibilities. You never knew whether a situation was for real or not until it was often too late. He knew he could think himself into a mind-numbing quandary. When the options were too confusing it was best to go with your instincts. Those seldom failed him.

Harris pulled close to McGinnis so he would not be overheard. "What do you think? Were we just fed a line of bull upstairs from your French friend?"

"What do you think?"

"I'm not sure," Harris was almost whispering. "Anything's possible."

"That's the key point, Harris. Anything is possible. Isn't that the first thing they taught you at Peary?"

"Yep."

"It's even possible that the London lab was hit by the French. Maybe they were competing with us in the bacteriological field. Or maybe it was a renegade group of SDECE agents who took the stuff and now are playing games by passing some of it around America. And since the French know it was some of their own, they have fed us this story about a Paris murder. The reason they can match the DNA code is they know who the perpetrators are. But they can't tell us because the whole damn operation isn't supposed to have happened. Just like we can't tell them about the real purpose of the London lab because it was never supposed to exist. And they've sent the bloodhound over here to see how close we are getting to finding out the truth."

"Jesus Christ, do you think that's what is happening?"

"Nope. Absolutely not. But that's how crazy you can make yourself if you start to think of the possibilities. You can't overemphasize that anything is possible in this business, but most of the time you overthink it. It's never usually as complicated as we make it in our own minds. You just have to let developments unfurl, and when we have enough leads then we can start to close in on these bastards. In the meantime a lot of people are getting sick, and that is why we are under the gun on this one."

"So what about the bloodhound? How do we get him back to Paris?"

"We don't. Not just yet. We'll tell Finch that he's being stubborn. I just think our French friend stumbled across part of the team that we're looking for. And I just don't believe we are dealing with multiple teams like Phillips suggested. I think it's one and the same. Our boy upstairs is on the right track. I want to let the bloodhound run a little and see if he can pick up a fresh scent for us."

CHAPTER 14 ⊨══════◄───────

San Francisco
December 17
12:30 p.m.

"The mass is ended. Go in peace." Colby finished blessing the congregation, his hands swinging in wide arcs forming the Christian cross. He felt a tremendous relief. The communion service had gone without a hitch. None of the other priests had second thoughts about encouraging him to personally serve the hosts. And he had made it through the entire mass without a single error. Or at least none that he could think of. The amphetamine in his system still worried him. There were moments when he felt he was almost on automatic pilot. A cold sweat would break out on his upper lip, small beads of salty perspiration running into the corner of his mouth. He would focus very intently on what he was doing at that precise moment. Then he would realize that his mind had been wandering and he didn't remember the past several minutes. Or at least he had not focused on what he was doing. He was merely going through the motions. That worried him. Had he made an error? Had his accent slipped? He would nervously look at the altar boys or the front rows of churchgoers to see if he had earned any disturbed or puzzled looks. Once he confirmed that everyone looked satisfied, he would breathe a small sigh of relief and promise to be more alert to everything that transpired. Although he had never had a problem during the many rehearsals for the mass, he did not want to make his first mistake at a time when he could least afford it.

As the hundreds in the pews began leaving the church, he wanted to smile but he did not dare. The fifty-five polished brass organ pipes to his left began filling the open space with a deep resonance. The children's choir, girls in lacy, pink dresses and the boys in pressed white shirts and little blue bow ties, began singing the "Hallelujah" chorus. Colby was sure that Handel intended the soaring spiritual sound of his music to be handled by stronger voices. Although the melody was beautiful and the voices clear as crystal, the words sounded like tin. It was as if someone had turned the treble much too high on a stereo set. Suddenly Colby felt a tugging at his left elbow. He looked down to one of the altar boys who had served the mass. Colby reached out and grabbed at air. "My chalice," he muttered to the youngster. The young hand reached to the top of the altar, grabbed the chalice, and gently pressed it into Colby's hand. He allowed himself to be guided by the altar boy to the sanctuary where the bishop and several priests were waiting. As Colby entered the room, the bishop strode over to him. Clad in brocaded-silk gold robes, a white silk cap covering the top of his head, the bishop clasped Colby by both shoulders.

"Father Vasquez, thank you for a beautiful service. I am Bishop O'Hara. I am sorry I was almost late for the service, but we had some problems this morning at the archdiocese. I want you to know that I meant every word of what I said in the homily. You do have the support of the entire church in the Bay Area. Whatever we can do to help, we will try."

"Thank you, Your Excellency. Your words were most kind. They filled me with the holy spirit. God bless you." Colby imagined he would become nauseous if he continued the dribble. He was also extremely anxious to get away from people who had just been infected with K-7. "Your Excellency, may I tell you something in private just for a moment?"

"Of course, Father Vasquez." The bishop led Colby near a large oil painting of the Virgin Mary ascending into heaven, surrounded by a dozen cherubs. "Is there any problem?"

"Yes, actually, Your Excellency, there is. And I am quite embarrassed to have to mention this. I hope it does not create too much of an inconvenience. As you may know, I am a diabetic."

"I did read that in an article about you, Father."

"Well, I am not that well. Actually, I am feeling quite ill. I think my blood sugar must have gotten quite high from all the traveling and the change in diet. And like a fool, I left my syringe and medication at the hotel room. I believe I need some insulin before I can continue the rest of the day's events."

"Father Vasquez, it's absolutely no problem. I will send someone right now to fetch your medical equipment, and he will bring it to you right here while you rest." The bishop twisted his head and looked over his right shoulder. "Mr. Clarke, will you please come here?"

"Oh, no, Your Excellency." That was the last thing Colby wanted. The operation required his presence at the hotel. "I think it's better if you don't just send someone to pick it up. I know when I am having a real problem, and this is unfortunately one of those times. After twenty years on this life-saving medication, I know my body and its limitations. It has kept me alive. It will be much better if I travel with the gentleman to the hotel. Then, instead of having to wait for him to pick it up and then return it to me here, I will get the insulin when I arrive at the hotel—at least half the time it would take the other way."

The bishop looked very concerned. "Listen, Father Vasquez, maybe we should take you to the hospital or . . ."

"Oh no!" Colby whispered so as not to be overheard, but he emphasized his words slowly for the bishop. "That is why I wanted to talk to you alone for a moment. I do not want anyone to think I am ill, because I am not really—I am just a person in need of his medication. If I don't get it soon I will definitely be sick, and that is why I would like to move now. If you take me to the hospital it is unnecessary and moreover will ruin the rest of the day's events. The press conference means a great deal to me. My statement must be delivered. I have not traveled this far just to say mass. Please, Your Excellency, just tell them I am returning for a moment to the hotel for some papers I forgot to bring with me. In fact, I do have some photos of the murder victims of the death squads. I will be back here in less than half an hour if your driver is as good as the taxi driver who brought me here. Then I will be as good as new and we will all have a successful and eventful lunch and press conference."

The bishop's face showed that he had given in. He nodded his head. "All right, Father. You know what is best for your body. We'll tell the press you will be right back for the photo opportunities." He turned to face the man standing behind him. "John, please bring Father Vasquez to his hotel. The good father is going to retrieve something from his room. Wait for him downstairs in the car. I want this as quick a round trip as possible. Get him back here before 1:00. Bring the car around to the back parking lot so we can get him out of here without going through the press and crowd."

While Colby waited for the driver to reappear, he asked another altar boy to place his chalice inside his leather case and to bring it to him. Two earnest young priests had approached him. Colby could tell from the pious expressions on their faces that they were anxious to talk about the problems of Central America. It was the last thing he wanted to do.

"Excuse me, is there a seat I can use while I wait?"

Bishop O'Hara pointed his finger at one of the young priests. "A chair for our friend. And please leave Father Vasquez alone for a couple of moments. He has had a long trip. If it had not been for the national day of protest planned in El Salvador for yesterday, we would have had the good father arrive a couple of days earlier in order to conserve his strength. Let him recuperate in peace."

Colby managed a weak smile, murmured "thank you" in the general direction of the bishop, and slowly lowered himself into a drab, olive-colored metal folding chair that was placed behind him.

San Francisco police are accustomed to their share of crackpot calls. The Bay Area has long attracted the rebellious and fringe elements in American society. From the beatnik era through the free speech movement, to the free sex and drug pandemonium of Haight-Ashbury, San Francisco has led the nation in the bizarre and avant-garde. Black Panther fund-raising events, armed feminist communes, Patty Hearst and the Symbionese Liberation Army, and a host of other radical elements have created a reputation that serves as a magnet, drawing undesirable and alienated people from around the country. A former San Francisco mayor summarized it best when he told a local newspaper, only half in jest, "Our city is like a giant box of cereal. Someone turned the country at an angle and all the flakes came tumbling here."

Only ten years earlier, in broad daylight, a city councilman had murdered the city's mayor and the first openly gay supervisor, right in City Hall. A jury later acquitted the murderer of the most serious charges, having accepted the defense counsel's claim that his client suffered diminished capacity, evidenced by the large intake of Twinkies. Sugar had supposedly affected his better judgment and led him to kill his former friends. The jury bought it and the "Twinkie defense" was coined. It was that type of place.

The people most accustomed to dealing with the fringe element were the police. They knew anything was possible in the city by the bay. That is why the police have a standard rule: no matter how wacky the information sounds, it must always be followed up. There were enough horror stories of duty officers who had summarily dismissed emergency calls about transvestites dressed as nuns running amok with knives in a downtown department store, or a boy barking like a dog throwing quarter sticks of dynamite at passing cars from a freeway overpass, or the like. San Francisco duty officers no longer dismissed callers as cranks until they had sent a squad car to check the information. That was a bad break for Colby.

The call came in at 12:15 to the Park station, which was shrouded in fog on the western end of the city. Built shortly after the devastating 1906 earthquake and fire, the Park station is one of the oldest in the city. Resembling a Spanish mission more than an official government building, it had remained the same while the rest of the once largely deserted area had become a crowded corner of the city. After the Second World War, Kezar football stadium had been built directly behind the station house. Although the 49ers had moved on to modern Candlestick Park, Kezar remained empty, a massive and quiet memorial looming over the precinct. A golf driving range had been constructed on part of the abandoned Kezar parking lot, and at least several times a day one of the power golfers would send a ball flying against the back of the station, now heavily reinforced with plasterboard. Only those police newly assigned to Park would jump at the first couple of balls that slammed into the building like a run-amok bat wielder. The duty officer sat at a wooden counter set behind bulletproof glass on the left side of the tiny foyer. Except for a wall lined with cigarette, candy, and soda machines, the duty officer was isolated from the rest of the station, which started behind a pair of swinging double doors.

Officer Randy Poppovich, a twenty-two-year veteran, was on duty that December afternoon. It had been a slow day. Two juveniles driving while intoxicated near Golden Gate Park. A vandalism case at the Japanese Tea Garden. A fistfight between a United Parcel delivery man and a bank clerk. If all his days were this quiet, he would look forward to the duty watch. But that was the danger. You never knew what was going to come into the station. Night duty was the worst. It brought out the real crazies. There were shifts when he couldn't even take a coffee break, between juggling the prostitutes for booking and dealing with several irate callers reporting everything from stabbings to four-alarm fires. This was more like it. It gave him an opportunity to read the *Chronicle*'s sports section from cover to cover. The 49ers were in the national championship game on the coming Sunday. Poppovich didn't have to work and had planned a tailgate party with almost twenty friends. He didn't have tickets to the game. They were just going to party in the parking lot, and then they would stay and watch the game on television. It was the next best thing to sitting on the fifty-yard line. The phone rang right in the middle of an article about Joe Montana, the 49er quarterback, and his fashion-model wife. Those sports stars had all the luck. A million-dollar contract and a model for a wife. Nothing like Poppovich's 210-pound, five-foot, three-inch bride.

"Hello, Park station, Poppovich here."

At first he thought there was heavy static in the background. Then he realized it sounded more like paper or cellophane being rubbed over the mouthpiece of the other receiver. "Hello?" he shouted into the phone again.

A mumbling greeted him on the other end. He strained to listen, could hear a male voice, but could not make out any of the words due to the scraping over the mouthpiece.

"Something is wrong with your phone. Do you have anything on top of it? Talk directly into it or call me back. I can't understand a word you are saying."

"Is this better?"

Some of the material covering the mouthpiece had obviously been removed. The caller was coming in quite clear, with only a slight muffling.

"Much better. Can I help you?"

Suddenly the male voice, which had sounded very ordinary just a moment ago, turned extremely hoarse and again unintelligible. It sounded like a demon had possessed the other end of the phone. Poppovich sighed and rolled his eyes skyward. This caller needed an exorcist more than a policeman. He hadn't had a crazy in several days. Guess he was due for one. He listened for a moment, but couldn't understand a word. A definite loony-tune.

He placed the receiver close to his mouth and shouted, "Hey! I can't understand a word you are saying. If you have something to report I will listen to you. But if you are going to fool around, I am going to disconnect this call."

Silence. The caller was obviously thinking about what to do. Paper over the receiver had merely muffled his voice beyond recognition. His attempt at disguising it left it unintelligible. Poppovich couldn't wait to hear what was next. He could hear a bare whisper.

"What?"

"Can you hear me?" came the soft response from the other end.

"Not really. I'm hanging up now."

The voice on the other broke into fast and clear conversation. "Okay, listen real good, scum bag, because I'm saying it once and that's all. That spic priest in the paper from El Salvador is a Commie cocksucker. He wants our boys out of Central America so he can fly the red flag together with the rest of the queers down there. But we aren't going to let him do it. Understand? It's too late to save his asshole. He's lucky we didn't take him out when he was bastardizing the cathedral this morning. Our bullet finds him before he talks to the press. Let it serve as a warning to anyone else. Death to traitors!" The phone went dead in Poppovich's hand. He shook his head in dismay. Shit! It was his bad luck to be on duty when a call for a political assassination came in. He flipped the newspaper in front of him to the news section and turned the pages until he saw the small article he remembered passing earlier. "Salvadoran Clergy Sends Activist Priest for San Francisco Fund-raising." That's the target. The article even mentioned the cathedral mass the caller had just raved about.

In twenty-two years on the force, he had developed his own feelings about whether the calls he received were true or false alarms. His batting average was damn good. This one was a fake. He would bet as much on that as he would on the 49ers. The caller was an obvious amateur who couldn't even make a decent death threat. He was probably a former veteran who thought we should be kicking some ass in Central America and was fed up with every northeastern liberal in Congress as well as every peace-loving priest from south of the border. It's just that this jerk took his frustrations out by calling in bogus death threats instead of writing his congressman. Probably even lived in the area and just decided to call the closest police station. This call should never have come into the Park station. For godsakes, they were halfway across the city from the cathedral. The crazy could have at least had the courtesy to call the central downtown receiving station. But Poppovich knew that all incoming calls were automatically recorded on large reel-to-reel machines running around the clock at the downtown headquarters. This bumbling call was already preserved for posterity. On the slim chance that he was wrong and the call was a real threat from a real assassin, he knew he had to notify nearby units to provide extra protection for the clerical visitor. If he didn't follow up and it turned out that the demon voice on the other end was real, he would be pounding the beat in the city's deserted docks. Although a foot patrol might help him lose the extra forty pounds his doctor told him had to go, it was no way to spend your midyears on the force.

He picked up the receiver and dialed an internal number that put him in contact with the general police dispatch unit. He explained the call he had received and within a minute the announcement went out on all squad-car radios. Police were told to respond to St. Mary's Cathedral and at least four officers were to stay with the visiting priest for the remainder of his high profile day.

"Father Vasquez, the car is here." One of the priests approached Colby, who was still sitting at the side of the sanctuary, his head held in his hands. Rumor had already spread that Father Vasquez was ill, and there was legitimate concern in the hushed tones of those gathered. Colby stood up very slowly, as though weakness was about to bring him to the floor. The young priest tried to put his arm around Colby in order to provide support, but he clumsily shoved the upper part of his shoulder into Colby's chest. Colby played the bump for all it was worth. He let himself fall over backward, secretly breaking his fall with his left hand. With his right hand he threw the white cane toward the ceiling, and as he crashed into the ground he let out a short scream. Again the dark glasses flew off his face and the blank white eyes stared hopelessly at the horrified onlookers. A group of laypeople and clerics ran over to help him, shoving the profusely apologizing young priest to the back of the room.

"Father, are you all right?"

"Can you walk?"

"Is anything broken?"

The questions came like a torrent. Colby raised his hand to stop them.

"Please"—he made his voice sound as weak as possible—"I am all right. Just please put my glasses back on and give me my cane. The chalice also. I must go to the hotel now. Please."

No one said another word. A group of arms helped lift him to his feet. Someone gently placed his glasses over his ears and rested them a little low on the bridge of his nose. He adjusted them as someone else wrapped the fingers of his right hand around the end of the white cane. An altar boy, still in his black cassock, brought the leather valise. "I have your chalice, Father. I will bring it to the car with you."

Colby nodded. Two people walked with him down the wooden staircase. Colby walked hesitatingly. At one point his foot slipped from under him and he was spared another spill only when his escorts helped prop him against the wall.

He was putting on a great show. He wanted to ensure that his witnesses remembered the terrible state poor Father Vasquez was in after the mass. It would make more sense when they found the priest dead within an hour. When he reappeared at the hotel the plan was simple. Colby would demand the driver wait for him in the car. A bellboy would guide him to his room door and then be dismissed. Once Erica saw he was safe, she would administer an injection of potassium chloride to the still sleeping Father Vasquez. That drug would cause a rapid increase in the heart rate, edging near 180 beats a minute. It would simultaneously constrict the blood vessels and heart valves. The result was like forcing water at high pressure through plastic pipes. They burst. Usually the veins in the soft part of the brain tissue ruptured. It made a perfect autopsy. Aneurysm in the brain. Heart failure. No possible earlier diagnosis. Death instantaneous. While Erica administered the lethal dose to Vasquez, Colby would quickly remove his clerical garb, the beard and hair gel, and return to his regular clothes. With a scrubbing solution he would rub his face, neck, and hands in order to return his skin to its natural lighter shade. Finished in less than ten minutes, they would leave the hotel appearing to be just another tourist couple about to visit the sights of San Francisco. There would be nothing unusual for anybody to remember.

Meanwhile, all the witnesses would have the same testimony to give once the impatient driver went upstairs to see why Vasquez was delayed, and discovered a dead body. Vasquez arrived in San Francisco, was picked up at the airport by friends, came to the cathedral and said mass in front of hundreds of supporters, was taken ill, then brought to the hotel where he died in his room. What a sad story. Everyone who saw the dead body would be so distressed they would fail to notice the height difference of the dead man or the slight weight variation from Colby. Anything that seemed unusual to them would be explained away as part of their grief, the distortions of the dead man. The K-7 infection would be underway and no one would be the wiser as to how it was planted.

If it hadn't been for a right-wing crackpot in the city's large Spanish community making a harassing call to a nearby police station, it would have worked like a charm.

The first squad car pulled up in front of the cathedral ten minutes after the call came on the radio. The two officers inside had been partners for less than two months. Judy O'Reilly was a third generation cop, her father and grandfather having preceded her. Her ruddy cheeks and strawberry blond hair marked her Irish heritage. Barely satisfying the minimum height requirement for the police force, her 105 pounds increased by almost twenty-five percent by the time she finished attaching the standard gun, handcuffs, nightstick, holster, and walkie-talkie to her hips. Steven Wong had been on the force for less than a year. He was one of only three dozen Chinese officers in the San Francisco police. Traditionally excluded based on height examinations, combined with an historical disdain for police work among Chinese families, Wong represented the new American-born Chinese generation. His thin, clean-cut face was offset with bushy, blue-black hair cut into an almost punkish, spikey style. More American than O'Reilly in many ways, the young Chinese officer had just returned to the job after spending a two-week honeymoon in Hawaii with his childhood sweetheart.

Wong stayed in the driver's seat of the squad car while O'Reilly walked into the cathedral to check on the status of the priest. She wanted to explain the situation to him privately, before Wong and the second pair of officers came inside. She genuflected in front of the altar and then continued to walk toward the rear of the church. She shook her head in dismay as she looked around the cavernous interior. Certainly didn't look like any church she had attended when she grew up. As she neared the sanctuary door, a pair of priests emerged.

"Excuse me, Father, but where can I find a Father Vasquez? He's supposed to have just finished a mass here."

"I'm afraid you just missed him by a couple of minutes. He wasn't feeling 100 percent so he went to his hotel to get some medication."

"Where is he staying?"

"Is there any problem, Officer?"

"No, Father. We just have some information to pass on to him. Where can I find him?"

"At the Hyatt Regency near the Embarcadero."

"Thank you, Father."

O'Reilly hurried out of the church, this time not even pausing to kneel before the altar. Wong knew she was out too quickly to have seen the priest. She was in a slow trot. He started the engine knowing that they had not arrived at the right place.

"What's the matter?" he shouted at her through the window as she neared the car.

"He just left to go back to the Hyatt at the Embarcadero—not feeling well. Call the dispatcher and tell them to cancel the second car for here and get the closest car in the area over to the hotel. We'll meet them there."

"No, I am absolutely sure. You must stay in the car. I will be fine on my own. You must believe me!" Colby was having trouble persuading the bishop's friend that he should be allowed to go to his room on his own. They were inside a black Chevrolet Camaro idling in the curved driveway in the rear of the hotel.

"But, Father, you were weak at the church. What if you lose your strength on the way to your room?"

Colby was getting quite exasperated. He really did not have time to argue with this moron. "Here. I will solve your misgivings." He turned in his seat and rolled down the passenger window. Leaning his head outside he saw two bellboys near the revolving entrance door. Deliberately he turned his head in all directions, playing to his blindness, as he shouted "Bellboy? Is there a bellboy here?"

One came running over. "Need help, Father?"

"Yes, my son. Just walk me up to my room. Will you be so kind as to do that?"

"I'd be happy to do that, Father."

"And then when you are done you are going to do me another favor. Please come down here and tell my friend here that I safely made it to the room. He worries about me."

"No problem."

Colby turned back in his seat and set his body in the direction of the driver. "Is that okay?"

"That's all right, Father Vasquez."

The bellboy opened the passenger door and helped Colby outside. Taking him by the right arm, and with Colby walking in half steps, they proceeded into the hotel. They entered the clear bullet-shaped elevators that rode along the inside walls of the hotel, overlooking the main lobby that was modeled like a modern day hanging garden of Babylon. At the nineteenth floor the bellboy led the priest to his room. They did not speak to each other the entire way. Colby was anxious to end this masquerade and be finished with the San Francisco segment of the operation.

"There you are, Father. Home at last."

"Thank you." Colby reached into his pocket and pulled out a handful of money. "Here, take out two dollars for yourself."

He watched the young man peel away two crisp dollar bills and then return a ten and three one-dollar bills to the priest's jacket pocket. The benefits of blindness. It induced honesty.

"Thank you, Father. I put the extra in your jacket."

As the bellboy walked down the corridor to the bank of elevators, Colby placed the key into the door and entered the room. Erica was pacing at the far end. She sprinted over to him.

"How did it go?"

"Fine." He ripped his glasses off and threw them on the bed. He glanced at the still propped figure of Vasquez. "Any problem with the sleeping beauty?"

"None. I've just been alternately bored and worried to death."

Colby bent over the dresser mirror and pulled down the lower portion of his eyelids with one hand and then with the other hand reached in and removed the white contact lenses. "God, I hate these things. You actually feel like you might go blind." He straightened, stretched his back, and blinked his eyes rapidly. "It was too high-risk. There were too many possibilities for discovery on this infection. And I still didn't like spraying the goddamn stuff only inches in front of my face."

"I told you that there was no chance of infec—"

"I know. There's absolutely no chance of infection. You told me once. You told me a hundred times. I still didn't like the whole operation. It was ridiculously high-risk. We could have infected people easier with a mass spraying."

"Yes. But I've told you that I need to know the identities of the people who are infected. We know the people on the guest list in New York and we know most of the people at the mass today from the archdiocese invitations. It's vital for research purposes that I monitor the results of these infections on a controlled group of victims—"

"So that you might know the progress of the germ. I know. I've heard it. I just don't like it. There were too many chances for someone to have discovered me today. I didn't feel good about it since the time I first heard it in the briefing." Colby had removed his black shirt and started applying a cleansing lotion to lighten the dye on his skin.

"Well, look, it worked. You made it."

"Yeah, yeah. Let's get out of here. Finish the job with the priest. Put him out of it for good."

Erica had already prepared the syringe. It rested in a linen napkin on top of the color television. Colby glanced at the 20 cc's of concentrated milky liquid inside the tube. Next to the K-7 killers, Erica's syringe looked like the dark ages. She grabbed the needle and walked toward the sitting Vasquez. She unbuttoned the sleeve of his shirt and rolled it above his elbow.

"Come here for a moment." She looked at Colby. "Put one hand around his bicep and the other around his forearm and squeeze." Colby did as requested.

"There, that does it." Erica looked at the bulging veins caused by Colby's pressure. She aimed the needle for the longest of the pumped veins and slid the tip of the steel point under the skin. Just as she started to pump the syringe into the unconscious priest, she jumped at a loud knock on the front door. A woman's voice froze Colby and Erica in shock.

"Father Vasquez, it's the San Francisco police. Please open up." O'Reilly was surprised they had made it to the hotel before any other squad car had arrived. Never a cop around when you needed one.

Colby let go of Vasquez's arm. The vein slipped under the layer of fatty skin and the tip of the needle popped out of the arm. Colby held his hand up to indicate silence. Still bare-chested, he softly tiptoed toward his leather case across the room on the dresser.

"Father Vasquez, are you okay in there?"

"Goddamn it." A man's voice. There were at least two of them outside the door. The woman spoke next.

"Are you sure you saw him go inside here?"

"Absolutely. I just took him up here less than five minutes ago." Now a third voice. The bellboy was there as well.

Colby reached inside his case and withdrew the sixteen-round, 9-millimeter automatic pistol. He unlocked the safety. The click was almost inaudible. He always carried his weapon with a full clip and a bullet in the chamber. It never needed cocking. Just a flip of the safety and Colby was ready to kill. Turning to Erica, he placed a finger over his mouth indicating silence. He hoped the unwanted visitors would go away if they thought he had left the room. If he had a few more minutes, his work would be finished. Erica had already drawn the pistol from her purse. She had gathered the needle and vial of potassium chloride with her free hand and placed them on the edge of the dresser.

"Father Vasquez, if you don't answer in a second we are going to open your door with a passkey and come inside."

Colby waved frantically at Erica and pointed for her to go into the bathroom. He grabbed his case and the black shirt he had worn during the mass and reached for the cleaning solution. But he had too much in his arms as he also tried to balance the two-pound SIG Sauer pistol.

The jar slipped out of his fingers, tottered for a second on the edge of the dresser, and then crashed to the floor, shattering across the carpet. He couldn't believe it. He had dropped glass a hundred times on carpeted floors and the padding had always prevented it from breaking. The one time he needed silence he couldn't have it!

It was the woman again. "Father Vasquez!" The sound of keys entering the lock followed. He turned to run into the bathroom so that he could have the element of surprise but he knocked directly into Erica as she passed him. As they bumped each other hard, the front door swung open. Colby knew he had no more time to plan a defense. It was blown. His pistol arm swung up in an arc from his waist emptying the hollow point slugs in a straight line at the door. Each shot sounded like a small cannon in the narrow confines.

The first two slugs tore into the bottom of the swinging door. The third shot past the two cops and caught the bellboy in the knee. It shattered the bone. As his body collapsed, the next bullet struck him in the nape of the neck, severing his main artery, and sending a stream of blood back into the hallway. It wasn't until the fifth shot left Colby's gun that Wong returned the first .38 caliber volley from his small handgun. His shots were wild and hit the wall high above Colby. O'Reilly jumped backward out of harm's way just as the next bullets tore into the doorjamb near her face. Colby had focused now on the young Chinese officer only feet in front of him. Erica was pressed against the side of the bathroom door, her gun having fallen on the floor in the collision with Colby. She dared not move. Wong started to turn his pistol in Colby's direction, the tip of the revolver moving toward Colby's abdomen. But he never had a chance to get off another shot. Colby just kept his finger on the automatic trigger and the pistol spit out the remainder of the clip as he aimed his hand toward the young officer. The bullets tore into Wong, descending from the shoulder and working to the groin in a close pattern. The young officer's gun flew into the air and crashed against the back of the hallway as his body spun around, slammed into the door, and then crumpled in a heap near O'Reilly's feet.

Colby knew the other cop was only around the edge of the door. She couldn't know how many of them were inside the room. It was suicide for her to proceed any farther without seeking backup. He would not let her get that far. He reached down for Erica's pistol, slowly resting his on the carpet near his feet. Suddenly O'Reilly swung into the doorway; her five-foot, three-inch frame seemed even smaller with the pistol held in front of her. It flashed through Colby's mind in an instant. How stupid was she? He couldn't believe that she was continuing the fight when she should be getting more help.

"Don't move, motherfucker!" she screamed at Colby. His hand was only inches away from the second gun. "Touch it and I'll blow your fucking head off! Hands up!"

He stared at her for a second. Her voice trembled with equal parts of rage and fear. Then he heard a small cry. Somewhere down the hallway a child was crying. He could tell O'Reilly heard it and was also concentrating on it. Then they both heard a voice. It sounded hysterical. "What's going on down there?" came the wail. Colby had seen it happen before. People near a gunfight. So petrified that they reacted in ways that were totally illogical. Sometimes running into the cross fire. The voice was getting closer. "What's happening?"

O'Reilly kept her gun trained on Colby, both hands holding the weapon aimed at his chest. "Stand up, motherfucker, now, or I'll shoot you!" Then she cocked her head back just a fraction and shouted even louder, "Don't come any closer! I am a police officer. Call the police department. Tell them there has been a shooting."

"Where? What do I tell them?" The voice was near the door.

O'Reilly took one of her hands off the revolver and swung it in back of her. "Get out of here. Now!" she screamed at the top of her lungs. Her eyes darted to her side only for an instant. It was all the time Colby needed. His hand swept to the pistol on the floor, and as he grasped it he started pressing the trigger. Nothing happened. He froze. Erica hadn't taken the safety off her weapon. Shit! He rolled forward onto the floor as he snapped the safety to the side with his other hand. O'Reilly recovered and started shooting her .38 at the blurring figure in front of her. Her first two slugs tore into the carpet only millimeters from Colby's legs. The third bullet found its target, ripping into his shoulder, settling deep inside his back. By the time O'Reilly was able to press the trigger three times on her single shot revolver, Colby had trained the now ready automatic at the top of her torso. As the burning from his shoulder started to spread over him, he pressed the trigger and the volley of bullets cut into O'Reilly's neck. Each hollow point slug left a large gaping hole and in an instant the uniformed body flew into the hallway, the head held to the torso only by a few glistening tendons.

"Let's go!" He grabbed Erica. She hesitated for a moment, immobilized by the battle she had just witnessed. "Now!" he screamed. She looked at him and started moving. Colby grabbed everything he could see. He shouted at her, "Get my case, and your needle. C'mon, don't leave anything here."

They ran down the hallway, Colby still bare-chested, bleeding profusely from his shoulder wound, a pistol raised high in one hand, the other arm holding on to his black shirt. Erica was only steps behind, carrying his case in both her hands, the syringe, his pistol, and whatever else she saw that belonged to them thrown inside. They ran past a young girl, no more than twelve, sobbing hysterically near the doorway. That was the girl who had inadvertently saved Colby's life. Colby punched the elevator button again and again. They were on the nineteenth floor. There was no chance of getting down the staircase before the place was swarming with police. The gun battle had lasted only a minute, but it was enough time for emergency calls to go out from the hotel's switchboard. If someone downstairs thought quickly they would cut off the elevator service, trapping Colby and Erica on their floor or on the staircase. And then there was always the problem of hotel security. He had noticed them when he arrived. They carried concealed weapons bulging under their jackets. Probably snubnose .38s. Just like the slug he had in his back. Whoever said being shot didn't hurt either didn't know what he was talking about or had never been shot. It hurt like hell.

The elevator Down light turned off as the elevator stopped at their floor. Good! At least nobody was bright enough to turn off the power. Yet. As the door slid open Colby stared directly at four Japanese tourists, cameras dangling around their necks. He pointed the gun straight at them and screamed, "Out! Now!" They froze in fear. He shot a single slug over their heads into the back of the glass-enclosed elevator. Colby's bullet shattered the largest section of curved glass, sending thousands of sharpened splinters flying about the lobby nineteen floors below. One of the Japanese men screamed. The one closest to the door ran from the cabin into the hallway. The other three followed only half a step behind, ducking, as though that would save them from a bullet. As the elevator door started closing Colby leaned forward to stop it. The rubber siding slammed into his wounded shoulder. He gave out a short yell like a wounded animal. Erica ran in behind him. "Goddamn it!" he gasped as he rolled into the cabin and the door closed behind.

Both of them could hear screams below as the glass began striking the lobby. He pulled Erica down to the floor and crouched next to her. "My gun." She grabbed it from the case. "In the side of the case, another clip. Put it in. If we've got any chance of getting out of here it's by you using that thing as well as I do." She fumbled inside the case. He peered over the edge of the broken glass. He could see several security men with walkie-talkies and raised pistols, waving guests out of the lobby. When they arrived at the lobby they would be sitting ducks. They were at the tenth floor and moving down fast. Colby reach up and pressed the button for the eighth floor. The stop would give them extra time. It might also confuse security as to whether they were getting off on that floor. The advantage they had was that security had no idea what was coming down the elevator. They didn't know whether the door would open to reveal a policeman, a criminal, or no one.

"I've got it." Erica held the gun on her lap while she removed the empty chamber and snapped the full one into place. "What now?"

Suddenly the elevator slowed again, this time stopping on the fourth floor. No button had been pressed. Colby's eyes widened. He motioned Erica to slide on the floor to the far side of the cabin. He moved to the front and lay near the door. As the elevator stopped and the door slid open, Colby raised his weapon, ready to empty it at the first thing that moved. His eyes focused on them at the same moment his finger tensed on the trigger. A woman and what looked like her daughter, about to get on the elevator. Colby barely stopped himself from pressing the trigger. Both women stared in horror as the elevator door slid completely open and paused for a moment.

Facing them was a bare-chested man, blood covering his shoulder, pointing a gun directly at them. At the far side of the cabin was a young woman, her eyes wide, also aiming a gun at them. Both women started screaming in unison just as the elevator door closed. That would also throw off the security people, Colby thought. They won't know what to make of a fourth-floor stop with screams that could clearly be heard through the elevator's gaping hole.

"They've only had a minute or two to figure it out. They're not professionals. You'll get out here," he ordered Erica. He reached up and hit the mezzanine button. "There's a single flight of stairs to the right. Get down those stairs right away. I want you on the staircase covering this elevator as the door opens. If you see anyone, shoot them." Erica nodded her head. The elevator stopped once again on the mezzanine. Colby assumed a cover position near the front of the cabin, but when the door opened the floor was empty. "Go!" Erica stayed crouched and darted out the elevator, the leather case dangling from one hand and her pistol held high in the other. Damn it, he thought, she better be able to do this or they were finished. The elevator made its final approach to the main floor. Colby turned so that his wounded shoulder faced the door. He lay flat on the floor and cradled the pistol under his stomach. He turned his head toward the door but pretended his eyes were closed. As the door opened he didn't hear or see anything. Then the first voice crackled over a walkie-talkie. "There's a dead body in the elevator."

The answer came back through the static. "Get it."

Two men in light grey suits ran toward Colby and tried to reach the elevator before the door closed. Colby could see through his squint that they both had pistols. The elevator door began sliding shut. A black security guard just got his hand inside in order to strike the door to make it reopen. A middle-aged blond guard started to step inside the elevator, his gun pointed at Colby. In an instant Colby rolled backward, exposing his pistol at the same moment he pressed the trigger. The first bullets caught the closest guard in the gut, splitting his stomach. The black guard didn't even get his gun into a firing position before a 9-millimeter round tore off the top of his forehead, splattering parts of his skull and brain into the lobby. Colby heard shooting outside the cabin. He recognized the sound of the SIG Sauer pistol, and the return fire of a smaller revolver. He rolled out of the elevator and onto the grey granite floor. Chips of the polished stone flew into his face as several bullets exploded into the floor directly in front of him. Then they stopped. He looked up in time to see another security guard fall from his position behind a group of potted trees. To his right, a fourth man, the one who had been guarding the exit, was dead.

"It's safe!" It was Erica. "There were four all together. We got two each! Let's go!"

He stood up and ran a step behind her. Now that was more like it. She was as good as he had hoped. They burst through the lobby door, both holding their guns high in the air. The front was deserted, the gunfight forcing people away from the hotel. Both of them could hear the wails of police sirens drawing closer. Colby ran into the street as a large burgundy Cadillac DeVille approached. He pointed the pistol directly at the windshield and the car screeched to a stop less than a foot away from him. He ran around to the side and shoved the tip of his pistol into the small open crack of the side window. "Get out now or die!" The driver, an elderly gentlemen in a suit and tie, fumbled with the door. He was petrified. Colby swung the door open and grabbed the man by the top of his tie. Yanking him out of the car, Colby virtually threw him onto the street. He jumped into the car at the same moment Erica leaped into the passenger side. Colby slammed the gas pedal to floor, and as the Caddy started screeching down the street, the first squad car, its lights blazing and siren blasting, turned the corner. It caught site of the speeding Cadillac and didn't even hesitate in picking up the chase.

Colby's wound was killing him, a searing pain spreading throughout his torso. His left arm was almost useless; only the right firmly grasped the steering wheel.

The Cadillac gained momentum up to nearly seventy miles an hour as it shot straight down Bay Street toward the docks. He ran two red lights and at one intersection a pickup van slammed its brakes, screeching within inches of Erica's face. The police car had been joined by two others, all three in close pursuit. Colby let his foot off the gas, and as the car decelerated he jammed the wheel to his left. The 4200 pounds of steel screeched into a side spin and then straightened when he jerked the steering wheel to the opposite direction. Again he hit the gas pedal to the floor and started up California Street, one of the steepest hills in the city. One police car missed the turn, sliding into a trio of telephone booths at the far corner, but the other two made it and started the climb in pursuit of Colby. The wail of their sirens seemed to close in on the speeding Cadillac. At Montgomery Street, in the heart of the financial district, Colby ran a red light, crashing through a crowd of dozens of pedestrians who miraculously missed being hit by the hurtling vehicle. At each new street corner the roadway flattened and the Cadillac would shoot off the top of the hill and crash onto the flat part of the intersection, then begin the rapid ascent up the next hill only to repeat the bone crushing experience.

As he approached Grant Avenue, the left lane was blocked by a stalled cable car. Then, over the top of Nob Hill, two more police cars started down the grade toward him. One swung sideways to block the roadway on the far side of the cable car, while the other squad car came over to the wrong side of the street, and started driving directly toward him. It was like a game of chicken as both cars bolted toward each other. At the intersection it appeared they would both slam head on. But at the last second Colby whipped the wheel to the right and the Cadillac swerved from California Street onto Grant Avenue. The police car caught the end of Colby's bumper and the contact forced the squad car to spin wildly to the right, slamming broadside into the stationary cable car, which teetered for a moment before sliding off its tracks and crashing onto its side. Several passengers in the cable car flew into the intersection; one was crushed as the car settled over him.

The first police car zooming up California Street in pursuit of Colby tried to avoid the accident but turned too far to the right and crashed through the picture window of Hibernia Bank at the corner, momentum carrying the car into the bank and embedding it into the cashier's counter. The second squad car tried to swerve around an elderly Chinese man who had been thrown from the cable car, but it came too close to the accident scene, the front wheels striking the edge of the overturned trolley. The speed with which the car had been traveling was enough momentum for it to start flying as though it would pass over the scene of the accident like an Evel Knievel stunt. But suddenly gravity took control and the vehicle paused in midair before plummeting back to the ground. It fell at an angle, and when the underbelly struck the edge of the cable car, the car flipped over backward, smashing the sirens and flashing lights on the roof. It slid an entire block down the hill. Only the third car maneuvered its way through the bodies and the twisted metal and glass to successfully follow Colby onto Grant Avenue.

Colby had his eyes locked on the rearview mirror. He almost thought that all of his pursuers had been lost until he saw the flashing yellow and red lights turn the corner nearly two blocks behind. Grant Avenue is a single, narrow lane that runs through the heart of San Francisco's Chinatown, the largest and most congested Oriental community outside the orient. Even on the best of days traffic is notoriously slow. The side streets and alleys leading off Grant are almost as congested. Colby knew the police would be up to him in a moment unless he took drastic action. "Hold on!" he screamed to Erica. He yanked the steering wheel to the right, floored the gas pedal, and the Cadillac lurched over the curb and started flying down the crammed sidewalks. People screamed and barely jumped out of the way. Wooden cages filled with live chickens were demolished, and feathers and chunks of the birds splattered around the street. The Cadillac kept swerving along the narrow sidewalk. Sometimes Erica's side of the car crashed into the small storefronts, and sparks would fly from the ripping metal as she covered her eyes, the store windowpanes shattering in succession. At Kearny Street, Colby plowed through an oriental-styled telephone booth that flew onto the hood of the car and smashed the windshield before tumbling over the roof and slamming onto the sidewalk. The glass from the windshield flew inside, stinging their faces, but they clenched their eyes shut to stop the splinters from blinding them.

The police had followed Colby onto the sidewalk and chased on the same route. They were only half a block behind when they saw the Cadillac strike the telephone booth at Kearny Street, and less than a quarter of a block behind when the telephone booth slammed into the middle of their path. They swerved back into the roadway and their car slid across the street, knocking a row of crispy ducks hanging from a metal rod; the birds splattered onto the car and across the windshield. They straightened out the car and started back down Grant when they saw a pickup truck crossing the intersection. The policeman hit his brakes and the car spun in a circle. He pressed the gas to break the spin, but the tires slipped and the car shot over the curb and slammed through the window of one of Chinatown's largest restaurants, the Golden Dragon. The force of the crash sent the car flying through the assembled diners, the wooden tables breaking like matchsticks before the metal battering ram. The squad car finally stopped when it hit the rear wall, right at the kitchen's main gas line. Even though Colby and Erica were three blocks away at the time, they could feel the force of the explosion. Erica turned in her seat and Colby looked through the dangling rearview mirror. A ball of flame, like a slow-motion picture of a sun spot, mushroomed from the storefronts and enveloped the middle of the street. The sound of the explosion filled their car.

He couldn't see anything behind the dark smoke that now covered the avenue. But he knew that nothing had made it through that explosion. He took his foot lightly off the gas pedal and made a right turn onto Broadway, San Francisco's red-light district. Not a squad car in sight. They had had a chance to get him and they had missed. He glanced at Erica. She was beaming.

"We are completely blown," he spoke to her in gasps, the pain in his shoulder numbing his senses. "We must get help from headquarters to get out of here alive."

She nodded. "No panic." Her voice was surprisingly calm. Despite the madness of the past thirty minutes, her professional instincts had taken control. "It's what you always told me. We take things one step at a time. Turn here." She pointed down steep Montgomery Street. "We get you dressed, dump this car, and then I get somewhere to fix you. Lucky you're with a doctor. Then we contact headquarters."

He made the turn. "But we are blown! Headquarters may wash their hands of us!"

"What, are you mad?" She was strong. It had a calming effect on him. "We have the virus. Enough of it to wreak havoc and start a new war. We are like walking atom bombs. Headquarters will get us out of here because it's better than leaving us on our own with the vials. Don't worry. We didn't go through this today just to end up dead. We are making it out of here, and we will finish our mission."

He looked at her as he pulled the car onto the side of the roadway, underneath the Oakland-Bay Bridge. Her eyes were on fire. There was no denying her will or bravery. He started to talk to her, to tell her how difficult it was going to be, when he felt the dizziness envelop his head. He saw her lips moving but he couldn't hear anything. Then he felt himself falling over and he crashed unconscious into her lap.

CHAPTER 15 ═══════════

Bolling Airfield, Washington, D.C.
December 17
2:00 p.m.

"We've got the break!" Hodson panted as he sprinted through the swinging doors of the airport security command center. McGinnis and Harris were closeted in a far corner, isolated from most of the personnel at Washington's military air base, nestled on the banks of the Anacosta River. A military transport jet was in the final stages of preparation for a flight that would get them into San Francisco in less than five hours. That should give the spectrum system and the local Company office enough time to isolate the infection site. They hoped it would give Hodson enough time to come up with a name for them to go on. From the smile on his face, it looked like he had made it with time to spare.

"What's the good word, old chap?" McGinnis mockingly called to Hodson as the Brit looked around the room, failing to see them in the corner. He turned his head toward the rear, noticed McGinnis sitting against a large wooden desk, and ran toward him.

"Don't piss around," he said as he held a sheaf of papers in the air. "I've got crucial information for you wallys." Hodson pulled a battered, grey metal chair toward the desk and sat down in front of McGinnis. Harris came around the front of the desk and stood directly behind Hodson, trying to block the view and conversation from anyone who might be nearby. Hodson scanned the area, and when convinced that no one could hear him, he lowered his voice and began talking rapidly.

"We've found their traveling names. I'm sure of it." He handed a sheet of paper to McGinnis. "I've come here to tell you about this even before debriefing Finch, because I assume you two need to know it before you land out there. There are two we are virtually certain of —the man is David Colby, supposedly a Swiss national, and the woman is traveling as Erica Cane, an American who works in Silicon Valley."

"How are you sure these are the names?" Harris asked while he craned his neck to look at the papers in Hodson's lap.

"Because when we ran checks on every possible way that someone could be at the murder scene in Paris, then depart to any other location, or combination of locations, and arrive in New York, we ended up with a master list of 1902 people who came into the Big Apple. The next part of the computer check was to follow up to see where those people went after getting to New York. We had to pull more than forty research analysts from Phillips's department to check airline, car rental, and train directories, plus calling many of the people for independent verification. Of the 1902, 1279 were coming into New York only on a stopover and had left before the hit at the Waldorf. Of the remaining 623, only 5 remained in New York long enough to have been there for the first operation and then travel on a commercial liner to San Francisco in time for the second infection the computers picked up a couple of hours ago. We tried to individually contact the five, and reached three. They have been eliminated as suspects. The final two are the names I just gave you. And we have further confirmation. First, Colby and Cane are supposedly in Europe on business trips. Both are five days late in contacting any family or business associates. That means that from a day before the London station was wiped out, our two traveling Americans have lost contact with the outside world. Now what does that tell you?"

The question was addressed to McGinnis, but Harris answered as though he was almost mumbling to himself. "That means they are probably dead somewhere, their passports used by part of the Soviet team."

"And what else does it tell you?" Hodson turned to look at him.

"It means that the Soviets had picked these people out as targets because they probably resembled the operatives involved."

"Exactly! The VKR had to have a team established just in order to locate the right identification papers. While they needed people who wouldn't be missed immediately, the single most important factor is that the agent can travel, without incident, on the victim's photo. I'm sure that both the real Colby and Cane are dead somewhere and may not be discovered for a long time, if at all. But we've been able to get the originals of their passport photos from the agencies where they applied, and here they are.''

Hodson handed two eight-by-ten-inch blowups to McGinnis. Harris walked around the desk and stared over McGinnis's shoulder at the photos. Hodson noticed surprise register in both their faces as they stared at the picture of the very attractive Erica Cane. She certainly did not fit the stereotype of a VKR agent. The Soviets were adept at recruiting women for their special squads who more closely resembled Olympian bodybuilders than a girl you would take home to Mom. McGinnis stared intently at the photos. "He looks familiar somehow." He paused for a moment and looked closely at the man. "I can't quite place it, but there is something remotely familiar about that face." He looked puzzled.

"Sure," Harris joined in, "that's because he looks a little like the Dutch actor Rutger Hauer. You know, *Blade Runner*, the—"

"Don't be a jerk," McGinnis admonished him. He finished the last gulp from his third postlunch coffee, and turned to Hodson. "These were the same names that traveled from London to Paris?"

Hodson shook his head. "No. They didn't use those names to leave London the day of the lab wipeout. We know from the forensic matches that a relatively young, Caucasian man was present in London, Paris, and then New York. We assume that's Colby. As for the woman, she wasn't in London, but she was definitely in Paris and New York.''

Harris was twisting a paper clip as he spoke to Hodson. "How do we know these are the same two people who let off the K-7 earlier today in the Frisco area? How can we be sure these two aren't a decoy and somebody else is involved in the S.F. infection? I mean for all we know, they just landed in San Francisco, and then they caught the next plane to Hawaii or the orient or some such place."

"Wrong." Hodson had a smug look on his face. It was clear that he was not finished with his news. "We checked the S.F. hotels' guest directories and we found our couple. They checked in at the Fairmont Hotel the night before we picked up the infection."

The Fairmont. McGinnis had been there several years earlier. Nice taste for a couple of Russian killers. "When are they due to check out?"

"They've listed themselves as one week guests. But that is clearly a cover. We've already dispatched local Company boys to wait for them at the hotel. If we corner them, we've got to make sure they have the virus before we take them. They aren't any good to us without the entire K-7 supply. We've taken rooms on either side of theirs. No sign that they are inside. We are establishing listening surveillance as soon as possible so when they return we can find out a little about them."

"Any idea who they are in the Soviet roster?" McGinnis asked.

"Nothing. We ran the photos of the real Colby and Cane through the computer identifier for all known Soviet and eastern bloc agents and we came up empty-handed. That's not surprising since these passport photos of the victims may only generally resemble the real killers. The machines are so damn smart that they need real precision for a match. There are probably enough variations in the facial features to throw off the computers. I have two researchers going through the Soviet files by hand to see if they can come up with the likely candidates. But they had nothing by the time I left to come here."

Harris tapped McGinnis on the shoulder and nodded with his head toward the front of the security room. A marine lieutenant colonel was walking toward them. McGinnis rose and stretched his arms. "I guess it's time for us to get going. Nigel, anything else we should know before we take off?"

"Just that we've got every possible exit from San Francisco covered. Their names kicked up in a computer search of rental car agencies. They have a nice navy blue Chevrolet Caprice. It's still sitting in the hotel garage. So wherever they are, someone else is moving them around. We're sending in a forensic team to sweep the car. They might have some preliminaries by the time you arrive."

The young lieutenant colonel stopped a half step behind the sitting Hodson. He gave McGinnis a crisp salute. "Sir, the transport is ready. Your bags and equipment are loaded. If you'll come with me I will escort you aboard and you can get going."

"Just one moment, Colonel." It was more of a question than a statement from Hodson. "Let me talk to them one more minute and they'll be ready to join you."

The marine officer looked at McGinnis to get an indication of whether the delay was warranted. McGinnis nodded his head imperceptibly. The marine stepped back to a nearby desk and waited.

"We've got red flags on their names sitting at airport reservation programs, car rental agencies, and all train and bus depots. People have to show ID today in S.F. in order to buy a ticket anywhere. I want to make sure they are still there when you arrive."

McGinnis began walking toward the marine and then paused for a moment. "Nigel, you didn't tell me where they were staying the other night in New York."

"That's because we don't know. Unfortunately, they didn't turn up on any hotel within a sixty-mile radius of the city."

"So that means they might well have been with other agents while they were there. They might well be on their way out of San Francisco in another agent's car. You can only guarantee me that 'David Colby' and 'Erica Cane' won't leave San Francisco before I get there. But you sure as hell can't guarantee me that those two Soviet agents will still be waiting for Harris and me."

"Unfortunately, you are right."

McGinnis patted Hodson on the back as he started leaving the security room. "Nigel, you and your goddamn machines. I've got to admit they are faster than a hundred gumshoes put together. And you know you've done a pretty little job on getting us this much. But I sure am going to be pissed off if I fly all the way to Frisco and those two are gone. Do what you can back at headquarters and try to make sure they stay there. And one last favor. Don't have those morons at the local Company office try anything before I get there. Tell them that's a direct order from the chief of field operations."

"Anything else?" Hodson asked as the two agents joined the marine officer and started walking through a sealed double door. "If you need any help, call me." Hodson lifted his arms in a mock bodybuilding pose.

What a lunatic, McGinnis thought as he proceeded through the doors, only half a step behind Harris. That's why he trusted him. Lunatics had to stick together.

The bloodhound was still in Washington. Finch had made it clear to him that he was not allowed to follow his friend McGinnis out of Washington. He didn't even know exactly where McGinnis and his new young partner had gone. But McGinnis had indicated it was still in the United States and had promised to telephone once a day. That was incentive enough for Bouchet to remain in Washington for several extra days. He could coordinate the work at home just as efficiently as if he were there.

He was on the second floor of the French embassy. The military attaché was in Belgium for a NATO meeting, so the bloodhound had taken his spacious office. Bouchet had already given the early Regency-style office his distinctive stamp. Four ashtrays were filled with fuzzy pipe cleaners, and the office was filled with a musty odor, evidence of his black tobacco. He had cleared the top of the massive, black-lacquered desk and had spread his notes in an organized fashion along one side. On the other half of the desk he kept neat stacks of classified cables arriving from SDECE headquarters, all containing updates on the forensic work as well as the search for an x-ray match of the skeleton found in the Hotel Raphaël. It was the latter quest that consumed Bouchet's time.

If he could identify the dead body, he knew it would bring him one step closer to identifying the people whose genetic traces were discovered in the hotel room. He knew it was a long shot to find a medical record that matched the dead man. Even with the peculiar skeleton left at the Raphaël, it was unlikely that he could unmask its identity in several days. The NATO central files had proven fruitless. Interpol reported no match. Britain, West Germany, Italy, and Spain had searched their own national police files and found nothing. Military files in half a dozen western European nations had proved worthless. The American military drew a blank. The Canadians had several close medical histories with osteomyelitis, but nothing that matched the exact skeleton of the dead man. Bouchet drew on his pipe and thought of the possibilities. The victim could have been from the middle east or South America and all the searching would have been in vain. The pathologists could tell that the body was not Asian or African, and although they believed it was not middle eastern, they did not completely rule it out. From the skin's melanin levels, the forensic team had virtually eliminated northern and central Europe as a home for the mutilated body. Bouchet pulled a beige file folder from his leather attaché, and, pinching it by the tip, he let several glossy pictures slip onto the desk. They were three dozen photos of the body found in the Raphaël. Photos taken from every possible angle, blown up to eight by ten inches. He reviewed them once again as he had every day since the body was discovered, hoping they would provide him with a lead. He methodically turned each sheet over, pausing, as if embedding the images deep into his mind.

Then he saw it. His heart beat ever quicker. Could he have missed something like that through so many earlier reviews? He reached into his attaché case while he kept his eyes focused on the blown-up picture of the dead man's testicles. With his right hand he held the photo close to his eyes and squinted as if he was trying to focus on a minute detail. His left hand first fumbled in his attaché case, then on the floor next chair. His hand ran over the file folders, past the pens and pencils, into a tape recorder, on top of a bottle of stomach antacid, and then he finally found what he was searching for—a precision optical magnifying glass. He brought it in front of the photo and placed it above the penis. There it was. Hidden by pubic hair, the outlines of a small scar. It appeared discolored, although it was difficult to tell through the thick hair. But to the bloodhound it looked like a light circle of blue, the remnants of a bruise. Or, if his suspicion was right, the discernible sign of a tattoo. The bloodhound pressed the magnifier closer to the picture. His eye almost rested against the glass. He could not make out anything more.

He placed the photo down on the desk and dialed the telephone number to his own SDECE office. It was 7:00 p.m. in Paris. Three rings, then four. Was it possible that everyone in his section had already left for the evening? He could not believe it. He was finally on the edge of making some progress, and he couldn't get someone to answer a telephone. Maybe he should have gone back to Paris—staying in Washington was not the most practical choice. Nervously he started tapping the end of his pipe against a heavy glass ashtray. Just as he was ready to hang up and dial the main switchboard, the phone was answered on the eighth ring.

"Hello."

"Hello, who is this?" Bouchet asked.

"Hello, who is this?" Standard procedure was never to identify yourself on an SDECE line until you first knew whom you were speaking to on the other end.

"This is Bouchet. Mauriac, is that you?"

"Oui." The bloodhound was relieved. The twenty-eight-year-old agent who answered the phone was trustworthy and meticulous in his attention to detail. Those were two attributes Bouchet required for the upcoming assignment. Mauriac continued talking, "Colonel, where are you?"

"Washington. At the embassy."

"Are you on a secure line?"

"Yes. I am talking from the attaché's office. His line is better than ours. Or at least that is what they say here. Listen, Philippe, I need you to do something for me right away and I cannot tell you how important it is."

"If I can do it, then I shall."

"You remember the corpse we found several days ago at the Raphaël?"

"Yes."

"Well, I want you to go across the yard to building six and downstairs to the pathology department. You get the chief on duty and tell him it is an emergency that requires his immediate attention. If he has any questions then tell him he should check the standing order from the Action Directorate. This matter is of pressing urgency."

"What is it you want him to do?"

"I want him to inspect under the corpse's pubic hair, in the upper left corner, a mark that might have been a tattoo. If I am right, it has been removed. Have him apply some radium-tinted acid. If it's a tattoo, the original will be etched across the dead skin once he applies a black light source. He can do it in ten minutes. I've seen it happen, so don't accept any answer that says come back in an hour. And don't let him tell you that he has no one who can do it. I could do it myself if I were there. It's simple. Now I will wait here by the telephone until he is done, and then you are to call me back and give me the results. Understood?"

"Yes, Colonel, I shall do it immediately."

"One more thing, Philippe. When is your shift over?"

"Actually, it was to finish in thirty minutes. I have been here since ten this morning."

"And who is on duty watch next?"

"Hubert." Bouchet grimaced. Hubert, after thirty-five years on the job, was biding his time until his pension activated. He had long ago lost the zeal for intricate intelligence work. Hubert was exactly the type of agent the bloodhound wanted to avoid during this investigation.

"Then I must ask you yet another favor. I may have some follow-up work tonight, depending on what, if anything, the good doctor finds. I want you to do that work. Not Hubert. Understood?"

"Yes, Colonel."

"Good. Now get going."

The bloodhound leaned back in the comfortable dark green leather chair. He swiveled slowly from one side to another. He took his pipe from the ashtray and slowly relit the remaining tobacco. The heady aroma of the black tobacco filled the spacious office. Bouchet thought of the mark. He couldn't discern it. But its location had heightened his interest. In the search for genetic codes and a detailed medical history of the skeletal structure, the significance of a simple body mark may have been overlooked. Just a couple of days earlier everyone in the pathology department was convinced that the skeleton had such a distinctive medical history that it should be easy to find a military jacket that matched it. He knew they were too optimistic. Even if he had the bones of the hunchback of Notre Dame, he would still have to search millions of computer files. And if those computerized files drew blanks, as they had in this case, then millions of additional files were left in friendly and not-so-friendly nations, and they all had to be checked through a painstaking hand search, if at all. And if the man never was in the military or in jail, all those searches were a waste of time. It was extremely difficult, no matter how unusual the body. And within the turnaround time he required the information, it was nearly impossible.

Bouchet rose from the chair and paced in circles around the room. It used to drive others crazy, and they would often plead with him to stop moving and to remain seated. But by walking, his nerves calmed, the mind rested, and he seemed to think clearly. Now, alone in the attaché's office, he paced to his heart's content. The telephone's ring startled him. He looked at his watch as he strode to the desk. Less than twenty minutes. Excellent work by the youngster. That is, assuming that he was calling with an answer and not a problem.

"Oui."

"Bouchet?"

"Who is this?"

"It is Dr. Berenger." Typical, Bouchet thought to himself. If a doctor was going to be bothered with work in the early evening, he was going to take credit for the information by calling it in himself. Poor Mauriac was probably standing only a couple of meters behind the credit-hungry doctor. "I have stopped some work I was doing on a Corsican brought in last night in order to turn my full attention to your problem, Colonel."

"Thank you, Doctor. Was it worth the diversion?"

"Yes. I saw the mark the minute I pulled the corpse out. As you know, I did not do the original work on the body."

Of course not. But you probably would have missed it as well. But Bouchet didn't say that. "I realize that, Dr. Berenger. What did you find?"

"A tattoo that had been quite precisely removed. Almost surgically, and then covered with a laser cross-linking to bar further identification. But the radium-fortified acid did reconstruct a basic form. It appears to be a hand, or fist to be more precise, hitting something that looks like a block of wood or sheet of steel or something. And the wood or metal looks as though it is breaking up."

"Doctor, could it be a fist striking through a group of chains?"

"Yes, that is it! I am looking at a magnification here on the screen. It is not wood or simple metal splintering. It is a jumble of chains. That is it."

Not just any tattoo. It was just as he thought. La Mano della Morte. The hand of death. It was the underground symbol used by the early founders of the radical, left-wing Italian terror group, the Red Brigade. The first several dozen who constituted the core membership had adopted the tattoo as a symbol of the proletarian uprising they hoped to lead against the fumbling Italian bureaucracy. It was their secret, their identification to bar outsiders and infiltrators from penetrating their society. But after the first arrests, coupled with the advent of informers, the tattoo became a mark of Cain, not a badge of honor. Just as the blood tattoos on the underarms of Nazi SS troopers had been displayed with pride during the war, afterward they became the identifying marks that allowed hunters to verify their catch. The hand of death was the same for the Red Brigade. Within a couple of years its use was stopped. Only a handful of early members retained the mark. To have removed it would have been considered an act of cowardice. Even when the Carabinieri had the Red Brigade on the run during recent years, those early leaders who were captured still proudly displayed the distinctive blue symbol. But the one on the Raphaël corpse had been professionally removed by someone who never wanted the affiliation discovered. Why was a founding member of a left-wing terror group turning up dead at the Raphaël with traces of a top intelligence tool, selenium paper, all over the tub? Were the Soviets using western European terror groups for their new strikes against the west? Had the Red Brigade penetrated a source inside a national spy network? Bouchet didn't like the turn in the case, but at least he was pleased he had a lead to pursue.

"Dr. Berenger, that is excellent work. Is Mauriac there?"

"Yes. He's right in the room with me. One minute, Colonel."

"Colonel."

"Philippe, go back to my office and telephone me here at the embassy. I want you to call someone in Rome. I would do it myself but you're probably going to interrupt his supper. And there are few things that can put an Italian into a bad mood faster than interrupting a meal. So on the way to my office, practice up on your most gracious pleading. I want to hear from you in five minutes. You have a lot of work to do."

CIA headquarters was nearing the second shift of the day. There was a lot of activity in the hallways and near the main offices of the western wing, the covert section of the building. The telephone emitted a quiet buzz indicating that it was ringing. The person in the high-back leather chair, his face buried in a classified update on the search for the VKR team, swiveled and pulled the telephone receiver to his ear. There was silence for a moment. Then a gruff male voice on the other end uttered the words "They are blown." The person behind the desk gently placed the phone's receiver back into its cradle and neatly placed the multipage printout into a corner of the desk. Then he quickly rose from the chair and walked out of the office and toward the war room. The search for the bioassassins had just taken a critical turn.

CHAPTER 16 ⊨———

San Francisco
December 17
5:00 p.m.

Erica closed her eyes and inhaled deeply, the air slowly filling and then rushing from her lungs. She had to relax. Although she appeared calm, her stomach and nerves were in turmoil. How could they be anything but? She was a scientist, goddamn it! Not a trained killer. The mission's objective had always been clear. She had been promised by headquarters. She would only accompany Colby to ensure the virus was correctly planted. Her main responsibility was to monitor the initial infection sites and prepare the victim profiles for follow-up research. Part of her work was to adapt the virus to field conditions and safely maintain it at all times. If Colby needed her assistance in any other aspect of the operation, and headquarters repeatedly assured her that he was the best agent available and would never need her help, then she might have to provide him a second hand. A second hand, her ass! She had to kill the contact agent in San Francisco because Colby thought it was a good experience for her. Just as she was recovering from her first kill in a decade, she was involved in a close-range shootout at the hotel, with bullets flying everywhere as she watched more than half a dozen people get blown apart. Again, she had to kill two of them with her own hands—hands that were meant to be in the laboratory, not in the field leaving behind a trail of bodies. This was not part of the deal.

Now she had almost had a heart attack while her one-armed partner flew a two-ton Cadillac through the streets of San Francisco without any regard as to whether he killed both of them or not. Well, she did care. She was not prepared to die. And now she was sitting in a car that half of San Francisco was looking for, and her partner was bleeding profusely from a bullet wound that had caused him to collapse unconscious on her lap. She was on the verge of hyperventilating. Again, she drew the air in gulps through her open mouth and slowly exhaled. She placed her right index finger against the underside of her left wrist and felt the steady and strong thumping. She opened her eyes and twisted her head to watch at the second hand sweep across the face of her watch. Twelve heartbeats in six seconds; 120 beats a minute. She was a mess. But if she didn't force herself out of the car and into action, she would momentarily find herself surrounded by police cars. She knew she could not be taken alive. If she was, headquarters would ensure her death in jail before she could talk. No one could stand for the public disgrace that would follow the bungling of a major strike inside the heart of the United States.

She took one last deep breath, opened and closed her eyes very wide several times, and then mustered the strength to shove Colby's torso off her lap and across the front seat. Reaching into his bag, which was nestled near her feet, she searched for one of the pistols. At first she didn't feel it. Then she glanced at the floor and saw it on the corner of the rubber mat; evidently it was thrown from the bag during the mad chase through the San Francisco hills. Pulling the pistol into her lap, she cocked a shell into the chamber, and slid it under her wool blazer. Before stepping outside, she scanned the vicinity through the Cadillac's shattered windows. Only a few cars passed along the quiet waterfront street underneath the massive blue-grey steel structure of the Bay Bridge. There wasn't a police car or a pedestrian in sight. Pulling the car's visor down, she flipped open the lighted vanity mirror and matted her hair so it did not look so wild. She wiped a smear of lipstick from the bottom of her lip, and then, convinced that she looked as normal as she could under the circumstances, she stepped outside the Cadillac.

The first car approached from the south. It was a Jeep with two men sitting in the front. She couldn't see whether anybody was in the back seat. It was not a good choice. She let them pass. The next car was half a block behind the Jeep. It was a light blue Toyota Corolla. As it approached, she could see a young blond woman in the driver's seat, a pair of large sunglasses obscuring most of her face. Next to her was a young child, possibly a girl, no more than five or six years of age. The back appeared empty. Erica did not have the luxury of waiting all day for the ideal car. This one would have to do. Stepping away from the Cadillac and into the roadway, she blocked the Toyota's path. Erica waved her arms across her body indicating that she wanted the car to stop.

The driver had not seen the stalled Cadillac off the side of the road. She was driving the way she always did: her eyes locked directly on the roadway in front of her. Penelope Giovanni, Penny to her friends, had just celebrated her thirty-fourth birthday the day before. Everything was going right for the young Italian-American girl. She had been married for seven years to a young dentist with a booming practice. Two early miscarriages were distant memories now that they had their first child, Agatha, nearly five years ago. Just six months earlier, her husband's spiraling business had allowed them to move out of their four-room condominium and purchase an $850,000, three-thousand-square-foot home in Sausalito, a sleepy but wealthy bedroom community only ten minutes north of San Francisco. Complete with a large in-ground pool, a tennis court, and three manicured acres, it was the life she had always dreamt of while in school. Two cars, his a BMW, at least two pampered vacations a year, a country club membership, all of the trappings of the up-and-coming family filled their satisfactory life.

Penny had visited San Francisco for a birthday party for one of Agatha's friends. The kids had gathered at Fisherman's Wharf where they spent the day wandering in awe through the wax museum and the local amusement rides. Penny could never have imagined in her wildest dreams that such a simple trip to the city would lead her into terror that would inalterably change her peaceful life.

Penny was about to turn onto Bay Street and head toward the Golden Gate Bridge when she was startled by the sight of a woman stepping directly in front of her car and frantically waving her arms urging a complete stop. It was a reflex reaction. She slammed on the brakes. If she didn't she would have struck the woman. The car screeched to a stop, Penny reaching out and putting her arm across the chest of her daughter. There was no need to do it since the three-point seat belt firmly held Agatha in place, but Penny's protective instincts had taken over. If she had time to think about the sight of the pleading woman barring her path, she probably would have swerved the car into the opposite lane and speeded past the scene. Penny just wasn't the type of person to get involved with other people's problems. She had enough on her mind and certainly did not want to get involved in any emergency. Not if there was trouble. And since this section of road was fairly well traveled and it was the middle of the day, it was not very difficult to justify to herself that some good samaritan would have been along in a couple of minutes. But she had not had the time to contemplate all of that before her reflexes caused her foot to hit the brake pedal.

The car came to a stop almost ten feet in front of the young woman. Penny tried to size her up. She was pretty but also disheveled, as though she had been running or sleeping in her neatly tailored suit. Erica started running toward the car. Penny instinctively reached to the side of her door and made sure the lock was depressed. Then she looked at Agatha's door and made sure the lock was also in place. When she turned back toward her side, Erica was at the window. For a brief moment, Erica studied Penny. Frosted blond hair, an attractive but soft face, pink lipstick, dangling rhinestone earrings—this was a pampered yuppie, not someone who was going to put up a good fight. It reassured Erica.

"Please, help me, my car has just broken down. If you could just drop my baby and me, she's inside the car"—Erica looked over her shoulder at the Cadillac—"at the nearest gas station, I would really appreciate it."

Penny looked at the smoldering wreck less than thirty feet in front of her. One entire side of the car was torn apart, as if it had been peeled like a banana. Smoke was pouring from under the front hood. Although she was looking at the car's rear, it appeared that all the side and front windows were smashed. Something was definitely wrong here. This car had not just stalled. It looked as though it had been through a demolition derby and lost. She was about to let her foot off the brake and accelerate away from the scene when suddenly the glass next to her face shattered. It happened so quickly that she didn't know what first alerted her senses—whether she heard the smash or saw the splintering glass from the corner of her eye. Both sight and sound seemed to register simultaneously. Then a millisecond later she felt the sharp edges of glass hit her face and she let out a short but penetrating scream. "Agatha!" She didn't even think about what caused the window to smash, she just thought about protecting her young daughter from the flying splinters. Agatha screamed at the same moment, filling the car with a wail of anguish. Penny's foot slipped off the brake and the car started to edge forward, but then she slammed the pedal to the floorboard, again jolting the car to a stop. She had to concentrate on her daughter, not on a moving car. As Penny turned toward Agatha, Erica slipped her hand through the shattered window and pulled up the lock. With her other hand she swung open the door. Just as Penny leaned over her daughter, she felt a sharp jolt against her neck, the sensation of cold metal pressed against her skin.

"Look at this, bitch!" The voice from the other woman was no longer pleading. It was an order. The voice almost trembled with rage. From the corner of her eye Penny saw the long end of a pistol barrel stuck against the side of her neck. She thought she would faint. Her foot fell off the brake pedal and the car started sliding forward again, but Erica was already halfway into the front seat. She jumped into the car and shoved Penny farther on top of her daughter. Before the car could gain momentum she pressed lightly on the brake and closed the door.

"If you make a single move I will blow your fucking head off! And if you don't stop that goddamn brat from screaming I am going to blow her head off in front of you. Shut her up!"

Penny started patting Agatha and hurriedly stroking her brow, pushing the light brown hair off her forehead. Her daughter's face had drained of all color and her eyes were wide with fear. Penny reassuringly whispered to her. "There you go, honey. Please, honey. There's nothing to be afraid of. Everything is okay now. Please, for Mommy, stop crying now."

It had taken less than a minute to hijack the car. Erica drove the Toyota next to the driver's side of the Cadillac.

"I will have this gun with me all the time. If you try anything stupid I am going to kill you and your daughter. Now get out of the car with me. I've got something here that you're going to help me with. Fuck it up and you've blown it for your daughter. Understand?"

Penny was biting her bottom lip. It felt as though it was about to burst. She was on the edge of tears, her body paralyzed with fright.

"Do you understand, bitch?" Erica screamed at the top of her lungs, the gun pushed near Penny's chin. Penny nodded her head rapidly. Agatha started crying again.

"Leave her. Come with me, right now."

The two of them left the car and walked to the driver's side of the Cadillac. It was the only door on the car that still worked. Penny felt a weakness in her knees, and she braced herself against the side of the car. She could not allow herself to faint, to be removed from protecting her daughter. Her fear for what the gun-wielding woman in front of her could do to Agatha consumed her. Erica looked up and down the road, and once she was convinced that no cars were in sight, she turned toward Penny.

"Look, all we have to do is to slide him across this seat." It wasn't until Penny heard the word *him* that she realized someone else was in the car. She glanced inside and gasped. A bare-chested man, covered in blood, was lying faceup on the front seat. Penny's head felt light.

"Grab hold of yourself, bitch!" Erica's harsh voice startled her. Erica reached with her right hand and grabbed both sides of Penny's cheeks. She squeezed them so hard that the lips puckered. "If you lose it now, you won't be any help to me. And if you're not going to help me then I am going to have to get someone new. But before I do that I am going to blow your and your daughter's brains out. Understand?" Erica's voice rose with anger. Her eyes were wide, maniaclike, and her nails cut into the side of Penny's face. Penny tried to nod her head. Her eyes pleaded to let her face go. "Good." Erica pushed her head back. "Now get your pretty little hands in here and help me get him into your car."

The cars were less than two feet apart, just enough to let the doors open on each. Erica climbed partially inside the car, still gripping the pistol in one hand. Penny hesitatingly reached inside and grabbed Colby's belt around his trousers. "Pull!" Erica grunted as she pushed against his good shoulder. His 180 pounds of deadweight seemed as though it would not budge. Penny strained to move the body, the veins on her arms popping up against her thin skin. Slowly he started to slide across the vinyl seat. Then suddenly the momentum gathered and the body slid over the seat and dangled halfway out of the car. Penny flew backward against the Toyota as Colby came toward her. She looked at Erica, still inside the Cadillac, and wondered whether she could get inside the Toyota, start the engine, and drive away before Erica could climb over the body and get out of the Cadillac. Her eyes gave away her thoughts. "Don't even think about it, stupid!" Erica screamed at her. "I can use this better that you can do your nails, honey. You wouldn't make it inside the car before I splattered you all over your daughter's window."

Penny looked over her shoulder at Agatha. The child was wide-eyed, staring at her mother. Penny had never seen her so panicked. She turned back toward Erica.

"I wasn't thinking—"

"Save the bullshit."

Erica climbed over the top of Colby, carefully pointing the gun in Penny's direction. A motorcycle zoomed past the parked cars but didn't even take notice of the events on the road's shoulder. It appeared to be two stalled cars and a couple of women helping each other. Colby's body was hidden from the roadway by the passenger side of the Cadillac. Again, Erica surveyed the road, and when she was convinced that no traffic was in sight, she bent over the body and placed her hand along his throat. She felt the steady and strong beat. "You'll be okay," she murmured to him. Gently she ran her fingers along the side of his face and then looked at Penny.

"C'mon, we just have to get him into your car. Let's do it right now, because if the police arrive while I am still here, you're going to be involved in one hell of a shootout. Honey, there's no way they're going to care where they shoot. So let's get out of here."

Penny reached down and grabbed him around the waist. On one of her hands she felt a cool film of blood spread across her palm. She felt nauseous but summoned her strength. She had to be strong for Agatha. If it was the only way she could survive, she was determined to pull this man into her car. His body seemed easier to move, the vinyl of the car's seat no longer sticking to his bare skin. His legs slid from the car and his head lightly hit the concrete as they pushed him flat. Erica looked at Penny.

"I'm going to put this gun inside the waistband of my trousers. If you try anything, you better be damn sure that you are going to beat me to it. Are you in a gambling mood?"

Penny shook her head no.

"Good." Erica reached over and opened the rear door on the Toyota's passenger side. Then she bent and placed her hands under Colby's armpits. "Grab him by the legs and push up and toward the car as I pull." Together they grunted and strained under his weight. But slowly he was lifted several inches into the air and together they shuffled the couple of feet toward the Toyota. Erica backed into the car, stooping her head low, and when Colby was halfway in she rested his torso and pulled the pistol from her trousers. She climbed over his body, joined Penny outside, and helped twist his legs into the car. The Toyota's rear seat was small and he was crammed into half the space. Erica studied him for a moment. It might not be very comfortable, but the bleeding would slow now that his torso was higher than the rest of his body. She could apply a bandage while they drove.

"Nice work." Erica turned toward Penny. "Now get inside and start driving."

"Where do you want to go?" Penny felt as though it were a nightmare. She hoped that any moment she would wake up and Erica and the bleeding man would be gone.

Erica leaned inside the Toyota and reached into the front seat. She grabbed Penny's purse and shook the contents onto the rear floor mat. Reaching for the wallet, she flipped it open with one hand, and a plastic row of credit cards unfurled. Holding it near her face, she spotted the right card—the driver's license.

"Let's see now. I think we'll go to 1074 Paradise Drive in Sausalito. What do you think of that?"

Erica had chosen Penny's home. She saw the fright settle across her hostage's face. It horrified Penny. It meant the ordeal was not going to end quickly. She was not just going to transport these people to another place, but they were now about to invade her home. They were going to bring the terror into her household. "But I can take you anywhere you—"

"Shut up and get inside! Where I want to go is where I just told you. And I know this area as well as you do. One wrong turn, one mistake on the way home, and I'll kill you as certainly as I am standing here. Understood?"

Penny nodded and began walking toward the driver's side. Erica had bluffed about knowing the area. She knew Sausalito was across the Golden Gate Bridge, but that was the extent of her knowledge. She would have no idea if Penny drove toward a police station instead of her house. But she figured that the bluff would work. Penny would have to risk a bullet in the head if she wanted to test Erica's credibility.

As the engine to the Toyota kicked on, Erica propped herself in the back seat and pulled off her pantyhose. She then swiveled and faced Colby, using the nylon to form a bandage on his wounded shoulder. Penny pulled the car around the Cadillac and onto Bay Street. The rear speaker of the car radio, which had been playing since the ignition was turned on, was blaring a Billy Joel ballad. Erica needed silence to concentrate.

"Will you turn that goddamn—"

Her words were cut short by the sound of a ticker tape, which interrupted the rock and roll. "This is a special KNEW news bulletin. A San Francisco police spokesperson has just reported that Father Enrique Vasquez, the priest who opposed the military abuses in El Salvador, was the victim of an attempted assassination today during his visit to San Francisco. Details are sketchy at this time, but it appears that two assassins, a man and a woman according to witnesses, were waiting for Father Vasquez in his room at the Hyatt Regency. The attempted assassination follows a threat against the priest's life by an unidentified terrorist group. The threat was made to the San Francisco police department, who were in the process of providing extra security to Father Vasquez when they stumbled across the assassination in progress. At this time, Father Vasquez is in emergency surgery at St. Mary's Hospital. At least two police officers and five hotel employees were also shot in the melee at the Hyatt. Their conditions are not known at this moment. Both of the assassins, one of whom might have been wounded, escaped in a burgundy 1980 Cadillac DeVille, license number A574985. We repeat, the attempted assassins of Father Vasquez are last reported driving a 1980 burgundy Cadillac DeVille, license number A574985.

"We repeat, an assassination attempt against Father Enrique Vasquez, the visiting antiwar prelate from El Salvador, has apparently been foiled while in progress. We will update you on this important, breaking story as it develops."

Billy Joel was in the final refrains of his song. "Turn that off, now!" Penny's trembling arm reached over and flipped the knob silencing the radio. The car was absolutely quiet, except for the labored breathing of Agatha, sitting rigidly in her seat. Erica glanced into the rearview mirror, and stared into Penny's eyes. Although they were focused on the road, they were filled with terror. The realization that she was captive to political assassins had added to her sense of horror.

But if Penny had glanced into the mirror and looked at Erica she would have seen a totally different picture of the woman who confronted her outside the car just moments earlier. Relief had spread across Erica's face. They weren't blown. She and Colby were convinced their mission had been foiled in midstream. Their roles as intelligence agents who had used Father Vasquez in order to carry out a deadly operation would be known within days. Now they were protected. Evidently a threat on the good priest's life had been made to the police. They had fulfilled the roles of the assassins for the police and the rest of the world. There were still problems. Colby needed treatment. The virus had to be stored safely. The CIA was still combing the country for them. Now the San Francisco police, and probably the FBI, were looking for them as political murderers. And, according to the radio report, Vasquez was still alive. It probably happened when the police knocked on the door and the needle popped out of his arm as she was administering the potassium chloride. Damn it! What a lousy break. If he lived long enough to tell the police that he had never been at the mass; it could lead the investigation to the K-7 infection. They would know a lot about Colby's general appearance, height, build, and they might be able to pick up forensic evidence from the church. That would be bad. But she couldn't worry about it now. Their cover was still intact. People might be looking for the killers of Father Vasquez, but nobody was looking for Erica Cane and David Colby. Control would let them know if there was a problem in that regard, and so far everything was quiet.

She placed her jacket over Colby's chest, and held him against her as though he were sleeping. He was her first concern. She had to make him function. Then together they could worry about getting out of San Francisco. They had three more infection sites planned for their mission—Chicago, Dallas, and Miami. The one thing that was certain was that they were not going to make the 5:00 p.m. flight to Chicago. The K-7 infections would have to wait for Colby's recovery.

CHAPTER 17

Rome
December 17
10:00 p.m.

The telephone call that the bloodhound had had his young assistant place to Rome caused as much consternation as expected. It resulted in fifteen hours of panicked activity in almost half a dozen Italian towns. The official who received the call was indeed in the middle of supper, a consecrated time in Italian family life. The young Frenchman on the line from Paris had refused to telephone later or be dissuaded from passing his rather lengthy message in full. His superior, Jean-Claude Bouchet, badly needed the assistance of the Italian, and it had to be done immediately and off the record.

The man in Rome who got the first call was fifty-four-year-old Captain Vincenzo Pagannini, chief of the state police's antiterrorist squad. His five-foot, eight-inch frame carried nearly 250 pounds, most of the excess the result of the heavily oiled and cheesed pastas that he dined on nightly. Not that the chunk of fried parmesan for breakfast, or the afternoon pint of chocolate gelato, or daily bottle of red wine, didn't add to his expanding girth. When he was younger, despite a prominent nose, he had often been compared to the British actor James Mason. He still shared the bushy salt-and-pepper eyebrows, the thinning hair slicked straight back, but that was where the similarity ended. Now the years of second pasta portions with heaping servings of cream sauce had puffed the skin and expanded the features. He looked like a million other well-fed Italians, rushing blindly toward early, high-cholesterol deaths. But his new size fit more with his temperament. Always a brusque man, he now resembled the proverbial bull in a china shop. Born the tenth of twelve children in the northern industrial town of Modena, which is famous for producing Ferraris and Lamborghinis, he had had an exceptional career from his earliest days with the Italian police. Scrupulously honest, he had arrested his first provincial commander for distributing bribes for local land barons near Naples. It had caused a tremendous row within the police and in the press. Although many fellow officers viewed him as a traitor to the uniform, he earned the respect of millions of Italians, frustrated at seemingly endless civic and public graft. Over the years he developed into something of a folk hero. He had led the investigations that placed Antonio Abruzzi, the Don of Dons, into a Sicilian prison for life for heroin trafficking. He was photographed personally kicking in the door to the country villa, north of Florence, where Angelo Tarazzi, the speaker of the Italian senate, was held by kidnappers. When two Mafia lieutenants offered him $2 million, packed into three suitcases, just for looking the other way when a drug shipment arrived in Genoa, he pretended to take the money only so he could later break the drug connection and place nearly sixty-five high-ranking Mafiosi in jail.

Over the years he had also developed a reputation as a fearless cop. Shot by his enemies on three occasions, he often returned to work, highly profiled in the press, still covered with bandages and slings. Near the Spanish Steps in Rome he persuaded a bank robber to release twelve hostages and substituted himself. For nearly seven hours he sat with a sawed-off shotgun, called a Lupo, tied into his mouth. When the thief finally fell asleep, he calmly undid the booby trap set around his head and arrested the man. It was only natural that during the 1970s, when Italy was rocked by bombs and kidnappings from right-wing terrorists like the New Front and left-wing radicals like the Red Brigade, the police and public clamored for Pagannini as the best choice to fight them.

He was a thirty-three-year veteran of the arcane bureaucracy that constituted the Italian police. It was not difficult for him to understand why his French friend would want an urgent request to proceed out of channels. The paperwork to merely start a file could take two weeks in Rome, and near the Christmas holidays it was almost a certainty that nothing would be done until the new year. Not that the French were much better in their own cumbersome paperwork machinery. That was why Pagannini, Bouchet, and a dozen other investigators in Europe, in police, military, and intelligence agencies had developed and maintained an "old boy" network. It operated outside the normal bureaucracy. Based on an intricate web of friendships and loyalties, the network facilitated multijurisdictional investigations without ever raising the political hackle that many of the cases could generate. It was possible to follow up on a hunch or a lead in another country without ever having to clear the request with the foreign office or the diplomatic corps. Not only did the network make life easier for the men involved, but coupled with inevitable church holidays or government strikes in Italy, it was often the only way to get work done.

The incentive to cooperate in the network was the realization that it was only a matter of time until you needed the assistance of the person who was now asking a favor. Bouchet had helped on so many occasions that Pagannini had lost count. The bloodhound helped them track fleeing Mafiosi in the south of France as well as break an arm of the Red Brigade that had established a Parisian base of operations. On the other hand, Pagannini had come to the bloodhound's assistance on several delicate cases. His favorite one had been nearly five years ago when a Libyan terrorist, suspected of several Paris bombings, was quietly biding his time in the luxurious Italian lake country. Pagannini and several of his most brutish deputies had abducted the startled Libyan in the middle of the night, drugged him, and drove him across the French border in the rear trunk of an Alfa Romeo. When the Libyan woke the next day in Cannes, he found the bloodhound standing over him with an M-70 submachine gun. A French court later held that the Libyan crossed the border of his own free will and the case was marked as another tribute to Bouchet's sleuthing ability. It was certainly much better than trying to process a long extradition case that would either end in failure or the escape of the Libyan. Bouchet owed him one for that. Now he obviously intended to add to his debt list.

After receiving the call from Paris, Pagannini informed his wife and four children that he had to return to the office for emergency work. He truthfully told them that he didn't know what time he would be home. It took him nearly thirty minutes to drive to the downtown headquarters of the antiterrorist squad. Located on Via Frattina, only blocks from the Coliseum, the 1904 Beaux Arts building was reminiscent of many striking architectural gems that dotted the center of the Italian capital. All five floors of the simple beige stucco structure had been converted for the use of Italy's most advanced law enforcement agency. The two apparently wooden doors were reinforced with steel and concrete panels, making them bombproof to anything short of a bazooka blast from less than twenty feet. The windows were double-reinforced and bulletproof. The top of the building had heat and touch sensors so that anything weighing more than fifteen pounds would set off the interior's elaborate electronic warning system. Access was gained by visual identification from a high-definition video system which swept the front of the building. Unless the guard posted at a second-floor desk could verify the identity of the person seeking access, the reinforced front doors remained locked.

Pagannini parked his Fiat nearly two blocks away. He always chose a different location so that anyone planning an attack against him would not discover an easy pattern. Besides, his friends were always nagging him that he needed to exercise more. Do it. Just like the Americans, they used to tell him. Screw the Americans and pass the grated cheese he used to tell them. So on this night he decided to give in to their requests. He walked the two short blocks to his office.

A skeleton crew was staffing headquarters. He took the tiny, single-cabin elevator to the fourth floor. Another thirty pounds and he would have to enter the cabin sideways. He groaned when he flipped on the light in his office. Neatness was not his strength. Stacks of papers, file folders, and notepads were piled haphazardly, everywhere from the massive oak desk against the far wall to the chipped birch wood credenza, even to the floor, where the papers covered most of the high-tech, grey industrial carpet. Somewhere under the papers on his desk was a ten-year-old picture of his wife and their children. More important to him right now, somewhere under the desk papers was half a Kit-Kat bar, his favorite candy. One thing those Brits knew how to do was make good candy. Nice and sugary. Cadbury's chocolate cream-filled eggs for Easter. Mmmm. His mouth was watering. He had to go nearly a mile out of his way when driving home in order to stop by a food shop that stocked the Kit-Kats. To avoid the detour, he normally stocked up on them, at least two dozen at a time. It sounded like a lot but it really wasn't. He had a cup of espresso at least four times a day and would break off one of the slender wafers to enjoy with the dark, brown liquid. But this had been his last one. Half a bar left. He would have stopped in the morning on the way to work, but how was he to know he would be coming to the office so late at night.

He removed his beige overcoat and threw it across the tattered leather sofa that filled the left side of his office. He had barely made himself comfortable in the enormous, swivel leather chair behind his desk when a young staff officer knocked at the door and entered.

"The espresso you wanted, Captain."

He nodded. "Close the door on your way out."

He gently lifted the white china demitasse, which was stained around the edges to a light brown from thousands of espresso servings. While he sipped the steaming, bitter liquid, he searched frantically with his free hand through the clumsily stacked papers. In less than a minute he found it. He knew it from the soft texture, melting chocolate covering his fingertips. His pudgy fingers brought the candy out from the papers and into his mouth in almost a single movement. It was the trademark of an experienced and serious eater. A bite of chocolate, a sip of espresso, both hands working fast to the face. The only sound in the windowless room was munching and slurping. His eyes reflected his contentment. It was the least he deserved for having to cut his dinner short. But then of course it was polenta, a fried cornmeal saturated in butter and olive oil, and that would always be good cold the next day. He finished the Kit-Kat and put each of the fingers of his right hand into his mouth and sucked off the remnants of chocolate. He tipped his head back as far as it would bend to get the last drop of espresso. He felt it coming as he put the cup on the corner of his desk. The belch echoed off the walls of his office. Much better. He wiped his mouth with the back of his hand and picked up the telephone receiver. He was ready to work.

Bouchet had been waiting in his Washington hotel room for nearly an hour. He picked up the receiver on the first ring.

"Hello."

"Bouchet, is that you?"

"Yes. Vincenzo, thank you for calling me back. How are you, my friend?"

"Good, and you?"

"I could be better. I will be better if you can do something for me. But it isn't so easy."

"It better not be easy for having to get me to the office at almost 11:00 at night. I want a challenge tonight. The more difficult the better."

Bouchet smiled. He was always amused by Pagannini's style. The Italian blustered and bluffed his way past criminals and terrorists and even pulled the wool over many of his equals in law enforcement. He never admitted defeat and always jumped at the hardest cases, even if in his heart he felt it was hopeless.

"I have a body in Paris—"

"If you have a body in Paris what are you doing in Washington?"

"Vincenzo, I want you to solve one matter at a time for me."

"Just wondering. I was in Washington three years ago for the international police association convention. Have you been to the Lion d'Or restaurant? They have a rum mousse that I still dream about."

"Vincenzo, if you can help me on this matter, I promise to personally fly the rum mousse back to you."

"Then I will do it for you immediately!"

"Please, let me get this out."

"Of course, my friend, I am sorry, I just haven't spoken to you since the last time you needed a favor."

Again Bouchet smiled. Pagannini was just reminding him that he now was owed several favors. The bloodhound had no doubt that the Italian would call in his markers at the appropriate time.

"I have a body in Paris of a young white male that someone obviously left behind to remain unidentified. And, as you can imagine, that is exactly why I want to identify him. As we are speaking, I am having some photos and autopsy reports faxed to your office. Destroy the reports when you are finished, they are classified and you shouldn't be seeing them."

"But I shouldn't even be talking to you without getting approval from the provincial commander. Shall you get me permission to see the reports and I'll ask the commander when I can talk to you?"

"You know what I mean. Just don't leave them around your office as a serving tray for an order of zuppa inglese."

"Ah, you know my weaknesses." Pagannini wished that Bouchet would stop mentioning food. It was making him hungry and that made it difficult to concentrate on the details of the conversation.

"As you will see from the pictures of the corpse, we do not have any fingerprints or any face to go by."

Pagannini could tell this was going to be an ugly murder. He hated that. A gun in his face didn't scare him. A bomb under his car wouldn't faze him. But a lot of blood bothered him. He never admitted that to anyone of course, not even to his wife. He just endured the slightly queasy feeling that always overtook him when faced with a gory scene. It was a shame since the chocolate and espresso were just starting to digest and he worried the pictures would disturb his stomach.

"If the police were the only ones handling this case, it probably would have been closed and marked unsolved. But whoever left it in Paris did not expect the SDECE to find it. We have done all types of tests. We know the man was left-handed, and involved in a labor-type job, the muscle density and joint arrangement spelling that out. From his body we have a genetic print, but we don't have anything to match it to. His height, blood type, and all the other pertinent info in the report is coming to you."

"What about his teeth?"

"They were there. We are sending you a dental x-ray and a tooth chart. But the best identifiers are some features on the skeleton. There is an entire list of unusual fractures, which might help match him against a file. He also had a fairly rare bone disease, osteomyelitis, and that would narrow it down considerably."

"So why am I getting this wonderful file? Why me?"

"Because we can tell from his dental work there's silver and tin alloy in the fillings. That means the dental work was done in your country, probably the north. They don't use that damn stuff anywhere else in the world. It falls out usually in five or six years."

"Ah, that's a terrible slander. I've had six fillings like that for nearly forty years, and mine have never budged."

"Yours are probably impacted with food residue."

"Very funny, my friend. Tell me, how do you know that the dental work wasn't done by a northern Italian who moved from my country and did the work in his new adopted home? Or are you sure that it wasn't done that way to look as though it was Italian?"

"Because he had a mark, a tattoo, hidden beneath the pubic hair. Our lab reconstructed it. It's La Mano della Morte."

Pagannini's head straightened and his eyes widened. The news of the tattoo was like an electric charge to his body. He listened intently as Bouchet continued.

"Unless this corpse was impersonating an early Brigade leader, which I don't think he was, then we might have one of your early trouble-makers. I don't know anything more than that. Honestly. I have to follow my best hunches, just as you do in your work. My hunch tells me that the body is something you can find in your department. I feel a terrorist link. You just need to check your files against the incoming papers and let me know if you show any rough match against the physicals."

The hand of death. There were not many of those around. Pagannini knew most of them by heart. Some were dead. Others were in prison. Which one could be turning up in Paris? He couldn't imagine.

"I will check my own personal notes and files."

Bouchet did not take that offer lightly. Pagannini might be disorganized but he was a copious note taker. Matched with his excellent recall, he was a walking computer on the Italian terrorist trade.

"I would appreciate that."

"When do you need an answer?"

"Actually, I could have used it earlier today for a meeting. But considering I am just getting to you now, how about anytime tonight."

"You are kidding?"

"Unfortunately not, Vincenzo. It is very important."

"But I have almost 1800 terror suspects on file." Pagannini didn't mind starting the work tonight, but finishing it was a nightmare. It could certainly cut into breakfast.

"Just look for the match on the fractures. Just look for the osteomyelitis. That shouldn't be difficult. We're not talking about the latecomers, just the early players. That has to narrow it way down."

"That assumes that the file has the information. We might have a suspect who just doesn't have a complete file."

"I appreciate the shortcomings, Vincenzo. Please. I would not ask you at this hour if it was not urgent." There was silence for a moment. "I mean it when I say I will bring over the rum mousse."

"It's a deal. I will do my best and call you if I see anything that resembles your mysterious dead body. Again, Vincenzo Pagannini and the services of the state antiterrorist department will come to your assistance!" No one had ever accused him of modesty.

"Thank you."

"Do not mention it."

I won't, Bouchet thought, I am sure you will remind me.

Pagannini took the elevator to the second floor, the fax and telex room, to receive the photos. He had had enough exercise for one night. It was preferable to wait for the interminably slow elevator than move his quivering mass down the nearby flight of stairs.

The pictures were waiting for him. They were as gruesome as expected. He felt his stomach turning. But the young police lieutenant who was manning the electronic equipment was staring at him. Pagannini flashed one of the full body shots, in vivid, horrible color, toward the lieutenant. "This is what happens to Italians who get involved with the wrong people in Paris. Now I must clean up the matter." He shook his head as though dismayed by the burdens of his job.

"Can I be of any assistance, Captain?"

Pagannini looked at him intently for a moment. "Maybe you can help.

Do you have anything to nibble on? I had to skip my dinner to come in tonight, and I haven't had a thing to eat since lunch."

"No, Captain, but I can ask the rest of the staff."

"Well, don't leave your station unattended, but see if you can call around. If you find something, I would appreciate it."

"Of course, Captain."

Pagannini took the photos and printed pages back to the elevator and to his office, where he again closed the door behind him. As he settled into his leather chair, he pulled out the photos and placed them face-down on top of a stack of papers in the middle of his desk. He did not need to study the gruesome prints. What could they tell him? Was he going to identify the torso? Not likely. Instead, he reviewed the medical evidence gathered by the French. Blood type AB negative. That was rare. The teeth were filled with cavities as well as two caps on the lower left side. That was distinctive. Onto a separate piece of paper he marked the unusual characteristics from the skeleton—the fractures of the left ankle, right shoulder, the smashed index finger, the broken nose, and the two bullet wounds. He drew a line and under that wrote "osteo-myelitis." He knew that was the skeleton's most unusual characteristic. In the back of his memory he had a faint recollection of that disease having something to do with one of his suspects. Was it one of his suspects or someone he helped another country look for? He wasn't sure. His memory might be damned good, but he couldn't remember the details on every criminal and lowlife he had come across in the past thirty-three years.

He buzzed for the corporal on duty in the computer command room on the fifth floor. It sounded fancier than it really was—two large Olivetti 1130s, four printers, and a couple of desktop work stations. The computer room wasn't as important as the places it had access to—Interpol's main computer bank, the memory systems for the Italian police, and the declassified files for Italian intelligence. The corporal arrived in less than a minute.

"Corporal Gandolfo, take these papers with you. You haven't seen them, understand? Copy them and bring a set back to me. The full description of what we are looking for is in there. It's a single man, now dead. I want you to start searching army files for the past five years to see if there is anyone with his characteristics. If you get nothing with that, go back to the next five, and then if that turns up nothing, go back to the next five. He's estimated to be in his early thirties, so that should cover enough time. Let me know the moment you come up with anything."

"Yes, Captain. What file name does this go under?"

"None. Mark it as my personal request."

Gandolfo crisply saluted, spun on his heels, and walked toward the door. He was almost out of the office when Pagannini called to him. "Excuse me, Corporal."

He immediately spun around and came back into the office.

"I forgot to ask you. Do you have anything to snack on? I haven't eaten in a day."

"No, Captain, I am sorry. Lieutenant D'Orio already called me to ask."

"Dismissed." Pagannini waved his hand at him. Not one of them knew how to live right. How could they spend a night shift in this desolate building without packing food to maintain their strength? It didn't make any sense to him. No wonder they were all so emaciated. Gandolfo was pale and thin. Not enough meat on his six-foot frame to tempt a cannibal. He was probably a jogger. Pagannini shook his head in dismay. He didn't know what to make of the new talent in the police ranks. His stomach was grumbling. Maybe work would divert his hunger.

For the next two hours he pored through 100 of the 128 files he had gathered, all distinguished on the cover sheet with an imprint representing the hand of death. These were active files of early members who were still alive and not imprisoned somewhere. Almost every one had a complete medical history, either from service in the Italian army, from their first arrest, or from files appropriated from a local family doctor. None of them came close to matching Bouchet's corpse. He glanced at his watch. Nearly 1:00 a.m. He knew it would be slow going. Although he would finish the first batch of files in less than an hour, it would take him a couple of days to go through all of them. And he was still juggling three ongoing investigations about which the bloodhound would have no concern. But it was the holiday season, and he could probably delay them to the start of the new year. Slowly he shifted in the chair, perspiration having stuck his wool trousers to the tufted leather seat. He hated it when his pants soaked through. He rubbed his face with his hands. After he finished these files he would call it a night. Someone else in the department could always review the papers, but he did not like authorizing that unless he was there. These were his personal papers, filling three standing locked file cabinets. Each manila file was packed with his own notes and markings. They were different from the files maintained in the central computer system and he jealously guarded access to them. He would have entrusted his deputy of fifteen years, Gregorio, to plow through them, but he and his wife and three children were in Sardinia for the holidays. He should never have let him go on holiday. It was guaranteed that once you let your staff go away, the most important cases were sure to crop up.

There was a soft knock on the door. "Come in."

It was Gandolfo from the computer room. "Excuse me, Captain, but I have something for you."

"Excellent! Come inside, Corporal. Don't stand at the door. I won't bite. What did you discover? A match for the body?" Pagannini's voice showed a trace of excitement at the thought that his work could be over.

"No, Captain. Perenti, you know, the guard on the second floor . . ."

"Yes, spit it out, Corporal!"

"He had a bag of brazil nuts. I have taken what he had left." The young officer held up a clear plastic bag partly filled with lightly toasted nuts. A broad smile spread across Pagannini's face. "Excellent work, Corporal. I was feeling faint. This should give me a boost of energy. Especially if you will be so kind as to make me an espresso." He picked up his empty demitasse and offered it to Gandolfo.

"Of course, Captain."

As Pagannini handed him the cup, he asked, "How is the search going for a match on the body?"

"I have fed the computers all the pertinent information on the dead body and they are conducting a search through the army files first. It will take at least four to five hours."

"It's doing the search on its own?"

"Yes, Captain. It is like automatic pilot. It will stop once it gets to a file that matches and will pull the material for a hard copy. Oh, speaking of hard copy, I have the photocopy of the material you gave me. I must return it to you."

"Do this instead. Get me the espresso, then retrieve the papers, and then why don't you join me here in the office. I would like you to review some files with me for the next hour or so. It will cut our time in half. And meanwhile we won't lose anything upstairs. You can check the computers' progress every twenty minutes or so."

"Yes, Captain."

Pagannini waved his hand to dismiss the young officer. He turned to leave. Pagannini cleared his throat. "Excuse me. Corporal. The nuts."

"Oh yes, Captain, I'm sorry, I wasn't thinking." He dashed to the desk and placed the bag directly into Pagannini's chubby hand.

"Go," Pagannini commanded.

They were all so eager to please him. At times like this it was useful. But at other times their fawning drove him crazy. His wife told him it was the curse of celebrity status. Maybe so, but it was a price that he was not always willing to pay. He leaned back in his chair, stretching his arms over his head, the chair creaking under the strain of his shifting weight. What set of files should Gandolfo review? He opened the plastic bag and grabbed a handful of nuts. He could feel the salt on them. Good. The unsalted ones were tasteless. He popped the entire handful into his mouth. It was like water to a parched tree, his mouth salivating at the introduction of food. He thought of the files while he ate. Maybe Gandolfo could begin reviewing those without a tattoo identification. It was possible that the tattoo had been missed. Maybe the suspect had it removed before he was arrested or first came to the attention of the police. In that case it might not be in his file. Pagannini leaned over the desk, crunching his shoulders and resting his chin in one hand while he continued to throw nuts into his mouth with the other hand. How could he have missed a tattoo? The hand of death was a critical mark as far as the antiterrorist squad was concerned. It would be tantamount to overlooking the fact that Adolf Hitler was also a Nazi party member. Over the years he had developed key informants inside the terror groups. It was one of the reasons the Italian authorities had such success in cracking the back of the assorted anarchists and killers. Those informants had supplied information on all of the early founders of the left- and right-wing cells. He would be shocked to have missed one. Maybe his mistake was in searching only the files of those he knew to be free. More than eighty were incarcerated, most in Italy. Yet he would know if any of those in Italy had recently escaped. None had. If one had escaped from another country, he would be one of the first to be informed. But screw-ups had taken place before. It was possible that one of them had escaped and turned up dead in Paris. Unlikely, but possible. Yet he couldn't overlook the chance, no matter how slight. He looked down at the bag. Not a nut left. Damn it. It was barely enough for a church mouse. What type of snack was this? He lifted his hand out of the bag and one by one sucked the salt from his fingertips. A light knock on the door again interrupted his thoughts.

"Captain," Gandolfo muttered as he walked in, holding the demitasse in one hand and a sheaf of papers in the other. He placed the espresso on a clear patch of wood on top of the cluttered desk. "Where do you want me to put these, Captain?" Pagannini grabbed the cup of steaming coffee, brought it to his lips, and indicated with his other hand for the corporal to wait one moment. He blew on the hot liquid and then slurped half the cup down his throat. "Ah, *perfetto*, Corporal, you make a good espresso." The young officer smiled at the compliment. He stood in front of the desk still holding out the papers. "Oh, the papers. Any- where. Put them anywhere." Pagannini waved his hand over the room.

"I want you to help me review these files. They have my personal notes in each of them. If you have trouble reading any of my hand- writing, just ask me. There"—he pointed with his thick arm to the far file cabinet—"in the top drawer, in the first section, is a group of about eighty files. Take those and start reviewing them over there on the sofa. See if you come across anything that matches the description of this dead body. I would get the files for you, but my leg has been bothering me recently." He had had enough exercise for one night. The corporal was thirty years his junior.

"No problem, Captain." The young officer carefully walked around the stacks of paper piled on the floor, careful not to disturb any of them, and finally reached the far cabinet. He grabbed a large handful of manila envelopes and proceeded to the sofa where he spread out the papers.

They sat in silence for the next fifteen minutes. The only sound was the occasional burp from Pagannini. For some reason the salt and es- presso had not settled well in his stomach. He probably didn't have enough polenta earlier in the night. He knew when he needed more food. He counted the number of files still in front of him. Twelve. He would be home in no time.

"Captain!" The corporal slowly rose from the sofa while looking intently inside a manila envelope. "Captain, I think I might have found something." His voice trembled with excitement. Also with nervous- ness, since he did not want to bother Pagannini with a false alarm.

"Don't just stand there, Corporal. Let me see it."

The young officer gingerly stepped over the papers on the floor and approached Pagannini. He handed him the file. "Look, Captain, the right age, blood type, osteomyelitis, everything."

"Shhh." Pagannini held up his hand to indicate silence. He looked inside the file. There was the mark of the hand of death. The medical file was not included in its entirety. Only a yellow sheet of paper with his own notes. He did that on some of the files, but usually when they were inactive. He quickly skimmed the yellow sheet. Blood type—AB negative. Born March 10, 1951. Distinguishing medical characteristics under the heading "X-Rays": broken nose, right finger, left ankle, shoulder. And then he saw it. Prominently marked in red ink. "Osteomyelitis. Visible bone damage in right hip."

"This is it!" Pagannini forgot for a second that the young officer was in the room. He was totally absorbed with the file. He flipped it closed to look at the cover. Salvatore Amalfi.

"Idiot!" Pagannini swiveled the chair toward the corporal. "Stupid! This is not an active file! You grabbed the files of the dead terrorists. Amalfi was killed nearly five years ago when a bomb he was working on blew up, destroying him and half the townhouse he was in! Idiot!"

"But Captain . . ."

"But what! You think he was resurrected from the dead to appear in Paris a couple of days ago?"

Gandolfo was clearly worried that he had made a major mistake. He stammered. "But, Captain, the match is so close."

"Yes, but they are only my rough notes. The full medical record is never kept in the files of the dead ones. There are no dental records here, nothing else. Go pull Amalfi's file from the army computer. Now. Then we will see the inconsistencies. Then I will show you why you are an idiot!" He waved his hand at the shaking corporal. Gandolfo spun on his heels and left the office.

Fool. Where was his deputy when he needed him? He trusts someone to review his own files and the fool can't even grab the right ones. Looking through the records of a dead man. Pagannini shook his head. He opened the file and looked at it again. Amalfi was thirty-three when he was killed. That's where he had remembered something about osteomyelitis. Now it made sense to him. He looked at the attached internal report. Fifteen pounds of plastic explosive had blown out two floors of an old townhouse in the south of Rome. No body was discovered. Just fragments of skin and bones. The match for Amalfi came from the reconstructed dental work. The teeth found at the scene matched. Amalfi was dead. He flipped the file into the center of his desk. What was he supposed to believe, that the man had come back from the grave? Preposterous.

The young corporal was back in less than fifteen minutes. He knocked on the door. "Come in," Pagannini bellowed. "Do you have the army medical file?"

"Yes, Captain."

"And what inconsistencies does it show to the body in Paris?" Pagannini reached out and grabbed the file from the young officer's hands.

"It shows every possible inconsistency, Captain."

"What?" He started to look at the computer printout.

"According to the army medical file, your notes are wrong."

"What?"

"His blood type is O positive, he did not have the fractures you listed, and he does not show any x-ray sign of that disease, oste—"

"Wait a minute. This is a different file. You've pulled the wrong file."

"No, sir. I checked it twice myself. It is Amalfi's file."

Pagannini flipped through the report. Nothing matched his yellow notes. Impossible. He might be disorganized, but he was scrupulous about one thing—the right notes on the right suspect always ended up together. Having seen the file jogged his memory. He distinctly remembered the osteomyelitis issue with Amalfi. They had looked for the right hip bone as an extra source of death confirmation. But when they had enough from the teeth, they no longer needed it. The army had to make a mistake. The age of the person in the army file was right, so were the general descriptions of size, weight, hair, and eye color. But the internal characteristics were all off. It was impossible.

"The army has made a mistake, Corporal. This file is misplaced under Amalfi's name. I know he was arrested in the late 1970s. Pull the central police file on him."

"After I saw the inconsistencies in the army report, I took the liberty of doing that, Captain. Here it is."

He offered a second computer printout to Pagannini, who hurriedly grabbed it from his hand. "It is an exact match of the army report. Your notes must be wrong."

Pagannini looked up at the corporal and stared into his eyes. The corporal jumped back for a second, the severity of the look startling him. It had been another error to suggest the mistake was on the part of the captain.

"Corporal, I do not make such fundamental mistakes. That is exactly why I keep my own personal files on this slime."

With a great effort he placed both his hands on the desk and pushed himself up from the chair. "Corporal, make both of us a double espresso. This is going to be a long night. We are going to find out what the hell is going on here."

CHAPTER 18 ⇐══════━━━━━━━

San Francisco
December 17
8:00 p.m.

McGinnis looked back at the cathedral one final time. What a weird church, he thought as he shook his head in disapproval. "You drive, kid," he yelled to Harris, tossing a jangle of keys over the hood of the black Ford Thunderbird.

"But I don't know the city like you do," Harris replied as he deftly snatched the keys from midair.

"I'll tell you the directions. I just want to rest for a couple of minutes."

"Rest" was an understatement. McGinnis had just spent five hours in a military transport that was intended to move heavy equipment, not delicate flesh-and-blood merchandise. He understood the security reasons for the military flight, but it didn't mean that he couldn't wish it had been a civilian carrier. You only had to fly in the belly of one of the Army's green monsters to appreciate the luxurious comfort of a fifteen-inch wide seat on a wide-body. He often heard other passengers complain about the cramped conditions in the economy section. They had obviously never been in active duty in a war zone. He gently rubbed his left side, trying to massage away a small cramp. Probably from his kidneys getting bounced around for several hours.

He glanced at Harris. At least boy wonder was staying quiet. The lack of sleep was catching up to both of them. It was already 11:00 p.m. eastern time, and there was half a day of investigative work ahead of them.

They had been met at the airport by a local Company agent, a jerk McGinnis had served with on a European operation nearly ten years ago. McGinnis took the briefing papers and excused him—the last thing he needed was a damn Agency chauffeur sticking with him everywhere he went in San Francisco. Hell, he knew the city by the bay as well as any place in the States. He had fallen in love with its natural beauty more than twenty years ago when he and his wife had spent their honeymoon there. They had wanted to go to Hawaii but couldn't afford the longer trip. San Francisco turned out to be an unexpected delight. They spent their days along the cool Pacific beach and their evenings over fresh, cracked crab and endless bottles of locally grown wine. It was the ideal romantic start for a marriage. Unfortunately, it was downhill after the first two weeks. Being back at work, usually halfway around the globe, had a lot to do with that. But McGinnis and his wife had visited San Francisco on three more vacations, and each rekindled part of that early magic. The Agency had also sent him through at least half a dozen times on official assignments. He was sure of one thing— he did not need a driver whom he didn't like and who didn't know a useful thing about the case.

The sealed confidential reports told him everything he needed to know. He opened the cover and flipped through the pages once again. During their flight, Hodson had obviously had the computers working overtime. The new infection had been isolated to the top of Geary Boulevard, the location occupied by the Roman Catholic cathedral. He had learned all about the morning mass filled with visiting dignitaries and press. He also knew that the priest who said the mass was in critical condition at St. Mary's Hospital, the subject of an assassination attempt within an hour of the mass's completion. Two murderers had gotten away, but left behind a long trail of evidence. The CIA had already moved its forensic squads onto the scenes. Members of the cleaning team had swept the church, the hotel, and the getaway car found abandoned under the Bay Bridge. San Francisco police and the local FBI had been notified by Washington that national security issues might be involved in the attempted assassination, and that as a result, CIA personnel would be part of the investigation. None of the other law enforcement personnel spoke to the CIA agents. Spooks were never very friendly. Small talk was not their forte.

McGinnis pointed his finger across the dashboard and Harris made another left turn.

"So what do you think, McGinnis? Is this the same guy we were dealing with in New York?" Harris looked at his quiet partner to make sure he was paying attention.

McGinnis was staring out the window. A couple of black streetwalkers had attracted his partner's attention, although Harris was sure the gaudy but bulky "women" were transvestites. "Hey, McGinnis . . ."

"Yeah, yeah, I heard you, keep your hat on," McGinnis mumbled as he watched the passing flesh trade. "Well, so far, there are a lot of possibilities." He straightened in his seat, rubbed both of his hands over his face as if the vigorous shake would activate his brain, and then turned toward Harris.

"They told us at the church that the priest was left alone for some ten minutes before the mass started. Now our boys know that the heaviest concentration of the virus is around the tabernacle safe where the communion hosts were kept. That means the fucking communion probably passed the K-7 into the audience. We also know that by the time the spectrum system picked up the first atmospheric violation, the priest had already arrived at the church."

"So you think this Vasquez is part of the plot?"

"Maybe. Maybe not. Hard to say from what we know. It's possible that our warning buzzers didn't start ringing the exact second that K-7 was first in the atmosphere. In that case, the infection might have happened just minutes before Vasquez arrived, and then our dear father is innocent. Then the entire church staff, the altar boys, and some of the local bigwigs are suspect. But headquarters is already running a background check on all of those possible bad guys, so we should know shortly whether there's anything unusual with that group.

"The second possibility is that the priest was involved, but was not part of the original team."

"You mean he was forced to do it?"

"No. From the little background they gave us on Vasquez, you couldn't force him to do anything. If he didn't take any crap from the generalissimos in his own country, I don't think he would take it from anybody here. If they threatened to kill him, he probably would have said a Hail Mary and then told them he was ready. Even if they were holding a hostage, somebody close to him, he wouldn't have sprayed a virus that would kill hundreds or thousands of people."

"Unless he didn't know it was a virus."

"Yea, it's possible. But unlikely. Hey, turn left here—another half a mile and we'll be right at the hotel. It'll be on the left-hand side. What was I saying?"

"You were telling me why you didn't think it was likely that he might have passed something not knowing it was a virus."

"Oh, yeah. Why would he voluntarily spray anything over something as holy as the hosts for a communion service? He wouldn't do it just to be a nice guy. And if they forced him by threatening him or kidnapping someone close to him, then he's sure as hell going to know that the thing they are dying for him to spray on the hosts can't be very good for you. These aren't the type of people who are going to give you a simple flavoring agent."

"So then you think he did it because he's part of their team?"

"No, I didn't say that. I just said I don't think they forced him to do it. And I don't know if someone else sprayed it before he got there. But my gut instinct tells me that he's not our guy. I mean, look at the capsule summary pulled by Phillips's department—this guy's clean. He isn't involved with any group or person that looks like a likely candidate to spread K-7 around our country. There are no Soviet connections. I just don't think he's our boy." McGinnis held his arm straight toward the windshield and pointed to the left. "There it is." Harris pulled into the Hyatt's underground garage.

They surveyed the cordoned-off portion of the lobby where the afternoon's shooting had taken place. Remnants of shattered glass, and eggplant-colored splotches marking the spots where bodies had crumpled were vivid testament to the ferocity of the battle. Harris paused for a second by the police guard in front of the elevator. It was as though he was trying to absorb the details of the fight.

"C'mon, kid. You can get souvenirs later." McGinnis tapped him on the shoulder. They entered the elevator and the police escort took them to the nineteenth floor. If the lobby looked bad, the nineteenth floor looked like a battle zone. They walked to the priest's room, past the uniformed police and suit-and-tie FBI agents, following the dots of blood along the carpet as their guide.

"Richard, I heard you were coming." It was Larry Novak, part of the Company's West Coast forensic team. Barely five-feet, five-inches, bald, and slightly overweight, he looked more like an insurance salesman than an intelligence agent. Novak had spent most of his career trying to transfer to Washington, exactly where McGinnis thought all careers ended from an overdose of boredom. But then McGinnis never thought of poring over stitches of fabric, droplets of blood, and microscopic traces of flesh and hair as being the most exciting work in the Company. But the fellows on the forensic team loved the detailed detective work they reconstructed from evidently empty locations. Novak was good; McGinnis knew that from earlier work on the Coast. He walked over toward McGinnis and Harris. Dressed in a dark grey three-button suit, starched white button-down shirt, navy-blue-and-maroon club tie, and a pair of spit-shined black wingtips at least a half size too big, Novak looked the image of the Washington bureaucrat that he so emulated. It only took a moment for Harris to decide he preferred the bloodhound's tailored clothes. Novak walked past Harris, reached out to grab McGinnis's hand, and gave it a hearty shake. "When I heard you were coming, I knew there must be something big going on."

"Nothing big, Larry. They just knew I liked it out here so much they decided to let me combine some business and work."

Novak patted McGinnis's blue sport jacket near the left armpit. He felt the handle of the Colt .45 automatic. "Sure. Business and pleasure. Going to do a little sport hunting while you're here?"

"Maybe." McGinnis wasn't in a joking mood. He didn't even crack a smile. Novak picked up the cue and turned to business.

"Aren't you going to introduce me?"

"Yea. This is Jimmy Harris, we're working this together."

Harris could have fallen over backward from shock. It must be the lack of sleep. McGinnis actually telling an old Company buddy that they were partners and not concluding it with some sarcastic remark. Harris reached for Novak's hand, but Novak had already turned around as he started to talk.

"Nice to meet you. Here, follow me, you two, I'll tell you what we've got so far."

They followed him into the room, past large blotches of dark red splashed about the corridor. Both McGinnis and Harris noticed the holes in the doorjamb from the stray bullets.

"We need this room for a minute," Novak announced to two uni-formed police. They looked at him with disdain, but without saying a word they quickly filed outside. Typical, McGinnis thought. Other law enforcement agencies hated the intrusion of Central Intelligence. CIA could make them do cartwheels under the guise of national security and the cops and FBI would have to do it. In their hearts they knew they had lost control of the investigation once the first spook came through the door with a federal authorization order. They would have liked to have given Novak a big "fuck you" but they had more common sense than frustration and instead they just followed his orders. Novak closed the door behind them. He faced McGinnis and Harris, who were studying an assortment of physical evidence stored in clear plastic bags, gathered in the center of the bed.

"We found a gold mine here. Five forensic traces, one belonging to a bellboy, now dead, and one to a hotel maid. The other three are in the preliminary genetic blowup phase, but we think we see where they are going. One belongs to the priest who was almost killed, that we're certain of. As for the other two, the beginning of the genetic pattern is matching, identically, the patterns we have created for two people you are evidently looking for; David Colby and Erica Cane."

McGinnis felt like someone had given him an injection of caffeine. His heart started pumping a little faster and he felt his senses sharpen. So they were here! He knew it! When he had entered the hotel lobby, he had felt it. His instincts told him that they had been in the priest's room. He couldn't explain the feeling. It was a gut reaction, an instinct that he always had. It was a blessing for intelligence work. There really was something to be said for working on your hunches. Especially if they were good. And his had never failed him yet. He knew that his quarry had moved on from New York, completed a new infection in San Francisco, and had somehow gotten involved with the priest. Novak continued.

"I don't know why you are looking for these two people, but as you know we have a team waiting for their return at the Fairmont Hotel, where there is a room reserved under their names. We have covertly entered the room and verified that they still have clothes there and they did stay there at least one night. We have pulled tracings from that room and are running a genetic print to make sure that these are all the same people."

"Anything else found at the Fairmont?" McGinnis turned to face Novak.

"No. Although the search was a light one. We didn't want to disturb so much that if they come back they would know we've been there."

"I want to go over there in a bit and do a full search. They aren't going to be coming back to the hotel if they were here. They are in real trouble. They can't play tourists anymore."

"Do you want me to tell the team at the Fairmont to start the search now?"

"No. I want to be there. Let's finish here, then I want to stop at the hospital where the good father is, and then I will go to the Fairmont. When Harris and I leave here you can notify them we will be there in forty-five minutes."

"Fine. Let me summarize quickly what else we have found in this room in the early phases. This"—he pointed to a group of glass splinters in a plastic bag on the bed—"surprised me. It has tracings of one of the most sophisticated cleaning solvents on the market. Not commercially available, it's so new that only a handful of countries have it."

Harris stared at the clear bag. "What type of cleaning solvent?"

"For makeup."

McGinnis looked up in surprise. Novak continued. "What's more, we have found traces of dark bronzing powder, a brown hair tint, and a state-of-the-art cover makeup, probably used to minimize a birthmark, scar, or maybe even a bad bruise. Also, traces of glue and some synthetic hairs from a wig."

"Did the priest have any makeup on him?" McGinnis asked.

"Not a trace."

It was a missing part of the puzzle, but now it made sense. He had not seriously considered the possibility—a disguise. The elusive Colby most likely cast as the blind priest. The more the thoughts raced through his head, the more sense it made. Handicapped victims were the easiest to mimic. The handicap gave the impostor a trait to emphasize. He thought back to the descriptions given to them at the cathedral—everyone seemed to emphasize the priest's blindness. They had all focused on the disability, exactly as the impostor had wanted them to. They vividly recalled how he had fallen on two occasions. A good stunt, McGinnis thought, but they could not remember in detail what he looked like. They merely said he looked exactly like his newspaper photo. Of course he would. It was probably that picture or a similar one that Colby had used to model himself after. The cover makeup was an interesting development. Maybe Colby sported a birthmark or a scar. That could help narrow the search for the right suspect, assuming the real Colby was in the Company's files and correctly listed with distinguishing marks.

Harris interrupted his thoughts. "You're thinking the same thing I am. Colby was the fellow in the church."

McGinnis nodded his agreement and then addressed Novak. "What has put the priest near death?"

"Potassium chloride, we think. We've got some chemical crystallization at a needle mark discovered on his arm. It looks like PC. We should have that confirmed within the hour."

Harris broke in. "But that stuff is as deadly as it comes."

"That's why we are hesitant in making a positive ID of the drug. But it appears to be that. We can only imagine that the cops interrupted at the exact moment the PC was being injected. Not all of it may have been forced into his vein."

Harris looked at McGinnis. "There was no political assassination. Colby and Cane were here as part of their mission. The priest was merely a way to get into the mass."

"Exactly." McGinnis was trying to imagine where they had fled after the unexpected gunfight. "Their plans certainly did not include this," he said as he swept his hand across the bullet-ridden room.

"That's for sure," replied Novak. He walked toward the door. "You see this spot of blood?" He leaned over and pointed at a red circle halfway between the bathroom and the doorway. "That blood is matching the genetic tracings for your Colby. So far, that is. The computers are still an hour away from a full DNA match, but it looks like it's going to be dead on. The same blood is in the corridor, the elevator, outside the front of the hotel, and also in the recovered car the two would-be murderers escaped in. If it's your Colby, then he's in pretty bad shape."

"Any descriptions from hotel staff?"

"We are still questioning them. One bellboy remembers taking them upstairs when they checked in early today. He remembers it because the priest was blind and it stuck in his mind. Two people were helping the priest at the time—probably the two you are looking for. He has a vague description of both. He's at FBI headquarters trying to reconstruct a look-alike photo on a computer screen."

"Why not show him some of our file photos of Soviet and eastern bloc agents?" Harris inquired.

"We don't have clearance for that yet. Finch doesn't want any civilian, aside from the local cops and FBI agents, to know we are here. Finch said the kid should come up with a description on his own. We can decide, independently, whether it looks like someone we know."

"Anything else of interest?" McGinnis looked into the bathroom but shouted the question over his shoulder.

"Nothing that we've come up with yet. You have a radio in your car?"

"Yep."

"Then I'll buzz you the minute we get the full DNA printout or if we scoop up something else here. By the way, can you tell me anything about what is going on with these two you're looking for? Everybody back at headquarters is so damn secretive it makes you think something major is under way."

"Would I look this calm if something major was under way?" McGinnis gave his first smile. It masked his uneasiness. "You know them at headquarters. Every year they classify more reports and cut out the number of people who know about operations. They are just leak paranoid, that's all. It's no big deal. Just a couple of people we would very much like to talk to."

"Oh, shit, Richard, there is one more thing I almost forgot to tell you. It's an important one. The bullets they used are for a SIG Sauer P226, a real nice piece."

McGinnis nodded. "I know it well. But it's a common gun."

"The gun may be common, but they were carrying some pretty damn sophisticated bullets. Theirs were hollow-domed, wad-cutters, with a densely packed capsule of mercury in the tip. They are like minibombs, exploding on impact and causing the damage of a .44 magnum, plus a little extra oomph. There aren't many special purveyors in the U.S. that can supply that type of hardware. One of the best is located in the Berkeley hills, a former special forces guy that sells his stuff to the highest bidder."

"Johnny Zarem?" McGinnis looked up from the front of the room.

"Exactly. Well, Zarem isn't anywhere to be found. His car—a nice, sparkling new Jaguar—is gone, and he's got a stack of phone messages that haven't been picked up in a day. We're still looking for him to see if he might be able to tell us something about how those type of bullets ended up in his own backyard. I'll let you know when we locate him."

"That's it?"

"That's it. For now."

McGinnis clapped Novak on the back as they walked down the hallway toward the elevators. Harris walked a couple of feet behind, closely studying the blood-splattered and bullet-ridden walls. "You can go back in when you're ready," Novak nodded to the two policemen. They broke a hushed conversation near the elevator bank and slowly drifted back to the room.

"You didn't take that from the room, did you?" Novak was staring at a paper clip in Harris's right hand.

McGinnis answered for him. "The kid has an unlimited supply of those. You want one?"

Novak ignored the rhetorical question. "I just wanted to make sure we weren't losing any possible evidence."

The elevator arrived, the police escort still inside. McGinnis spoke as he backed into the cabin. "Have you scraped the toilet yet, Larry?

Maybe you can tell me what they had for lunch and I will know where to go and ask some more questions?''

Novak looked puzzled, unsure for a second whether the request was real. Then he saw the glint in McGinnis's eyes. "You bastard, very funny . . ." The door closed as Novak shook his head and chuckled to himself.

"What do you think?" Harris asked.

McGinnis held his hand up to indicate silence. He didn't want to talk in front of the police operator.

Within five minutes they were inside the car and back on the city streets. This time McGinnis drove, no longer needing the rest after the conversation with Novak had charged his senses.

"McGinnis, why the hell would this Colby and Cane come all the way across the country to plant an infection inside a church?"

"If we knew that we'd be a lot closer to knowing who they were."

"But doesn't it seem a lot easier to you to just spray the damn virus in the middle of the street in a couple of large cities and infect masses of people?"

"Sure it does. If your goal is to kill off half the nation. But then you don't just have a two-person team do something like that. If they wanted to wipe us out, they would have taken the damn virus back to Russia and worked on it for a couple of years until they duplicated it. It wouldn't have been that difficult once they broke down the chemical components. Even Finch told us they only had enough supply to infect two to four million people. That's the worst case scenario—then it has to spread on its own. Anything can happen in the meantime. A vaccine, a cure, anything. So they aren't here to wipe out the entire U.S. of A. They would have done it very differently. Instead, they are here to cause some havoc. And they are certainly doing that. They obviously picked these targets a long time ago. You don't pull off operations as complex as the Waldorf job and the church caper without months of detailed advance planning. They almost seem to have picked targets that won't fit into a pattern, knowing then we have virtually no chance of figuring out where they will strike next."

"Do you think the operation by these two agents might be unauthorized? Maybe they have broken with the KGB and are doing it on their own?"

"Like I told you, anything's possible in this business. But I would be damn surprised if they were able to do this type of advance preparation without the support of the entire KGB. I would also think that Ivan would have pulled these two in by now if they were acting on their own."

Harris looked at McGinnis, the dull green lights from the dashboard casting an eerie pallor over his skin. "Unless the Russkies are looking for them and are having as much luck as we are."

"Maybe." They stopped at a red traffic light. "We're going to drive ourselves crazy speculating on why they are here. Instead we have to figure out where they are. Let's see if there is anything going on at the hospital. If not, maybe we can just shoot over to the hotel and see what their room holds."

McGinnis reached over with his right arm and unlatched a black aluminum box sandwiched underneath the dashboard. He then pulled out a small, round metal ball attached to a thin, coiled wire. He brought the steel ball to his mouth. What McGinnis had described to Novak as a mere radio certainly didn't look like one to Harris. It was the latest generation of mobile communications. Although it broadcast over public airwaves, a microchip inside the sending and receiving units ensured that all conversations were continuously scrambled with electronic noise that changed its format every ten seconds. Moreover, if someone was able to penetrate the scrambling and access the broadcast, the radio would automatically shut itself off, terminating the conversation until the uninvited eavesdropper was disconnected.

"This is McGinnis." The conversations were automatically routed through the main desk at the Agency's San Francisco headquarters, a lumber yard cover south of Market Street.

The response was crystal clear. "We're receiving."

"Give me an update on Vasquez's condition."

"Just spoke to the doctors ten minutes ago. Same. No change. Unconscious and still on respiratory support. Can't be spoken to yet."

"Listen. Get me Clark on this line. I need to speak to him."

Peter Clark was the regional director of the Company's West Coast offices. Although based in Los Angeles, he had flown to San Francisco to assist the team from Washington. He had no choice in the matter. Headquarters had sent word that McGinnis and Harris were on a priority mission and were to be granted every feasible request.

McGinnis pulled the car to the curb and waited for Clark to be patched through. He had stopped along Columbus Avenue, the heart of North Beach, the Italian neighborhood. Harris stared at the fresh pasta being kneaded in an adjoining store front.

"What do you need to talk to Clark about?"

"I've got an idea that may help to bring our visiting Russian friends out. I think—"

"Clark here." The connection was so good that it sounded almost as if he were in the car.

"Peter"—McGinnis had only met him once, nearly a decade ago, but formalities were not important at this point—"I need you to use some Company press connections to get something done for us."

"If I can do it, Richard, I will. What do you need?"

"I would like the news reports on tonight's radio and television, and tomorrow's papers, to carry the story that Vasquez is making a remarkable recovery. Couple that with the fact that the investigation for his killers is stalled. I would like the reports to suggest that the authorities are looking for a big break when they get a chance to talk to him later in the day. Make it sound like he's going to be well enough to spill his guts tomorrow afternoon."

"But, Richard, the guy is blind. Even if we were able to talk to him, what the hell could he tell us?"

"He is only missing one of his five senses, highlighting the use of the other four. He won't be able to describe the faces of the people we are looking for, but as good field agents they'll know he could be a wealth of information. He'll have information on accents, any unusual inflections, or any speech impediments. Maybe he had physical contact that could highlight age or unusual characteristics, any number of things. He was with them for some time. He's the only person we know who had contact with them and is still alive. They won't like that. Even if the risk is low because he's blind, they didn't intend to leave him alive, and they screwed up. It's a major mistake that he is still breathing. If they think he's getting better, and if they are still here, they are almost obligated to finish him off before he talks."

"But they'll know we will have the place crawling with agents and police. It would be suicidal for them to walk in."

"Yeah, maybe. But do me a favor, Peter. Humor me. Can you do it?"

"Sure. We've got some good local press contacts. Once the story gets out on the wire services, then other news media will automatically pick it up. You should hear the first reports within a couple of hours."

"Great."

"Are you going to the hospital now?"

"No. To the Fairmont. I am going to take some of your boys into their room."

"Don't you want to wait for their possible return?"

"They aren't returning. I want to see how they're traveling."

"You're calling the shots. I can be contacted anytime if you need me."

"Thanks."

Just as McGinnis was about to snap the microphone back into its cover, Clark's voice came into the car one final time.

"Oh, Richard, I almost forgot to tell you. I was notified by headquarters that Finch is on his way here. Phillips and Fitzgerald are coming out too."

McGinnis pulled the mike back to his mouth. "They are all coming here?"

"Yep. You guys must be on something pretty delicate."

"No. They just miss field work."

McGinnis snapped the mike back into the black box.

"Why are they coming here?" Harris looked at McGinnis.

"I'll bet Finch is coming because he feels the Soviets are still here and he wants this to be their last stand. We've got to pull them in this time. Two infections too many already. Finch is coming out here to ride herd on you and me. I've got no goddamn idea why Phillips and Fitzgerald are on their way. Shit. The only good thing about them striking in San Francisco was that we were able to get three thousand miles away from headquarters. Now headquarters follows us here."

"It won't be so bad, McGinnis. Especially if your idea for the hospital works."

"It's a long shot. You heard Clark. It would be a suicide mission for them."

"I know. But you and I know something that Clark doesn't. That is that these two VKR agents are already on a suicide mission of sorts. Clark doesn't have any idea why we are looking for them. He would crap if he knew they were part of a team that had eliminated an entire station in London and was now single-handedly passing bacterial infections around the U.S. I don't think these two agents are scared by much. If they think the priest is getting better, they are probably crazy or confident enough to think they can get to him and still escape. I mean, the hospital may be crawling with cops and agents, but it is still packed with civilians and staff. There are plenty of ways to get inside. Their problem will be in getting away."

"Not bad, kid. You keep hanging around me and you're going to start thinking like an agent all the time. I couldn't have said it much better myself."

A compliment from McGinnis. Maybe California had mellowed him a bit. It was certainly a different partner than the one who promised to smash his face just several days ago in Washington. Working around the clock together had softened each of them. Harris was no longer in a rush to prove how much he knew. He realized that McGinnis might be a little competitive, but his experience earned him some respect.

"You think we'll find any of the virus inside the hotel room?" Harris asked.

"What do you think?"

"Not a chance. They wouldn't leave it unattended. I guess it travels with them."

"Right again. But we'll have a look anyway."

"You driving?"

"In a minute. There's one priority we have to take care of before getting to the Fairmont."

Harris looked at him for direction. McGinnis slowly lifted his arm and pointed across the dashboard. Harris followed his finger and looked across the sidewalk and into the brightly lit window of Angelo's Pizzeria.

McGinnis whispered as though imparting a great secret to Harris. "Large, pepperoni, extra cheese, and anchovies. It helps the detective part of your brain work."

"What about the detective part of your stomach," Harris grimaced. "I can't stand anchovies."

"Then put them on half the pizza and hold your nose while you eat your slices. Now get out of here before I stop being such a nice guy and demand that they get spread across the whole pie."

"You're all heart."

Harris was out the door when McGinnis shouted. "And a six-pack of Coca-Cola. I want the real thing!"

Harris shook his head as he walked to the pizza joint. McGinnis might be pretty smart when it came to intelligence work, but he was a Neanderthal when it came to nutrition. A massive dose of carbohydrates would further tire them, and then the Coke's sugar would cause a blood-sugar reaction that would crash them even more. He hesitated before entering the parlor and almost returned to the car to tell McGinnis that it was a poor choice. But his better judgment took hold. A quick glance back at the car told him that McGinnis was not in a negotiating mood. He had to give in. The alternative, anchovies over the whole pie, was too terrible to contemplate.

CHAPTER 19 ══════════

Sausalito, California
December 17
10:00 p.m.

Agatha whimpered during the entire twenty-minute ride across the Golden Gate Bridge. Penny didn't need any prodding from Erica. She knew that the woman with the gun was irrational—Agatha's hysterical screaming could push her over the edge and endanger both their lives. She constantly reached out with her right hand and stroked her daughter's forehead. "Everything is going to be okay. Mommy loves you. Everything is going to be all right. Mommy's not scared."

Penny's words sounded hollow. She didn't believe for a second that everything was going to be all right. But she had to mask her fear. If it took control of her, Agatha would join her hysteria. It would overwhelm both of them. She had to remain rational—as rational as she could with a pistol held inches from her head. She didn't have to look in the rearview mirror and search for it. Knowing that the gunwoman was sitting directly behind was the same as if the gun itself were cocked and pressed against her skull.

During the drive to the Golden Gate Bridge Penny did not miss a single traffic light. She couldn't believe it. Almost every time she made the trip into the city, she was delayed in heavy traffic and missed at least half a dozen lights. While sitting in traffic for almost a minute, she hoped that someone in a neighboring car might notice that the man in the rear seat looked ill. Maybe someone would sense the panic and fright in her eyes. But she didn't even have the chance to find out if her terror was so easily telegraphed. Each time she approached an intersection the light turned green. The traffic was almost non-existent. Nothing was going right for her. The most difficult moment had been at the bridge toll plaza. No toll is collected going north, the direction they were traveling, so she did not have an opportunity to signal a token collector at the glass-enclosed booths only two car lanes removed. But the traffic at the toll plaza bottlenecks, even on the free passage side. As she slowed to fifteen miles per hour, she glanced at the uniformed and armed bridge personnel in the nearby surveillance booth.

Erica didn't give her much chance to contemplate the possibilities. "Don't think about it, stupid. Do you think you can let them know you have a problem without me putting a bullet into your little kid here? Do you?" Erica screamed at her.

Penny squirmed in her seat. Agatha started whimpering louder and faster. "Please," Penny pleaded, "I wasn't thinking about anything but getting you to the house."

The rest of the ride was quiet. Erica tended to the man in the back seat. After Penny had taken the freeway exit and was nearing her home, she heard a moan from the rear seat. He was waking up.

"I . . . where am I . . ."

"Shhh. Conserve your strength," Erica whispered. How different she sounds, Penny thought. The harshness was gone, a soft tone having replaced it. "You are going to be fine. We are on the way to a safe house." Those words sent a chill through Penny's spine. Terror gripped her at the thought of these two wanted murderers thinking of her home as their "safe house."

"How bad is it?" Colby barely nodded his chin toward his shoulder.

"Not bad at all. I have to check it more closely, but I don't think it pierced your lung. It looks like it just ripped into the lat muscle and probably cracked a rib or two. If I'm right, you're damn lucky. Because of the way you moved around, you lost a pretty good amount of blood. But once I get you inside a bed, I'll get the bullet out, and with a night's rest you'll be surprised how strong you'll be tomorrow. You'll be sore, but ready to move."

"What about the—"

"Stop. We have strangers in the car. Wait till we get inside."

Colby lifted his head up from the rear seat and stared forward. Penny looked into the rearview mirror, and when she made contact with his eyes, she quickly averted hers to the roadway. Even though his eyes were clouded with pain, she could tell they were reflections of a mean soul. Penny thought that when he was back to full strength, he and the gunwoman must make some team. One was bad enough to deal with, but both would be horrible. She started to shake. She pressed her hands down hard against the steering wheel and tried to calm them. Agatha must have sensed her fear. She started to cry a little louder.

"What the hell is a child? . . ." Colby again tried to lean forward.

"Don't worry. It's our insurance." Again the words sent a queasy feeling through Penny's stomach. Erica leaned forward and almost spit out the words, "Shut her up!" Now that he was awake, Erica was no longer screaming. She had lowered her voice to a hateful hiss.

They passed the Hotel Alta Mira when Penny took a right turn, proceeded up a sharp hill, then suddenly slowed to a crawl. "What's the matter with you!" Erica leaned forward and grabbed the top of her shoulder.

Penny bolted upright in her seat and the car lurched forward several feet. "Nothing! We're here!" Her voice sounded urgent, as though by imparting the information she was saving a life. Maybe she was.

Slowly she turned the car to the right and entered a driveway partially obscured by thick eucalyptus trees. The car crawled the fifty-foot driveway and finally pulled to a stop in front of a white, one story, ranch-style house.

"Is anyone else home?" Erica asked.

Penny shook her head no.

"What about your husband. Where the hell is he?"

"He's working."

"What does he do for a living?"

Penny didn't think fast enough to lie. She told Erica the first thing that came into her mind. It was the truth. "He's a dentist."

"Is that right, Agatha?" Erica turned to the little girl.

"Leave her alone!" Penny yelled and started turning toward Erica.

Erica raised the gun and put the barrel only inches from the front of her face. "Shut up, I want to hear it from her!"

"You can . . ." Colby started to speak from the rear seat.

Erica put her free hand in front of him indicating silence. She had the situation in control. He was still too weak to take command. He closed his mouth. Agatha started crying louder. "What does your daddy do, Agatha?" Only sobs. "If you don't answer me I am going to hurt your mommy. Now you don't want that, do you?" Agatha shook her head violently no. "Good, then what does Daddy do?"

"He's . . . a . . . a . . . dentist," Agatha forced out the words.

Penny felt relieved. She had told the truth. There was nothing to fear.. Suddenly Erica reached around the front seat and grabbed a large hand-ful of Penny's bleached blond hair. She yanked it back as if she was going to pull the hair into the rear seat. Penny's head jerked backward, slamming into the headrest, and her hair felt as though it was about to be pulled from the roots. She instinctively screamed.

"Don't lie to me, bitch!" Erica leaned forward and hissed in her ear. "What about that car?" She turned Penny's head toward a steel blue BMW parked in front of them. "How did he get to work? Walk?"

"He's—he's . . . at a convention . . . in Miami . . . honest . . . I swear it . . . he—he won't be back until tomorrow." Erica pulled tighter on the hair. Penny's voice pleaded for mercy. "I swear it . . . you can call his office. His answering service will tell you. Please!"

"So why did you lie to me?"

"I thought maybe . . . maybe you'd think he was coming home and you might leave."

"Why would I leave? Huh! You think he has a gun bigger than this." Erica pushed the tip of the barrel against the hollow of Penny's cheek.

"Uh, uh," was all Penny could mutter.

"I catch you on one more lie and I will really be pissed. Understand?"

Penny nodded her head yes.

"Good. Any other children?"

Again a negative nod.

"Any live-in housekeepers, gardeners, cooks, or the like, princess?"

"No."

"You mean it's just the two of us and the two of you? How cozy. If we had a fifth we could play poker." Erica released the hair and shoved Penny's head forward as she pulled the gun away from her face. "Now let's cut the crap and get inside."

They propped Colby on their shoulders and helped him shuffle into the bedroom in the rear of the house, where they laid him on the king-sized bed. There was a Jacuzzi in the rear of the bedroom and lush, hanging ferns filled most of the ceiling space. Large picture windows looked out onto a kidney-shaped pool in a high-fenced backyard. Al-though privacy was ensured, Erica ordered Penny to close the draperies. Then she had the radio turned to the local all-news channel.

Erica had Penny carry two high-back, red lacquered dining room chairs into the bedroom. She ripped long strips from the bed sheets and used the material to bind and gag Agatha to one of the chairs. Then she turned to Penny and waved the pistol in front of her face, "Now, you are going to help me get ready for a little operation. You have a first-aid kit?"

Penny nodded yes.

"Well, what are you standing around for? Let's go get it."

Penny led Erica inside the powder room, adjoining the bedroom, and pulled out a small blue plastic attaché case with a red insignia emblazoned on the front. Erica opened the lid and looked inside: a reel of white tape, four rolls of cotton gauze, a small bottle of iodine, and two boxes of bandages. Several of the plastic containers were empty. "This is it?" Erica asked incredulously. Again, Penny nodded yes.

"Your husband's a goddamn dentist. Doesn't he have anything better than this? Does he keep any of his dentistry tools at home?"

"Nothing."

"What about medications?"

"Whatever we have is on the first shelf there in the vanity." Penny pointed to the sliding mirror overhanging the pink marble sink. Erica slid the glass open and looked inside. Aspirin, Tylenol, Lomotil for diarrhea, Valium as a muscle relaxant, rubbing alcohol, and Betadine. Erica grabbed the large plastic bottles of rubbing alcohol and Betadine. The latter solution was a general disinfectant, similar to iodine, but more potent. It would come in handy.

She turned around and looked at Penny. "Do you have a manicure kit?" Penny pointed to the second drawer in the cabinet under the sink. Erica opened it and pulled out a small leather case. She laid it on top of the sink, unzipped it, and took out a pair of tweezers and a small pair of scissors.

"How about a sewing kit?"

"In the back of the same drawer. It's a red plastic case."

Erica reached to the back of the open drawer and removed the kit. She snapped it open and pulled out two large sewing needles. "Now the kitchen."

Erica followed Penny from the bedroom, down the long corridor, past the family room, into the natural-wood-styled kitchen. "Here's what I need. As I name them, you get them and arrange them on the sink. A colander . . . as many dishcloths as you have . . . you have an ice pick? . . . good . . . two large bowls . . . do you have a serving tray? . . . Good. And where are your knives?" Penny slid open a large drawer next to the refrigerator. Erica walked over and rummaged through it, bypassing short grapefruit knives, butter and steak knives. None of them seemed very good. She was a doctor by training although it had been years since she had used her textbook knowledge on a real person. She dreaded taking the bullet out, but she wasn't sure when they would get to a proper doctor. If the bullet didn't come out soon, he would have real problems. And that would mean real problems for her as well. The damn knife. It was one of the most important parts of the surgery. She could feel the perspiration breaking out on her forehead. Nerves. She leaned over and looked into the back of the large drawer. Finally she spotted it. A paring knife, with a wooden handle, and a six-inch serrated edge. She removed it and ran the blade across the edge of the counter. It cut a slim groove easily into the laminated plastic. She placed the knife next to the other materials Penny had gathered.

"Now I need a large pot, big enough for the colander to fit into. And also some strong wire. You have anything like cat gut?"

"Nothing like that. I have some rope and also some twine."

"No good." Erica paced back and forth in front of the kitchen sink. She needed something to sew the wound. Twine was no good. What would be around a house that could be used? "Is your husband a fisherman?"

"Yes, why?"

"Take me to his gear."

Again, Erica followed Penny through the kitchen and laundry room to the attached garage. Against a far wall, neatly laid out, were three fishing rods and several metal boxes. Erica opened the first one and saw what she was looking for. She grabbed a reel of nylon leader. It was thin but strong enough to close the wound. "Back to the bedroom," Erica commanded.

By the time Penny had returned to the bedroom, Agatha was already quietly sobbing through her gag. Penny started to go to her when Erica reached out and grabbed her arm. "Sit down. Now!" Whatever thoughts Penny had of resisting were overcome when Erica pushed the gun near her face. Penny sat in the spare lacquer chair and Erica proceeded to bind her firmly to it. Before she could place a final strip of cloth into her mouth, Penny started talking as fast as possible.

"My husband is going to call me soon. He'll call in several hours. He always does. If he doesn't talk to me then he's going to be worried and he'll have a neighbor come over and check us."

Erica straightened up and hovered directly over Penny. "Now, now, princess, don't be worried. He'll call, and then you're going to talk to him. And when you sound a little funny you're going to tell him it's something you ate or that you might have the twenty-four-hour flu. And if he wants to talk to his lovely daughter you're going to say she's taking a nap and you don't want to disturb her. If you say anything to him about what's happening then you guarantee that your husband will have the distinct pleasure of hearing your and your daughter's brains splatter against the telephone receiver. Understand?''

Erica seemed almost tranquil. She no longer yelled or screamed. Getting off the roadway and into a secluded house had calmed her. And she didn't need to raise her voice. Her words carried the intended threat to Penny, who merely nodded her head. Penny was even losing her fear. She was becoming resigned to her fate, and felt as though the tragedy was just beginning to play out.

"I have some work to do, but before I do . . ." Erica grabbed the strip of bed sheeting dangling near Penny's throat and stuffed it into her mouth. Agatha continued sobbing, but the cloth so muffled the sound that even Erica was not bothered. Erica left them alone with the half-conscious Colby lying across the bed.

She walked outside to the car and retrieved the black leather duffel containing all of their possessions. Most of Colby's makeup material was haphazardly tossed into the bottom, his pistol resting in the center, spare bullet clips at the side, a crumpled towel from the hotel and Colby's priestly garb on top. Erica bypassed all this to pull out a separate padded leather pouch. On one side of the pouch were the individual containers holding the encapsulated K-7 and a small metal canister with undiluted virus. The other half of the bag contained seven vials and half a dozen syringes. They were her medical liquids, her traveling pharmacy in case of emergencies during the mission—emergencies exactly like the one with which she was faced.

One vial contained potassium chloride, the assassination liquid used on Vasquez. Another was morphine, which would come in handy. A third contained the Benzedrine she and Colby had used. Another vial was Solu-Medrol, a steroid that she carried in case of life-threatening hypersensitivity. A fifth contained lidocaine, a local anesthetic that she would use in the operation. The sixth bottle had epinephrine, a cardiac stimulant used to counter heart attacks. The final bottle contained one of the few drugs she considered a true wonder aid, penicillin. She had used it on many occasions to treat numerous problems. She would use it again tonight. She withdrew the morphine, the lidocaine, and the penicillin. She filled the largest syringe with 25 milligrams of morphine. A second syringe was filled with two million units of penicillin, all she had. The contents of the small vial of lidocaine were emptied into a third syringe. It provided only 10 cc's. Damn it. She should have taken larger vials with her. The lidocaine would only numb the muscles and skin for twenty minutes. He was going to go through some real pain. She gathered the rubbing alcohol, the cotton gauze, and bandages, and, together with the syringes, placed them neatly in a straight row at the foot of the bed.

Then she walked back to the kitchen. She ran water from the faucet until it filled half the large stainless-steel pot before grabbing it by both handles and placing it over the gas flame on the range. The high setting quickly brought the water to a boil, and she carefully placed the colander into the pot. Into that she dropped the scissors, the pair of tweezers, two sewing pins, nylon fishing line, the ice pick, seven medium-sized dishcloths gathered by Penny, and the paring knife. She looked at her watch. 3:45. The instruments would be as sterile as they were going to get by 4:00.

She unscrewed the cap to the Betadine and slowly poured some into two glass bowls on top of the counter. Then she took one of the bowls and the rest of the bottle of Betadine and returned to the bedroom. She needed to do a nonsterile cleaning of his wound. It would give her a chance to examine the injury.

She sat on the edge of the bed and tried to compose herself. This was not right—her training had not been for operating on people. Certainly not in settings as unprofessional as this. Trying to settle her nerves, she took a deep breath and stretched her arms in front of her. Colby should not sense her anxiety. She grabbed the rubbing alcohol, took some gauze, ripped off a long strip, and then soaked it in the alcohol.

Colby was lying on his abdomen. "Can you push yourself a little to the back?" she asked him. "I need to look at the spot the bullet went into."

Slowly he maneuvered his good arm underneath his frame and pushed so that his wounded side faced her. She placed the wet gauze on top of the bed, leaned to the side, and brought up the morphine-filled syringe. Lightly grasping his good arm, she bent it at the elbow, and then slowly sank the needle into one of his protruding veins. "You'll feel better in a couple of moments." There was no reason to delay administering the first dose of the narcotic. The examination and early cleaning was going to be painful. Although the morphine would leave him semiconscious, in forty-five minutes he would need another dose. He would unfortunately remember this day in all too much detail.

She leaned over the bed and studied the bullet hole near the top of his shoulder. The skin around the small hole was red and puffed. She pressed against the open wound with her fingers and pushed hard around the inflamed edges, forcing some blood to ooze. There was no sign of the bullet near the entrance. She took the gauze, ripped the soaked strip in half, and rubbed it in and around the hole. He grunted when she probed her fingers into the tip of the wound. The coagulated blood lifted off easily. She tried to find the bullet, but couldn't feel anything like a metal slug. When she leaned farther to look at his lower back she was surprised to see a large, purplish bruise had spread across the latissimus dorsi muscle. That quick discoloration meant a lot of bleeding had taken place under the skin. The bullet might have lodged lower than she expected. Its location was critical because it would determine whether she had to cut into the bullet wound or to create a new incision. If a new cut was required it would be much messier, releasing the large amount of trapped blood gathered just under the skin. But that couldn't be her deciding factor. The cut had to be at the closest point to the bullet. She pressed against the back, in and around the large bruise, hoping to feel the bullet's hard tip. Again she had no success. Damn it. With the remainder of the gauze she lightly rubbed the wound once again, wiping away the small amount of blood that was now dribbling out. She looked at her watch. It was two minutes until 4:00. "You can rest on your stomach. I need to get your pants off." He nodded weakly. One look at his glazed eyes told her the morphine had taken hold. She untied the laces on his heavy black shoes and slipped them off his feet. Then, forcing her hands under his stomach, she unclasped the black trousers, and with a great effort, slowly slid them down the bed and over his legs. She did not remove his underwear. The operation was going to be very messy. There was no reason to let him spend the night in blood-soaked pants.

She ran back to the kitchen and took a fork from the utensil drawer. There was no other way to get the colander out of the boiling pot. Reaching into the top of the pot, she grabbed one of the colander's handles with the tip of the fork, and then quickly yanked it out of the water. By touching the tip of the colander with the fork, it was no longer sterile, but that wouldn't affect the rest of the operation. She dropped the colander into a serving tray, which she had placed into one side of the double sink. Grabbing both handles of the boiling pot, she moved it over the sink and poured the contents into the colander, the instruments and cloths falling into the metal receptacle. A small cloud of steam passed in front of her, and she leaned backward as far as possible to avoid being burnt.

She pushed the faucet into the other half of the double sink, turned on the hot water, and pulled the glass bowl containing Betadine near her. Then she took a bar of soap resting on the back edge of the sink and vigorously washed her hands, working the soap into a lather and forcing it under her nails. For nearly five minutes she continued the careful scrubbing. Then she placed her hands into the bowl of Betadine and worked the orange lotion into a lather as she finished the sterilizing process. Reaching into the colander, she grabbed one of the sterilized towels and wiped her hands dry. Then she wrapped that towel around the unsanitary handle of the colander, grabbed it with her left hand, and clasped the clean handle with her other hand. She carried the pot of instruments back to the bedroom and rested them at the foot of the bed.

He was still on his abdomen. The massive purple bruise covered half his back. You poor bastard, Erica thought. She looked back at Penny and Agatha, bound tightly to the chairs, less than ten feet away. Well, here goes. She tapped him gently on the side. "Roll back a little. I need better access to the wound."

There was a momentary hesitation, and then he pushed himself with his good arm and moved his body back several inches. It was enough for her to work. The bullet had to be found. With the ice pick she carefully peeled away a ridge of the skin around the hole and took a deep breath as she moved the index finger of her free hand to the opening. Slowly she pushed her finger inside the wound. Colby's muscles in his neck and arms tensed as she entered him, and he moaned as she kept pushing it into the soft muscle tissue, following the bullet's path. "Hold on," she encouraged him, "this won't last long." He was trying his hardest not to cry out. Even through the morphine, the pain was powerful.

In the background the radio news was commenting on a new Iranian offensive at the port city of Basra. She had blocked it out as she concentrated on Colby. But over the sound of the radio she heard the sound of Agatha. She was grunting in apparent disgust. Erica kept pushing her finger inside and, without even turning, addressed her hostages. "If the two of you don't like this, then keep your eyes closed. I don't want to hear a peep out of either of you. I'm a little rusty at this operating crap, so maybe I should practice with the knife on one of you. Hmmm?" She turned her head slowly and stared at both of them. Agatha's eyes bulged with fear. Penny seemed calmer. It was the look Erica had seen before in hijacked passengers when they were about to be killed by terrorists. They had passed the stage of fear and had accepted the upcoming bullet. She could probably start cutting Penny with a knife before the look of terror would settle back across her face.

In a moment her finger could not move any deeper. It was shoved to the base of her knuckle. She tried to wiggle her finger to each side feeling for the bullet, but she only felt the warmth of soft muscle tissue. The fact the bullet had traveled that far shocked her. It probably lodged deeper in his back, causing the large bruise. She had to find it. Slowly she withdrew her finger, the intrusion now causing a small amount of blood to stream from the wound. Colby barely made any noise. He was as strong as she expected. He was doing his best to make it easy for her, and she admired his courage. "On your stomach." He rolled over.

Again, she bent close to his back and pressed deeply into the discolored skin. The bullet had to be there. Each push into his bruise brought a slight moan from Colby. "Not much longer," she assured him. It was a lie. She knew it was just beginning. Finally, near the lower part of the rib cage, she felt it. Just the hard end of the slug. A relief rushed over her. It was in a good location. He was one lucky bastard. From where she felt it, the bullet must have passed into the lat muscle, grazed the lower tip of the scapula, and then embedded in a rib. That's what it felt like to her. The rib was raised up, the bullet shoving the bone nearer to the surface. If the rib hadn't stopped the bullet, it would have certainly collapsed his lung. He was very lucky.

She reached to the side of the bed, took one of the sterile cloths, and dipped it into the bowl of Betadine. Then she carefully wiped the large bruise, sterilizing it for a new incision. When she finished wiping him, she grabbed four of the other cloths and placed them around the bruised area, leaving only a six-inch patch of exposed skin. The towels would have to catch most of the blood during the surgery. Even with the cloths, the bed would be a mess.

She grabbed the syringe with the 10 cc's of lidocaine and felt the area where she intended to put the incision. It was puffed from the internal bleeding. Quickly she jabbed the tip of the needle just under the outer layer of damaged skin and injected a couple of drops. Within fifteen seconds the lidocaine had forced the skin to blister. This is what Erica needed in order to penetrate unobstructed into the surrounding muscle tissue. She pushed the syringe deep into his back until the tip struck the damaged rib. His body jerked when the steel point hit the bone, a short yell coming from his mouth. She didn't say anything to comfort him. It was difficult for her to imagine how painful it was. She hated causing him the pain, but it was to save his life. He couldn't live more than thirty-six hours with the bullet inside. Infection, blood loss, and ruptures could lead to death. It had to come out.

The remainder of the lidocaine was injected directly into the muscle tissue, and then the needle was withdrawn. That would give him twenty minutes of numbness. She moved as quickly as possible. First, she leaned over and grabbed the knife. She stared at it for a moment as she placed the sharp tip against the skin. It was not a great instrument. But it would have to do. Grabbing the ice pick in her other hand, she pressed the tip sharply into the skin over his bruise. He didn't flinch. The lidocaine had taken hold. She put the ice pick back into the colander, straightened herself, and pushed the paring knife half an inch into his back. She cut straight down in a vertical line and created an incision of almost 2½ inches. It was a long cut, but was necessary to get at the bullet.

She placed the index and middle fingers of her left hand at a sharp angle so she could separate the tissue that had just been sliced. The blood began running from the cut. With her right hand she pushed the knife into the center of the incision and through the swollen tissue. In a matter of seconds she had touched the edge of the bullet with the tip of the knife. She heard the faint sound of scraping and felt the tension run up her hand. Working the knife in a tight circle, she widened the incision, making access to the bullet easier.

She removed the knife. He was grunting, trying to hold back the pain, but the lidocaine was already wearing off. Just hold on, she thought, this is the worst of it. She reached into the colander and clasped the tweezers. With her left hand she again pushed open the skin and simultaneously pushed down on the cut. The blood poured out in a steady stream, soaking the washcloths draped over his back, and dripping onto the bed. With her right hand she shoved the tweezers in as far as they would go, and felt them finally hit the slug. She pushed the tweezer heads together, and slowly withdrew. Damn it! She had missed the bullet. Cold sweat was running into her eyes and Erica brought the back of her hand to her forehead and wiped it clean. She took a deep breath and once again pushed down on the wound and inserted the tweezers. Erica jammed them in as far as she could, grinding away the muscle tissue to clear a path to the bullet. Again she felt the metal slug, slowly pushed the pincers together, and withdrew the instrument. Relief rushed over her as she saw the smashed metal slug pop out of his back.

She threw the tweezers and slug on the floor next to the colander. "Just a couple of minutes and you'll be fine." He was moaning. Any other person would have passed out by now. If he was conscious this far, he was probably going to stay awake for the entire procedure. It was time for more morphine. Grabbing the syringe, she injected another 5 milligrams of the narcotic into a vein on his good arm. That should help him through the stitching, she thought.

She grabbed the final two sterile cloths in the colander and used them to soak up some of the excess blood that had run over his back and legs. "Please push up, just a fraction on your side." He amazed her. Under the narcotic's hold, and with a 2½-inch hole in his back, he still managed to follow her requests. He pushed himself up so the bullet wound was more accessible. While the pressure caused by his movement forced more blood out of the incision, she had to make sure the original bullet hole had not opened up from the stress of the surgery. If it did, it would also need stitches. Erica put her head close to the wound. There was minor bleeding, a red stain having spread on the mattress under his arm, but it didn't need to be closed. She reached to the floor, grabbed a piece of gauze, and soaked it in the bowl of Betadine. The she brought the wet gauze to the bullet hole and stuffed it inside. It must have burned like a match struck on the inside of his skin because even through the morphine haze he screamed. She grabbed the ice pick and stuffed the Betadine-soaked gauze deeper into the wound. She would bandage it after she had stitched his back.

She gently nudged him onto his abdomen and reached to the floor for the penicillin. Near the top of his healthy shoulder she injected half the syringe's contents directly into the muscle, hoping it would battle any infection. She looked at the straight incision on his back, a thin line of blood still running down to his buttocks. The blood was everywhere. The bed was soaked through to the mattress. He had to be closed immediately. Grabbing the bowl of Betadine, she brought it over his back, peeled away the skin around the incision, and poured the antiseptic directly into the opening. His body jerked on the bed and his hands grabbed the top of the bed sheet as he gave a curdling yell. "Almost done . . ." She seemed to be trying to assure herself as much as him.

Again she reached to the foot of the bed, this time grabbing the nylon leader. Shit! In all her haste to operate, she had forgotten to thread the nylon through the two sterilized needles. She leaned over the side of the bed and retrieved the two needles from the bottom of the colander. Her hands were shaking for the first time, the anger at such a simple mistake distracting her from the work at hand. She tried to thread the nylon into the eye of one of the needles. Goddamn it! The line was too thick. It wasn't going to fit. Panic set in. "Get hold of yourself. Everything is going to be fine. It's almost over," she kept repeating. Grabbing the ice pick she tried to sandwich the tip into the needle's eye in order to enlarge it. The pick would not fit. There was no choice. The hole had to be expanded even if it meant that she would make it unsterile. She put the end of the needle into her mouth and clenched it between her two front teeth. Biting hard on the thin metal she bent it, slightly expanding the hole. Again she tried the nylon. Just enough fit so she could pinch it through. She did the same with the second needle.

One final time she separated the skin along the incision with her fingers. At a hospital the doctors would have first sewed the underlying muscle tissue with dissolvable thread. Then they would have used a synthetic thread to close the skin. None of that was available to her. The muscle tissue couldn't be closed with nylon. It would cause serious infection in less than a day. Instead, she was forced to close everything together with very large stitches. Starting at the bottom of the cut, she pushed the needle deep into his back and pulled it through the other side, taking large gobs of tissue in each movement. She would swing the thread back toward her, then repeat another big loop, closing chunks of meat each time. When she had finished sewing the cut, she bent over and clasped the pair of manicure scissors, brought them to the tip of the nylon line, and clipped it.

She wiped her brow with the back of her hand. Her blouse was stuck to her chest and back, soaked with perspiration. The worst was over. Her body relaxed, and the tension began leaving her muscles. Reaching down to the first-aid kit she pulled up the tape, cotton bandages, and strips of gauze. For the next ten minutes she carefully bandaged both wounds. When she finished, she administered an additional 5 milligrams of morphine, his moaning being the indication that the effects of the narcotic needed a reinforcement.

She was exhausted. But she still returned the instruments and bottles to the kitchen. She also took several large velour bath towels and spread them three deep over the bed. At least they would prevent him from sleeping on damp blood all night. Several pillows spread on the floor made her makeshift bed. When she had finished, she stood by him and stretched her arms and arched her back. It was at that moment she realized how tense she had been. Her spine cracked as she leaned backward, relieving the pressure in her lower back. Again, she reached upward, trying to loosen the knots of muscles throughout her body. Although the effects of the Benzedrine were wearing off, her brain was charged from the surgery, the adrenaline pumping hard. She needed something to relax her. She walked to the living room, where she had earlier passed an open bar. Reviewing the assorted bottles, she reached to the second mirrored shelf and grabbed a half-full liter of Chivas Regal. Returning to the bedroom, she sat on the edge of the bed, twisted off the cap, and put the bottle to her lips. Before she took a gulp she looked over at Agatha and Penny. Again, Penny's eyes were filled with fear. Erica wondered what had prompted the change. Maybe Penny feared that drunkenness would make Erica meaner. Well, she could relax. Erica didn't intend to get drunk—she just wanted to relax enough to sleep. She held the bottle up in the air and smiled at them. "Cheers," she declared, then she put the opening of the bottle to her mouth and took a long swallow of scotch. It stung her throat and burned her chest as it passed down to hit her stomach like a firecracker. That's exactly what she needed. As she put the bottle to her mouth again, her ears picked up the report she had been waiting for. She froze. Penny noticed the change and also paid attention to the clear voice on the radio.

"And, repeating tonight's top story. Father Enrique Vasquez, the Central American peace prelate, who was the subject of an assassination attempt earlier today at his hotel room at the Hyatt in San Francisco, has been removed from the critical list. According to doctors at St. Mary's Hospital, Father Vasquez was suffering from shock upon his admission to the hospital, and his condition was originally diagnosed as more serious than it was. He will be removed from any respiratory equipment tomorrow, and authorities are anxious to speak to him. According to an FBI spokesman, Dan Merritt, the investigation for Father

Vasquez's two assassins is stalled, and authorities are hopeful that the priest will have solid clues about the fugitives.

"The mayor tonight met with the families of the two police officers killed in today's bloody shootout. He offered condolences to the families of what became the ninth and tenth police fatalities in this, the worst year ever for police murders. Four private hotel security guards were also shot to death in today's bungled assassination attempt. Another twelve were injured in the high-speed car chase in which the two would-be assassins, described as a young Caucasian man and woman, escaped. Their getaway car was found abandoned near the docks earlier today.

"We repeat, Father Enrique Vasquez is recovering from an attempted . . ."

Erica tuned out the announcer. So she hadn't injected enough potassium chloride into the goddamn priest before the needle popped out. Shit! What a lousy break. Another fraction of a second and he would have been dead. Her mind raced. What could he tell them anyway? He was blind for godsakes. Vasquez didn't know what they looked like and didn't know their names. Although he had spent time with them, there was nothing substantive he could provide the police. He could tell them he had been knocked unconscious once they entered the room. And they would discover he never celebrated the mass. That would turn the investigators toward the scene of the infection. It could blow their cover for the continued K-7 mission. It might give the CIA a reason to go public with the information about the germ infections. Damn it. She should have jabbed the needle deep into his arm. It would be much better if he were dead. But how the hell could she get inside to kill him? The hospital must be like an armed camp. Colby would be useless until the morning. She had to talk to him. She wasn't too proud to admit when she needed someone else's help. The choices were overwhelming her better judgment. Although she wanted to contact the New York safe house, the call had to be placed from a public telephone. The residential phone of a stranger would not work—the safe house phones were electronically programmed to refuse a call from a private, unrecognized number. In any case, it broke every rule she had been given. She certainly couldn't leave Colby, Penny, and Agatha in the house on their own. She took another swallow of the scotch, this batch going down smoother than the first. As she started to walk toward the end of the bed, to sit peacefully and gather her thoughts, the telephone suddenly rang. It was a loud buzzing tone and it startled her. She looked at Penny, ran over, and roughly pulled the cloth in her mouth down to her neck.

"That's my husband. I told you."

The phone had rung twice.

"Remember what I told you. I am going to be listening to everything you say."

Erica ran back to the leather duffel near the side of the bed. Three rings. She pulled a pistol from the bag and ran to the light pink telephone on the side of the bed. Four rings. She grabbed it and pulled it as far across the room as it would reach. The cord stopped about two feet short of the chair to which Penny was tied. The fifth ring pealed out. Erica picked up the receiver in her left hand, reached out, and placed it against Penny's face. At the same time she raised her right arm, cradling the pistol in her hand, and placed it against Agatha's brown hair. The child began softly whimpering through her mouth gag. Erica listened to the one side of the conversation she could hear.

"Hi, honey. . . . No, I was in the bathroom, that's why it took me so long." Penny's voice sounded weak, as if it was on the verge of tears. But she had her eyes locked on Erica and the gun nestled against her daughter's head. It gave her whatever strength she needed at a time when she only felt like crying.

"I'm not feeling so well. I think it was some shrimp I had today at the party. . . . No, she's fine. She was exhausted from the party and is taking a nap. . . . Honest, I'm okay. Just a little nauseous. . . . No! Please don't have anyone check me. I'm fine, but I'm just not in the mood to see anyone. I just need a good night's sleep. . . . I love you too, honey. I'll see you tomorrow. . . . I will. Promise."

Penny turned her head away from the phone. Erica pulled the receiver to her ear and heard the distinctive tone of a dead connection.

"Nice job." She pulled the gun away from Agatha's head. Erica walked over to Penny and pulled the cloth strip back over her face until it rested inside her mouth. "You're smarter than I thought." Erica hovered near her for a moment. Penny could smell the odor of scotch. Then, without any warning, Erica reached out and slapped Penny's face as hard as she could. The crack of her palm across the smooth cheek sounded like an exploding firecracker. Penny's head jerked to the side, and a red blotch emerged where Erica's hand had struck her. Erica raised her hand again, high in the air. Short grunts, unintelligible pleas to Erica to stop, came in quick succession from Penny's throat. Her eyes asked for mercy. Then, as suddenly as Erica had started, she stopped. She walked back to the bed. She spoke without looking at her victim. "Don't worry. I'm tired tonight, princess." As Erica rested on the edge of the bed, placing the pistol on top of the blood-soaked satin spread, Penny dropped her head. In the background the radio gave a rundown of the record cold spell gripping the eastern part of the nation. The only other sound in the room was that of Penny sobbing.

CHAPTER 20 ⊨————

Rome
December 18
7:00 a.m.

Pagannini was enraged. Gandolfo's computers kept spitting back the same reports on the dead terrorist. The captain shuffled his massive frame around the crowded computer room, grunting and mumbling to himself. Occasionally he slammed his fist on top of one of the expensive machines, and other times just gave them a solid kick. Pagannini seemed to blame the computers for not having the information he wanted. The corporal performed the tasks asked of him in absolute silence. He was petrified that at any moment Pagannini's frustration and wrath could turn from the machines to him. The young officer kept wondering what he had done recently in his life to have deserved this night. Why couldn't this have happened on his night off or during the day shift? Gandolfo knew that if the pounding resulted in a damaged computer, he would have to answer for it. But if he reprimanded the enraged captain he was likely to get the next bash. He wished he never had found the damn file with the captain's notes that matched the corpse.

"It's not possible!" Pagannini paced near the entrance to the computer room. His agitation, combined with his fifth cup of espresso, meant that even walking didn't feel bad to him. How could Interpol, the Italian police, the army, and his own central command have identical medical files for Amalfi, none of which matched any of his notes? He already had the young corporal take the other files on the "hand of death"

Brigade members and compare their computer reports against his written notes. They all matched, eliminating the chance that he had mistakenly swapped the notes with another file. While that told him what had not happened, it didn't get him any closer to solving the puzzle on the Amalfi file. He was even more flustered when he tracked down the local family doctor in the northern mountain town of Spezia, where Amalfi was raised. The doctor was eighty-two years old and had not only treated Amalfi in the town of 3500 people, but had delivered him. In July, 1984, the doctor's office of nearly forty years burned down, destroying hundreds of patient files, including Amalfi's. The local authorities told him it was from a short in the electrical system. Pagannini cynically noted that the fire was less than a month after Amalfi was blown up in the Rome bomb disaster.

The only helpful information the doctor had was the vague recollection that Amalfi had once come back from a trip to Munich, sometime in the mid-1970s, and had spoken about emergency dental treatment for an impacted tooth. That would be another way to find a set of dental x-rays. But Pagannini's department could not even start that search until dentists' offices opened in Germany, and then it would be like searching for a needle in a haystack. They would have to call every dentist in Munich, assuming the eighty-two-year-old doctor was even right about the city. Then they would have to hope that the dentist was still in practice, and without knowing the exact year, they would have to find a file of a one-time patient, from at least ten years ago. Pagannini had little hope that the German lead would prove fruitful.

By 3:00 a.m. he was stumped and exhausted. But he also wanted to get a fresh start in the morning by having the physical files from the army medical center brought to his headquarters. That could be done by 7:00 a.m. Then he could determine with his own eyes whether the computers were somehow retrieving the wrong file. He was still convinced the computers were malfunctioning.

Returning to his fourth-floor office, he sat for a moment on the edge of his leather sofa. He was getting too old for this work. Placing his head into his hands, he rested for a moment before lying down. How could his notes be wrong? He was certain they weren't. Could the files be of the wrong person? Was it possible that someone had replaced the information in three of the most sophisticated crime data banks in existence? It was possible, but extremely unlikely. Who would have the ability to do that and for what reason? He had been reading too many spy novels. Things like that happened in books, not in real life.

After several hours sleep and a good breakfast he would feel better. Bouchet might need the information as soon as possible, but he would get it quicker if Pagannini was refreshed in the morning. He called his wife, woke her from a deep sleep, and informed her that he would be staying at the office overnight. She was disappointed, but after thirty-three years she was not surprised.

He removed his tan shirt, neatly placed his brown loafers near the side of the sofa, and left on his white cotton T-shirt and trousers. As he lay back, he wondered whether the couch was getting smaller or whether it was merely his imagination. Years ago he remembered inches of extra, soft leather on each side of him. Now his skin spread over the entire seating area and even hung a little over the side. Probably just his imagination. He started to think about the Amalfi file, but realized that if he didn't block it from his mind, he would never sleep. If he was to be useful in the morning, rest and relaxation were a priority. Instead, he thought of his dinner in Washington nearly three years ago. Little neck clams with a garlic and light butter sauce to start the meal. A small serving of fettucini noodles with a light cream basil sauce as a second course. The wild mushrooms and capers had perfectly ac-cented the noodles. Ah, the main course of fillet of salmon in a hol-landaise sauce so thick you could stand a spoon in it. The last thing he remembered was the lemon sorbet served to clean his palate after the main course. He fell asleep before he got to the rum mousse.

He thought there was a tapping in the pipes. It barely penetrated his deep layer of sleep. He kept his eyes closed so that he would not completely wake, but the steady and light knocking became more per-sistent. The plumber had promised him after the third visit that he wouldn't have the damn noise anymore. When the furnace came on, he was told the heat expansion resulted in a continuous racket that woke him and his wife every night. Maybe he could block it out. With a great effort he turned his large frame over so that he would roll to the right of the bed. He felt his body starting to slide from the bed. His eyes popped open and he realized he was about to fall off the sofa in his office. His thick arm shot out and crashed into the carpet to stop the tumble, the adrenaline rushing through his system. The knocking continued. It was his office door. He couldn't believe what a deep sleep he had been in. Someone could have come into the office and killed him and he would have never heard them coming. He pushed himself into a sitting position on the edge of the sofa, shook his head to clear the cobwebs, and bellowed, "Come in, come in, I'm awake."

It was Corporal Gandolfo. At least the young officer had shaven and looked fairly well rested after less than three hours sleep. He had a file folder in one hand and a brown paper bag in the other.

"Captain, it is 7:35. I have followed your orders exactly. Here is the file on Amalfi. I was personally waiting at the army archives when they opened at 7:00, with your authorization order. I could only find Angelica's open at such an early hour. But together with the fruit mart I was able to put together something for your breakfast."

Pagannini stared at him for a moment. It was difficult to concentrate on what Gandolfo was saying. Pagannini had a foul taste in his mouth, the residue of too many espressos. He brought his hands to his face and rubbed the rough stubble. He must look terrible, although Gandolfo stared at him as though everything was absolutely normal. He could probably wear a pink tutu and Gandolfo would stand stiffly at attention and pretend it was all right. He was an ass-kisser but an efficient policeman. Pagannini reached out for the paper bag. "Thank you, Corporal. Well done. Put the file down next to me here. I will look at it in a moment. A man needs food to think correctly."

"Captain, what if the file doesn't match your notes?"

"Corporal, the questions can wait. But the espresso cannot. Please."

"I am sorry. Of course, Captain." Gandolfo gave a short bow and hurriedly left the office.

Pagannini opened the top of the brown bag and stared inside. A round roll of wheat bread studded with whole walnuts and finished in a honey glaze. Ah, one of his favorite treats from the little Angelica food shop. He took it out and placed it next to the file folder. Inside the bag, a clear piece of plastic was wrapped around a chunk, the size of his fist, of a light yellow cheese. He reached in, grabbed the cheese, and brought it to his nose. Romano. Parmesan would have been a better choice, but this would do. He glanced back inside. He shook his head. Two bananas. What was wrong with Gandolfo's head? Must be too little sleep. He had stopped at the Roman fruit market, one of the best in the Mediterranean, and he returned with two measly bananas. The market had a selection of fruits from around the globe. No wonder he looked like a beanpole. Gandolfo must weigh 160 pounds at the very most and he was taller than Pagannini. What type of Italian mother raised him so that he could bring such a breakfast and not hang his head in disgrace? Well, it would have to do. It wasn't enough for a bird, but it would have to wake him up.

Pagannini carefully unwrapped the cheese, placed it on top of the walnut bread, smashed it flat with his hand, and took a large bite. As he struggled to move the mass of food around his mouth, he picked up the file containing the thin military report. At that moment Gandolfo returned, holding the familiar white demitasse. Pagannini waved at him with the report, indicating that the espresso should be placed at his feet, on the carpet.

Pagannini looked up at the corporal. He opened his mouth to talk, but all Gandolfo could see was a mush of food, and all he could hear was a jumble of words lost in the mouthful of partially eaten breakfast. He hunched his shoulders to show Pagannini that he couldn't understand a word. Pagannini closed his mouth, worked on chomping the food for a moment, and then looked up once again.

"What's the matter? I look like I'm sick? Why two measly bananas?"

"Captain, I could not park the car. I thought you wanted the report as early as possible. So I pulled next to the market and yelled to the nearest vendor for a couple of the best pieces of fruit he had. That's what he brought me."

Pagannini had taken another enormous bite of the cheese and bread combo, leaving only a small piece. In another moment, he shoved the last portion of the makeshift sandwich into the corner of his mouth. He looked at Gandolfo and shook his head in dismay as he picked up the espresso cup and somehow managed to pour some of the liquid into a mouth that appeared ready to burst at the seams. Somehow, half the espresso emptied between his lips. The corporal stood at attention while Pagannini placed the army report on his lap and began reading the front page. This was Pagannini at his best—working and eating. He would flip a page of the report, then peel a banana. Adjust the report for easier reading and take another sip of espresso. Both his eyes and mouth moved quickly. The bottom of the second banana fell onto the report. He smeared it across the page as he picked it up. Well, at least they would know that Pagannini had personally read this file.

He barely finished eating the last morsel, never offering a bite to Gandolfo, when he slammed the report on the floor in front of him. He pushed himself up from the sofa and held his stomach as a belch came from his mouth. "Ah, that's better. Corporal, this file is the same as the ones the computer gave us last night. I must call a friend. Wait for me outside the office, and I will get you in a minute."

He had to talk to the bloodhound. If someone would know what to do with this puzzle, it had to be the Frenchman. The intercontinental connection was clear and the phone was answered on the second ring.

It was 2:30 a.m. in Washington. The voice on the other end sounded alert.

"Hello."

"Bouchet, it's Vincenzo."

"What took you so long?"

"You are funny for a man who just woke up. Look, I have a problem. Are you awake enough to follow me?" Pagannini thought of how groggy he had been only minutes earlier when his sleep was interrupted.

"Absolutely."

Pagannini smiled as he thought of the Frenchman vigorously shaking his head to clear his brain. He continued, "I found a file, my own personal one, that has jottings that match your body. I even remember something about this man. He was from a working-class family in a northern town, a student at the State University in Rome, when he became involved in one of the first Red Brigade cells. He was one of the most active and brutal Brigade terrorists. His name is Salvatore Amalfi."

"Amalfi? Wasn't he put away in prison several years ago?"

"Worse for you. He was put away by God—permanently. He was killed when one of the bombs he was making blew him halfway to Paris. Back in '84. We had an absolute match from the dental fragments left behind."

"So did you match the records I sent you against his full medical records? It can't be the same person."

"Ah, that's my problem." He couldn't stop the little burp that passed his throat and went right into the receiver.

"From the sound of that, it sounds like you might have a couple of problems, Vincenzo."

"No, if I didn't do that, my friend, then I would be in trouble. Excuse me, Romano cheese always does that to me." Bouchet smiled and shook his head as Pagannini continued. "My real problem is that when I checked his military and police files, there is a completely different medical history than the one listed in my personal notes. His original doctor lost his file in a fire, one month after Amalfi was supposed to be blown up. All other computer files are exact matches of each other. I list the fractures you show on your report, even the osteomyelitis, but the computers make us both look like we are crazy."

There was silence for a moment. "Is it possible that your notes matching my corpse belong to another file, to another person? My corpse was killed only days ago, not five years ago Vincenzo."

"I know that, Jean-Claude. But assume for a moment that my notes are correct. It's much too great a coincidence—all the medical items on such an unusual skeleton. If it was Amalfi in Paris, that means he didn't die in the Rome bomb blast. Maybe we made a mistake on the identification or maybe the death was staged. Isn't it possible, from the little found at the bombing that killed him, that we were left just enough fragments by which to identify the body and declare him dead?"

"Sure, it is possible, but you are talking about a very difficult job. Someone has to find a set of teeth that can be altered to match the supposed victim's, and then leave those at the scene. It's not easy, and often requires intricate dental work to make the job pass the scrutiny of a good pathologist. And now that the computer files don't match, it would mean that someone not only staged Amalfi's death, but then successfully replaced the real medical files in a number of strategic organizations with a new and altered set. Even we would have trouble doing that, Vincenzo. It is extremely complex, and I just don't think a terrorist organization has that type of sophistication or the necessary contacts inside the appropriate agencies."

"But it is possible, Jean-Claude?"

"Of course it is possible."

"And what would you do if you wanted to prove whether this dead body of yours might be the man who is supposed to have died five years ago? I am sure if someone replaced the medical files on him in our army and police files, as well as the one in Interpol, then they haven't left many stones unturned."

The only sound was the light static hiss of the transcontinental phone connection.

"Jean-Claude?"

"I am thinking, Vincenzo. Give me a moment."

Pagannini held the phone to his head while he grabbed a toothpick from his top drawer. As he waited for Bouchet's answer, he picked at residues of food stuck between his teeth. He wedged the toothpick between his teeth and when he popped the little morsels of food out of his mouth, they shot across the desk.

"Vincenzo, does he have a wife and child?"

"Wait a moment." He grabbed the file and flipped to the cover page. "No, single at time of death."

"Parents alive?"

"Wait a moment. . . . Yes, they were at least as of '84. The father, let's see, would be eighty-eight if he was still alive today."

"Check on it. It's important. But only if both of them are alive."

"Why, what's up? What good are his parents right now?"

"Please, just find out. Now. I have an idea."

Pagannini buzzed for Gandolfo, who ran inside the office.

"Go to the desk in the hallway and dial the number in this file. Say you are with the police, and you want to know if you are talking to either Mrs. Aurelia Amalfi or Mr. Guido Amalfi. If it's either of them, make sure that Salvatore was their son, and then ask whether their spouse is still alive. When you find out, come back and tell me. Hurry! This call I am on is costing the Italian taxpayer money!"

Gandolfo ran out the door, cradling the file under his arm.

"I heard that, Vincenzo," the bloodhound chuckled. "You and I both know that the average Italian doesn't pay any taxes, so don't worry."

"Very funny, my friend. Please, save the jokes for later. Now, tell me why both parents interest you."

"Vincenzo, we have preserved frozen samples of tissue and blood from the corpse we found. If you have two living parents then I need just 10 cc's of blood from each. If you run a genetic print for those two samples, then with my corpse I can tell you within almost 100 percent certainty whether or not he was their son. If he matches, then I don't care what the computer files say about the Paris corpse being dead five years ago."

"I like that idea." Bouchet was good. He knew the latest technology and how to apply it to solid intelligence work. Pagannini had never mastered the technological innovations as well as he should have. He didn't need to when he could rely on people as talented as the bloodhound. The corporal had been gone less than a minute when he reappeared at the doorway.

"Captain, I just spoke to Mr. Amalfi. He has gotten up every morning at dawn like he says he has for the past sixty years. His wife is still asleep, which he says is the same as she has done for the past fifty years."

"Excellent! Jean-Claude, did you hear that?"

"Yes. How can you get to them immediately?"

"I will send a military helicopter from Genoa. They will be in Spezia in less than twenty minutes. In Genoa there is an excellent forensic laboratory belonging to the state security police. While the helicopter is getting the blood samples you need, I will get the clearance from the security police to use their lab. We could have results for you by midafternoon."

That would still be morning in the U.S. "That would be excellent, Vincenzo. While you are doing that, I will call the Lion d'Or and make sure that they are making an extra order of rum mousse for tonight."

"Go back to sleep, you pain-in-the-ass Frenchman."

"On those kind words I will."

Pagannini slammed down the phone. "Corporal, patch me into the regional military command center in Genoa. And another espresso." He handed the white demitasse to Gandolfo. "And corporal . . ."

"The espresso first, Captain?"

"Exactly."

CHAPTER 21 ⇒━━━━━━

San Francisco
December 18
Noon

Lunch was the time to strike. Visiting hours were in full swing and the hospital was crawling with doctors and nurses on breaks and the start of new shifts. It was the time that Colby and Erica had chosen to finish the assignment against Vasquez. The morning news programs were filled with reports that the priest had been removed from intensive care and taken to a private suite. Law enforcement authorities were anxious to talk to him in the midafternoon. As far as Erica and Colby were concerned, the priest could never be allowed to remember anything about what happened to him. They were determined he should die.

Colby had reinforced Erica's decision. They were ready to move, despite his condition. Each had their first night's sleep in almost four days. Not that it had been all that restful. At times it was fitful for each of them. Colby had morphine-induced nightmares, images of jellylike blobs chasing him across a computer screen and slowly nipping off chunks of his backside. When he finally couldn't run anymore and lay in the roadway bleeding to death, he would partially wake, the headiness of the narcotic keeping him dazed. He would return to sleep and the dream would repeat itself. Erica told him in the morning that morphine, a derivative of opium, had a tendency to cause hallucinations. Addicts smoked it to "chase the dragon," to induce the poppy's peaceful dream state. Following the trauma Colby had suffered, it was little wonder that the dream state had turned to the terror state. The night was not much better for Erica. Despite the deep sleep that was common to her, Agatha's moaning had woken her twice. The child was dying to go to the bathroom and was almost crying in pain. Penny grunted through her gag, and pleaded with her eyes, urging Erica to untie the child and allow her to relieve herself. Both times she had obliged and another time she did the same for Penny. On each occasion she checked Colby before returning to sleep at the foot of the bed. At 3:00 a.m. she administered another 5 milligrams of morphine. The moaning caused by the throbbing pain subsided as the drug took hold. Yet, even with the interruptions, she was so exhausted that she managed to sleep almost seven hours until the alarm loudly buzzed. As a doctor, she knew that one night of good rest could compensate for days of sleep deprivation. It was the single most important thing they could have done in preparation for the rest of their mission.

The alarm had also woken Colby. Penny and Agatha looked as though they had been awake most of the night. Erica was not surprised. Tied to straight-back chairs, the sitting position restricted circulation and encouraged muscle cramping, and was not conducive to a restful night. Their fatigue should make them less of a problem during the remainder of the day. Colby was exactly as Erica expected him to be. He was extremely sore and stiff. She gently helped him to the edge of the bed and slowly tried to move his arm, but his wound limited his range of motion. She noticed that a light reddish-yellow stain had soaked through the gauze. It was time to change the wound's dressing. He kept looking at the mother and daughter, bound less than ten feet in front of him, but he did not ask any questions. He knew he would find out soon enough what had happened since he passed out.

Erica helped him to the bathroom where she removed his blood-stained underwear, carefully peeled away the bandages, and then assisted him into a shallow, warm bath. "Keep the soap and water away from the wound, just let the steam loosen your muscles," she commanded him.

During the ten minutes that he was washing, she first made a call to the San Francisco hospital where Vasquez was being treated. The news was not good. He was getting better. As she considered the consequences of his recovery, she prepared a large pot of coffee, threw half a dozen eggs into a skillet, and quickly scrambled them. The toaster kicked up lightly browned bread as quickly as she had ever seen one work. When the food was ready, she took him from the bath, helped him wipe down, and then draped him with a white, terry cloth robe she found in Penny's closet. As they sat and ate in the white-tiled breakfast room, she filled him in on what had happened since he had pulled the Cadillac underneath the Bay Bridge. Her problems getting his body out of the car and the aggravation caused by Agatha actually brought a smile to his face. Her news about the priest's fast recovery was not received as well. But his first concern was with Penny and Agatha.

"You should have killed them last night before sleeping," he blandly stated as he put half a slice of buttered toast into his mouth.

"Why? They can be useful to us."

"How? They could have gotten loose while you were sleeping and we could have woken up with police over our faces."

"But they didn't, and we didn't. I saved your life, and I think I did a pretty damn good job."

"I don't mean to say you didn't. I just think we should finish them this morning. Our entire operation is screwed up. We can't leave any more loose ends. We should have been out of San Francisco last night and in Chicago this morning. Headquarters knows we are in trouble. They certainly will when we don't meet the contact in Chicago. We've got to worry about getting pulled back in. Forget about the rest of the operation."

"But hostages can be good."

"Good if you think you are going to have to use them to get away. I suggest we don't need them. We will contact Control in New York this morning. We must do that immediately. It should have been done yesterday—"

"How the hell could I . . ."

"I'm not blaming you. I'm sure they are going crazy at being unable to find us. We must contact them and then wait to be reeled in." Colby grimaced, the pain in his shoulder obviously becoming intense as he became more agitated.

"What about the priest?" Erica asked.

"It's very high risk to go after him there."

She would not be dissuaded. "Yes. But if we don't, we have ruined the entire operation. If the virus is exposed then I will be unable to conduct the follow-up research that is so necessary. Our enemies will be alerted to us. Even if we stop the K-7 now, we will still have two good infections. That is not the best of all worlds, but it is enough to let us do our work. But we must leave both of the sites without a trace that we have been there. In New York we were successful. If we eliminate Vasquez, then no one is any the wiser for what really happened at the church. It's just another political assassination. But once they discover he did not say the mass and someone impersonated him there, they are going to have everybody and his brother poring over every inch of that church looking for what really happened. If they discover any trace of K-7, the whole operation is finished. We might as well not have come." She waited a moment for the words to sink in. "The priest must die. It's worth the risk."

He slowly sipped coffee from a large Minnie Mouse mug. "How would you intend to do it?"

"I've called the hospital this morning and said I'm from the arch-diocese and we want to know where to forward flowers and cards that are arriving at our address but are intended for Vasquez. He's being moved to room 501, a private suite, at 11:00. Respirators come off by 1:00. You will drive me there and wait a block away. I will go inside, get a nurse's uniform, and get inside his room long enough to set the potassium chloride into his drip. There will be lots of police, I know. But no one knows what I look like, unless they have the busboy from the hotel sitting in front of the priest's room."

"Well, maybe . . ."

"You know they aren't that smart. They aren't looking for a female nurse as the assassin. Not with official hospital identification. By the time they find the real nurse, you and I will be gone."

"How will you get the nurse's uniform and identification?"

"I'll take it. By force if I have to. What will that do? Increase the risk factor by 1 percent? Don't worry, I can handle it."

He sipped the coffee and stared at her. He wasn't sure if it was bravery or stupidity that pushed her to the hospital. In his condition, his shoulder throbbing incessantly, he would be virtually no help to her.

"I will give you thirty minutes from the time you leave the car. If you don't return by then, I will leave you behind. You still want to take that risk?"

"Yes."

"First, we will stop on the way into the city and call Control."

"No. Not until after we have finished the priest. If we call before, they will stop us from moving against Vasquez. It will be deemed too high risk. They don't care if the project is ruined. Their concern is whether we fall into enemy hands. We will call them after Vasquez is dead, and then we will have some good news for Control."

She had developed into an excellent field agent. Her instincts were replacing his, which were still at half-speed from the shooting. He nodded his head. "Agreed."

She led him back to the bedroom where she redressed his wounds with fresh bandages and gauze. The small syringe, half-filled with penicillin, was emptied directly into the incision before the new dressing was applied. She administered 10 cc's of Solu-Medrol in the upper portion of his arm, promising that would alleviate the throbbing. And although he felt fairly rested, she told him that the loss of blood would catch up to him in several hours unless he took some Benzedrine. He reluctantly agreed. The 15 milligrams of pure speed was shot into his veins just as the Solu-Medrol started to dull the ache in his back.

Erica helped him dress in some of Penny's husband's clothes. A pair of dark grey wool trousers fit well around the waist but were a little short. He carefully put on an oversized plaid shirt that easily covered the bandage on his shoulder. All the shoes were too small, forcing Colby to wear the heavy black pair he had used as part of his Vasquez disguise. A navy blue, double-breasted blazer completed the outfit. Erica had more luck rummaging through Penny's closet for something fresh to wear. She settled on a pair of navy blue, high-waisted trousers and a large white sailor's pullover. She finished her outfit with a California touch, high-top, pink and white Reebok sneakers, just half a size too large. Erica gathered all of their soiled clothing, her syringes, the K-7 packet, and the remainder of their goods, and placed them into the Toyota's trunk. In a final search of the bedroom closets, she found his and hers Burberrys raincoats. They would be perfect for the damp, misty weather.

By 10:30 they were ready to leave. The final decision was whether to kill Penny and Agatha. Colby was convinced they should both be dead. But Erica's argument carried the day.

"Look, you're not thinking rationally because of all the chemicals. It's not your fault, but listen to me for a second. It is almost impossible that when we call Control they are going to have an immediate route out of here. They aren't even sure what city we are in. So once we tell them, then it will take several hours, at least, and maybe more, to arrange for our safe exit. Agreed?"

"Agreed."

"So when we are finished with the priest, at least we know we have a place to return to as a safe house until we are ready to move. We'll be coming back here no matter what."

"So why not kill them? We can come back here anyway. What do we need them alive for?"

"They are our trump cards. If we need anything done that we cannot do ourselves, the mother will do it. She is petrified of what we could do to her daughter. And if we are about to travel, everyone is looking for two assassins, a man and a woman. They aren't looking for two women, a man, and a child. They are a perfect cover to the airport or wherever we have to go. If we make sure they are secure when we leave, they will be here when we return. If Control arranges for us to leave and we don't need their help, then we kill them before we go. But you are being premature."

It made sense to him. He wasn't sure it made sense because it was right or because he was not thinking clearly. But in either case he was ready to agree. He nodded. "What time does her husband return?"

"I saw his travel itinerary and double-checked his reservation with the airline. He doesn't even get into the airport until 9:00 tonight. We will be back long before then and can decide what to do before he arrives."

Before they left, Colby directed Erica in retying Penny and Agatha with the torn sheets and thin strands of wire. Towels covered and gagged their mouths. Colby tipped each of the chairs to their sides, crashing them to the floor, making it impossible for either hostage to move about. He leaned over Penny before leaving. "We'll be back in an hour. I wouldn't even think of trying anything in that time if I were you. Remember, I know where you live. No one can protect you twenty-four hours a day. You can't watch over your daughter every minute of every day. So even if you get free now, I'll be back to pay a visit, and I'll cut your daughter up in front of your eyes. You can bank on it. Understand?"

Penny's eyes seemed to say yes.

"Good. If you're real good, we'll leave here tonight. And you have my word that if you do as you're told, you, your daughter, and your husband will remain unhurt. I have no desire to hurt you unless you try to hurt me. Understood?"

Again Penny tried to nod yes, but since the chair had been toppled over, her neck was jammed against the floor. He patted her on the forehead. "Good." He had hardly ever kept his word in the past. There was no reason why this occasion should be any different.

The drive into the city was without incident. Erica drove. Although Colby claimed he was a good one-armed driver, Erica's vivid memories of yesterday's terrifying chase had encouraged her to sit behind the wheel. The traffic was light, and by 11:20 they approached Stanyon Street and the front entrance to St. Mary's Hospital. Two police cars were parked in front, and both Colby and Erica assumed that some undercover agents were posted inside. Yet, they still would have been surprised to discover that nearly a dozen undercover agents were inside the hospital disguised as everything from cleaners in the dining area to doctors and nurses on the various floors, to the salesperson at the lobby gift stand, even to fretting "family members" waiting for news of supposed sick relatives. They had no idea that McGinnis and Harris were also waiting on the fifth floor, inside the room where Vasquez was supposed to be recuperating. They were waiting for one of the murderers to walk through the front door to the room. Frustrated by the previous night's nonproductive search of the Fairmont Hotel room, both CIA agents were anxious for their trap to work. They had no idea their quarry had arrived.

Erica drove slowly past the front entrance, made a right turn on Hayes Street, and pulled to the curb near the next corner. She slipped on a large pair of Penny's sunglasses, placed the small vial of potassium chloride into her pocket, and looked at her watch.

"11:24. I will see you by 11:55. If not, you get the hell out of here and call Control."

"Hurry up and get back."

She left the car and briskly walked the block back to the hospital. She was amused by Colby. Even in his slightly altered chemical state, he was still superstitious about offering a simple "good luck." Since his wounded shoulder was being looked for by half of San Francisco, it was out of the question for him to come into the hospital and help. He hated waiting. Action motivated him during an operation. But on this occasion he was more useful in the car than if he joined her and served as a warning light to the police.

The Burberrys raincoat Erica wore was not heavy enough to provide protection against the cutting San Francisco chill. The wet cold swept inside the coat and sent shivers through her. She walked past the first police squad car with two officers sitting inside. They did not even bother to look at her. Past the double set of automatic sliding glass doors, she was finally met with a blast of warmth from the hospital interior. Near the gift stand she made a left and waited with a doctor and a wheelchair patient at the bank of four elevators. Not wanting to increase the remote chance that somebody could recognize her, she stared directly ahead to the elevator doors. Her hair was pulled into a tight bun, a change from the long, carefree style she wore in San Francisco the day before. Together with pink lipstick and light purple eyeshadow, which she had found in Penny's powder room, she looked quite different from when she had helped Vasquez at the Hyatt.

She knew that the second floor was intensive care. It was likely to be the hub of too much activity. The fifth floor was the new location for Vasquez and was probably crawling with uniformed and undercover agents. The third floor was her destination because it cared for the hospital's routine postoperative patients. It would be relatively quiet and provide the best opportunity to get at a nurse, alone.

She looked up at the elevator numbers on a large electronic board at the end of the hall. Two of the elevators were on the eighth floor. Two were still going up. She hoped they would be quicker when she had finished injecting Vasquez. She looked at her watch. 11:28. Four minutes wasted—she had to get moving. Suddenly she felt someone shuffle close behind. Whoever it was stood almost on top of her, nearly breathing over her head. She started to take a step forward when she heard the almost inaudible whisper, "What the fuck are you doing here?"

She froze. She thought that she must have misheard the voice. It couldn't have been intended for her. "Just get in and follow me." The whisper was almost unintelligible. The person behind obviously did not want to be overheard by the nearby doctor or patient. She turned her head as though looking back into the hallway. His face was staring directly over the top of her head. She couldn't believe it. The mission's Control agent, the emergency contact she had intended to call within the hour, was standing behind her. How did he know she was there? What was he doing there? Her mind was confused. Colby wouldn't believe it. The far right elevator finally arrived and she entered ahead of the other people. The doctor pressed "4," and the patient "5." Control pressed "8." She was speechless. What was she going to do about Vasquez? What did the agent know about the priest? Was it possible he was here on another assignment? No, it was too much of a coincidence. He must be at the hospital because of Vasquez and the mission.

The elevator was interminably slow. Control stood at the front of the elevator and did not acknowledge her existence. She didn't know him that well, but he seemed furious. She would have to wait to find out if her hunch was right. On the fourth floor, the doctor exited and a nurse got in. But she didn't press another button as the door closed.

That meant the nurse was either getting off on the next floor with the wheelchair patient, or she was traveling with them to the top floor. If that was the case, Erica would not get an opportunity to talk to Control. It was clear that he would not acknowledge her in the presence of anyone else. The elevator slid to a stop at the fifth floor, the patient wheeled himself out, and then the nurse briskly stepped into the high-tech corridor. Once the door closed he turned to face her. The minute he started to speak, even though it was a controlled whisper, she knew she was right about his fury. He was steaming.

"Idiot!" He hissed. "Vasquez is a ruse to get you here. He died this morning. They are waiting for you everywhere. The kid from the hotel is on his way here. You have walked right into it! Where's Colby?"

"Outside. Down the block in a car."

"Hurt badly? Can he travel?"

"Yes, he can travel. He's fine."

"Mission's canceled. You should have checked in much earlier. They were able to track the virus much better than we ever expected. They have your names and know all about New York and the church. You call New York today at 5:00 p.m. Pacific time and they will tell you where to rendezvous for an exit."

The elevator came to a stop at the eighth floor. The doors opened wide but no one got in. When they closed and the elevator started descending, he continued talking.

"Bring the K-7 with you. Everything goes out of America tonight. I will be there personally to make sure you get out safely. I have had to come here to protect you. This is a risk I never wanted to take."

The elevator slowed to a stop at the sixth floor. Control turned toward the button panel and quickly pressed "5" and then the lobby button. "Leave the hospital now! Stay low profile until 5:00."

When the doors opened a young nurse entered the elevator. She would never have guessed that the two people inside knew each other.

Erica's head was spinning. She barely remembered walking out of the hospital. The Americans were tracking the infections. The damn spectrum system must have been accurate enough to pick up the atmospheric variations. They had discussed it beforehand and were convinced the sensors were not sensitive enough to pick up the changes made by the virus. She had been wrong. That was a major mistake. And their names were known. The hospital was a trap. She would have been dead if she had not had the good fortune to run into Control. Maybe their luck was changing after all.

Halfway around the world events had moved with haste. The Italian military had dispatched a Huey helicopter with a medical team aboard. The residents of Spezia, the sleepy mountain town just north of Genoa, looked as though they had never seen a helicopter before. They gathered around the chopper as it dropped for a landing on the southern and flattest edge of the town. When the military doctors, resplendent in full uniform, stepped out of the massive Huey and asked for directions to the Amalfi house, word spread through the little village like wildfire. Everyone knew the Amalfis had been disgraced by a son who had been a leader of the Red Brigade. When he was killed, the family refused to even honor him with a burial ceremony. Now the army was arriving in helicopters to talk to the parents. What could be the problem? The other three sons were respectable. Two still lived in Spezia, one a mechanic and the other a cook. The third had moved to Milan and was involved in the fashion trade. Although there was some doubt about his sexual inclination, there wasn't any thought that he might actually be in trouble with the authorities. Those poor Amalfis. What could be their problem this time? A small crowd followed the two doctors to the Amalfi home.

Guido Amalfi, eighty-eight years old, was as feisty as could be. He was not going to let them put a needle in his arm for all the money in the world. They might as well kill him first. That's probably what they were trying to do anyway. He might be old and live in a little village but he read the daily journals. He knew about some disease in America that was passed with needles. That's it. They were trying to give him the new sickness. Trying to make him pay for what his Salvatore had done. "Out! Out!" He screamed it at the top of his lungs. The neighbors who had gathered outside could hear the screaming. It sounded like the elder Amalfi was being killed. Should they get help? Should they do anything to stop the two army men from hurting the gentle, elderly couple? While the gathering villagers debated what they should do, the army men followed their orders. If they had any difficulty obtaining voluntary compliance, they were to obtain blood samples at any cost, short of extreme violence. The key word was "extreme."

They did not view one of them holding Guido to the floor while the other ripped open his shirt and kept striking a needle into his arm in search of a vein to be extreme use of force. Aurelia, his frail wife, screamed at the army men to leave her husband alone. The screams raised anguish among the milling villagers outside the home. Some wanted to charge inside and do away with the army men. The Amalfis were friends. They did not deserve this. But cooler heads prevailed and the crowd grumbled but did not take action. On the fifth jab the needle found a tired vein and the medic pulled a syringe full of blood from the arm. One doctor kept holding Guido to the floor, which was no easy task, while the other approached Aurelia with a fresh syringe. She merely fainted. When Guido saw his wife fall to the floor and the other doctor lean over her and stick a needle into her arm, he was sure they had killed her.

"Murderers! Murderers! Why did you kill her?"

By this time some townspeople had arrived at the Amalfi house with shotguns and long-barreled rifles. "They're killing the old folks in there. It's horrible. Close your ears," the crowd would tell newcomers. Suddenly the door to the small stucco house opened and the two military men came out in a sprint. When they saw the size of the crowd and the tips of the guns, they simultaneously unlocked their holsters and drew their pistols. The crowd gathered tighter in front of them and blocked their path. Then Guido Amalfi appeared at the door, his shirt torn, his face contorted in apparent agony.

"They have that disease from America. The one with the needles! Be careful! They just killed my Aurelia and they have stabbed me with a needle. Look!" He held up his tattered sleeve and exposed his arm to the crowd. Mothers grabbed at their children and men backed up, creating a large pathway in the center.

"AIDS! Oh, my God, no!" someone yelled. Murmurs and little yells were heard in the crowd. The army had infected the Amalfis with AIDS.

"Watch out. Don't touch them. They have needles, get away from them." It was like they had given a magic password to leave unmolested from the town. They had all heard about the strange disease in America. Now the army was bringing it to the little towns. Those damn Americans. It must have something to do with NATO.

Once the medics were airborne they began performing preliminary tests aboard the helicopter, which doubled as a flying hospital. By the time they arrived in Genoa, at the main medical testing facility, they had already prepared the slides for laboratory work. In less than three hours, the slides had been analyzed for initial DNA patterns. Enough to give to Pagannini.

The captain was in the middle of a lunch of fettucini with a heavily peppered cream sauce and a small loaf of garlic French bread covered with anchovies when the Genoa doctors called with the information.

He didn't even wipe his hands as he wrote it on a sheet of paper. The ink spread around the paper together with blotches of grease and co-agulating sauce. When he hung up with Genoa, he immediately placed a call to the bloodhound, who eagerly transcribed the information, and then called his forensic team at the SDECE in Paris. He read the DNA print from the blood samples of Guido and Aurelia Amalfi. The voice in Paris had no doubt about the answer. "This corpse is their son."

"You are sure of that, Doctor? Absolutely sure?"

"Within a 99.9 percent certainty. You have just read me the blood patterns of his parents."

The bloodhound's next call was to Richard McGinnis. The night before, McGinnis relented and gave Bouchet his location and hotel number. He swore Bouchet only to use it in an emergency. As far as the bloodhound was concerned, this qualified. But McGinnis was not at his hotel. He had no other way to contact him. He called CIA head-quarters. First he asked for Finch. He was not available and wouldn't be for several days. John Fitzgerald? Neal Phillips? No one was there. The bloodhound had the feeling that the case was moving fast without him. He had just made a major breakthrough and no one was able to receive the news. The only other person he felt comfortable enough to talk with was the loony Brit, Hodson. He was there.

"Hello."

"Mr. Nigel Hodson?"

"Who is this?"

"Jean-Claude Bouchet, a friend of—"

"Sure, chap, I know who you are. I thought you had gone back to Paris, but the connection sounds nearby."

"I am nearby. They haven't gotten rid of me yet, Mr. Hodson." Hodson liked that type of frankness. He knew of Bouchet's reputation as a damn good agent. And he was a friend of McGinnis, which meant he couldn't be all bad.

"I have been trying to get hold of Richard McGinnis in San Francisco, but I can't seem to locate him. Can you help me?"

"No, sorry, I can't. I can't even waste much time talking with you as I've got my hands full here and if I don't get back to work, I'm just going to fall farther behind."

"Well, just one moment, if you would please. I was trying to get some information to Richard, which I believe may be critical to him on a case he is working on."

"Can I pass it on to him?" There was silence for a moment. "Hey, mate, I'm on the same side. I'm even on the same case as Richard."

The bloodhound had little choice. "The dead body that turned up in Paris, which you all showed some interest in, do you know it?"

"I know all about it."

"Well, you might be interested in knowing the identity. His name is Salvatore Amalfi, Italian, Red Brigade."

"You mean to tell me we may be dealing with a terrorist team, not a group of KGBers?"

"Since I don't even know what you are looking for, that is difficult for me to answer."

"All right, I understand. Listen, thank you very much for the information. I will check it in our systems and pass it along to Richard."

"One last thing."

"Yes?"

"When you check on Mr. Amalfi, I think you're going to find that he blew himself up in a Rome bomb blast in 1984. I think you should ignore that part of your file. I can assure you that the reports of his death were greatly exaggerated."

"You're sure of the identification?"

"Absolutely."

Hodson whistled into the phone. "Thanks again. I didn't have enough to do without trying to get some background on a resurrected terrorist. I owe you one for this, Jean-Claude."

"I'll collect from Richard." The phone connection was already dead. Bouchet started to dial again. It was time to interrupt Pagannini's mid-afternoon snack and to thank him for a job well-done.

CHAPTER 22 ⇒———————

Sausalito, California
December 18
2:00 p.m.

Colby was furious. More with himself than with anyone or anything in particular. His initial shock at Erica's unexpected meeting with Control had turned to anger. He should have known better. He should have checked with the New York townhouse before this. It wasn't completely his fault. Headquarters had decided it was too high risk to maintain daily contact during the operation. But no one had devised a safe way for the agents in the field to keep abreast of the hunt for them. If Colby had known that the CIA computers were successful in tracking infections, he would have altered their plans. The need for such elaborate disguises and complex operations would have been eliminated. They could have reverted to straightforward infections. There would have been no need to undertake such a ridiculous operation as Vasquez and the mass—they wouldn't be in this situation if it hadn't been for that venture.

"You've got to stop worrying about it," Erica tried to assure him as they drove over the Golden Gate Bridge on the way back to Penny's house. "The simple fact is that we didn't check in and they didn't create any means by which we could safely do that. It's their screw-up, not ours. Considering that the CIA is able to track the virus and they know our cover identities, I think we did a pretty damn good job of avoiding capture. They know it too. So all the worrying in the world is not going to change anything. You're too professional for this. So cut it out. You'll aggravate your wound."

"I'm trying. I'm trying."

"You're just not accustomed to failure. To you, since half the operation is incomplete, it's like you've let everyone down. Think about it. We came inside the U.S., started two major infections that they cannot do a single thing to stop, and we are going to get away tonight. That's not bad for less than a week's work."

He smiled at her. Her enthusiasm was admirable. She was like some American cheerleader he had seen in film clips about the States. Her attitude was good for him. He needed the reinforcement.

The early afternoon traffic across the bridge was almost nonexistent. He looked out the side window at the shimmering bay, the infamous Alcatraz prison in the distance, and the postcard beauty of the San Francisco skyline. It seemed so peaceful. He had never been to the west coast of America. Maybe, one day, he could return.

"Do you have any pain?"

"A little. A throbbing in the shoulder. And I can't seem to move it much without it stiffening up."

"That's normal. You should see how you would be without the medication. In bed."

"I'd probably be better off in bed."

"You can get some rest at the house. We have several hours of dead time."

They both looked forward to the short break. Now that the mission was officially canceled, it was as though a burden had been lifted from their shoulders. Their close brush with death the previous day had a profound effect on them. Now that they were about to enter the safety net from headquarters, there was a tremendous release of emotion.

They were just about to enter the partially obscured driveway leading to Penny's house when Colby realized something was wrong. He saw the glint of a flashing light bouncing off the front hood of the Toyota. "Keep going, don't turn into the driveway!" he commanded. Erica whipped the wheel back to the center of the roadway and kept climbing the short hill.

He tried to look down the road as he spoke to her. "Make a U-turn and go back down the hill."

"What is it?"

"I'm not sure yet."

She cranked the wheel to the left as far as it would go and gradually completed a U-turn. She pressed against the brakes and the car slowly slid down the road. Colby strained his neck to see over the treetops into the front of the house.

"Police cars!" he almost spit out the words. "How the hell . . ."

"I don't believe it!"

"Well, believe it. There are two there. Goddamn it, I knew we should have killed those two!"

Erica didn't say a word. She had made a major mistake by talking Colby out of his better instincts. Penny and Agatha knew exactly what they looked like. The police would have detailed descriptions. And the Toyota was probably being looked for everywhere. Colby read her thoughts.

"We've got to get rid of this car," he said, turning to face her. "Keep going, I'll tell you where to stop."

They both wondered how the police had arrived at the house. Her husband wasn't due home until tonight. What Colby and Erica didn't know was that it made little difference whether they had killed Agatha and Penny or let them live. What Penny had failed to tell them was that a cleaning woman came in daily at noon and spent two hours. One way or another, they would be discovered either dead or alive that afternoon. The police would be there shortly thereafter. The only difference would be that if they were dead, they couldn't provide descriptions.

"Stop here," he said, pointing to an open parking place alongside the curb. They were less than half a mile from Penny's house. He turned his head and checked the surrounding area. There were only homes, set back from the road, mostly hidden by the thick foliage—not a person in sight. Colby pulled a small, Swiss pocket knife from his trousers. "Give me a moment; some of these look like they should be easy."

He reached over with his good arm and unlatched the door. Swiveling his body to the side, he left the car and closed the door behind. She watched as he walked slowly next to the car parked in front of them, pausing for what seemed like only a brief moment by the driver's door. She knew he was trying to jimmy the lock with his blade. He kept strolling toward the next car. Again a pause by the door, his hand shaking as it tried to force the lock. She glanced around the area. She could not see anyone. By the time she turned to watch him, he had moved on to the third car. After a moment at the door, he raised his head and looked up and down the road. When he confirmed the area was empty, he suddenly opened the door and as quickly as his wound allowed him, slipped inside. She didn't need any further direction. Grabbing a handkerchief from her sweater pocket, she quickly wiped the steering wheel and the door handles, hoping to smear any fingerprints. She leaned under the dashboard and pulled the lever that popped open the trunk. Using the hanky to open the car door, she moved quickly to the rear of the car to retrieve the duffel bag, pushed the trunk down with her elbow, and then walked down the steep embankment until she reached the side of the third car, an early model bright blue Mustang. She opened the passenger door just as he successfully matched the wires under the dash that kicked over the ignition and started the deep-throated, 351-cc high-performance motor.

"What are we going to do?" Erica asked, a nervous edge evident in her voice.

"We're going to go back into San Francisco. When we first went to the hotel the other day, we passed a large multistory parking garage. We'll put this car in there. Even if it's reported stolen, the police won't look for it in a public lot. Almost directly across the street, on the diagonal corner, was a glass-enclosed multiscreen cinema."

"I remember it."

"Good. Because that's where we're going."

"To the movies?"

"They have a description of us now. What are we going to do until 5:00? Wait to be caught? I think not. In a movie house we are safe. In a modern cinema like that one, they are sure to have pay phones. We'll use one at 5:00 to call New York. I am sure they are working on getting us out of here as fast as possible."

Erica nodded. Her determination to let Agatha and Penny live had now placed them in additional jeopardy. He was not reminding her of the decision. She was grateful for the silence. As they drove down Van Ness Avenue toward the parking garage at the Jack Tar Hotel, they passed the corner cinema. Colby heard a groan and looked at Erica. He followed her eyes to the marquee on the other side of the street. Flashing lights announced *Rambo III*. He groaned in unison.

McGinnis was on his third coffee. That's if you could call it coffee. It was a light brown liquid that was squirted from a vending machine into a plastic cup after a quarter was deposited into the slot. The machine announced in bold letters that it was coffee. But McGinnis was almost sure they had forgotten to put the coffee beans inside. He remembered once that his son accidentally drank some dishwashing liquid left near the kitchen table. He wished his son was with him—he could tell whether the automatic coffee vendor had confused Folger's with Ivory. The first cup he had that morning he took black, just the way he preferred it. But when he realized the only similarity between the brown liquid and a good brew was that they were both hot, he decided to add sugar to the next batch. For his second cup he had deposited the quarter and pressed the coffee and sugar buttons. Same putrid odor and taste. If nothing else, McGinnis was persistent. On his third cup he pressed both "extra sugar" and "extra cream." That upgraded the taste to bottom-of-the-pot status. Well, at least the caffeine was working. He was staying alert on one of the most boring assignments—sitting inside a ten-by-fifteen-foot hospital room with Harris, waiting for some crazed Soviet agent to blast through the door. When no one appeared by 1:00 he had doubts that his plan would work. The radio and television shows had been announcing that the respirator was about to be removed from Vasquez. If they intended to kill the priest, they would have to do it before then. But as more time went by, he felt they had decided to pass. It must be because of the priest's blindness. They must have weighed the chance of his identification versus the risk of entering the hospital and decided the risk was too great. It surprised him. VKR agents were almost certifiably crazy. It might be a prerequisite for the job. But not storming the hospital was a rational choice. That's what surprised him: that a VKR agent could make a rational choice.

There was a triple knock on the door, the signal for authorized entry to the room. No one wanted to step inside unannounced on the off chance that a trigger-happy Harris or McGinnis could put a fast end to their career. "Come in," Harris called out.

It was Peter Clark, the Company's West Coast chief. "Fellows, I think you can get out of here. We've just been contacted by the S.F. police. It seems your two friends spent the night with a mother and daughter across the bay in Sausalito." McGinnis stood up. Harris looked like someone had just jabbed him with a sharp pin.

"They evidently kidnapped the pair at gunpoint, right where they abandoned the car used in the getaway from the hotel yesterday. They tied up the mother and daughter and then spent the night at the house. The two were discovered that way this morning by a maid."

McGinnis looked puzzled. "You mean that our two birds just left after a safe night and didn't blow their hostages' brains out?"

"I had a quick conversation with a captain downtown and he is only relaying to me what he picked up from the Sausalito police. The two of them evidently left this morning and promised to be back in an hour. They've been gone nearly three hours and there was no sight of them until the police just discovered, in the last half hour, the family car they had been using, abandoned about half a mile from the house."

"Was either of them injured?"

"The man was pretty badly hurt according to the mother. But the woman with him apparently was a doctor of some type and was able to operate on him last night. She doesn't know exactly what happened because she evidently kept her eyes closed most of the time. They are waiting for you at the house if you want to talk to them."

McGinnis seemed disturbed. "You mean no one has tried to set a trap for them if they are returning? Don't tell me there's just a bunch of cops sitting at the house like a warning flag in case the two of them come back?" McGinnis could feel the coffee churning extra acid in his stomach. God, he hated incompetence.

"Unfortunately, that's the case, Richard. This was under the juris-diction of the Sausalito police, a tourist town that has weekend drunk-enness as its biggest problem. I don't think you can blame them for not immediately thinking of how to set a trap for two international intel-ligence agents."

"Thanks, Peter. Jimmy, let's go and see what we can find out."

Harris grabbed his overcoat, which had been hanging in the room's only closet. Before they left, there was a second authorized knock on the door. Clark pushed the door open and revealed a young female police officer, disguised as the day nurse for the floor. "Mr. McGinnis, you have a telephone call at the front desk from Washington. Do you want me to transfer it to this room?"

"Please."

He hoped it wasn't business. It would be nice to get a single if only momentary break from this case. It was suffocating him, like he was punching away at a wet paper bag, exerting a lot of energy but not making any progress. A good double of Jack Daniel's would help relieve his frustration, but there wasn't a bar or bottle in sight. He picked up the receiver.

"Yep."

"Richard?"

"Yes." He could hear the accent. "Hodson?"

"Well, for godsakes, it took me nearly twenty minutes to track you down. You're harder to find than the damn people we are looking for."

"I'm surprised you found me at all, since this part of the operation was supposed to be airtight."

"Well, you know what they say, where there's a will, there's—"

"A way."

"That's right. Listen to me. Enough small talk. I've got some major news, but I want to pass it on to you directly. I don't know quite what to make of it, but I don't like it. Can anyone hear me?"

McGinnis looked up at Harris and Clark, both nearly five feet away, and in the midst of a conversation. "No, you're clear."

"Richard, your friend Bouchet called me this morning with an ID on the Paris corpse."

McGinnis felt vindicated. He knew the bloodhound was one of the best in the business. He came through! "Soviet?"

"No. I bloody wish it was. It would make our job a lot easier. Now just listen to me and try not to act surprised or show that anything is out of the ordinary."

"Fine."

"Bouchet IDed the body as a Salvatore Amalfi, former bigwig in the Red Brigade." Hodson paused to let that disclosure sink in. McGinnis had to catch himself from saying something. What the hell was a Red Brigade member doing in the middle of an operation this sophisticated? It was beyond their ability, of that much McGinnis was certain. Hodson continued. "I was as surprised as you. But wait, the best is yet to come. This Amalfi chap is supposed to have blown himself up back in '84 when a bomb he was making prematurely exploded. It looks like the death confirmation made by the Italians, based on some tooth fragments, was faulty. And someone has gone to a lot of trouble to cover this fellow's past. All the medical records on him have evidently been swapped in police agencies. It's a sophisticated cover-up. Not an everyday insurance scam. Richard, you following all of this?"

"Yep."

"Well, here's the kicker. I try to run our file on Amalfi and I'm blocked. His name is listed under a Delphi program and the whole thing is locked up tighter than a mouse's asshole." McGinnis was really having a difficult time keeping his mouth shut. "But I got inside the file to take a look."

"How did you . . ."

"Richard, they are my computers, for godsakes. If anyone can figure out a way to pierce their security, I better be able to. I designed the damn system."

"Where are you right now?"

"Don't worry. I am not talking to you on a Company line. You think I want this conversation recorded? I am on a safe private line and your hospital line is as good as any we are going to get. Now pay attention."

Harris was waving his arm to get McGinnis's attention. He was pointing to his watch, indicating that it was time for them to get moving. McGinnis raised his hand indicating just another moment. Harris returned to his conversation with Clark.

"According to the Delphi, Amalfi was not killed by his own bomb. He was supposed to be eliminated as part of an antiterror team led from the Company. The man who led the team that confirmed the kill on Amalfi was your old friend Neal Phillips. Now I don't know what's up here. Either Amalfi screwed us and got away and Phillips doesn't know it. Or Phillips helped stage Amalfi's death, in which case I think he has a little explaining to do."

McGinnis's mind was racing, but he tried to appear as calm as possible. "I agree. I will see what I can do. Anything else?"

"Isn't that enough for one day?"

"Thanks. Seriously. You've done well."

"I know. I just don't know what you Yanks would do without me. I think—"

McGinnis had already put the receiver down. He looked at Clark. "Peter, I haven't seen Neal Phillips yet. Is he in from D.C.?"

"Sure. So much brass has come in that I'm afraid the local office will never recover. Phillips, Finch, Fitzgerald, they are here in force. They want this thing wrapped up as soon as possible."

"Thanks." McGinnis grabbed his raincoat and tapped Harris on the shoulder as he left the hospital room. He was sure that Clark was right. They all wanted it over as soon as possible. After talking to Hodson, he just wasn't sure they all wanted the same results.

CHAPTER 23 ⟹————

San Francisco
December 18
5:00 p.m.

It was a fitting end to their ill-fated mission. They had checked with
the New York townhouse at 5:00 p.m. The rendezvous with Control
was set for 11:00 p.m., at Fort Point, an 1870s Russian fort now converted into a national monument and tourist haven, located directly
underneath the base of the Golden Gate Bridge. Colby knew the location
and was certain it would be deserted by the time he and Erica arrived.
It was on a rocky and desolate point jutting into the water where the
bay met the Pacific Ocean. The nearby water currents and waves were
so treacherous that the U.S. Army, who owned the land, closed the
point to the public after sunset.

When he returned to Erica in the theater, he told her the news. "It
must mean they are taking us out by boat. From a pickup at the point,
we could be in the ocean in minutes. Then we'll probably transfer to
an oceangoing vessel. It's a good departure point for getting out of
America. We're lucky to be in a port city. If we had had this problem
during our next phase, in Chicago, it would have been much worse
for us."

"It is much worse for us," Erica whispered to him. "If we have to
stay out of sight until 10:00, that means we have to sit through two
more Rambo showings." She rolled her eyes. Even he had to smile. One
showing was bad enough. But three could cause brain damage. Yet,

they both had to admit there was one scene they liked. At one point in the movie, when Rambo is wounded with a metal spear sticking in his back, he performed self-surgery. Instead of merely pulling out the spear, as John Wayne would have in the old westerns, Rambo invented a new operating style. First he pushed the spear through his body until it came out through his abdomen. Next, he took a large caliber bullet, chopped off the top with his commando knife, and then poured gun-powder into each wound. He finished off this medical wonder by hold-ing a lighted torch to one side of his body, and long flames shot through his body and out each hole, cauterizing the wounds. Erica and Colby found the scene very amusing.

"Thank God he wasn't there to operate on me last night," Colby told Erica.

"If I had only seen this movie before I had to get that bullet from you, I would have blown it out with some plastic explosive," she in-formed him.

But aside from that one moment, the film was tedious. Bodies blown from the sky every two minutes seemed too close to home after their travails of the past two days. Sitting through the film once was difficult. Two more times in the crowded theater would be deadly. But the way their luck had been running it wasn't surprising.

Erica had given Colby the final 5 milligrams of morphine at 6:00. It helped him through half of the second show. At 9:00 they prepared to leave. Colby thought it best to arrive early, positioning themselves to ensure that only a proper evacuation team arrived at the rendezvous. He was tired of leaving things to chance. It had worked against them every time during the mission.

Together they walked to the pay phone near the large staircase in the lobby. He pulled a registration card for the stolen Mustang from his trouser pocket. He telephoned 911. They answered on the second ring.

"911."

"Hello, 911, this is Andrew Sheldon. I am so sorry to bother you, but I have just found out that my brother had borrowed my car and hadn't told me. I thought it was stolen. Now, my son has been looking for it for several hours, and I don't know if he called you reporting it stolen. If so, I need to cancel that report, because everything's fine."

The woman on the other end of the line sounded totally confused. "You want to report a stolen car?"

"No, I don't know if my son reported my car stolen, since it was missing before, but now I discovered my brother had merely borrowed it and hadn't told me. I could just kill him for causing me all this embarrassment."

"Well, if your car was reported stolen, you can't just cancel the report over the telephone. You have to come into a station and sign a report that the car is in your possession."

"But, that's just it. I don't know if it was reported or not. If I give you my name and license number can't you check to see if my son called in?"

"Why don't you just ask your son?"

"He's still out looking for the car. He doesn't know I have it back. So I can't ask him."

By this time the 911 operator was totally confused. She decided it was easier to pacify the caller than to expend energy figuring out what happened. "What's your name, car make, and license number."

That's more like it, Colby thought. "As I said, I am Andrew Sheldon, the car is a 1970 bright blue Mustang Mach I, and the license is ADT6547."

"Wait a minute." Colby could hear the click of computer keys being pressed in the background.

"We don't have any report of your car being stolen."

"Oh, then my son must have had the good sense to have held off in calling you. Thank you for your help, Officer."

Colby gently placed the receiver back. "Dumb. Bureaucrats are the same all over the world. A prerequisite for the job is stupidity. Well, some news is good. Our only means of transportation has not been reported stolen. We can use it to get to Fort Point."

McGinnis and Harris introduced themselves to Penny as FBI agents. They found her to be helpful, even though she was dreadfully tired and still recovering from her all-night terror. The most interesting information was that the man, although groggy most of the time, seemed to lapse between perfect American, and then slightly broken English. It was an accent she couldn't quite place, but it reminded her a bit of Arnold Schwarzenegger, whom she had recently seen in a movie. She heard the accent when he appeared to be in the most pain, during the makeshift surgery she described to them. To the two agents, that meant Colby was not American. He was obviously trying to maintain English as his cover language, but under the narcotic and in the stress of the surgery he couldn't control his enunciation. His real origins were showing through. Schwarzenegger. Although he is Austrian, Colby could easily be eastern European or Russian. Americans were notoriously inept at distinguishing foreign accents. As for the woman, the fact that Penny identified her as an American didn't mean anything. Any Soviet agent worthy of an assignment as important as the K-7 infections would certainly be so well-versed in America and in the language that they could pass as a true, red-blooded citizen of the stars and stripes. The woman wasn't the wounded one, and it was no surprise that she did not lose control of her American inflection, even during the stress of removing the bullet.

The information about the makeshift surgery was helpful. All agents were given courses in emergency medical treatment, but not to the extent with which she was evidently familiar. She was likely a doctor, or at least had medical training. That could narrow the list of suspected Soviet or eastern bloc agents. Although, after speaking to Hodson, McGinnis was no longer convinced the bioassassins were merely VKR agents. The dead Red Brigade member in Paris told him there was a terrorist connection. The CIA files were filled with information, most of it generated from Neal Phillips's department, about Soviet support of the international terror network. In previous operations the KGB manipulated some terror groups into executing high-risk missions. The K-7 infections would be ideal for terrorists bent on maximum disruption of society. It would also be the perfect cover for the KGB. They could hide behind the skirts of the terrorists and proclaim total ignorance.

The only wrinkle was that the dead Brigade member was supposed to have been killed by Neal Phillips's squad some five years ago. According to Hodson, it was a bomb explosion. There could have been a leak inside the CIA, a Russian mole who was providing information back to the Kremlin. In that case, the KGB might have known in advance about Neal Phillips's antiterrorist team and the details of their planned operations. If the KGB had that information, they could have staged Amalfi's death. Phillips and his team would confirm the kill with tooth fragments, as they did in this case, and close the file. Then that "dead" terrorist would become the perfect tool for the Soviets. He would have a new identity. They could cover his tracks by replacing his old medical files in different agencies around the globe. He would be a trained killer, indebted to the Soviets for saving his life, and no one would ever be looking for him since he was supposed to be dead. That made a lot of sense.

The only other option that McGinnis could think of was that Neal

Phillips had somehow not killed the Brigade member, but reported it as a kill anyway. He couldn't understand why Phillips would be involved in that type of deception. Phillips might be a goddamn pain in the ass, but he was also a patriot.

McGinnis had informed Harris about the details of Hodson's call. He had debated it for a while, but in the end decided Harris should know all the facts, so at least he could understand why McGinnis made the decisions he did. Harris was his partner, and while the kid might be a little rambunctious, he was trying his best. He even had a good idea once in a while. Given enough time, he might even turn into a decent agent.

Night had fallen by the time they finished with Penny at 6:30. She had given them descriptions of both her captives. The problem was that the gunwoman sounded like millions of others, and the description of the man was heavily influenced by his injury and the blood all over his torso. She recalled more details about the extent of his bullet wound than about his features. However, one thing she distinctly remembered was a prominent scar on the left side of his face. McGinnis took notes on the physical details of the kidnappers. When he finished, he thanked Penny for her time, and, together with Harris, started the trip back to San Francisco.

There was nothing else for them to do in Sausalito. The house was already being swept by an Agency forensic squad for fingerprints and other evidence. McGinnis knew that the bioassassins would not be returning to their "safe" house. They had probably passed outside hours ago and seen the police cars. Damn it! Another opportunity to set a trap was wasted.

When they reached San Francisco, McGinnis did not immediately drive to local headquarters or to their hotel, the St. Francis, on Union Square in the heart of the downtown district.

"Where are we going," Harris asked.

"We're going to first take a long shot with Hodson's computers. Then we are going to play the 'I don't trust anyone game' for the rest of the night."

"How do we play?"

"I'll show you the rules. If we have anything to worry about with Phillips, he should show his hand shortly. Things have gotten pretty bad for the two K-7 killers. If they have a line inside the Company, they have to pull on it soon. We're just going to be watching." McGinnis stopped the car at the curb on Bay Street, only several blocks from the gaudy, neon-lit Fisherman's Wharf. "Give me a couple of quarters, kid. I've got some calls to make."

"Can I listen?"

"You bet your ass. And later you can buy me a drink. But right now the quarters will do."

Harris gave him a handful of change. They left the car and walked to the open air phone booth only ten feet away. It was a typical San Francisco winter evening. The fog had settled and the dampness cut right through the clothing, no matter how thick the sweater or coat.

McGinnis dropped the first quarter in the slot. He pressed the seven digits and then blew into his hand, trying to warm himself. Harris was huddled directly behind him, hoping that his partner and the small phone booth would block the gusty winds that swept in off the bay. Harris could only hear one end of the conversation.

"McGinnis here. . . . Not much. A mediocre description. Nothing really on voice patterns. The cleaning squad doesn't have anything yet, it's too early. I'm going over to look at the impounded car the Sausalito police have. . . . Maybe not, but I want to check it anyway. . . . I will probably grab a quick hamburger or something on the way back. . . . We will do it tonight. . . . We have to map out a better plan for to-morrow. . . . Oh, I almost forgot, is Neal there? . . . Oh, I just wanted to ask him a question on his intelligence reports. I need to know what he has on VKR biotechnology experts. It's just a hunch I want to follow up on. . . . See you."

He turned to Harris, who was now pacing back and forth trying to stay warm. "That was Finch. Everything's at a crawl tonight. No new leads. They seem to think something might break tomorrow. Everyone wants us to get geared up for a final move then. Phillips is already back at the hotel. Too quiet. That's why I'll bet you ten bucks to your one that something's on for tonight. I just feel it."

"McGinnis, I think I feel it too. It's colder than a witch's tit out here. I'll wait in the car."

"You sissy," McGinnis yelled at him. "You should at least have the decency to stay here with your elders. You've got those damn hard muscles to keep you warm."

"Sure. Maybe if I catch pneumonia they'll let me get eight hours sleep around here."

"Don't bank on it." McGinnis dropped another quarter into the phone and dialed the hotel. "Any messages for 1801?" In less than a minute he had placed the receiver back.

Again he turned to face Harris, now cupping his hands near his face and trying to blow hot air into them. McGinnis laughed. "Hey, for a kid who grew up in New York you certainly don't seem very comfortable here in sunny California."

Harris didn't look happy. "Yeah, well you heard what Mark Twain once said about Frisco. The coldest winter he ever spent was a summer in San Francisco."

"Maybe you and Twain have more in common than a weakness for the cold. Can you write, kid?"

"McGinnis, can we do the jokes in the car. Who called? The Carson Show? Are they booking you yet? You've got to be the funniest spook on the circuit."

"Cute. Listen, all bullshit aside. I got a call from Ace Hardware, the parts are in. That's Hodson. But he left a different number. Let's try it."

McGinnis dropped in a quarter and dialed the number with a Virginia area code. "I need another $1.20 for the first three minutes. Let's see here." He peered into the palm of his hand, looking for the correct change, and quickly dropped the coins into the slot.

"Come on, Hodson, answer for godsakes," McGinnis muttered to himself. The wind had picked up and was whipping around the corner. It caught the two agents full blast. Harris held up his hands as though he were surrendering, and McGinnis nodded that he should get inside the car. Harris had just closed the passenger door when the phone in Virginia was answered on the fifth ring.

"Hello." McGinnis heard the accent. He never got tired of the clipped British enunciation. It just made simple English sound classier.

"Hodson?"

"McGinnis, thank God you got my message. I don't know what you are coming up with out there, but I thought I'd fill you in on a little extra snooping I did. Maybe some of it will make some sense to you."

"Make it fast. I've got three minutes on this phone. I don't want you calling back to leave a trace on your number."

"This is brief. I just decided to take a look inside the other cases Phillips directed as the antiterror chief. Besides the resilient Mr. Amalfi, it seems as though the Company eliminated four other terror kingpins before the Operations Division canceled the entire program on the grounds it was too risky. One of the cases involved an IRA bomber who was killed in a drunk driving cover. Head on into a speeding train. Although the body was badly mangled, there was a lot of it left for an autopsy. The pictures are in the file. I don't think anyone got away there. A second case was a Basque terrorist leader who supposedly killed his wife in a marital argument and then took his own life. I have seen the photos of the dead man. It looks like a closed case. The third was Ayotallah Rinay Banha, leader of the radical fundamentalist sect in southern Beirut, responsible for some prominent western kidnappings. He was almost beheaded in a bizarre accident when a prayer platform he was on during the feast of Rammadan collapsed. They found him underneath with a steel pipe almost through his neck. Everyone concluded it was a freak accident. But the photos again show the full body.

"The final case was one of the most vicious chaps inside the West German terror group, the Baader Meinhof. His name is Christian Valdor. Cold son of a bitch. Responsible for their bombing and kidnapping programs. Blown up by a rival faction in September 1984. Only some hair and tooth fragments left behind. No pictures of a body. Maybe it's just a coincidence, but it's the same modus operandi as the Amalfi case."

"You've seen a file picture of Valdor?"

"Right in front of me. He's six feet even. Would be thirty-six years of age if alive. Light, sandy hair, straight and full. Deep green eyes. Fair skin. Lean, but muscular body type. Pretty interesting fellow. File attributes thirty-two known kills to him, including the Munich assassination in front of TV cameras of the U.S. military attaché to NATO. Only son of a very wealthy Bavarian industrialist, he has a Ph.D. in political science, 162 IQ, speaks seven languages like a native. File says he's a master of all forms of death, from martial arts to the latest bombing techniques. Also renown as a master of disguise."

"Distinguishing marks?"

"A facial scar. From a police billy club in a student riot in 1970. Supposed to run from the corner of his left eye to the middle of his cheek."

McGinnis suddenly forgot about the cold. His heart was pounding fast. Hodson may have stumbled across the wounded K-7 killer. The Schwarzenegger accent that Penny had heard. It wasn't Slavic. It was German!

"Hodson—"

An electronic voice interrupted. "Please deposit another fifty cents for the next five minutes." McGinnis fumbled again with the change and put in sixty cents by mistake.

"Hodson, I want that photo faxed to my hotel."

"Sorry, can't Richard. I'm looking at it on a computer screen. I could be fired just for getting inside the electronic file. I can't make a hard copy. The best I can do is to electronically transfer the photo onto a computer screen, if you have a digital modem."

"Forget it. Anything else on this Valdor? Any wife? Any woman that he used to run with in the Baader Meinhof?"

"Nope. Real loner type. Leader, but not with women. No personal life to report of."

So the female K-7 killer might not have come from the Baader Mein-hof. "And no women in any of Phillips's antiterrorist jobs? Not even a female target slated for a hit but saved by the program's cancellation?"

"I don't know about that. The computer doesn't show what operations were planned but canceled by the director's decision."

"All right. Nigel, I've got to get going. I want to play cat and dog tonight with some of the boys out here. Let me see if I can have as much success as you're having back there on the machines."

"Good luck, Richard. Be careful. Phillips hates your guts and would love to hang you out to dry. If he thinks you're looking after him when you are supposed to be chasing some VKR agents, he'll have your ass."

"Relax. He's been trying to have my ass for twenty years. It'll be another twenty and he still won't be any closer. I'll call tomorrow in the a.m. for a check-in." McGinnis slammed the phone down and rushed back to the car. Now that the news had settled in, he felt the weather again. Mark Twain was right. It was too damn cold.

Except for a strange look from the usher, Colby and Erica left the theater without attracting any undue attention. They paid the $5.50 at the Cathedral Hill parking lot and began the trip along Van Ness that took them onto the approach to the Golden Gate Bridge. Immediately before the toll plaza is a parking lot down a small hill to the right. Erica made the turn, but instead of pulling inside the lot, she continued straight and entered the Presidio, the military base nestled on the edge of San Francisco Bay. In less than a quarter of a mile, she slowed in front of a metal chain blocking access to a side road. Erica killed the lights while Colby got out and removed the chain. After she drove onto the road, he replaced the chain and quickly reentered the car. For several hundred yards they drove along a narrow, two-lane road covered with a dense canopy of eucalyptus trees. After another quarter of a mile the tree cover ended and the road twisted along the side of the bay. The base of the Golden Gate Bridge faced them and they were both surprised at its massive size from such a close perspective. Directly in front of the Golden Gate, on the very tip of the land protrusion, was a two story brick fort, complete with gun windows and barred cells. It was difficult to see the fort in much detail since there were no lights along the road. Although a full moon was in the sky, it was hidden by a thick, low fog that had settled over the bay. Only the eerie glow of yellow dots, suspended more than a hundred feet from the ground, barely showed through the mist. They were the fog lights along the Golden Gate Bridge.

Their car crawled along at less than ten miles per hour. Erica did not want to take the chance of hitting anything, but she didn't want to turn on the headlights for fear of attracting the military police. Those army patrols came by twice a night to ensure that young partyers had not sneaked into the grounds. Like clockwork, they arrived at midnight and at 3:00 a.m. If their rendezvous took place at eleven, Colby and Erica did not expect to be near the fort by midnight. They had no desire to attract the police.

Suddenly Erica hit the brakes hard. Colby lurched forward and then settled back roughly in the seat. The short but loud yell indicated that his wounded shoulder had just taken the brunt of the jostling. "What the hell happened?" He looked at her with a mixture of confusion and anger.

"There." She pointed through the windshield.

He squinted and peered through the glass. "What? I can't see a thing."

"Another chain. We almost ran into it."

"Good eyes." Again he left the car, found the opening in the large metal chain, and dropped it to the ground. He replaced it as Erica drove into the lot. Little things like that worried him. He was only four years off forty and might not be as strong or fast as he once was. His endurance was good, but he was not as powerful as ten years earlier. Not that little things like bullets and knife wounds didn't help to age you prematurely. But not seeing the chain bothered him. At thirty-six, his eyes should not give out on him. He hated aging. Nothing worse than a retired agent, sitting around a country house getting fat on beers and boring the neighbors with reminiscences about the good old days. Someone had to shoot him if he ever got like that.

"Where do you want me to put this?" she yelled out of the car's side window.

"What? I can't hear you." Even though she was less than twenty feet away, the sound of the crashing waves along the rock embankment obscured her words. Combined with the din of the constant traffic running along the metal floor of the Golden Gate Bridge just above them on the top of the rocky bluff, it was difficult to hear someone unless he was directly on top of you. As he walked toward her, he could feel the mist from the waves as they crashed against the man-made barrier, just ten feet to his right.

"I said, where should I put this?"

He looked around the lot for a moment. "There." He pointed to the far left corner, almost obscured by the protruding rock ledges. "I don't want them to know we are here until they are inside the lot."

She started to drive away. "Wait!" he called out to her.

He shuffled to the car window. "Look, I'm going to walk the grounds and see what it looks like. Why don't you stay in the car." He looked at his watch. 10:02. "Control won't arrive early. It'll take me only ten minutes to look around. I'll come back to sit inside the car with you. It's freezing here."

"I'll keep the heater on."

McGinnis stopped at the Avis rental car agency on O'Farrell, only seven blocks from the St. Francis Hotel. It was time to switch cars. Everyone in the Company knew the car assigned to him and Harris. They needed something innocuous, and different from what they had. A light grey Volvo fit the bill, even though McGinnis would have preferred an American car. Without a reservation, it was the best he could do. They transferred two bags from the trunk of their Thunderbird to the new rental, and then Harris parked the Company car in an all-night lot across the street. McGinnis signed for the rental, picked up Harris, and drove back to the hotel. He pulled the car into an open parking space along Post Street, directly in front of the St. Francis's side entrance. He had not told Harris about the Valdor identification. There was no reason to. Not yet, anyway. He pulled a latch on the dashboard and Harris heard a pop. It was the trunk. "C'mon, I'm going to show you how the game is played."

Harris and McGinnis got out of the car. Harris watched as McGinnis pulled out a nylon sport bag buried near the spare tire in the trunk and started rummaging through it. "What's that?"

"Just a couple of things I picked up from Clark. They are little gadgets that could help us track our elusive pair. Now they are going to help us track anyone that moves out of here." He looked up at the hotel as he pulled out a plastic bag filled with what appeared to be quarter-sized magnets. He also retrieved a black box, no larger than a pack of cigarettes, and placed it in his raincoat pocket. McGinnis slammed the trunk closed. "Follow me." Harris dutifully obeyed.

They entered the hotel on Post Street, proceeded directly to the rear bank of elevators, and took the first one to the basement garage. McGinnis walked around the garage, stopping at three cars, each time taking out a small metal disk and bending over near the rear tire-well. After he stood up, the disk was hidden from view, attached to the car's metal frame. He spoke to Harris as they walked around the parking lot. "These are the best available, kid. They allow you to fall several blocks behind the lead car and still keep track. The box in my pocket gives a directional identifying beep for nearly a mile. And the disks themselves don't send off any electromagnetic currents, so even sweeping the car won't disclose their existence."

"Who are we following?"

"Don't know yet. I'm putting them on the cars used by Phillips, Fitzgerald, and Finch."

"What if more than one of them leaves at once?"

"I'll opt for Phillips. He's got some answering to do."

"How do you know they are going anywhere?"

"Don't. Just a hunch."

"What do you expect to find if they do go out?"

"I've got no idea. That's why I want to find out." McGinnis stopped between aisles and looked back at Harris. "No more 'twenty questions.' Not now, please."

Harris held up his hand and indicated that he understood. The more they were together, the better he realized what made his partner tick. There were times McGinnis preferred silence. Usually it meant he was reviewing options. He was never daydreaming. There was always some-thing going on in his head, and you could almost always bet it had something to do with the investigation. When they first met, Harris thought the silence was directed personally at him. He interpreted it as McGinnis's dislike for him. Now he realized that McGinnis would ask for the same quiet time even if he were sitting next to Raquel Welch. Harris was more than pleased to afford him some silence.

When McGinnis finished planting the bugs, they returned to their car and sat inside. It was now a waiting game.

"How long will we wait?" Harris wondered.

"If they don't go anywhere by midnight, I'll send you for a pizza. Depending on how long that holds us, we'll play it by ear."

Great. Harris's stomach churned at the thought of another pizza like the one they had had the previous night. The pepperoni and extra cheese had sat in his stomach like a rock. It still felt like it was blocking some part of his intestines. Anything but another authentic Italian pizza.

Harris's wishes were granted. At precisely 10:30, the little black box resting on top of the dashboard began emitting a soft, intermittent beep. A small yellow light also began flashing on the front of the box. "Someone has kicked on one of those cars." McGinnis straightened in his seat and turned on the ignition. He kept his eye on the rearview mirror. The exit from the hotel garage was about twenty feet behind his car. The third car out of the garage was a tan 1987 Chevrolet Camaro. "Here's our pigeon," McGinnis notified his partner. It was the car assigned to Neal Phillips, and both Harris and McGinnis identified Phillips as the driver as he accelerated past. The black box now had a red light flashing in the direction of Phillips's car. McGinnis slid the automatic gearshift lever into drive, checked the traffic behind him, and pulled into the roadway.

"What if another one of them leaves while we're following Phillips?"

"At least the light will go on telling us they've turned on the car. We'll know if someone else is moving, but we're not going to be able to do much about it. Phillips will be enough for tonight. I haven't seen Phillips on a field case in a long time. I'm just interested in seeing what he's up to."

They followed the Camaro at a safe distance of almost a block. Twice they missed traffic lights and had to speed and weave through traffic to catch up; the black box helped them make turns they would have ignored. Suddenly the yellow light started flashing. "He's stopping and turning the ignition off somewhere ahead," McGinnis announced as he peered through the windshield trying to spot the Camaro in the maze of traffic. Harris bent his head, looking for the car. "I see it!" he exclaimed. He's pulled up near an awning for the Portman Hotel, but I don't see him getting out."

A car honked its horn at McGinnis, who was idling his car in the middle of the intersection. Suddenly he yanked the steering wheel to the right and made a turn onto Hayes Street.

"Do we go on foot from here?" Harris asked.

"No, we don't go anywhere. It's a trap. Remember, I worked with Phillips in southeast Asia. He was my first commanding field officer and I learned a lot of things from him. In Saigon, if you thought you might have a tail, you just pulled over at random to the side of some busy street. Then you waited a couple of minutes to see what happened. I'll bet you a week's wages that Phillips had his eyes locked on his rearview mirror for several moments before he pulled over. He was looking for any familiar car. Our Volvo doesn't mean shit to him so we're okay. Then he wants to see if anyone he recognizes drives past him. Lucky we were holding to a long tail, because if we were half a block closer we would have had to pass him and he would have fingered us." McGinnis made another right turn onto a one-way street.

"The other thing he looks for is any car pulling to the curb just a moment after he does. That's usually the sign of a tail who is making the same moves you make. We didn't fit into any of the categories. So far, so good."

"What will he do now, and what are we doing?"

"He'll sit there for a couple of minutes. He wants to make sure he didn't miss any car. He also wants to be absolutely sure no one on foot is looking for him. By the time he is satisfied that he's alone, we'll have come around the corner and should be ready to pick him up once again."

"And what if he's left the car and gone into one of the buildings?"

"Then we're fucked, kid, and 'Uncle McGinnis' was just plain wrong. We'll find out soon enough."

They climbed the short hill back toward the intersection they had left only minutes before. Suddenly the beep started from the black box and the yellow light began flashing. "He's back on, kid. Just like I thought he would. Once an asshole, always an asshole."

Harris shook his head and smiled. "You've got him down pat, McGinnis."

"They didn't teach you that little trick at Peary, did they?"

"Yeah, but I wasn't very good in 'tailing 101.' Will he stop again?"

"Nope. He thinks he's clear. Now he'll relax a little, which will make him sloppier. As a result, we'll be able to keep him on a shorter leash."

They followed Phillips along the piers to the Embarcadero, north on Bay Street past the majestic, Roman-inspired Palace of Fine Arts, and onto the approach to the Golden Gate Bridge.

"Where the hell could he be going?" McGinnis muttered as much to himself as to Harris.

"It's the same route we took when we went to question the woman today. You don't think he's going to ask her questions himself, do you?"

"It's almost 11:00 at night. I doubt it."

As they neared the toll plaza, the traffic bottlenecked and slowed to a crawl. Phillips was about twenty car lengths in front of them. Suddenly the red indicator on the black box changed direction and pointed to the right instead of straight ahead.

McGinnis was puzzled. He didn't know about any turnoff immediately before the toll booths. Stretching his neck, he tried to look over the tops of the cars in front of him. "Where the hell could he have gone? What did he do, just make a right turn into the bay?" He picked the black box off the dash and shook it. "Is this damn thing on the fritz? Did you see anything, Harris?"

"Not a thing. I didn't even see him turn. Just keep going up a little farther. There"—he pointed ahead and a little to the right—"that sign says 'United States Army: Presidio,' and underneath it says 'Fort Point, National Historical Monument.' There must be an exit up there."

McGinnis felt like a fool. "For Chrissakes, I know the point. I went there with my wife nearly twenty years ago. Only then it wasn't a national monument. It was just an old boarded-up fort with more rats than tourists. Maybe Neal's going sightseeing."

In another moment they both saw the exit and made the turn, following the flashing indicator on the box. They had only traveled a couple of hundred feet when the arrow switched directions again. "Damn it!" McGinnis was perturbed. "He's really moving around now. Must be getting closer to his final destination." He pressed the accelerator and picked up speed. In a minute they had come to a stop sign at a crossroads. The red light was flashing toward the left. But a heavy metal chain blocked access to a small roadway. Suddenly the yellow light on the box started flashing and then both lights went off. The beeping stopped.

"He's pulled over again. He went down that road. For Chrissakes, he did go to the point. That's where he turned, and now he's stopped down there."

Harris started to open the car door. "I'll let the chain down."

"No! Wait a minute. It's starting to come back to me. I remember the road down there. There's nothing else around, just ocean, rocks, and the fort. If we take the car down there, even if we're dark, he might see us coming. We can't take that chance." McGinnis turned the steering wheel hard to the left as he spoke to Harris. "We're going to put this thing in the parking lot on top of the hill. If I remember correctly, at the edge of that parking lot is an observation deck. It looks right over the fort and the tip of the rocks that jut into the bay. That's where my wife and I stood on our honeymoon and first saw the fort. We would never have known it was there otherwise. If my memory serves me right, we can climb over that deck and go right down a short hillside and drop in on Phillips from behind."

He pulled the Volvo into the rear of the lot and slammed on the brakes. "There's the deck!" McGinnis pointed to a concrete circle less than twenty feet away. He reached under the dash and pulled the lever that opened the trunk. "Grab the bags. We don't know what goodies we'll need."

Harris yanked the nylon duffels from the rear of the car and slammed the trunk closed. McGinnis was already on top of the observation deck and Harris ran over to him. "Keep low," McGinnis called to him in a loud whisper. "We don't want anyone in the bridge's security tower to see us." Harris crouched over and joined his partner. "Put these on and look over here. What can you see?" McGinnis handed Harris a pair of what appeared to be very thick sunglasses with a small protruding three-inch microphone from the bridge of the nose. "They're infrared. And they have one of the best unidirectional mikes in the business. It will pick up from about 100 yards if you point it right at your conversation source." Harris slipped on his pair while McGinnis pulled a second pair from the bag and put them over his eyes.

"That's the fort for godsakes?" Harris asked.

"Yep."

"Bigger than I thought. Christ, why the hell would you want to be down there?"

"Because you don't want anyone else to see what you're about to do. Look into the parking lot behind the fort."

Harris glanced over. "I see Phillips's car."

"And look farther toward the rear of the lot."

"I see another car."

"Exactly. I don't think our friend Phillips is alone. We'll check for ourselves."

McGinnis unzipped the second duffel and pulled out two large, dark grey vests. "Slip these over your head and under your jacket. It might look ugly, but it will keep you warm. It's going to feel like subzero down there. Only the Russians could be stupid enough to build a fort at the coldest spot in California."

In less than a minute they had the vests securely under their jackets. McGinnis slung one bag over his shoulder and stepped over the three-foot concrete barrier. Harris picked up the second duffel and followed only a step behind. Once they were on the other side of the wall, the din of the traffic diminished and the sound of the waves crashing against the rocks 100 feet below became the loudest noise picked up by their eyeglass microphones. They slowly descended the rocky grade leading to the back of the fort. Although it was usually not a dangerous descent, the fog had soaked the ground and covered the rocks with a fine mist, making the hillside slippery. They had barely gone ten feet when Harris's foot slid off a large rock. He threw his arms out and stopped what had appeared to be an inevitable tumble.

"Be careful!" McGinnis warned his partner. "One bad step and you'll fall the rest of the way to the fort. And if that happens, you won't be the only casualty. You'll alert whoever is down there and then I'll be a sitting duck as well."

Harris paused for a moment and took a deep breath as the wind from the bay whipped around him. "It's cold as a son of a bitch out here."

"That's part of our advantage. Whoever is down there with Phillips doesn't expect any party crashers in this weather."

"Do you hear any voices down there?"

"Nope. They are probably in one of the cars or on the other side of the fort, near the water. We won't know until we get a little closer. Come on."

McGinnis led the way. He carefully climbed down the face of the incline, using solid chunks of rock to steady himself. The noise from the crashing waves was getting louder.

"McGinnis, are you sure they can't see us coming?"

"Take off your glasses."

Harris removed the thick framed eyeglasses. "Shit. I see what you mean. Or maybe I should say I don't see."

The fog was thick and close to the ground. As they dropped in on the back of the fort, visibility was severely impaired. Even so, McGinnis thought it was fortunate they had both worn dark trousers, shirts, and jackets. There was no reason to tempt fate.

It took them nearly six minutes to climb down the grade and reach a dirt lot behind the fort, separated from the parking lot by a chain link fence. Both McGinnis and Harris peered through the fence links. Harris leaned toward McGinnis's ear and whispered over the roar of the ocean. "I don't see anyone in the cars."

McGinnis gave him an "okay" signal with his hand, signifying he agreed. He turned to go in the other direction, leading to the west of the fort and coming to the edge of the walkway next to the ocean. If they followed that path it would take them to the front of the fort, the portion that was obscured from their sight. McGinnis waved his hand in a big arc, signaling Harris to follow. They both crouched low, in part to avoid being seen and in part to block out the wind that whipped like a mobile freezer off the bay. When they arrived at the back of the fort, they pressed their backs against the brick wall, clinging to it and slowly moving toward the ocean pathway. Suddenly McGinnis put up his hand signaling them to stop. He pointed to his microphone. Harris strained to aim his mike and pick up the sound that had stopped McGinnis. He heard a noise, like the dull roar of an engine. It was getting closer. Now he could hear it clearly over the sound of the waves. A motor was approaching, and it sounded like it was coming from out on the bay. What the hell could be coming here in this weather? McGinnis indicated that Harris stay put as he proceeded around the edge of the wall. In fifteen seconds McGinnis reappeared at the corner, this time waving for Harris to follow. He looked frantic.

Harris quickly sprinted around the corner of the building. McGinnis was crouched behind a dozen large garbage cans that had been stored for the night. He was peering through cracks between the cans. When Harris leaned against the cans and peeped through the slits, he saw what had caused McGinnis's agitation. Less than thirty feet in front was Phillips. He was bundled inside a large raincoat. About ten feet in front of him were a man and a woman. They were also in raincoats but looked like the cold was wearing them down. The man was crouched to one side, as if the cold was actually hurting him.

"Look," McGinnis whispered excitedly, "there's our man. Look how he's compensating for the shoulder wound."

It was like someone had turned a light on in Harris's head. Of course. It was a wound. He wasn't slumped to his side because of the cold. That was the man who had spread K-7 in New York and San Francisco. The woman next to him was probably the other half of the team. And they were talking excitedly to the chief of intelligence for the CIA. Harris couldn't believe what he was watching. What the hell could be going on here? Phillips was gesturing wildly, and the woman seemed to be infuriated.

"There!" Harris pulled on McGinnis's jacket. "Look, approaching the wall along the edge of the bay. A boat."

McGinnis stared at the water and saw it. It was a small fishing vessel, no more than a forty footer. That had been the sound of the motor they had heard only minutes earlier. A boat was going to do a pickup. As it slowed near the concrete embankment, it stalled. Phillips gave it a wave of his hand and a small flashlight blinked rapidly three times from the captain's cabin. The waves were too rough for it to float next to the wall, so it had to drop anchor.

"Richard, why can't we hear anything?"

"You've got to push the microphone exactly between the cracks of the cans. Then you won't be able to see, but you'll hear what is going on."

Harris aimed the middle of his glasses to the largest space between the cans. McGinnis did the same. The boat and the waves made a lot of background noise, but the voices still came through.

The woman was screaming, "You can't just let it sit here with nothing being done. It's not the purpose of the mission!"

Phillips sounded enraged. McGinnis knew the sound of fury in his voice. It had been directed at him many times in the past. "For the final time, the decision is out of my hands. It comes from the top. You have to get out of America, and the only time is right now. The vessel is going to be at the coordinates in two hours. If you aren't there, you aren't going to get picked up and out of here safely. Valdor, get her going!"

The name "Valdor" hit McGinnis like a jolt of electricity. Hodson was right. McGinnis knew that damn Englishman was a genius with those computers.

"I can't convince her of anything," the wounded man answered in perfect English. "Anyway, she saved my life and I at least owe her something for that. If she wants to stay, I think it's suicidal, but she has a right to end her life that way if she wants."

The woman turned toward the man Phillips called Valdor. "I don't want to end my life that way. It's just that if I don't stay to monitor it, then what was the purpose of killing everyone in London? We still won't know anything more than we knew in the laboratory!"

Phillips yelled toward the boat. "Bring the raft to the edge of the wall. They are leaving with you in one minute and they'll be on." A man began lowering a five-foot rubber dinghy into the water. The shore was only fifteen feet away.

"Bullshit, I will!"

My, McGinnis thought, she is feisty.

Phillips looked away from her. "Valdor! Too much is at stake. You know it! Talk to her alone for a moment! We've been at this for nearly fifteen minutes. This is asinine!"

McGinnis moved his head back so he could watch the three of them. He rubbed his hands together in a vain attempt to fight the cold. That son of a bitch, he thought as he stared at Phillips. He had never liked him—now it made sense. He was dirty.

Phillips turned his back to the couple while they huddled together. Within a moment they seemed to be engaged in a heated discussion. But they were too close to the water to be heard. The waves pounded their words into an inaudible jumble. McGinnis angled his head so he had a fuller view of the entire scene. As he surveyed the grounds, he noticed Phillips make the telltale movement. He had slipped his hand under the front of his raincoat. As Phillips swiveled around he pulled out a MAC-10 machine pistol. He started to fire it in an arcing movement. Valdor had seen the spinning figure out of the corner of his eye. By the time Phillips started firing, Valdor had pushed the woman backward across the walkway, and he had fallen flat on the ground. The .45 caliber bullets from Phillips's gun slammed into the concrete path, ripping up chunks of stone and sending them disappearing into the mist. None of the initial volley struck either of the targets. Nice shooting, asshole, McGinnis thought. The woman was reaching for a pistol under her jacket when Phillips finally focused on her and sent a stream of slugs, splitting her abdomen and lacing the front of her face. She crashed back against the thick concrete columns used as supports for the interconnecting iron chain that was supposed to prevent tourists from falling into the bay. As her body slid down to the ground, the unused gun still in her hand, Phillips spun to face Valdor.

Valdor was still lying on the ground, his mobility cut by his wound. His mind was racing. He was furious that he had been stupid enough to walk into such a trap. How could he ever have trusted them? The chemicals. The goddamn amphetamines screwed his judgment! He had drawn his pistol, and although the fog blurred his vision, he started emptying his magazine at the image of a diving Phillips. Valdor brought down the angle of his pistol. He probably would have struck Phillips in another split second, except the man in the dinghy had arrived. His first task was to let a shotgun blast blow a hole into the back of Valdor. The force of the shot slid Valdor's body across the pavement. The gun flew out of his hand. When he came to rest, his body just lay lifeless, the hundred pellet marks the only sign of the force that had struck him down.

McGinnis and Harris had already drawn their weapons. McGinnis with his trusty Colt .45, holding nine slugs, while Harris had a new 9 millimeter with fifteen hollow point bullets in the clip. "Keep the glasses on," McGinnis told Harris. "It'll make things easier to see."

They ran around the garbage cans just as Phillips and the boatman were starting to move the dead woman. McGinnis screamed, "Don't move! Don't move! Drop the weapons! Drop the weapons! Now!"

Phillips looked over his shoulder and saw the two agents running toward him, their pistols held in both hands, aimed directly at him. His mouth dropped open. "McGinnis! I don't fucking believe it!"

"Drop the weapons!" McGinnis and Harris were less than ten feet away. The man standing next to Phillips held out the shotgun as though he was about to drop it to his side. But McGinnis noticed the grip. It was still locked on the trigger.

"Drop it, fucker!"

The man whipped his wrist back and the boom of the shotgun bellowed at them. Both Harris and McGinnis began firing at the tall figure next to Phillips. The .45 caliber and 9-millimeter slugs tore into his head almost simultaneously, dropping him backward. His body spun into the iron chain, tripped over the top, and fell past the ledge into the bay. Phillips still had not straightened up from his crouch over the dead woman. After his accomplice fell into the bay, he dropped his machine pistol.

"Straighten up, pig!" McGinnis was screaming. "Are you okay, kid?" he yelled over his shoulder to Harris.

"Fine. And you?"

"Great. That piece of shit was a lousy shot." McGinnis came on top of Phillips, grabbed him roughly by the collar, and pulled him straight up. He shoved the tip of his Colt into Phillips's face. "Just like you, asshole," he screamed at him. "You're too cheap to hire a good shot." He was shaking Phillips. He dropped his hand from his collar and brought it around in a roundhouse punch that caught Phillips on the side of his nose, splitting the skin and cracking the bone. Phillips fell over backward onto the pavement.

Harris rushed over and pulled on McGinnis. "Stop it, Richard. Stop it. We've got to bring him in."

"Listen to your partner, stupid!" Phillips had propped himself up on one elbow and wiped the blood away from his lower face. "You think you're smart. You don't even know the half of it, McGinnis. You couldn't give up, could you? You had to be the big hero. Well, you've really fucked up this time!"

"I have? You think you're going to get the presidential medal of honor for being here tonight with two terrorists who have just started bacteriological war in our country? Have you lost your mind?"

Phillips stood up and pressed the back of his hand to his face, trying to stop the flow of blood from his broken nose. "Terrorists, my ass! They were ours! How does that strike you, jerk-off?"

McGinnis and Harris looked at each other, shock settling across their faces. McGinnis glanced over his shoulder to look at the still bodies of the woman and Valdor, as if he was trying to make sure he and Phillips were talking about the same people.

Phillips snorted as if he was in total control of the situation. "Yes, you heard me right. They were ours."

"You're full of shit, Neal. You've always been. I heard you call him Valdor. He's Baader Meinhof. I know all about him. And I know you signed a report saying you had him killed over five years ago. I also know that another fellow that mysteriously survived your killing, the Red Brigade member Amalfi, was the corpse that turned up in Paris a week ago. Since when have terrorists become part of the Company?"

Phillips shook his head as though he were lecturing a remedial child. "For a guy who has been in the field for twenty years you don't know much about the way we run things, do you? Your young friend is supposed to be stupid. You should at least have an ounce of brains, McGinnis. Sure, Valdor and Amalfi were terrorists. At least to the rest of international terror. But they were CIA from the first day each got involved. We pushed them to become some of the most brutal enforcers in the terror network. We even set up a highly public kill for Valdor, of an American army officer."

McGinnis interrupted. "You mean you helped him kill our NATO rep in Munich?"

"Yep."

"Why? What the fuck was going on? Were you one of the them?"

"You still don't see it, do you. I always told Finch that you were lucky, not smart. He never believed me. This proves it. You're lucky enough to have gotten this far, but you still don't know what the hell it's all about. We helped them set up big kills, including a couple of our own expendable fish we threw in, so that they would have credibility inside the terror network. And it worked. Both Valdor and Amalfi moved along into the upper echelons of international terror. By helping them kill a couple of dozen people, we saved the lives of hundreds and maybe thousands of innocent civilians. Over the years they passed us some of the best information on pending terror operations. The public will never know how many *Achille Lauros*, TWA hijackings, or Munich Olympic massacres were averted because of those two moles."

McGinnis had lowered his voice. He was no longer screaming from anger, just loud enough to be heard over the waves. "So if they were two angels, why did you have their deaths faked back in '84?"

"What happened in May 1984? Think, McGinnis. May. Big headlines."

McGinnis hesitated for a moment before answering. "The Company's deputy chief of European Operations, Tom Welles, defected to Moscow."

"You win the big prize. Welles was the highest ranking Company man ever to go to the Soviets. And he took a lot of information with him. We had to scrap our entire informer support program in Europe, change codes, methods of access, and close front companies. It was a disaster. Welles also knew about the Pandora Operation. That was the code name for working our people into the inside of the terror networks. We were sure he had blown both Valdor and Amalfi. The Soviets would gladly have given that info to the Red Brigade and the Baader Meinhof and built up some favors. We took that chance away from them. We got congressional authorization for an antiterror squad, and then hit at some big names, making them look like accidents. The Iranian, the IRA bomber, and the Basque were all real bad guys that we blew away. Amalfi and Valdor were the real reasons for the whole antiterrorist squad. We needed a way to make it look as though they were dead without arousing too much suspicion. If they were the only ones killed, it would have smelled fishy to the Soviets. Instead, we made sure several others had life-ending bad luck at the same time. Valdor and Amalfi just blended into the rest of the news. Only by making them die could we stop their real deaths once their role with us was exposed. So, although we lost them as terror informants, we gained two capable agents, who were even better than before, because they had no past. They could become whomever we wanted them to be."

"And you had their medical records switched?"

"Of course I did. Did you ever know me to run a slipshod operation? I didn't want these fellows ever to be identified again. The names Valdor and Amalfi died in bomb explosions and that's the way I wanted it."

McGinnis nodded his head toward the dead woman. "And what about her?"

"Well, I hope this isn't all too much for your pea-sized brain,

McGinnis, but she was one of our scientists inside the London lab that was wiped out last week. Real name—Sandra Everingham. *Doctor* Everingham to you."

"But all—"

"I know, I know. Everyone in the London station was killed. Wrong again, dumbo. Everyone assigned to the London station was accounted for in the forensic identification. What was left of the bodies after the place was bombed and torched? Bone fragments and some teeth. If I could leave behind samples in 1983 that were good enough to get Amalfi and Valdor listed as dead, don't you think I've even gotten better in the last five years? Everingham was listed as dead. But she was alive as you two dummies."

"And what the hell were they doing planting K-7 around the U.S.? Don't tell me they had both gone bad and had exceeded the scope of their authority. I won't buy that bullshit."

"I wouldn't tell you that. I don't think you're as stupid as you look, McGinnis. These two followed orders exactly. They just didn't know they were being used in a slightly unusual scheme. Part of what the two of you heard in the Washington briefing was right. The London lab had begun unauthorized research on an offensive chemical weapon. By the time we found out about it, they had started live experiments in Asia, and the thing looked like a monster weapon. And it wasn't long after that they developed an ironclad antidote to the virus. You didn't know that. We have the stock of antidote back in New York. The whole program could have revolutionized the entire balance of power. A weapon to cripple the enemy, but one from which we could all be protected. But when we approached the top of the Company for authorization to pursue a full blown development program, with a complete first strike capability, the boys upstairs said no. Can you imagine it? We present a weapon that can make nuclear arsenals obsolete, and they are afraid to go ahead. And you know why? Because the damn political appointments made after Helms retired had no balls. They were afraid to break the treaties with the Soviets. They were afraid of upsetting at first, détente, and now, glasnost. Bullshit! The Soviets haven't changed. They would still ram it up our asses if they had a chance! And while we get soft in the head over here and think they are our bosom bodies, we are getting ready to get our heads handed to us. So something had to be done to wake up the goddamn bureaucracy and political leadership. We had to give them the balls they didn't have!" Phillips voice had risen to a crescendo. He was on the verge of hysteria, his arms waving wildly in the air, and his face contorting with anger.

"So I used Amalfi and Valdor for the London operation. Then I eliminated Amalfi because he had been injured in London and was a risk to move. I couldn't leave behind a single loose end on this one. Then, Valdor and Everingham came in to plant the infections here. Not a lot. Just five large cities. We sold Dr. Everingham by telling her that the groups were controlled, small population samples that she could monitor. She jumped at that chance. She was one of the codevelopers of K-7 and believed that further experimentation was the only way to verify the drug's accuracy and potency. Valdor was used because he was one of the best. He would do anything for the right price.

"Here's the little part that Valdor and Everingham didn't know. I never intended for the infections to be placed and just run their course. Instead, all the paperwork and all the clues at the scenes were made to look like the K-7 caper was a Soviet job. We even doctored files inside the main information computers showing that K-7 was a virus the Soviets were improperly working on since the early 1970s. We decided that since we had to plant some infections, we might as well strike against people we weren't that keen about anyway. Like the Democratic party hierarchy and the damn neoliberal establishment in New York. Or all the peaceniks in San Francisco. Maybe we could get rid of some unwanted dirt from our own society!" Phillips was foaming at the mouth, having worked himself into a frenzy.

"And once the President and the military were informed that the Soviets had sent a terror team inside our country to spread a bacteriological weapon, that would have been the fucking end of glasnost and détente. The cold war would have switched back on in an instant. And then we were prepared to stage a mammoth research program to try and find a cure to the dirty Russian chemical weapon. And in about four months, once the panic really started to settle in, presto—we would turn up with the 'newly developed' antidote. Not only would the cold war be back on, but the CIA would be the savior of the country. We could have had anything we wanted in the new political atmosphere. We were changing the course of history, you jerk. You two bozos were supposed to go along and do your investigation and conclude it was a Soviet operation. And Valdor and Everingham were supposed to stay one close step ahead of you and then get away. You would get patted on the back for a job well attempted. But you got lucky. A has-been, borderline alcoholic who is over the hill and a young kid who doesn't know his way around Langley. What a pair of losers! I can't believe you fucked this up!"

"You're the loser, Neal." McGinnis sounded somber. The story from Phillips had numbed him. He wasn't even responding to the insults. "You're going in with us. It's over. I've had a tape recorder running in my pocket the entire time. A nifty idea from Hodson. I've got your little speech down for posterity."

"You big dope. Do you think I would have done this all on my own? Do you?" Phillips's face was contorted in a weird smile.

McGinnis tensed. Harris looked around the area. Phillips kept screaming. "Do you think I just came this far to be taken in by you two stooges? No way! What did you do? Follow my car here? Did you check the trunk for extra riders?"

McGinnis spun around, scanning the area. "You're full of shit, Neal. You're alone."

"He's not full of shit, Richard!" McGinnis spun toward the back of the fort. His mouth dropped open. It was as though someone hit him in the chest with a hammer. Tony Finch was standing less than twenty feet away, a Uzi cradled in his arms. He was walking toward McGinnis and Harris.

"Don't look surprised, Richard. It's nothing personal. But Neal is right." Finch's voice sounded very calm compared to Phillips's frenzy. "It's much bigger than any of us. This is history in the making. You can't stand in its way. I would never have assigned you to this case if I thought you were going to break it. I never wanted it to come to this." He stopped a couple of feet short of Harris. "Take off those silly glasses and drop your guns, gentlemen, we're going for a little walk. Neal, pick up your gun."

McGinnis knew that once they dropped their weapons and Phillips was rearmed he and Harris were dead men. If he had any chance to live, it was to act immediately. He hoped Harris was thinking the same thing. He screamed, "Now, Jimmy!" spun his pistol under his torso, and aimed at Phillips, who was crouching to recover his machine pistol. Two .45 caliber slugs hit Phillips in the temple. Even through the noise of the wind and waves, the sound of his skull caving in could be clearly heard as his body flew across the walkway.

Harris had been prepared for action. When McGinnis shouted, he started raising his pistol toward Finch. But Finch had been one of the best field agents the CIA ever had. His desk job may have taken a millisecond off his reaction time, but he still had the instincts and timing of a good jungle cat. He laid a burst of the Uzi at Harris, ripping into his chest and sending him sprawling across the gravel at the base of the fort.

McGinnis and Finch spun toward each other simultaneously. Each emptied their weapons in the vicinity of their opponent. But they also dived for the ground to avoid being hit. It made their fire go wild, and none of the bullets hit their target. McGinnis, lying flat on the walkway, aimed his pistol at the rolling figure near the fort. Just as Finch came to a complete stop and turned over to fire his Uzi, McGinnis rapidly pressed the trigger three times. With the help of his infrared glasses he saw two bullets strike the brick wall behind Finch, but the third struck its target, hitting him near the neck, causing the Uzi to fly from his hands and land near his side. His body slumped to the floor. Finch tried to lift his head, but it fell back to the ground, slamming against the stone floor.

McGinnis quickly stood up, his gun still trained at the prone figure of his commanding officer. He looked at Harris. There was no sign of life, a line of bullet holes across his chest. The sons of bitches! He sprinted across the pathway to where Finch lay. He couldn't detect any breathing. He bent down to feel for a pulse in his neck.

It happened so fast he couldn't even react. Finch reached out, grabbed the barrel of the Uzi, and swung it as hard as possible at McGinnis. The butt of the steel gun struck McGinnis in the lower leg, cracking the bone through the skin. He gave out a curdling yell as he collapsed to the ground. His Colt .45 flew from his hand as his leg broke, the pain causing an involuntary spasm throughout his body. Finch was lying next to him. He tried to turn the Uzi around so he could fire at McGinnis. But before he could, McGinnis pushed himself to the side and with his healthy leg, kicked the submachine gun out of Finch's hands. It landed nearly five feet away. But as fast as McGinnis had gotten rid of the gun, Finch was on top of him. He clawed at McGinnis's face. One knee came up and caught McGinnis in the groin, forcing an excruciating pain to spread through his abdomen. McGinnis brought his hands up and locked them in a solid grip around Finch's throat. He pressed as hard as he could, digging the thumbs deeply into the neck, trying to cut off any air to the windpipe. He could see the bullet hole, just half an inch from his grip. The blood was pouring in a steady stream from the wound. Another minute and Finch would pass out.

Finch's hands were flailing. With his right hand he clawed at

McGinnis's eyes, knocking off the special glasses, and scraping a finger into one of the eyeballs. McGinnis squeezed both shut, trying to keep the hands from inflicting permanent damage. But Finch was strong, and McGinnis felt as though his eyes were about to be gouged. He slipped his right hand from Finch's throat and slammed it into his stomach as hard as he could. His fist sank into the soft part of Finch's abdomen, forcing the breath from his attacker's body. But Finch still clawed at the eye sockets. McGinnis took his other hand from the neck and punched straight up toward Finch's face. His knuckles first scraped teeth and then landed solidly into the bottom of Finch's nose, the impact splitting the skin and forcing the cartilage to ram into the forehead. Finch let out a spine-curdling yell, the blood splattering over his face and onto McGinnis. I have him now, McGinnis thought. He's finished. And he would have been in another moment. But McGinnis was so intent on finishing the fight, that he didn't see Finch grab a rock the size of his fist. With all the strength Finch could muster he brought it down on top of McGinnis's forehead. He heard the skull fracture as the skin split from the hairline to the eyebrows. McGinnis's hands dropped to his side. He looked up through dazed eyes, blood pouring into them, a light-headedness overtaking him. He felt removed from the scene as Finch grabbed him by the lapels of his jacket and partially picked him up. Then he realized that Finch was slamming him into the brick wall of the fort. Again and again his back and head cracked against the wall. Then Finch let him drop to the floor, and McGinnis crumpled into a sitting position, propped against the base of the fort.

Finch walked over and grabbed the Uzi. McGinnis knew it was over. He rolled his head to the side and stared through his stupor toward the ocean. Finch was saying something to him, but he couldn't understand the words. He could only hear muffled sounds in the background. There was liquid in his ears. Why couldn't he hear? Then he blinked his eyes. He tried to concentrate through the red film that had formed over his retina. He couldn't believe it. Valdor was not dead! The assassin was kneeling near the spot where he had been shot, cradling a gun in both hands. He was pointing it toward McGinnis and the fort. Who would get him first? Did it matter whether he died from a terrorist's bullet or one from Finch? He heard the sound of gunfire. It was the last thing he remembered. He slumped over and fell to his side.

CHAPTER 24 ━━━━

She received the call just as she finished her coffee break, her first of two as manager of a women's lingerie boutique. She savored the breaks from the hectic pace of retail sales in downtown Washington. Her sales-clerk merely told her there was a man on the phone and he wouldn't identify himself. Probably a husband who was looking for a gift for his wife but was too embarrassed to come in—had decided to do some phone shopping. Might even be a dirty call. Those came in occasionally, but they almost never requested the manager before delivering their abusive harangue.

It was Jimmy Harris. He had always been pleasant to her since the events in San Francisco. He knew how difficult it was for her to maintain composure when she visited McGinnis at the hospital.

Not that it was easy for Harris. It had taken him nearly three weeks in the hospital before he was strong enough to be released. He was still in physical therapy, only about 85 percent of the way to becoming himself once again. The bulletproof vest that McGinnis made him wear that final evening had saved his life. One of Finch's 9-millimeter slugs entered under the vest and lodged in a kidney. Another bullet shattered his collarbone, and he had a couple of scars on his chin that were going to stay with him for life. But anytime he was frustrated about his progress, he merely had to pay a visit to McGinnis's bedside. The damn doctors didn't even know if he would come out of the coma. It tore

Harris apart to look at his partner in that degenerative state. Like death in every way except for the machines pumping air in and out of the chest.

But whatever anguish it caused Harris, it was much tougher for McGinnis's wife and son. She had lived with him. She had borne their child. She tried to discourage their son from going to the hospital too often. That's not how she wanted him to remember his father.

"Elizabeth?" There was excitement in his voice. He sounded as if he had won the lottery.

"Yes, Jimmy."

"They just called me. He's awake!" There was silence for a moment. She wasn't sure she understood him correctly. Maybe he was talking about someone else or something different. "Elizabeth! Didn't you hear me? Richard's awake. This morning at 6:00. He buzzed the nurse with the emergency call button. Evidently, it has taken them hours to get him off the breathing equipment. The first thing he did was ask for some aspirin. Said he had a great headache. Can you believe it?"

She couldn't speak. Tears blurred her eyes. It felt as if someone were holding her throat. Nothing would come out.

"Elizabeth, have you heard anything I've said?"

"Yes." It came out in a whisper. He could hear the tears in her voice.

"I'm going over there now. They told me to call you and to meet you there. They want to talk to him later today, but for a couple of hours he's ours. Okay?"

"Okay." She placed the receiver down. She didn't mean to be rude but she knew Harris would understand. She couldn't talk on the phone. Someone said something to her but she walked past them. She grabbed the keys to her car from the drawer behind the cash register and told one of the salesclerks that she was taking the rest of the day off because of a personal matter. The rest of the employees saw the tears. When a person cries you can't always tell if it's for sorrow or happiness unless you ask. No one asked. They assumed her sick husband had finally died.

It took her less than fifteen minutes to arrive at the hospital. She was lucky to make it safely, driving in a daze the entire journey. Today the corridors did not seem so sickly. The oppressive air of death did not hang over them. She noticed Harris standing outside the room. He shuffled down the hallway and grabbed her in a solid hug. He looked at her, tears in his own eyes.

"Have you seen him?"

He shook his head. "I thought you should be the first."

She placed her palm against the side of his cheek. "No, you come in with me. It'll do him good to see both of us at the same time. I want to see him first before calling Andy. I've got to see how he is with my own eyes before I have our son come here."

"C'mon let's go."

She tugged on Harris's jacket just as he started to push open the door. It was almost as though fear had taken her over. She had entered that room so many times during the past three months, and the sight had always been so horribly numbing that she had developed a fright about the entire place. She couldn't quite believe that this time everything would be fine. Harris grabbed her hand. His face reassured her. It was going to be all right. "Let's go in." His voice was confident.

Harris pushed the door open and allowed her to enter first. A nurse was sitting by the bedside. McGinnis was propped up in the bed in a sitting position. He was still a shadow of his former self, but he was clean-shaven, his hair had been washed and combed, and a new set of hospital pajamas covered the scars still on his body. He looked better than at any time she had seen him since he arrived at the hospital. He had at least returned to the world of the living. When he focused on Harris and Elizabeth, his eyes looked as though someone had lit a bulb behind them.

She ran over to him, Harris only a step behind. The nurse signaled to Harris that she was stepping outside the room but would be close by in case they needed her. Elizabeth paused at the side of the bed and stared at him for a moment. She couldn't believe that God had answered her prayers. He had ended the ordeal. But instead of doing it the way she expected, by taking his soul, he had revived the body. She leaned over and squeezed him around the neck and then kissed him softly against his chapped lips. A small tube remained in his nose. Another two still trailed into his arms. He looked frail. His skin still had a yellow pallor, the result of too many days under the hospital's fluorescent lights.

"My breath may be a little bad, so be careful." His voice sounded hoarse and he had difficulty talking clearly with the tube in his nostril. But they were the first words she had heard from him in three months. They were words she never thought she would hear again. More tears filled her eyes. "Now don't start crying. It'll ruin my bed sheets."

"Same old McGinnis," Harris chimed in from the back. He leaned over Elizabeth, reached out, and grasped McGinnis's hand. There was real warmth in the grip.

"I thought you were dead," McGinnis said as he looked up at the smiling face on the young agent. "They told me this morning that you were still alive."

"Even the team that discovered us evidently thought I was dead. They were ready to mark me DOA when one of the paramedics tried a stethoscope on me and heard the faint murmur of a heartbeat. Your vest did a lot more than keep me warm."

"Typical." McGinnis rolled his eyes. "Played dead so I had to do it all on my own. Well, you know what they say, once an—"

". . . asshole, always an asshole."

"I'm glad you paid attention." He looked at Elizabeth. "They tell me you've been here every day." His fingers were weak but they gripped the edge of her wrist. "That helped me. I know that helped me." He squeezed her wrist as hard as he could.

The nurse opened the door. "I'm sorry, but the doctors want to prep Mr. McGinnis for a CAT scan. It'll be over in less than an hour, and then you can stay and visit with him until he gets tired. If you can leave now, the doctors are coming."

Elizabeth felt like telling them to go to hell. They had her husband for three months and had poked him with every instrument they had. Now he was hers again. At least he was alive. They could have him later. But she knew she wasn't the priority as long as he was in a government hospital. They weren't worried about his emotional well-being. They were worried about making him well so they could interrogate him, just as they had done with Harris for three weeks. She wasn't going to let it drive her crazy. She had him back. That's all that mattered for now. She leaned over and kissed McGinnis once again on the lips.

He managed a weak smile. "Best damn medicine I've had in a long time."

"We'll be back," Harris said, and reached out and touched his hand.

"Is that a threat?" Again McGinnis tried to smile.

"Like I said, funniest spy on the circuit. Once Carson knows you're getting better he's sure to book you on the *Tonight Show*."

"Harris, before you go. One thing. Is everything cleared up? They came to talk to me this morning but I was too dazed. Doctors told them they can't start until later. But no one told me a thing."

"They want to debrief you first." Harris also glanced toward Elizabeth.

"Fuck the clearance crap. She's okay." At least the coma had not dampened his feisty spirit.

"They found your tape. It was a lifesaver. Together with Hodson's help, they've pieced together a pretty good picture of what happened. Two agents on Finch's staff have also been flushed out of the woodwork. The fellow who was the boatman that night was on Phillips's staff. They also found the antibody in Finch's private vault in his New York townhouse. That stopped a potential disaster. The Company used press contacts to plant stories that a virulent strain of Legionnaires' Disease had been discovered on both coasts. Over 100,000 people were innoculated—anyone who might have been anywhere near the infection sites. Only thirty-six people died."

"Time to leave, folks, the doctors are here," the nurse said as she popped her head back through the door.

Harris turned to look at her. "We're leaving now, nurse, just one moment."

He looked back to McGinnis. "No one told you anything else?"

McGinnis shook his head.

"When the Company found us, they had the boatman, Phillips, Finch, the two of us, and Dr. Everingham."

"What about Valdor?"

"No boat. No Valdor."

McGinnis's mouth dropped open. An image flashed through his head—of Valdor, a mist surrounding him, on his knees firing a pistol. He could see the image of Finch jerking forward and then turning in amazement to face his killer. The pistol McGinnis thought was intended for him had been emptied instead into Finch. He looked back at the two of them, shock evident on his face. "Don't worry, honey," Elizabeth said, patting him on the hand. "It's over."

Valdor had made it. No, he thought, it was just beginning.